CW00921651

FEY TOUCHED

Changeling

ARISTA HOLMES

Amazon Print Error 3/9

Copyright © 2023 by Arista Holmes

All rights reserved.

No portion of this publication may be reproduced, stored or transmitted in any form or by any means, electronic, mechanical, photocopying, recording, scanning, or otherwise without written permission from the publisher or author.

It is illegal to copy this book, post it to a website, or distribute it by any other means without permission.

This book is entirely a work of fiction. The names, characters and incidents portrayed in it are the work of the author's imagination. Any resemblance to actual persons, living or dead, events or localities is entirely coincidental.

Arista Holmes asserts the moral right to be identified as the author of this work.

Cover Design by GetCovers.com

Editing by Nicole Wilson at Evermore Editing

Ebook ISBN: 978-1-915913-00-5
Paperback ISBN: 978-1-915913-01-2
Hardcover ISBN: 978-1-915913-02-9

First edition.

Contents

For my mum,
who always made sure I knew magic was real, and
anything was possible.

Thank you and Happy Birthday.

Changeling

Noun

A child believed to have been secretly substituted by fairies for the parents' real child in infancy.

1

In the nocturnal peace of Lizzy's bedroom, lit only by the dim shards of light from a newly risen crescent moon, the thud of her jewellery box snapping open as it hit the hard wooden floor seemed amplified.

The sound pulled an involuntary wince to her features and forced Lizzy to freeze, her eyes wide with barely controlled panic. Her arms tightened around the folded clothes that had knocked the box to the floor in her haste, and her half-packed bag sat conspicuously on her bed, while Lizzy waited to see if the bang would betray her.

She froze in place, not even daring to breathe as she strained her hearing, listening for any sounds of movement in the house. When she heard nothing, Lizzy released her breath in a sigh.

She brushed her long, dark hair away from her face, relieved her actions hadn't summoned her best friend and turned back to her bag.

Booker would be furious with her when he woke in the morning to find her gone. Lizzy knew the Fey Court wouldn't waste any time before dragging him in to answer dozens of questions. They were sure to ask about her whereabouts. About how she'd managed to sneak out of his home without him noticing. About what her plans were.

She was placing Booker in a terrible position, and yet Lizzy also knew she didn't have a choice.

She had to leave.

She couldn't stomach sitting at home, doing nothing, while her mother was missing.

Missing and presumed dead; Madeline Hail's official status. And that had been the Fey Court's final word on the latest delegation of fey that had travelled to, and gone missing in, the mortal realm almost a month ago.

Lizzy had tried to grieve and move on, like she was expected to. She'd tried going to classes and distracting herself by practising her fey magic. Booker had even let her move in with him, until she turned eighteen and the court laws would allow her to live alone, but Lizzy couldn't settle.

She couldn't stop the feeling in her bones that her mother was still alive somewhere.

Shoving her armful of clothes into her bag, trying to make as little noise as possible, Lizzy then quickly turned to pick up the box.

She crouched down and began gathering up the jewellery pieces scattered across her floorboards, tossing them back into their individual compartments. Her movements were swift and careless, unwilling to waste any more of her limited time than she already had.

As her fingers brushed over a distinctive silky surface, Lizzy paused and, against her better judgement, lifted the familiar pendant to hang in front of her face.

It was formed from four inky black pearls, held in place with frames of delicate goldwork to form the shape of rounded fey wings. She couldn't make out the intricate pattern of veins carved across them, as the night's shadows blended against the green-black of the pearl's surface and muted the shine of the gold that framed them, but Lizzy didn't need to see them to know they were there.

She knew the intricate design of swirling metal, carved veins, and silky pearls as intimately as her own face.

It belonged to her mother. The only memento, besides herself, that her father had left behind. Lizzy had long ago been promised it for her eighteenth birthday.

It was still a few weeks away, but Lizzy slipped the gold chain over her head and pressed her hand against the pendant as it settled against her breastbone, cool and somehow reassuring, like she was carrying a piece of her parents close to her heart.

Shaking herself, she eased the lid of the jewellery box closed and shoved it back onto her desk before returning to stand beside her bed, running through her mental checklist once more.

Dried food, clothes, spare shoes, and all the precious gems she could conveniently lay her hands on to buy and bribe information.

After another moment of quiet consideration, Lizzy pulled the thick blanket off her bed, roughly shoving it into her bag, in case the mortal realm was cold.

With her final checks done, and the sharp crescent of the moon tracking its way steadily across the sky, she tied her bag closed. She slung it over one shoulder, but Lizzy only managed two steps towards the door when she heard movement in the hall outside her room and ground to a halt, her heart pounding.

The only other person in the house was Booker, and panic clawed at her throat as she listened to her oldest friend approach her room on quiet feet.

If he found her like this, he'd try and stop her. Or worse, he'd want to come with her, and while Lizzy loved Booker like a brother, the last thing she wanted to do was drag him into the middle of the mess she was about to make.

Desperately glancing around her room for a solution, her eyes landed on the window. For a split second, she seriously considered the jump from her room to the ground, debating its merits as an escape route.

If she hadn't been lacking the signature wings all female fey should bear, Lizzy wouldn't have thought twice. Instead, her hesitation cost her the chance to flee or hide, and now it was too late.

Her bedroom door opened slowly, swinging wide to reveal the frowning features of her best friend. Standing there, Booker leant his tall form against her doorframe, effectively blocking her path, a yawn wide enough to crack his jaw escaping him.

"What, in the realm, are you doing?" Booker asked her on a heavy exhale, his sleep-coated voice rumbling quietly as he ran a weary hand through the tufts of bed-mussed blond hair in a vain attempt at smoothing them into place.

"Nothing," Lizzy answered, wincing. It was too short, and too sharp, and she hoped he was still drowsy enough to miss her tells.

Her hope sank when Booker paused in his grooming to blink at her owlishly. It took a couple of seconds before her abrupt answer seemed to register, but when it did, his frown deepened into an outright scowl.

"Lizzy, you're fully dressed in the middle of the night, with a bag packed, and the best you can come up with is 'nothing'?"

"What are you doing up, anyway?" she deflected, but she could hear her voice still wasn't right.

She might be able to lie to a stranger, but lying to Booker was different. She watched anxiously as irritation chased frustration across Booker's features before he finally crossed his arms and raised an eyebrow.

"Whatever you dropped woke me. I knew you had to be up to something disastrous, you usually swear when you drop things," he explained dryly. "So, what's going on?"

Despite him catching her red-handed, Lizzy still hesitated. Booker had been her best, and only, friend for most of her life, and she hadn't wanted to repay that loyalty and friendship by putting him at risk by dragging him into her plans.

She met and held his steady green gaze for a long moment as she considered several different answers to his question, all of them lies.

She should have known better than to try and keep him out of things.

Booker had always been at the centre of her plans, ever since he planted himself by her side when they were still children, and Lizzy grudgingly relented to his questions.

Booker's discovery of her escape had ruined any chance of the plausible deniability she'd wanted to give him. One trip inside Booker's mind by the Court's master of telepathy was all it would take.

And if plausible deniability wasn't on the table, Lizzy saw no reason to keep lying to him. She resigned herself to giving him the truth and shook her head with a sigh.

"I'm leaving," she admitted, fingers tightening around the strap of her bag when Booker rolled his eyes, bracing herself for the fight she was sure was about to come.

"That much I'd gathered from the packed bag. Where and why?" he prompted, beginning to sound more alert in response to her evasiveness. "I thought we agreed that staying with me was the best place for you, until you hit eighteen?"

They had, and it was. Her only other alternative had been to become a ward of the Court, and Lizzy had never been more grateful Booker had a good half a year on her in age, but that was another reason she'd wanted to slip out undetected.

She knew full well her plan was obstinate, childish, ridiculous, and borderline insane... not to mention illegal. But she had to do it anyway.

Shifting her weight, nerves closing her throat, Lizzy lifted her chin and took a calming breath. It helped, a little, and she forced herself to speak and answer Booker's questions.

"I'm going to the mortal realm to search for Mum," she said, relieved to find that her voice was steady, and unwavering, despite the thrumming beat of her heart against her chest.

Silence.

She'd expected shouting, or laughter, but Booker just stared at her in silence.

Lizzy cleared her throat, heart still thumping hard enough to make her feel sick. As she dropped her gaze, she saw Booker finally stir into action, pushing off the doorframe in a sharp movement that made her jump, drawing her eyes back to his.

"You're not joking," Booker muttered, shaking his head. "Lizzy, are you insane?" he snapped, his voice raising as the argument she'd predicted finally arrived. "You can't go to the mortal realm! You're not even considered an adult yet! Even if you could sneak past the court sentinels at the fairy circles, they would track you down and drag you back in a matter of hours."

Despite the tension Lizzy could see in his frame, she couldn't stop the scoff that escaped her at his words. "The Fey Court wouldn't risk anyone to bring me back, and without Mum here, you're the only person who'd even try to make them."

"It's court policy," Booker shot back, voice sharp and eyes narrowing, "adult fey accept the risk of vampire attacks. They accept they might not return, but children, unaccompanied by a chaperone, are to be brought back—"

"Oh come on, Booker! Be realistic!" Lizzy finally snapped, interrupting his recitation of the fey laws. "You know they wouldn't bother for me, I'm not exactly fey material! Just look at me!"

She spread her arms wide, challenging him to do exactly that, but Booker refused to shift his green eyes from her determined gaze.

Despite his stubborn refusal, Lizzy could see Booker press his lips together hard. She saw the way his hands clenched into fists, half hidden beneath his crossed arms, and she knew he understood exactly what she meant.

With her long, dark hair, Lizzy didn't look like a fey should. Not as light and willowy as was normal for a fey either, and while her eyes were the same bluebell colour as her mother's, the warm tan she gained from time spent beneath the summer sun marked her as strange and other amongst the permanent pale etherealness of the residents of Arbaon.

The most damning difference, however, was her complete lack of wings. An integral part of all female fey; their absence from her form had caused her to be ignored at best and outright ridiculed at worst, until Booker had made himself her friend.

She was right about the Court's indifference, and Booker knew it.

The longer the silent standoff continued, the more signs of his frustration Lizzy could read in his face. She could almost hear him trying to think up another reason for her to stay, and Lizzy let her arms fall back to her sides with a sigh.

"You said it yourself; adults take the risk of not returning. They're not going to look for her, or the rest of the missing fey. I have to go, Booker. I have to know what happened."

"So what was your plan then?" he asked, voice turning sharp and taking on a bitter edge that made her wince. "Sneak out in the middle of the night, sweet talk the sentinels so you could slip past them, and leave me to answer the Court's questions?"

Lizzy didn't have an answer that wouldn't hurt him, so she chose silence. Booker shook his head in disbelief while a short, sharp laugh escaped his throat.

"You know Maddy wouldn't want you doing this, don't you?" he asked, invoking her mother's name.

Lizzy flinched in response as pain lanced through her chest.

Booker's voice softened as he kept going. "She wouldn't want you risking your life for this, and she certainly wouldn't want you to run off, alone and unprep—"

"Then she shouldn't have gone and gotten herself—" *killed* hung in the air between them. Unspoken, but heard by both.

Lizzy turned away from the rising sadness in Booker's face and shook her head. "What else can I do? I can't sit here not knowing, Booker. I've tried and I just can't. I'll go mad."

Another moment of tense silence overtook them both as Lizzy avoided his gaze. Her hand rubbed at her chest while the pain in her heart subsided, and she waited for Booker's decision.

It was when Lizzy heard him heave a heavy sigh that she risked glancing back up at her friend. He had the palms of his hands pressed against his eyes, and as she watched, they raked up through his nest of blond hair in abject frustration. But there was defeat in his slumped shoulders too as he dropped his hands to his sides, and Lizzy tentatively began to hope.

"Alright, fine," Booker grumbled, "can you give me ten minutes?"

"For what?" Lizzy asked, cautiously hoping that he was about to give her a head start before alerting the Court, but Booker's features shifted from tired frustration to open amusement at her question.

"To pack a bag, of course. If I can't talk you out of this ridiculous plan of yours, then I'm coming with you."

"What?" Lizzy spluttered. "No. Booker. I can't drag you into this—"

"No?" he repeated, cutting her off and lifting a disbelieving eyebrow. "I either come with you, or I go straight to the Court, right now, and have them stop you. What's it going to be?"

It was on the tip of Lizzy's tongue to tell him that he wouldn't dare. To challenge his ultimatum with a scoff and an eyeroll, but a quick study of his features and she swallowed back the words. He was serious, and she shook her head in confusion.

"Why?"

"I have a whole list of reasons," Booker said with a shrug,

"starting with the fact that I don't want to explain to the court officials why I didn't stop you. Followed quickly by the fact that Maddy was important to me too... but mostly because you're my best friend, you idiot. I'm not going to let you go wandering off to the mortal realm without me."

Lizzy could feel the tears burning her eyes and she launched herself at Booker, burying her face against his sleepshirt-covered chest.

He caught her easily, arms sliding around her shoulders in a tight, familiar hug, and Lizzy felt him sigh in relief at her surrender.

"Thank you," Lizzy muttered, and she felt the vibration of his quiet hum of acknowledgement against her cheek.

"When this explodes in our faces, don't say I didn't warn you," Booker muttered, drawing a watery laugh from Lizzy before she released him with a grin.

Booker knew better than to draw attention to her tears. With nothing more than a soft smile, he turned around and left her, heading back to his room so he could pack a bag for their impromptu trip.

Lizzy waited until she could hear him rummaging around in his wardrobe before she let herself wipe away the tears that had stained her face.

The tight band of fear that had settled around her chest was easing. Relief began to creep into the cracks in her armour with the knowledge that she would now have Booker at her side, and she suddenly felt like the chances of finding her mum just got infinitely better.

2

Lizzy had chosen the small collection of fairy circles on the edge of their village. Unlike the main arboretum in the central city, it wasn't guarded by a large number of sentinels.

Since most fey had no desire to leave the realm of Arbaon in exchange for the mortal one, the court sentinels were little more than a warning system. Their orders consisted of watching for unscheduled activation of a portal from the other side and deterring curious children.

Booker had taken the lead, directing them both through the sleeping village, creeping along the dusty dirt roads as fast as they dared.

Every time they came to a corner, Booker checked the next street to make sure they didn't bump into anyone taking a late-night stroll.

The last thing either of them wanted was to be forced into answering awkward questions about the bags slung over their shoulders.

Booker was already eighteen, an adult under Arbaon law, but Lizzy knew her presence on the streets, late at night, would bring too much attention.

As they approached the wooden fence that surrounded the arboretum, Lizzy's steps slowed and she stared at the small copse of sacred trees.

Ash, birch, oak and hawthorn, all acting as portals between the two realms. Powered by the fairy circles growing in a wide ring around the base of each tree.

The stems of inactive, white-capped glowshrooms were aligned with the trees' deep roots beneath the soil, even as their twisting limbs stretched up, tall and dark, against the night sky. Lizzy felt a surge of relief and gratitude well up in her chest that she had Booker's reassuring figure at her side.

"Ready?" he asked, keeping his voice low as he leaned closer to her, and Lizzy braced herself before nodding.

As he scaled the fence, Lizzy watched him with narrowed eyes, his movements quick and determined, and his long coat seemed to give him no trouble at all.

Then he was dropping to the grass-carpeted ground on the other side. The soft soil muffled his landing, and Lizzy moved to follow.

Booker had a good six inches on her in height, and Lizzy found herself struggling with her bag as she climbed, but by the time she managed to swing her legs over the top, Booker was already waiting to help her down to the ground.

They moved together into the shadows cast by the portal trees, keeping back from the winding pathways through the grove and trying to stay out of sight of patrolling sentinels.

"Which portal do we need?" Booker whispered as they moved deeper into the trees, and Lizzy forced herself to offer a casual shrug, hoping Booker wouldn't realise quite how flimsy her plan actually was.

Lizzy stepped over a line of pale glowshrooms, taking care not to damage them. The last thing they needed was the sentinels raising the alarm.

"I don't have any way to activate a fairy circle, so we need to find one being prepared for the morning transportation. So, just... look for the blue light of activated glowshrooms."

"Do you even know which one Maddy went through?" Booker

asked, voice raising in concern, but he fell silent when Lizzy shot him a sharp look of warning.

"Unless you have a way to activate it, then it doesn't matter which one Mum went through," she reminded him. "We can figure out where she arrived once we're in the mortal realm—"

Lizzy cut herself off when she spotted a patrolling sentinel approaching along one of the neatly trimmed pathways. She grabbed Booker's hand, dragging him behind a large hawthorn to hide.

Booker pressed the pair of them as close to the tree as he could, lifting the hood on his wool coat and using the dark material to blend with the shadows.

In tense silence, they watched the sentinel wander down the path. Her wings fluttered in open boredom, but their luck held and the sentinel never glanced in their direction.

It was only when she was finally out of sight and they were in no immediate danger of being overheard that Booker continued their discussion. This time he kept his voice low and quiet, all but hissing his complaints in her ear.

"Lizzy, do you have any idea how big the mortal realm is? Without knowing which portal Maddy used—"

"Getting out of here is the hard part," Lizzy deflected. "Once we're there, they won't follow us. We'll have time to figure everything else out but, most importantly, we'll be that much closer to Mum."

Lizzy didn't give Booker a chance to argue, turning to glance around the tree they had hidden behind, scanning the pathways for any more sentinels before stepping out, ready to move on.

"Come on, we need to find an active circle before one of the sentinels finds us," she said, tugging a silently sulking Booker along with the light grasp she still had on his hand.

They didn't have to go much deeper into the arboretum before Booker pointed out the bright blue glow of an active fairy circle, and Lizzy immediately headed towards it.

Her excitement, and the hope for answers, distracted her until she almost walked headfirst into another of the court sentinels.

Only Booker's grasp on her hand, and the large trunk of a huge oak, kept the sentinel from spotting her and raising the alarm.

Lizzy turned to Booker to thank him but silenced herself with a grimace when Booker pressed the fingers of his free hand against his lips before tapping at his temple—a silent request for telepathy.

Glancing at the sentinel standing by the active circle, Lizzy watched the woman, hoping she would walk onto the next leg of her patrol. Lizzy let several long seconds pass, but the sentinel didn't appear inclined to move any time soon, and Lizzy reluctantly turned back to Booker and nodded her acceptance.

There was a tiny twitch at the corner of Booker's mouth, a familiar sign he was focussing his powers. Seconds later, Lizzy wrinkled her nose and bit her lip at the uncomfortable sensation of something wriggling against her skull.

"*This would be so much easier if you didn't fight it every time,*" came the quiet voice in her mind, and she shook her head.

"*I wouldn't fight it if it didn't feel like a fly buzzing against my ear,*" she grumbled, glancing back at the sentinel before adding, "*What are we going to do about her?*"

"*You had to find the fairy circle with a permanently stationed sentinel, didn't you?*" Booker complained, but with their thoughts linked, Lizzy could almost taste the reluctant amusement behind his words.

"*How was I supposed to know?*" she shot back, and the strange sensation of a simultaneous laugh and sigh brushed across her mind.

"Fine, fine, lemme think for a moment..."

Lizzy couldn't help but grimace again when she felt the pressure in her head change. Booker retreated and sank into his own thoughts, but the connection remained and she could still feel him thinking.

In an attempt to distract herself from Booker's mind, Lizzy watched the stationed sentinel pace along the same small stretch of path.

Lizzy's active dislike of telepathy was just one more thing that set her apart from other fey. Its use was a normal part of fey society, but she had always shied away from the contact unless it was with her mum or Booker.

Someone inside her head had always felt too intimate and a little foreign to Lizzy, and yet there were some fey who communicated almost exclusively via telepathy.

Lizzy had made it a point to avoid those fey as much as she could.

She felt Booker's attention return to her. The slow deliberate press of his mind against hers. Booker was always careful not to startle her, so by the time his voice floated through her thoughts once more, Lizzy had prepared herself.

"I'm going to distract her," Booker said, and Lizzy turned to stare at him, eyebrows raised.

"How?"

"Do you trust me, or not?" he replied. Booker was being careful to keep his thoughts guarded, but Lizzy didn't need to be inside his head to know he wasn't as confident as he was pretending to be. The way he wouldn't meet her eyes told her that much. They'd known each other too long for his well-practised bravado to fool her.

He must have sensed the argument brewing in her mind. *Or*

perhaps, she mused, *he can read my face as well as I can his.*

Before she could respond, Booker continued quickly, "*Look, just be ready to make a run for the portal if this goes sideways,*" he told her while dropping his bag into her hands.

Before she could summon any kind of answer, Booker had broken the connection between their minds. He stepped away from the tree, leaving Lizzy to lift his bag onto her empty shoulder and hope he knew what he was doing.

She watched him from her hiding spot as he made his way out onto one of the cultivated paths. Booker was still hidden from view by a blind corner, created by the branches of a portal tree, but it only took half a dozen paces before he was in sight of the sentinel.

The woman was quick to straighten from her bored slouch, her wings flaring in preparation to take to the sky, her hands grasping at the long wooden shaft of her bardiche.

Its curved blade tilted towards Booker, the pale blue light of the glowshrooms glinting off the sharp edge of the weapon, and Lizzy's concern escaped her in a soft hiss.

Booker's pace slowed, and his hands lifted, but he kept advancing on the woman, and Lizzy's heart continued to hammer against her chest until the bardiche pointing at Booker finally retracted.

Since she couldn't make out what was being said, no matter how hard she strained, Lizzy turned her attention from Booker to the sentinel. While she still couldn't make out their words, the sentinel's face was an open book. Her features shifted from wary to confused before sliding straight into panic-stricken.

It was enough to reassure Lizzy; whatever Booker had intended, it was going to plan.

When the sentinel's wings flared, fore and hind both lifting away from her body and hooking together as she launched herself into the air, Lizzy's jaw dropped open in shock.

The sentinel's body twisted fluidly in the air, turning towards the town centre. She braced the shaft of her weapon against her chest as she flew into the night, disappearing into the sky without a single look back over her shoulder.

"Lizzy!" Booker's hissed call snapped her wide-eyed gaze down from the sky and back to her friend, who was beckoning her urgently. "Hurry up, she won't be gone long!"

Jerking into motion, Lizzy tightened her grasp around both their bags and jogged over to Booker's side. He didn't let her stop, hooking his hand around her elbow and sending them both running towards the oak tree surrounded by the active circle; a perfect ring of glowshrooms, glimmering and throbbing bright blue, full of fey magic.

The instant their feet crossed the ring of 'shrooms and pressed against the soft grass, the blue light pulsed brighter. Racing across the ground beneath their feet like a shockwave, it closed in on the sacred tree, hitting the base and running up the oak's trunk before sinking into the deep cracks between the bark and turning its surface translucent while the 'shrooms became washed out and white once more.

Then an aurora of warning lights lit up the sky above them.

"Squirrel shit!"

"Keep running!" Booker snapped back, tugging on Lizzy's arm when her steps faltered at the light display they'd inadvertently triggered.

The humming vibration of fey wings filled the air behind them, and Lizzy realised the aurora must have summoned every court sentinel in the vicinity.

She kept running, heart in her throat, until she and Booker hit the still glowing trunk of the tree and passed through it.

Bright blue faded to black. Like the aftermath of an explosion, or from staring into a fire too long and then looking away. She was weightless, and Lizzy had just enough time to realise the whole sensation felt disturbingly like falling before her feet slammed into solid ground.

Her legs gave way beneath her from the force, and Lizzy dropped their bags. Her hands snapped out in front of her, slamming hard against damp grass, barely halting her forward momentum and stopping herself from smashing face-first into the grass.

Booker's anxious panting beside her suggested her experience wasn't a unique one, but Lizzy pushed through the moment of disorientation.

Rolling over, she stared wide-eyed at the tree they'd travelled through, then scrambled backwards across the soaked soil and away from the fey portal.

Despite her reassurances to Booker earlier in the night, Lizzy still half expected the sentinels to follow them through at any moment, determined to drag them back to face... whatever the punishment was for unauthorised portal access.

As she watched, heart in her throat, the glow faded from the tree. It leached out from between the cracks in its bark and sank into the soil before disappearing entirely.

"We did it," Lizzy breathed. It took a second or two for their success to sink in, but then she released a loud, relieved laugh as it hit her.

"Booker, we did it!" she repeated before flinging herself at her friend. Her arms wrapped around his neck in a hug that knocked him back down onto the grass, pulling a groan of complaint from his throat.

"You had doubts?" he huffed breathlessly, and she released him with a grin.

"How did you get rid of the sentinel?" she asked, moving back so he could sit up. Booker shrugged in answer, but there was a small twist to his lips that told Lizzy whatever he'd done, Booker had thoroughly enjoyed it.

"I told her Crisan had sent me to get her, and that she'd looked furious," Booker explained. Reaching for his fallen bag, he climbed to his feet, holding out a patient hand to help Lizzy up.

"Crisan?" she repeated, accepting his help and frowning. "As in Fiona Crisan, captain of the court sentinels?"

"That's the one."

"And she fell for it?"

"I think you're forgetting how much of a bitch Crisan is," Booker said lightly. "No one wants to get on her bad side."

Lizzy snickered as Booker glanced back at the now-inactive portal and shook his head. "Can we get out of here now? I feel like the tree's going to reactivate at any moment..."

"Absolutely," Lizzy agreed. Picking up her bag, she slung it over her shoulder and turned to examine their surroundings, more than ready to figure out where exactly the portal had spat them out.

3

It was still the middle of the night, but the similarities ended there.

When Lizzy and Booker had stepped into the fairy circle, they had been surrounded by the carefully curated collection of sacred trees. Now they were standing on a large patch of grass with the lone oak they had arrived through standing at their backs.

Even the moon looked different, Lizzy noticed, hanging full and round, despite the light cloud cover hiding the stars overhead.

Beyond the green were what looked like streets, paved in uniform square stone slabs, with lights on top of tall poles that stood at regular intervals and bathed their surroundings in pools of harsh orange light.

Lizzy hesitated, glancing around as she tried to find something she recognised but each direction looked the same. Rows of buildings stretched out into the night, further than she could see.

Their doors were sealed, their windows dark, and Lizzy felt her fingers tighten on the strap of her bag as a wave of doubt crashed over her.

"You have no idea which way to go, do you?" Booker groaned, and the threat of his imminent teasing banished her hesitation. Booker wouldn't let her live it down if she admitted to being lost, so she did the first thing she could think of. She lied.

"Of course I do," she answered, clearing her throat and pointing towards the nearest row of orange lights, "it's this way."

Without looking at Booker to see if he'd bought her bravado, Lizzy started across the green, hoping they would stumble over something she recognised before he called her on her bluff.

"And what makes you so sure?" he asked, scattering her hopes to the winds, even as he fell into step beside her. Lizzy forced herself to roll her eyes like she wasn't making everything up on the spot.

"There are lights," she told him, "and where there are lights, there are people. If there are people, Booker, then there's going to be an inn—"

"A hotel."

"—a hotel, and then we can stay there for the night, and figure out where to go next in the morning."

"With what money, Lizzy?" Booker prompted, and she shot him a glare.

"I have gems to trade, of course. I'm not a complete idiot."

"Did you fail the class on the mortal realm, by any chance?"

"Why?" she asked sharply, coming to an abrupt stop, her suspicion rising at the amusement in Booker's voice, and when she turned to face him, his green eyes were almost glimmering with barely restrained laughter.

"Because humans don't work in trade anymore. Unless we can find some kind of jewellers to sell them to tomorrow, those gems of yours are worthless here."

Lizzy stared at Booker for a long moment, disbelief battling with despair in her chest, before her shoulders slumped and her eyes slid closed.

"Tell me you're joking?" she pleaded, but her friend's quiet laughter said he wasn't. "How did I not know that? And stop laughing!" she added, voice sharp as she slapped the back of her hand against his arm, but the reprimand did nothing to smother his amusement.

"What are we going to do?" Lizzy moaned. Pushing her hair off her face with a groan, she struggled to reorganise her plan. If her gems were useless for bartering, then everything was at risk of disintegrating before it even began.

"This was your idea, why do I have to come up with a solution?" Booker shot back, still grinning. Despite his words, he slung an arm around her shoulders and tugged her into his side reassuringly, starting them both walking towards the street once more.

"Well, you're now the self-appointed brains of the operation," Lizzy muttered, calming under the comforting weight of Booker's arm. Trusting him to find a solution to their current dilemma, she continued her earlier observations of the human town they'd found themselves in the middle of.

The portal they had arrived through seemed to be acting as a sort of central point to the town, and Lizzy felt a rush of relief that they had arrived in the middle of the night. While humans couldn't perceive fey magic, a couple of teens crawling across the grass in open panic might have raised a few eyebrows.

As the pair of them stepped off the grass and onto the smooth stone slabs that seemed to pave the street, she began to study the buildings more closely. They were all uniformly rectangular, put together with red brick, and there wasn't a single thatched roof in sight.

They didn't look residential to her, but it was becoming clear her knowledge of the mortal realm might not be as solid as she had believed it to be.

Beyond the fact her gems were useless, nothing around them looked familiar. Nothing like her teacher, Master Weylan, had described in his lessons and she glanced back at Booker, her curiosity piqued.

"How do you know so much about the mortal realm, anyway?" she asked. "You didn't even take that class."

"I didn't take it because Weylan is an idiot who's never set foot here," Booker muttered. He glanced around briefly before turning them both down a street that, to Lizzy, looked no different than all the others.

"I read my dad's journals," Booker continued, his voice growing soft and quiet. "He and Mum came here a lot. Especially when they were trying to convince the Court to reimplement regular contact."

"Ah..." Lizzy couldn't think of anything else to say. Booker didn't talk about his parents often, and she didn't want to press him further. Instead, she slipped her arm around his waist in silent support and accepted the gentle squeeze around her shoulders as wordless thanks.

They moved down the street, their footsteps against the damp pavement the only sound disturbing the night air until Booker huffed out a soft sigh.

"So, I'm thinking if we wander around the town tonight, we can try and spot a store that looks like it might buy your gems. It'll let us familiarise ourselves with the layout a bit too, so we don't get hopelessly lost every time we turn a corner," Booker began slowly.

"Once we've got some of the local currency we can find somewhere for breakfast, and ask about a hotel. That'll give us somewhere to sleep while we figure out where to go next. Sound good?"

Lizzy hummed as she considered Booker's plan, stepping over a small puddle that had collected in a dip on the pavement.

She glanced up at the sky again, but the clouds had grown thicker as they'd walked, coating the moon in inky shadows. It wasn't raining, but the damp night air had already sunk through her light linen clothes and settled against her skin.

"It sounds miserable in this weather," she grumbled, wrinkling her nose in distaste, "but what choice do we... have...?" Lizzy's voice trailed off as a sudden chill raced along her spine.

For a second, she thought it might be nothing more than the cool night air, an unexpected breeze against her damp skin, but then she heard a sound behind them. The slap of something against the stone that she almost put down to their footsteps bouncing off the buildings, only it echoed wrong.

A little too fast, a little too soft.

Lizzy stopped and turned, Booker's arm falling away from her shoulders, but despite the almost ominous orange glow of the lights lining the street behind them, Lizzy couldn't see anything out of place.

When the sound she'd been hearing abruptly stopped, her skin began to crawl.

"What is it?" Booker asked, his voice quiet and wary, and Lizzy knew he was reacting to her tension.

"I think... someone might be following us."

"The portal deactivated, and no one here knows us."

Despite his reassurances, Booker's voice had dropped to an anxious whisper, and Lizzy swallowed, shaking her head while she continued to scan the street behind them for any sign of movement or a shadow out of place.

"I don't think it's fey..." she told him, voice just as quiet before taking a step back and bumping into Booker, pressing her frame against his in an attempt to make him move without having to tear her eyes away from the street.

"A human? Lizzy—"

"Let's just go," she pleaded, fear bubbling up through her stomach, burning her throat. She didn't want to argue, she wanted to run.

Lizzy didn't know what she was afraid of, but she couldn't fight it off either.

"Please, Booker."

A nerve-wracking moment of silence followed her request

before Booker grabbed her hand and tugged her around with a quiet, "Alright, this way."

He quickly led them down more streets, taking seemingly random turns, and within moments Lizzy felt hopelessly lost. She wouldn't have been able to find her way back to the portal if she'd wanted to.

The moment they'd continued walking, the strange slapping sound had returned. Faster now, and close enough to make her shiver. Lizzy kept sending anxious glances over her shoulder, trusting Booker to tug her through the maze-like town.

Without warning, the sound changed. It seemed to overtake them, and Lizzy ground to a halt.

They were in the middle of a cobblestone street that passed between two buildings, the narrow pathway only a little wider than Lizzy and Booker walking side by side and with no space for the regular orange street lights that had seemed so eerie only ten minutes ago.

Despite the close quarters, they had somehow been overtaken, and Lizzy turned to stare up at the rooftops as the answer came to her too late.

It had only taken a moment and Lizzy's hand slipping out of his grasp for Booker to notice she'd ground to a halt. He turned back to check on her, eyes wide with concern.

"What is it?" he demanded, voice still quiet but filled with urgency. "What are you looking at?"

Lizzy didn't answer him. It didn't matter that they'd been tracked from the rooftops, not when the person trailing them had moved ahead.

Lizzy dropped her gaze from the buildings, staring down at the end of the narrow street. Booker turned to follow her gaze, and immediately backed up to stand beside her.

The glow of the orange street lights ahead of them were no longer ominous, but reassuring. It summoned a desire in Lizzy to step closer, to seek out the safety of a well-lit area, but their path forward had become blocked.

A woman stood at the far end of the alley, her hands clasped against the small of her back with the narrow street opening out behind her into a fresh part of town.

It was as beyond their reach as the portal back to Arbaon.

Before Lizzy could summon her voice to call out, the stranger began to move closer. One slow step at a time. Bright blonde hair hung around her face in long, lank strands and swayed with her movements.

As she approached, Lizzy felt her heart rise to sit in her throat, the source of the sound that had been following them through the town became obvious and she found herself staring at the woman's bare feet, mesmerised and horrified as they slapped against the damp ground.

A dark dress fell to the stranger's knees and merged with the shadows cast by the buildings on either side of them as she approached. Her head tilted to one side as though curious, but twisted too far over in an unnatural manner, and everything about her made Lizzy's skin crawl.

"I don't know what I did to get this lucky," the woman purred before suddenly giggling like a child, her hands springing up from her sides fast enough to make Lizzy flinch back and press against Booker's side.

Lizzy's fearful reaction didn't seem to have any effect on the woman, and she tangled her fingers together and pressed her hands to her chest.

She continued her slow, measured approach, but with each steady step, she twisted her body. Back and forth, swaying until her skirt spun around her knees, giving a deceptively innocent appearance.

As she moved closer, Lizzy realised her light blonde hair almost gave the woman the appearance of a fey, but the unrestrained manic glee in her bloodshot eyes and the twisted expression creeping over her face placed her firmly on the wrong side of terrifying.

Neither Lizzy nor Booker needed the connection of telepathy to begin retreating as one, but the strange woman didn't change her pace, only matching their movements and releasing a delighted laugh.

"Where are you going?" she snarled darkly, snapping from amused to furious in a heartbeat and tilting her head to the opposite side.

The movement made her seem even more broken, like her neck had no support. The angles reminded Lizzy of a puppet with its strings cut.

"Don't you want to play?" Her voice shifted from its dangerous growling into a high-pitched, almost singsong, tone.

She began to chant then, a chilling rhyme, hopping onto a new square of stone pavement with each beat of her song. Advancing ever closer and Lizzy felt her hands begin to shake.

> "Two young fey-blood walking 'long the street,
> How will I choose which to eat?
> Knock them out, and break the boy,
> Then turn the girl into this month's toy!"

"A vampire," Booker breathed, and Lizzy almost stumbled, her limbs shaking with the desire to turn and run.

But it was too late now. The vampire was close enough Lizzy could see the sharp teeth of a predator behind the woman's delighted grin, and a second later, she lunged.

4

"No!" Lizzy screamed as the vampire dove for Booker, almost too fast to track. Its hands outstretched, twisting until the fingers resembled grasping claws.

The vampire never reached Booker.

Instead, it slammed hard against the force of Lizzy's telekinesis.

The invisible blow sent the vampire careening back down the narrow street, a furious snarl escaping it, even as the creature twisted in the air like a cat and landed on all fours.

Lizzy's reaction had been primal and instinctive, but she didn't know what to do next. She held the mental force in place, pushing back against the vampire.

"Come on," Booker gasped, sounding shaken to the core, but Lizzy couldn't turn her attention away from the vampire as it began to fight against the push of her mind.

"I can't... I have to... focus..." she spluttered, jaw tensing in concentration. Booker cursed when he figured out what Lizzy couldn't say. If she turned to flee, the shield would dissipate and the creature would be on them before they made it onto the next street.

"What the rot are we going to do?" he hissed, watching the vampire finally stagger upright, and push towards them with a single slow step, its grin widening when it found it could still advance, albeit slowly.

Lizzy didn't have an answer for Booker's frantic question. She was out of ideas and couldn't risk letting her focus falter to consider alternative solutions.

"I was going to be kind," it snarled, taking another slow stride towards them, leaning into the force of Lizzy's mind as though fighting against a strong wind.

"I was going to keep you in a pretty room, with toys and lace," the vampire continued, bracing bare toes against the hard ground before pressing towards them in incremental steps.

"Telepathy's not working," Booker added, voice wavering with almost palpable fear, and Lizzy swallowed hard against her growing terror as another strand of hope shattered.

"But now, fairy-child, I think I shall just devour you here, in the filth and muck, like you deserve!"

The vampire's voice had lifted into a playful lilt once more, and the chill that had first warned Lizzy they were being followed returned, prickling across her skin.

There was a madness in the vampire's wild, bloodshot eyes, and Lizzy's concentration almost faltered as it moved another step closer. Cackling in delight, its grasping hands stretched out, clawing at the air, pulling itself forward another step.

Lizzy grunted from the strain, her brow furrowing against the pounding headache rising in her temples, while the seed of a desperate plan began to form.

She watched the way the vampire pressed against her telekinesis, leaning forward until it was almost parallel to the ground.

If she could make the creature stumble, fall, it might give her and Booker a moment of opportunity. A tiny chance to try and flee.

It was reckless, and Lizzy had serious doubts about their chances of success, but she couldn't hold the vampire back much longer. Either the pain in her head would force her to withdraw, or the vampire would reach them through brute force.

"Be ready," Lizzy muttered, making her decision and stretching out her hand blindly for Booker's, not daring to tell him the rest of her plan and risk tipping off their attacker.

"Ready for what?" he shot back, panic coating his every word.

Lizzy didn't answer, but that didn't stop Booker from clasping her hand in his. The familiar feel of his palm against hers grounded Lizzy as the vampire giggled, seeming to delight in their fear, and its tongue ran over its lips like it was tasting the air.

A soft whimper escaped Lizzy, the pain in her head almost blinding as the vampire took its time in pressing closer across the last few feet. Forcing its way steadily through the telekinetic barrier Lizzy was struggling to maintain.

"Lizzy..." Booker's voice was a low warning as the monster before them cackled, her outstretched hands almost close enough to touch, but Lizzy remained still.

Waiting. Waiting for their best chance.

It was only as it prepared to take the final step forward, to bring its grasping, claw-like fingers within range of the two fey, that Lizzy moved.

"Now!" Stepping back and to the side, shoving Booker along with her, Lizzy released the mental barrier the vampire was fighting against, and it staggered forward, its straining limbs sending it crashing into the ground.

Lizzy's head throbbed with pain, and she swayed with exhaustion, but Booker didn't falter. He took the opening Lizzy had provided and ran with it.

His fingers tightened around hers as he dashed towards the end of the street, heading for the orange glow of the street lights and tugging her along behind him.

She did her best to keep up, but the world was spinning around her and nausea churned in her stomach at the furious snarls from the vampire on the ground behind them.

Lizzy could barely stay upright, let alone run, and she grew cold, shuddering as the realisation hit her; they were going to die.

Booker was going to die, and it was all her fault.

In the moment it took her to get lost in her growing despair, Booker came to a dead stop right in front of her, snapping Lizzy out of her spiralling thoughts when she crashed into his back.

Her free hand lifted to grasp at the sleeve of his coat. "What—?"

"Get out of the way," a new voice snapped, interrupting Lizzy's half-formed question.

Booker reacted instantly, pushing them both back from the speaker and trapping Lizzy's still disorientated form between the wall of the building and his shoulder.

A tall shape moved forward in a blur of motion like that of their attacker, making Lizzy gasp and press her back harder against the rough stone of the building, but it made no move to lunge for them. Instead, the dark shape flung itself at the vampire.

The shape, she quickly realised, was a man and as the vampire turned to snarl at them, he planted his curled fist against the creature's jaw in a blow that sent its head snapping backwards with an audible crack.

The punch drew blood, an unnatural shriek of rage from the vampire's throat, and a sound of surprise from Lizzy, her eyes wide and fixed on the fight.

"We should run, Lizzy," Booker prompted, "while it's distracted."

He took an encouraging step away from the building and towards the main street, still bright with the orange lights, but Lizzy couldn't make herself follow him, despite the tugging on her hand.

Her head still ached, and the world remained unsteady, but the fight held her mesmerised.

The fey weren't natural fighters. They had declared it uncivilised centuries ago, but the movements of the stranger didn't look uncivilised. They were smooth and controlled. Almost like a dance Lizzy could feel, but didn't know the steps for.

He wasn't wearing any kind of armour Lizzy recognised either. Just a shirt without buttons or lacing, and trousers in a stiff, blue fabric that somehow still managed to move with him.

The only thing that looked armoured or reinforced were the heavy boots he used to kick the vampire back a few paces.

Seconds later, the newcomer had traded fists for two short blades, slicing at the vampire as the creature lunged for him again, forcing it to retreat or bleed.

Only minutes ago, Lizzy had believed the vampire to be the most dangerous thing in the mortal realm. As she watched the stranger close in, grabbing the monster and slamming it into the building before his weapon sliced across its throat, Lizzy began to re-evaluate that belief.

Blood flooded out from the vampire's severed neck. Its claw-like fingers scrabbled at the stranger's broad shoulders in a desperate attempt to escape his grasp. It gurgled, the sound forcing Lizzy to swallow back the taste of burning acid, but the man never faltered, watching the vampire die with a cold, stoic expression.

The clawing hands fell limp. Its head drooped and its eyes slipped closed, but the stranger continued to hold the body pinned to the wall for another long moment before stepping back swiftly and letting it drop unceremoniously to the ground.

As it hit, it disintegrated in a soft splash, leaving behind a foamy pile of red against the damp street that looked like it had been expelled from someone's stomach. The only evidence of the man's kill.

Lizzy's hand snapped up from where she'd been clinging to Booker to press against her mouth, struggling not to be sick at the sight, while Booker swore quietly at her side, sounding as shaken as she felt.

Their reactions drew the stranger's attention, his head spinning around until his gaze settled on Booker before flicking down to land on Lizzy.

In an instant, his features twisted and a growl escaped him, prompting Lizzy to step back as far as she could, still trapped between Booker and the wall.

The stranger lunged for her in the same way he had the vampire and she could do nothing but release a startled yelp.

Booker stepped between them, a snarl on his lips and his hand still clasped around her own, like a lifeline. "Don't touch her!"

The stranger's attack faltered at Booker's command, and he staggered sideways to lean against the building. One of his blades dropped to the ground and he raised his now-empty hand to his head with an audible groan of pain.

"Enough!" he ground out between clenched teeth, the word half request, half demand.

Lizzy saw the twitch on Booker's face, telling her he'd brought his telepathy into play. She knew he must have flooded the other man's mind with a cacophony of noise to force him to falter and she squeezed Booker's hand.

It was a gentle reassurance she was fine, even as she struggled to slow her breathing, but a moment later, the line of Booker's shoulders softened and the stranger blew out a sigh of relief.

The stranger's pain-filled expression had begun to fade, but Booker stayed in his position between their rescuer and her.

"Who are you?" Booker asked. "You're not like... her..." he fumbled, indicating the now foamy red mess congealing against the pavement, and the other man gave a dry, humourless laugh as he straightened slowly.

"I should be the one asking questions," he snapped. "What the hell is a fey doing running around alone, protecting a vampire."

"I'm not a vampire," Lizzy snapped, "we're both fey."

"Is that so?" the stranger asked, running his eyes across her, assessing, and Lizzy could almost taste the disbelief rolling off him.

"It's true," Booker confirmed, and Lizzy caught the flash of surprise on the stranger's face before he hid it and shrugged. He bent to collect his fallen blade, slipping both weapons into sheaths strapped to his legs before speaking again.

"That still doesn't answer my question. What are you both doing wandering around, alone?"

"Why is that any of your business? Who are you?" Lizzy demanded, eyes narrowing as she fought back the fury at his easy dismissal of her honesty.

"I just saved your lives. I think the very least you two owe me are some answers," the man offered back calmly. Lizzy had every intention of telling him where he could shove his answers, but Booker squeezed her hand and she fell silent, turning to her friend instead.

Lizzy didn't need telepathy to read Booker's intentions. They were written all over his face. The brightness in his eyes, the hint of an arched eyebrow. He was asking her to trust their rescuer.

Whatever he'd glimpsed in the stranger's mind, it was enough for Booker, and Lizzy pursed her lips in irritation before surrendering. If Booker wanted to trust him, she would trust Booker, but that didn't mean they had to tell him everything.

Spinning her gaze back around, she found the unnamed man watching them, features sharp and alert as he patiently waited for one of them to answer his questions. Lizzy released a heavy sigh to give herself another moment to think.

"We're looking for a missing fey delegation," she said. "They came here about a month ago, and never returned to Arbaon."

"Just the two of you?" he asked, and after another moment's pause, Lizzy nodded.

"Right..." the man said before huffing out a soft sort of laugh and shaking his head.

"You don't believe us?" Booker asked, but the stranger merely offered a nonchalant shrug.

"I think if a whole delegation went missing, then sending two people to track them down is stupid. It's just asking for two more to go missing. But that's above my pay grade."

Something in the man's frame had relaxed at their answer, and he stepped closer to them, finally giving Lizzy a clear look at his face.

The first thing she noticed up close was how tall he was. With her nose level to the man's sternum, Lizzy needed to tip her head back to meet his gaze, only to find storm-cloud-grey eyes already staring back at her intently, shadowed by heavy brows.

She'd thought his hair to be black, hanging to his shoulders in loose curls and making his tawny skin appear paler than it was, but as he stepped out of the alley's shadows, she could see it was actually a dark auburn colour.

A short, matching beard softened the line of his jaw, but everything about him spoke of a leashed strength. All hard lines and sharp angles, except his eyes. Despite the way they pierced through her, there remained a softness to them that made Lizzy want to trust him.

The snarl as he'd lunged for her flashed through her mind, and Lizzy squashed the thought ruthlessly. She glared instead, focussing on her irritation and stubbornly resisting the urge to flinch away from him.

"Are you going to introduce yourself?" she demanded, and for a moment, there was almost a smile on his lips before it vanished and she was left wondering if she'd imagined it.

"Are you?" the stranger shot back, but before Lizzy could snap at him, Booker answered.

"Booker Reed," he offered, placing the hand that wasn't still curled around her own against his chest, "and this is Lila Isabelle—"

"Lizzy," she corrected, her voice sharp, "Lizzy Hail."

She glared at Booker for handing her first name to a stranger and he grimaced, offering her a wide-eyed look of apology until she relented.

Glancing back at their rescuer, she found him studying them, his attention sliding between her and Booker with calm consideration before humming and finally offering his name in return.

"Andric Roche," he introduced, "kavian hunter."

"A what hunter?"

"Kavian?" Lizzy asked, her question clashing with Booker's, and Andric blinked at them in unmasked surprise.

"The... woman that attacked you," he explained, "she was a kavian."

"A vampire," Booker said slowly, as though double-checking the wording on a particularly complex piece of Arbaon law. "You call them kavians here?"

"No," Andric answered, beginning to frown at them in open confusion, "kavians are different. I'm a vampire."

Andric had a sneaking suspicion his night was about to go from mildly entertaining to annoying at record speed.

When he'd heard the snarls of a kavian, the last thing he'd expected to find had been a couple of fey still alive enough to attempt an escape.

A *couple* of fey. He still wasn't entirely sure about the woman, Lizzy.

Her skin didn't have the near-translucent etherealness of the fey, and she had no wings he could see. On the other hand, the young man at her side was protective enough that Andric found himself inclined to believe them on principle.

Until he pointed out the difference between a kavian and a vampire, and the pair of them stood gaping at him in stunned silence.

Admittedly, Andric had only been half-listening to his mother's talk of council procedures. Still, it seemed likely officials would have briefed all fey arriving from Arbaon on the current state of the mortal realm.

"How old are you two, anyway?"

A mixture of curiosity and suspicion drove his question. As the adrenaline from the fight drained away, he found himself studying them with narrowed eyes and a fresh, critical gaze.

They were both dressed in typical fey garb. Shoes woven from leaf-like fibres, matching trousers and shirts in light linens of cream and blue, and the young man, Booker, had a long dark coat. Each of them only carried a single small bag, and Andric's suspicions grew.

"You seem very... new... to the mortal realm."

"Ah, well—"

"Old enough," the girl, Lizzy, growled, jabbing her companion in the side and silencing his words.

Andric smothered a grin for the second time since he'd met her. Consistently, and furiously, stubborn. Her attitude was refreshing, but he pushed down the admiration and focused on his suspicions instead.

Forcing his expression to reveal nothing, he considered what to do with them.

He couldn't let them wander off alone. Kavians were wild, rabid, and uncontrollable, and while they usually travelled alone, they could also hear fey blood humming with power. It would draw more of them in, like flies. Leaving the two companions to fend for themselves would be a death sentence.

"I think I had better take you to someone who knows more about this than me," Andric muttered, mostly to himself, as his thoughts turned to his employer.

He didn't let himself wince, but he wasn't looking forward to revealing how close to Speculo School he'd been staying. He'd been hoping to keep that little tidbit a secret until after his mandatory leave had run its course.

"Come on, follow me, I'll drive you up to speak with Thomas Walcott," he told the pair, not giving himself a moment to second-guess the decision.

Andric moved to step past them, heading towards where he'd parked his car for the evening's hunt, but Miss Hail's voice stopped him in his tracks.

"And what if we refuse?" she demanded, voice sharp and reluctant, and Andric bit back a laugh before turning to meet her electric-blue eyes that were sparking at him furiously.

He let one eyebrow raise, the sole trace of amusement he allowed on his face, but it only seemed to amplify her irritation. Instantly, her features twisted into a scowl and her hands curled into furious fists.

"Lizzy," Mister Reed groaned, but the girl never wavered and Andric admitted himself impressed.

She'd watched him dispatch a kavian, with blades and blood, but he could find no fear in her features as she stared him down, challenging him.

She was going to be trouble.

"Then, Miss Hail, I shall be forced to assume you're both lying to me, knock you out, and take you anyway," he announced lightly, as though he didn't already suspect the pair of concealing their real intentions. "I promise you, however, coming with me voluntarily will be a much more pleasant experience."

They didn't have a choice. He knew it, and Booker Reed knew it. Andric held her gaze, letting her see that he wasn't about to take no for an answer and, begrudgingly, the realisation sank into the lines of her face.

Even then, she only seemed to back down with great reluctance. Offering a short nod of agreement before she heaved a sigh, Miss Hail pulled her hand free of Mister Reed's, only to cross her arms in open disapproval, forcing Andric to bite back another grin.

"Fine. Lead the way," she ordered. If not for the bitter tone to her voice, Andric might have believed taking them to the local vampire stronghold had been her plan all along.

"This way," he invited, indicating the far end of the alley with a sweep of his arm before heading towards the main street he'd arrived from.

After only a couple of paces, he heard them both fall into step behind him. They kept their distance, but he didn't fault them for their caution and calmly led them through the streets.

As they walked, he let himself fall into practised habits. Scanning the shadows for the blur of a kavian, while keeping his sensitive hearing focused on the fey at his back.

Patrolling the quiet little town of Hockley had become a regular nightly occurrence for Andric while he waited out his mandatory leave.

He'd stayed at his family's home almost a week before he'd had to get out. Get away. He hadn't been able to stand watching his mum grieve for his brother, so he'd made his way back towards Speculo.

But his mandatory leave meant he couldn't, shouldn't, be heading back to the school at all. It was why he'd spent the last fortnight living out of a hotel room.

While not ideal, it had still been an improvement on the grief that coated every corner of his home, and Andric had taken to spending his nights hunting any kavian stupid enough to try heading in the direction of Speculo School.

Being forbidden from active duty was one thing, but Andric was still a trained hunter. Even without the safety of the castle's wards and walls, or the support of his fellow hunters, he'd tracked down and killed as many kavians as he could.

And if it helped to distract him from his grief, then that was nothing more than a bonus.

"Lizzy," he heard hissed from behind him, "stop antagonising the man who just saved our lives!"

Their voices pulled Andric's mind away from imagining the disappointment on Headmaster Walcott's face when he walked into the old vampire's office. Instead, he let himself concentrate on the conversation the two troublemakers at his back were trying to keep quiet.

The pair were doing a good job; they were staying several paces back and speaking in hushed tones. If he were human, or fey, he doubted he'd have noticed their murmured argument at all.

Unfortunately for them both, being a vampire gave him a distinct advantage.

"It's not my fault he's acting like a—"

"Please," Mister Reed pleaded quietly, cutting off his companion's scathing comment. With Andric's back to them, he didn't bother smothering the amused grin that spread across his face.

"This might be exactly the kind of opportunity we were looking for," Mister Reed continued, and Andric sobered in response. He kept half his attention on the surroundings but found himself focussing more and more on the two fey.

"What do you mean?"

"These vampires seem well established in the mortal realm. They might have resources we can use. They might be able to trade your gems for local currency without arousing human suspicions. They might even already have some leads about what happened to Maddy. Let's just see how this plays out."

His answer was silence, but Andric was more interested in what he'd managed to glean from Mister Reed's words than in Miss Hail's possible response.

That the pair of them hadn't been able to differentiate between a kavian and a vampire had been concerning enough on its own. But now, it sounded like the two following him had little to no knowledge of the mortal realm at all. Let alone the state of the vampire-fey political climate.

The fey had chosen to seal themselves inside Arbaon for almost four centuries after the emergence of the kavians. It had only been during the last three decades that the Court had begun to re-establish communication with the Vampire Council.

Despite that, it sounded like the two following him were fresh from the sealed realm. Like they'd had no contact with vampire officials at all, and they seemed to lack any knowledge about how the mortal world had changed in the absence of the fey.

It only made Andric more certain that leaving them to their own devices was a bad idea.

He had to get them to Walcott. For answers, if nothing else. But if the pair were as alone as they seemed, Thomas Walcott was in the best position to help them.

Most telling, however, was the newly learned name, Maddy. With that small insight into their motivations, Andric hoped he had the first clue to the puzzle Miss Hail and Mister Reed presented.

"... but if they can't help, we move on," the young woman behind him muttered, breaking him from his thoughts. "We need to find out what happened, not get tangled up in... this."

The silence behind him suggested Mister Reed had agreed with her caveat, but Andric had faith that Headmaster Walcott would be more than capable of outsmarting the young woman.

They were approaching his car, and as he pulled out his keys, Andric had to force down a grin.

Just how outdated is their knowledge? he wondered, before pressing the button in his hand to unlock the vehicle.

The car beeped. The lights flashed once, telling him the doors were unlocked, and Andric turned to face the pair of fey. He waved a casual hand at the car and watched them come to a wary stop.

"You can fight over the front seat," he instructed, but neither of them moved for a moment. Unsurprisingly, Miss Hail reacted first and she leant towards her companion slowly.

"What... is it?" the young woman asked. Her voice was quiet, not quite a whisper, but Mister Reed only offered a shrug in response.

"It's a car," Andric answered her instead, voice a little weaker than he'd have liked.

He had expected the electronics to surprise them. He hadn't anticipated neither of them knowing what a car even was.

Miss Hail blinked at him twice, and he could almost hear her weighing the validity of his words before turning her attention back to the car and tilting her head to the side, studying it. Mister Reed watched her in silence, amusement painted across his face, and Andric found himself waiting for her verdict.

"Don't you need to wind up the front, or something?" she asked after a moment of consideration, and Andric felt his jaw drop.

"I think the term is 'crank it'," Mister Reed added.

"Not... not in the last... hundred years or so," Andric forced out weakly, and Miss Hail pressed her lips together in open annoyance.

He had no idea how either of them planned to survive in the mortal realm if they still thought cars needed cranking, and that gems were an acceptable form of payment. Their lack of knowledge regarding kavians was concerning, but it was no longer the most shocking aspect to their story.

"I see what you mean about Master Weylan being an idiot," the young woman said, glancing at Mister Reed briefly before turning back to face Andric.

"Where do we sit?" she asked, shoulders slumping in at least a temporary surrender.

It took a moment for Andric to calm his swirling thoughts, and he shook his head as he fought to focus on the question. He was beginning to wonder exactly what kind of mess he'd found himself in the middle of.

Instead of answering Miss Hail directly, he turned towards the car and pulled open the rear door.

"One of you can sit in the back; one of you can take the front seat," he explained, making the split-second decision to keep the pair as separate as possible.

"Looks like there's enough room for both of us back there," the young woman prompted. Her eyes were spitting blue fire at him again, and he almost shot her a grin of approval before he caught himself.

"In theory," he agreed, voice quiet, "but I don't know you two. Can't say I trust you overmuch, either," he added, exaggerating only slightly.

The girl was sharp, impressively so, and Mister Reed's abilities had already brought him to a stop once. While their ignorance was alarming, they were capable enough to be troublesome.

"I don't really want one of you sitting behind me," he added, "and since it's my car..." He trailed off with a shrug.

"Perfectly understandable," Mister Reed said brightly. "I'll take the back," he added, shooting a soothing grin in Miss Hail's direction.

Andric was quite certain Mister Reed's hand, settling light and brief against the woman's elbow, had been the only thing that halted the irritation lighting up her eyes.

Deciding not to antagonise the young woman any further, Andric bit his tongue and nodded. He gestured for Mister Reed to get in before he moved to open the front passenger door for Miss Hail.

Both of them stepped forward without comment, only parting at the last moment to each take the offered seats.

Andric spared a few minutes to make sure they both knew how to fasten the seat belts before closing the doors, blurring around the car, and sliding into position behind the wheel a heartbeat later.

"Rot! How did you do that?" Mister Reed cursed from the backseat as Andric clicked his seatbelt into position. Andric snapped his head round to stare at him in surprise, spotting Miss Hail's silent expression of shock at the same time.

"What?" he asked, cautiously glancing between the pair until Miss Hail blew out a soft breath of frustration.

"How did you move that fast?" she elaborated, her large blue eyes growing impossibly wide with a sudden realisation. "Is it a vampire thing?"

He didn't know whether to laugh or groan, so Andric turned around and shoved the key into the ignition.

"You two are so far out of your depth," he muttered to himself as the car came to life with a soft rumble, startling his passengers.

"Do they not tell you anything in Arbaon before shoving you through a portal?" Andric challenged, but he could hear his voice held more exasperation than he'd intended, and Miss Hail latched onto his tone.

Her gaze snapped up from studying the car around her to scowl at him, her glare boring into the side of his face as he bit back an instinctive apology.

Andric braced himself for another acidic comment or a fresh argument from the woman. Instead, she huffed out a harsh breath and settled back into the seat, turning to stare out of the window in silence.

"Hmm," Andric hummed in quiet surprise, but he didn't comment further, resisting the urge to spark up the woman's fiery temper.

Andric watched her from the corner of his eye. He wanted to get them on the road before either of the fey could change their minds and try to leap from the car, or run off into the night.

A quick check of the mirrors later, he put the car into gear. Pulling out of the parking spot, Andric breathed a silent sigh of relief as he got them on the path towards Speculo School and, with luck, some answers.

Every time the vampire spoke, something about what he said, or how he said it, sparked Lizzy's temper.

Even now, with nothing more than a soft hum that should have required nothing from her other than the ability to ignore it, the dismissive sound lit up her anger once more.

"'Hmm', what?" Lizzy challenged, her voice sharp as she turned from staring out the window of the strange vehicle so that she could narrow her eyes at Andric Roche.

The threat of a vampire attack once she reached the mortal realm had always been a possibility. One Lizzy had been willing to risk. But now they had discovered two factions existed; only one of which seemed to be in control of their bloodlust.

It made Booker's suggestion of using the vampire's connections a good one. Garnering their assistance was the smart move, but Lizzy was still torn.

If only they'd encountered a vampire a little less infuriating.

"I just expected more of an argument," Andric offered, shrugging one shoulder. "I was pleasantly surprised, Miss Hail."

"I didn't think explaining the education system of Arbaon, and the preparation procedures for portal travel, were important enough to make my headache worse," she snapped back, and the vampire glanced at her briefly before he returned his attention to the road.

"I didn't realise," he said, the apology ringing clear in his voice and soothing her anger just as quickly as he'd riled it. "Did you hit your head in the attack?"

"No," Booker offered from the seat behind her, "Lizzy used telekinesis to hold the vamp—I mean, the kavian back," he explained.

"And... using it hurts?" Andric questioned, but Lizzy shook her head with a sigh.

"Not usually, but she was pushing against it," Lizzy admitted.

He frowned, open confusion on his face, and Lizzy pressed her lips together, trying to figure out how to explain something so instinctual.

"Telekinesis uses the mind," she tried again, voice slow, "but it's still a muscle. Using it against an inanimate object, like... a piece of parchment, and against a person who's fighting against it, would be the difference between... punching a pillow and punching a grain sack. It's more of a strain."

"And what about you, Mister Reed?" Andric asked after a brief pause where he appeared to be considering her explanation. "Whatever fey trick you employed against me seemed very effective—"

"Telepathy," Booker answered, voice quiet but still managing to cut off Andric's question. "I did try it on her but... her mind..." He paused, and Lizzy glanced over her shoulder. He looked sick, but shook his head before continuing "I couldn't affect her mind. It was already screaming."

There were a few minutes of tense silence in the car after the disturbing revelation, but when Booker continued to avoid her gaze, Lizzy turned and settled into her seat.

"I would like to extend my apologies, however, Master Roche," Booker continued, his voice growing steadier as he spoke. "It's considered an extreme breach of etiquette for a fey to force our way into someone's mind. To connect without consent... and unlike a fey, you had no defences in place—"

"You don't have anything to apologise for," Andric cut him off. "I attacked, and you defended yourselves. As you should."

"Attack, or defence, fighting is not the fey way, and should the Court learn of my actions—"

"Well they won't hear about it from me," Andric said, cutting Booker off a second time, his voice tight.

Lizzy glanced at him, her curiosity piqued, and she noticed his hands clenched around the wheel he'd been using to steer the car, knuckles white.

"You don't agree with the Court's position?" she asked, watching his grey eyes flick over to her for a second before refocusing on the road, his grip loosening on the wheel. Just a little.

"I suppose it makes sense," Lizzy continued, "you're a fighter, after all. We saw that with the kavian—"

"If something is attacking you, determined to kill you, or worse, you shouldn't lay down and let them," Andric growled, and Lizzy let a small smile tug at the corners of her mouth.

"You're right."

Their vampire driver fell silent. Lizzy watched in amusement as he appeared to try and match her response to whatever knowledge he had of the fey. And failed, if his features shifting from a furious scowl to a confused frown was anything to go by.

"What do you mean?" he asked, shaking his head. "I thought the fey were against fighting. You were only apologising a moment ago for defending yourselves—"

"Booker was apologising," Lizzy corrected, her lips lifting into a genuine smile when her best friend sighed behind her.

"Most fey do not believe we should use our abilities offensively," Booker agreed, "but there are some who think our ways should... change. That we should be allowed to use them in life-or-death situations, like today. But it's not a common position to hold within the Court," Booker added.

Without even turning around, Lizzy knew Booker had shot her a look full of frustration.

"If you were to lodge a formal complaint with the Court about my illegal entry into your mind," he continued, "I could be in a great deal of trouble."

"Booker!" Lizzy hissed, snapping her head around to glare at him, but he huffed at her concerns.

"I'd rather we tell him, Lizzy," Booker argued. "At least if he knows he's less likely to get me unintentionally arrested."

"Arrested?" Andric spat out before Lizzy could snap back at her friend.

"While it was being investigated, yes," Booker said, ignoring the furious frown Lizzy still had fixed on him with practised ease.

"I wouldn't be charged, of course. I didn't dive deep enough into your mind for that. Only far enough to fill it with noise, but I would still be arrested, and held, while the Court investigated."

Andric made a soft sound of disgust, and Lizzy narrowed her eyes as she considered the tight grip he had on the wheel once more before deciding to expand on Booker's explanation.

"Arrested and investigated isn't the worst possible outcome," she said softly. "We can connect with surface thoughts for communication purposes. It's a standard part of our society, and many fey communicate telepathically all the time... but we can also deep dive into a person's mind. Search through their thoughts and memories.

"Connecting with surface thoughts without permission is frowned upon, and can be cause for official reprimand, but doing a deep dive without permission is... not good," she finished weakly.

"Deep diving into someone's mind can result in execution," Booker corrected.

Deafening silence settled over the car until Andric took a slow, deep breath in. His fingers flexed around the wheel before they relaxed slowly and he released the breath on parted lips.

"Alright," he said, a grimace twisting his lips, "and what about telekinesis? What's the problem with using that?"

"That it's crass, crude and uncivilised," Lizzy answered, her lips lifting into an amused smirk.

"That's it?" Andric asked, voice startled. He glanced around at them for a moment before returning his attention to the road, and Booker laughed as Lizzy's smirk widened into a grin.

"You clearly don't know much about the Fey Court," Booker offered, still chuckling. "For them, that's more than enough."

When she spotted Andric roll his eyes, Lizzy forced herself to turn away before she broke out into soft laughter. Instead, she focused her attention back onto the passing scenery.

The car fell into a calm quiet, much to Lizzy's relief. The newfound peace let the throbbing in her temples ease until it dissipated entirely.

As Andric continued to drive, they left the town behind them and the view outside the car windows shifted.

Stone streets and orange lights transformed into the shadowed darkness of a forest at night, and Lizzy found the familiar sight of the branches passing her by at high speed soothing.

The rumble of the car brought to mind the thrumming vibration of fey wings, summoning memories of times past. Of times when her mum had taken her flying through the forests of Arbaon.

Her shouts for them to go faster. Her head tipped back, the wind pushing her hair away from her face. Icy cold air hitting her lungs.

A pang of longing shot through her chest, a sharp ache that had her struggling to push back tears and seeking a distraction.

Blinking rapidly, Lizzy focused on the view again, letting her eyes try to lock onto an individual tree as it flashed past the window, but she couldn't.

They sped by too fast to track. A frown replaced the sharp sting of tears when she realised the speed they must be travelling at, and how much ground they must have covered.

Shifting in her seat, she turned to watch Andric instead of the passing scenery.

"Where are you taking us, anyway?" she asked after a moment, her voice quiet. "You never actually said."

There was a note of caution in her voice, despite not having intended the words to come out that way. She could tell Andric had noticed it too when he gave a soft, amused huff.

"If you weren't going to trust me, you shouldn't have got it the car."

"What?!" Booker squawked from the backseat, and Lizzy grit her teeth as her hands clenched into fists, panic gripping her throat.

"Relax," Andric responded to their reactions quickly, "I meant it as a general warning, not a specific one. Don't get into vehicles with strangers... but in this case, you got lucky. I've no intention of hurting either of you."

"You just happened to stumble over two fey being attacked by chance, then?" Lizzy growled. "And decided to help them out of the goodness of your heart?"

Lizzy hadn't liked Andric since the moment he'd lunged for her in the alley. She'd only agreed to follow him because Booker believed they could trust him, and she trusted Booker.

But now, his casually flippant comment had brought all her doubts and suspicions swarming up to the surface. It shattered the tiny, flickering hope that they had found someone genuinely kind.

Someone willing to help them, without having any ulterior motives.

Andric glanced at her for a moment, with an expression Lizzy couldn't read. Before she could figure it out, he'd turned away again, eyes fixed forward and jaw tensed.

She could see the muscle twitching there, like he was grinding his teeth, but he didn't say anything. A split second before she was about to call the vampire out on his nonanswer, he broke the tense silence, his words halting her half-formed rebuke.

"I heard her snarling," Andric admitted. "I'm a kavian hunter. Killing them is what we do."

His words were short and clipped, but he stayed calm despite what appeared to Lizzy to be obvious annoyance at their questions and clear doubt.

"As for where I'm taking you, we're heading towards Speculo School. The headmaster there has experience in dealing with fey."

"What do you mean 'dealing' with fey?"

"Have a little patience, Miss Hail," Andric shot back. "Once we reach the school—"

"I have no intention of being 'dealt' with," Lizzy snapped, and Andric drew a slow, deep breath in through his nose before sighing.

"I only meant... your kind are reclusive, at best. Headmaster Walcott is better positioned to know what aid we might give you in tracking down your missing delegation," Andric said slowly, obviously trying to keep his temper.

Booker's hand settled against her shoulder, a silent warning to let it drop, and Lizzy turned her gaze back to stare out the window. She studied the speed of the trees flying past the car and bit into her lip to silence another sharp comment.

This headmaster might know enough to realise she and Booker hadn't travelled legally through a portal, but they didn't have a choice.

Trying to leap from the car would be a death wish, and even if they could risk it, they had nowhere else to go. No other options. Not now they had left the town they'd arrived in far behind them.

"How much further?" she asked instead, irritation still thrumming through her and staining her voice.

"I'd say less than an hour," Andric answered. "Closer to thirty minutes, at this time of the morning."

Lizzy didn't respond, her mind too busy turning over all the various ways in which meeting with the vampires could go wrong, but Booker took advantage of her sudden silence, his hand still resting lightly on her shoulder.

"Won't we be waking this headmaster up?" he asked quietly. "It's hours until dawn..."

Lizzy hoped Booker was asking in an attempt to buy them more time. Time to get the lay of the land at this school. Time to get their story straight, or to at least link their minds so they could work together.

She spun back to the vampire, but Andric smothered her small spark of hope before it could ignite by simply laughing. A bright, loud sound, filled with genuine amusement, as a grin cracked across his face and Lizzy scowled in response.

"We're vampires, Mister Reed. By the time the sun rises, most of Speculo School will be tucked up in bed for the day," Andric explained, still chuckling through his words.

His open delight at Booker's question made Lizzy's fists clench once more with the urge to hit him.

"Not to worry, you two," he continued, seemingly oblivious to her frustration, "we'll get you some answers about your missing delegation before the moon rises tomorrow night," Andric promised.

Lizzy had to force herself to turn away from him, lifting the pendant at her neck to brush the cool pearls soothingly over her bottom lip, staring wordlessly out into the darkness.

She hoped the vampire was right, but she had a sneaking suspicion, like everything else that night, the meeting would end up going disastrously wrong.

The way Booker sank back into his seat with a heavy sigh, his hand falling away from her shoulder, told Lizzy he was thinking exactly the same thing.

7

Lizzy didn't know what she expected from a school of vampires, but she didn't expect the car to drift around a gentle curve in the road only to reveal a large stone building emerging, ghost-like, from amongst the trees.

Her mouth fell open at the castle sitting in the middle of the forest, and Booker let out a low whistle of appreciation from behind her.

Its tall spires stretched up into the skyline, black against the dark blue of the predawn sky. Beyond the stone wall that had guard towers scattered along its length, were hundreds of windows, all lit up with warm yellow lights, the glow welcoming them in out of the dark.

"It's huge! Are all your schools like this? How many vampires are there?" Booker asked, unmasked curiosity clear in the rapid-fire questions.

"There's one school per country," Andric explained. "The kavians are a constant threat, so if we need to gather in groups, like with a school, we choose single, easily defendable locations.

"Without access to fresh fey-made wards, strongholds like Speculo, guarded by kavian hunters, like myself, are the best we can do."

Lizzy had dozens of questions of her own.

How were the kavians different from the vampires, for starters, but all her questions would raise suspicions and garner questions in return. Questions she couldn't answer, so she bit her tongue and stayed silent.

Andric slowed the car as they approached the castle, its thick stone outer walls looming above them, almost four times as tall as Lizzy. The gates, two large, rectangular doors made of solid wood, braced and inlaid with broad bands of metal, stood slightly open but blocked most of Lizzy's direct view of the school.

As they drew closer, she pulled her attention from the gates to the guardians of Speculo School.

Two vampires appeared in the space between the open doors, almost flickering into view with their enhanced speed. Their hands settled on their blades, dual daggers like the ones Andric had used to dispatch the kavian earlier in the night.

Another flicker of movement on the walkway above the gate showed a third vampire with a long object in his hands.

Lizzy had seen pictures of muskets in her mortal realm classes. While the object wasn't exactly the same, it was similar enough to make her nervous and she didn't need to step out of the car to spot the tension in their faces.

She turned to Andric to ask if he was sure about their welcome, but the vampire beside her had already pressed something on the inside of the car door, and the window beside him slid open.

Surprise halted her words, and a moment later, Andric leant out of the new opening in his vehicle's door, a bright grin on his face.

"It's only me!" he called, and when Lizzy glanced back at the vampires outside the car, all of them had relaxed, their hands moving away from their weapons.

"What are you doing back already? You're supposed to be on vacation for another week!" one of them called back, a welcoming grin emerging from beneath his beard as he stepped forward. His movements were slow, for a pace or two, before he seemed to materialise beside the car, bending over to peer in and immediately frowning.

"What's going on?"

"They're good, Nameer," Andric reassured the other vampire. "I stumbled across a couple of fey in Hockley, about to be dinner for a rabid," he explained, and the other vampire's features twisted into an expression Lizzy could only describe as nauseous.

"It's dead?"

"Yes, but these two need to speak with Thomas."

"Makes sense. No one else around here would know how to handle fey."

Nameer's calm, mahogany-brown gaze slid over Lizzy and Booker in turn, frowning beneath a mop of tight black curls before he shook his head and stepped back from the car.

"Alright, Roche, I won't hold you up. You taking responsibility for bringing strangers in?" the vampire asked, while already signalling his fellow gate guards to let them pass before Andric had even finished nodding.

"Come and find me later," Nameer added as Andric settled back into his seat, "I wanna know why you're back early."

Andric didn't answer, but he did lift a hand in silent acknowledgement. A couple of hunters had pulled the gates open a little more, and Andric edged the car through before driving them deeper into the school's grounds.

"You work here?" Booker asked. Lizzy had been trying to figure out how to ask the same question without sounding accusatory, but somehow Booker had made it seem like innocent curiosity.

"I work where I'm assigned," Andric answered. His voice was quiet, calm, and Lizzy got the distinct impression being inside the walls of Speculo was reassuring for the vampire.

"But, for the last few years, I've been assigned to guard Speculo School and its surrounding grounds, yes."

He pulled the car to a stop, and Lizzy glanced around outside again, only to find rows and rows of more vehicles surrounding them in neat lines. They were in a myriad of colours and all differing shapes but they were clearly still cars.

"Okay, let's get you two up to the headmaster's office," Andric muttered, almost to himself, opening the door and stepping out of the car in one smooth motion.

Lizzy quickly unhooked her seat belt and copied Andric's actions, locating a handle and pushing the heavy door open just as the vampire appeared on her side of the car.

His movements slowed and Lizzy watched his gaze flicker over her bag as she slung it onto her shoulder, a grin creeping across his features.

"Fast learner, huh?" he prompted, moving to open the door for Booker instead.

"It's more that she's observant," Booker answered when Lizzy shrugged in response, but he fell silent when she narrowed her eyes in his direction.

It was a quiet warning. He might trust Andric, but she didn't yet. Booker turned to avoid her gaze, picking up his bag without further comment.

Andric either didn't notice their silent argument or chose to ignore it. He only paused long enough to close the car doors and to make it beep again before beckoning them both towards the school.

"Keep up. Let's try and avoid getting you lost in the crowds that will swarm the place once lessons let out for the night," he said, turning to lead them through the castle.

Lizzy didn't get a chance to examine the school as they moved through it. Struggling instead to keep the back of Andric's head in view as he strode down hallways and up flights of stairs at a pace that left her and Booker nearly running to keep up.

After the third set of stairs, Andric had to wait for them at the top as the pair staggered after him. By the time they caught up, Booker looked ready to drop to the floor for a chance to rest, prompting Lizzy to turn a furious glare on Andric.

"I'm sorry," he offered unprompted, glancing between Booker's breathless form and her anger, but while she swallowed back most of her irate tirade in the face of his apology, it wasn't what she wanted to hear.

"How much further?" Lizzy snapped, and Andric's features closed off once more, lips pressing together to silence whatever his immediate reaction to her snarled question had been.

Instead of answering her, Andric turned to Booker. He was leaning against the wall at the top of the staircase, still catching his breath, but he waved his hand, indicating he was ready to move along. Only then did Andric turn to gesture at a door halfway down the corridor.

"This way," he said, moving forward once more without glancing back at either of them.

Booker's hand on her arm stopped Lizzy from following him immediately, and when she turned to face her friend, he tapped his temple.

The relief that one of them was thinking clearly washed away her anger and she nodded. It only took a moment for the wriggling sensation of telepathy to crawl across her scalp and settle into a disconcerting buzz as they turned to follow Andric.

"*Good idea*," Lizzy sent across the link, and Booker's mind sparkled under her praise.

"We've no idea what we're walking into. It seemed like the safest option."

"If they contact the Court... If they send us back before—"

"*They won't, Lila*," Booker reassured. The comfort of his familiarity soothed her nerves and the familial affection he infused behind her name gave her strength she'd been missing since her mum had left for the mortal realm.

She only allowed two people the privilege of using her first name, and Booker took shameless advantage of it when trying to get her to listen to him. His voice in her mind was firm and unwavering, without a shred of doubt, and she glanced at him in surprise.

"*I won't let them,*" he continued. "*We'll find her, Lila, I promise.*"

A sharp knock snapped her focus away from Booker, and when Lizzy returned her attention to their guide, he was already lowering his hand from a heavily carved wooden door, only to press down on the ornate handle and push it open without bothering to wait for a response.

Using his free hand, Andric beckoned Lizzy and Booker into the room after him, and Lizzy struggled not to let her jaw drop like she had when first laying eyes on the school.

Rich wood panelling covered every surface, the floor softened only by thick rugs. Book-laden shelves sat on each side of the room, stretching from the floor up to the high ceiling and sporting the same ornate carving as the outer door.

Each side of the room had a ladder attached to the bookcases, presumably to reach the upper shelves, and in the middle of the room, an L-shaped desk sat nearly buried under various stacks of paper.

"*They must have cut down half a forest to make this room alone,*" Booker murmured into her mind, and Lizzy nodded in response before catching herself and stilling the motion.

"Good morning. Is Headmaster Walcott in his office?" Andric's voice cut through the quiet of the room, but instead of an answer, he received an excited gasp. A head of red-tinged brunette hair emerged from behind a stack of papers, and the newly revealed receptionist grinned.

"Andric! You're back!"

"Miss Harris?"

If she had to guess, Lizzy would have put the young woman who stepped out from behind the desk with a wide grin stretching across her delicate features at around the same age as herself and Booker but dressed in a crisp white shirt and a tight skirt she appeared older at first glance.

"You're not supposed to be back until next week," she said. Despite her scolding, her voice had an undercurrent of delight, and Lizzy's eyebrows lifted as she watched them interact.

"I guess you just couldn't bear to stay away from us all, hmm?" the woman prompted, tossing long waves of hair over her shoulder before blasting Andric with a clear expression of affection from beneath lowered eyelids.

"Miss Harris—"

"I told you to call me Mimi," she corrected, and Lizzy could feel Booker's amusement reach breaking point as he smothered a laugh with a sharp cough into his hand.

The woman's soft expression vanished, and she turned sharp hazel eyes to scan over Booker before settling on Lizzy.

"Oh, I'm sorry, I didn't see you there. Shouldn't you be in class?" she asked politely, but Lizzy could see the displeasure in the tightness of her shoulders.

"Nope," she offered back, shifting her bag on her shoulder before turning her attention to Andric, waiting for the man to explain why he'd led them here.

"They're with me, Miss Harris," he said, but the way the receptionist's eyes spun from Andric back to Lizzy, narrowing in sudden scrutiny, told Lizzy his choice of phrasing could have been better.

She had a calculating expression hidden beneath her mask of civility that Lizzy recognised from amongst the children of the Fey Court. It made the hair on the back of her neck stand on end, but she lifted her chin, refusing to give away how unsettled she was.

"Lizzy Hail," she introduced herself, "and this is Booker Reed."

The woman stared at her in silence until Andric shifted slightly. In an instant, a tight-lipped smile sprung onto her features, and she tilted her head in greeting.

"*Oh yeah, this one's going to be trouble*," Booker's voice thrummed against her mind, echoing her thoughts so loudly Lizzy almost missed the woman's introduction.

"Mia Harris," she said before returning her attention to Andric. "The headmaster is in his office, but he expressly asked not to be disturbed. I'm sure whatever these two troublemakers got up to can wait until—"

"It can't," Andric cut in, voice soft but firm. "Could you please let him know I need to speak with him."

Mia still hesitated. She glanced between Lizzy, Booker and Andric, but Andric patiently stood with his hands clasped behind his back, waiting.

Lizzy watched the woman swallow down the unspoken words Andric had interrupted before sighing and offering a reluctant nod.

"Very well. And what should I tell him the matter is regarding?" she asked, arching an eyebrow, as though challenging Andric to brush her aside again.

Lizzy hoped he would, but instead, his previously determined countenance wavered and Lizzy's eyes narrowed.

Booker's nervous curiosity buzzed against her mind as they waited, and she could see him from the corner of her eye. He was watching Andric as intently as she was, although with markedly less hostility, while they waited for the hunter's explanation of their presence.

Maybe he had felt their combined glares, because the moment Andric seemed about to explain their presence to Mia, he glanced back at them and paused, lips still parted to speak.

Lizzy wasn't thrilled about the flash of amusement she caught on his face, but she was willing to forgive it when Andric turned back to Mia Harris and shook his head.

"Tell him it's regarding a kavian attack in Hockley."

Lizzy also took a petty satisfaction in watching the colour drain from Mia's face as the other woman rapidly sobered.

The caramel freckles scattered across her nose stood out starkly as her complexion shifted from warm beige to ashen with an edge of grey, and her haughtiness evaporated in the face of Andric's half-truth.

"Alright," she said, her voice subdued, and she glanced over at Lizzy and Booker one more time. "Give me a moment. Wait here."

Mia turned on her heel and headed for a set of double doors at the back of her reception area. She knocked once before entering, exactly as Andric had, but the moment the doors closed behind her, Booker stepped up beside the remaining vampire.

"And who was that?" he asked, smiling as Lizzy rolled her eyes.

"Miss Mia Harris. She is a final year student here at Speculo School, so she helps out the headmaster by working as his receptionist, part-time," Andric answered, voice slow and wary, like he was expecting a trap, and Booker's grin widened.

"You know, she's—"

"Trouble," Lizzy interrupted, recognising the playful, taunting tone that had overtaken Booker's mind. She punched his arm before stepping past him and moving further into the room.

"Don't antagonise the vampire who saved our lives, remember?" she scolded through their link, and Booker's mind sighed against her own.

"You shouldn't judge people you don't know," Andric said, frowning at the pair of them, but Lizzy couldn't silence her sharp laugh.

"Mia Harris would flourish within the Fey Court," she added when Andric raised an unimpressed eyebrow at her reaction. "I might not know her personally, but I have known many, many people exactly like her."

She didn't say she'd hated every single one of them. It went without saying. The children of the Court had made her life a living nightmare, until Booker, and that silent knowledge drew him back to stand at her side.

She half expected another reprimand from the vampire, but before he could say anything, the doors at the rear of the office opened again and Mia stepped back into the room.

"The headmaster says he'll see you," she told them.

Andric straightened immediately, ushering Lizzy and Booker across the room ahead of him for the first time since they'd arrived at the school and, Lizzy noticed, giving neither of them any chance to make a final dash towards the exit.

8

Lizzy stepped into the office, her movements cautious, with Booker still glued to her side.

Its decor appeared to be an extension of the previous area. Floor-to-ceiling bookshelves lined the walls to the left and right, but Lizzy found her gaze drawn to the back of the room.

An older gentleman sat behind a large, solid-looking desk. His short, dark hair highlighted the frequent streaks of grey running through it, and his features held deep lines of age.

He sat with his back straight and his hands moved to clasp together against the surface of the tidy desk as he watched them enter the room.

"That's one old-looking vampire...!"

"We're so screwed," she sent back, and Booker's hand settled against her elbow in silent support as they advanced into the room.

"Headmaster Walcott," Andric greeted, breaking the old vampire's scrutiny of Lizzy and Booker as the door clicked closed behind them.

"I apologise for disturbing you so late in the day—"

"Not at all," the headmaster interrupted. "You mentioned a kavian attack in Hockley? I'm assuming these are the lucky benefactors of your unscheduled return to Speculo School?"

"Yes," Andric confirmed, stepping up beside them and holding out a hand in their direction as he began the introductions.

"Mister Booker Reed, and Miss Lila—"

"Lizzy," she interrupted sharply, "Lizzy Hail."

Andric paused, and Lizzy's fingers curled into frustrated fists at the quiet chuckle escaping the headmaster and the hint of amusement in Andric's voice when he continued.

"Of course, my apologies. This is Thomas Walcott, headmaster of Speculo School, and I think he can help with your delegation problem."

"Delegation?" Walcott asked.

"A missing fey delegation," Andric explained, and the headmaster turned his suddenly sharp brown eyes on Lizzy and Booker before humming.

"Well then, never let it be said that I don't extend my hospitality and aid to the Fey Court," the old vampire said, beckoning all three further into the office with a casually waved hand.

"Come on in, there's no point loitering in the doorway. Take a seat, and tell me all about this missing delegation," he invited.

Lizzy shared a glance with Booker before stepping forward. He stayed reassuringly close to her side, right up until they parted to settle into the chairs opposite the headmaster's desk.

Lizzy spared a moment to look over at Andric, watching him lean against one of the bookshelves. He hovered between them and the headmaster, his arms held loosely at his sides.

He reminded her of the court sentinels, relaxed but alert, and Lizzy got the sudden chilling feeling he was no longer their escort, but Walcott's sentinel.

Turning back to face the headmaster, Lizzy took a steadying breath, giving herself a chance to straighten out the half-truths she and Booker had already told before she began to speak.

"About a month ago, a fey delegation came here, to the mortal realm, and never returned. We're here looking for them, or looking to find out what happened to them."

"Only, when we arrived, we found that kavian instead," Booker added.

"Right," Lizzy confirmed, "Master Roche killed it and then, after we explained to him why we were here, he seemed to think that you would be able to help us."

The headmaster hummed and leaned back in his chair, a tiny frown gathering between his eyebrows before he turned his attention on Andric Roche.

"Fortuitous that you stumbled over them so quickly, Hunter Roche," he said. "It was lucky you were nearby."

"That's what I said," Lizzy grumbled to Booker, and she could feel him fighting back amusement while trying to remain alert to their situation.

"I wasn't that close," Andric said. "I heard the snarls. Figured I'd find the kavian standing over some poor human by the time I got there."

"Interesting," the headmaster mused, prompting Lizzy to narrow her eyes. His tone was too light, and she glanced over at Andric, only to find him avoiding her gaze, setting her nerves alight. She focused on Walcott instead.

"What's interesting?" she asked warily.

"Kavians aren't known for playing with their food," Walcott explained. His gaze had turned sharp again and the small smile on his face wilted away. "And fey are not known for defending themselves. That makes your survival all the more unbelievable."

"I'm sorry, which part of this don't you believe?" Booker asked. He sounded shocked and surprised by their doubt, but Lizzy could feel the cold calculations happening within his mind. He was looking for a way to twist words and bring the conversation back under their control, but Lizzy shook her head.

She'd told Booker if the vampires couldn't help they would leave, but as she attempted to remember their path through the school, she realised she couldn't. Andric's speed had made it impossible for her to pay attention to their route, and she felt her temper begin to fray.

"We didn't want to come here, you know," she snapped, shooting a glare at Andric for good measure, her teeth grinding together for a moment before she could force herself to continue.

"Your employee over there insisted we come, so if you don't believe us, or don't want to help us, that's fine by me," she spat, "we'll just leave—"

"I'm afraid, Miss Hail, things aren't as simple as that," Walcott said, his soft voice cutting her off surprisingly effectively.

She held the headmaster's steady gaze, her heart in her throat, and she could feel Booker's apprehension swimming around in the back of her mind. After a moment, the vampire leant forward slowly, letting his elbows rest against the surface of his desk with forced casualness.

"You, Mister Reed, are definitely fey," he said, but even as he spoke to Booker, his gaze stayed on Lizzy, and she swallowed hard against the frustration bubbling up in her chest.

She already suspected what was coming, and her hands clenched into fists, wishing she had some way to stop the accusations that were about to fall out of the vampire's mouth.

"But you, Miss Hail... you do not have the look of a fey and, unless you have them strapped down in what I hear is an exceedingly uncomfortable manner, you also do not bear the wings of a fey."

Wrong. Deformed. Freak.

"I'm aware," she ground out, her teeth clenching together with a roiling mixture of anger and a splash of embarrassment. She could sense Booker's concern in her mind, feel his worried gaze on the side of her face, but she didn't tear her eyes away from Walcott.

"Then I'm sure you can understand why I'm hesitant to believe your claims."

"Lizzy may not... look like a fey, but I assure you she is. We both are," Booker said. His voice was quiet but contained a familiar thread of steel. It reminded her of a shared childhood, and past tormentors verbally put in their place. It soothed Lizzy's embarrassment, just a little, at being called out so openly on her missing wings.

"You, or your family, could be being threatened to say such things, Mister Reed. Or you could have been tricked yourself, or any number of other situations," Walcott responded, and Lizzy's skin crawled under his unwavering gaze, but she refused to let herself squirm.

"What do you want me to do? Prove it?" Lizzy scoffed, but she fell silent when the headmaster nodded.

"Yes."

"I don't have to prove anything to you!" Lizzy growled, her temper flaring up again. "Regardless of whether you believe I'm fey, what I am not is a performing animal!"

She rose to her feet, fingers wrapping around the strap of her bag to stop her hand from curling into a fist. "If you can't help us then we'll leave—"

"Miss Hail, let me explain something," the headmaster said, interlocking his fingers lightly. "You are travelling with a fey, but you do not appear to be fey yourself. Considering the reclusive nature of the Fey Court, that implies you are either threatening Mister Reed, or have some form of leverage over him. If you are fey, as you claim, then surely you can understand my concerns."

Lizzy stood silent, her fingers still clenched tightly around the strap of her bag and her mind racing. The worst part was she did understand the headmaster's caution and should have known there would be questions about her appearance.

"*I didn't think of it either*," Booker grumbled into her mind, "*I'm sorry*."

Lizzy shook her head sharply, dismissing his apology, but her motion of denial made both vampires tense, and the headmaster rose to his feet.

"I cannot, in good conscience, allow you to leave with Mister Reed. Not when I do not know you or your motives. You either need to prove that you are fey, or we contact the Fey Court right now and they can examine your mind for answers."

"You can't do that!" Booker snapped, rising to his feet and stepping forward, placing himself between Lizzy and the headmaster, but Lizzy's mind was spinning.

If they summoned the Court, she would never find her mum.

The sentinels would drag her and Booker back to Arbaon. While Lizzy didn't know the precise punishment for unauthorised portal access, she doubted the Court would be lenient.

Cornered, and finding herself outmanoeuvred and threatened, Lizzy's teeth ground together as her temper bubbled over. She tuned out Booker's sharp words as he argued with the headmaster, but she couldn't block out his emotions.

His frustration and irritation buzzed away in the back of her mind, fuelling her growing fury as her gaze spun to settle on the vampire that had brought them there.

Andric Roche was already watching her cautiously, and she let her anger build in her chest, let her furious glare settle across her face in a near-snarl before lashing out with her telekinesis and sending a random shelf full of books flying towards him.

The thudding of books hitting wooden shelves silenced the argument between Booker and the headmaster.

Lizzy glared at the now-empty spot Andric had been standing in mere moments before and spun to find him, the thirty or so tomes continuing to hover in the air while she tracked where her target had fled to with his vampiric speed.

"Miss Hail—"

His voice came from her left and she flung the books in his direction with a twist of her mind, faster than she could turn her head to find him, but he was gone again by the time her gaze followed the sound.

"*Enough, Lila.*"

Booker's voice in her mind, and his warm hand on her shoulder, cooled her temper, but she didn't let the books drop. Instead, she slowly turned back to the headmaster, anger still painted across her features as she tilted her head to the side.

"Is this enough proof, or should I fling them across the room a time or two more?" she asked, voice quiet and cold.

"My apologies, Miss Hail. That is more than enough," the headmaster offered, voice just as gentle as Booker's had been within her mind. She hesitated a moment, but her friend's hand still on her shoulder squeezed gently, his mind buzzing against hers in wordless reassurance, and she finally calmed.

Carefully, Lizzy stacked the books beside the headmaster's desk before releasing them from her control with a sigh. She lifted a hand to rub at her eyes, her headache from earlier in the night returning with a vengeance.

"Please, both of you, sit down," Headmaster Walcott offered once more, his voice now warm and inviting, but Lizzy was too tired to wonder over the change.

She let herself sink back into the chair, but Booker stayed standing beside her, his hand still curled over her shoulder in silent support.

Lizzy saw Roche return to his spot against the bookcase from the corner of her eye, but as her anger subsided, embarrassment had begun to take its place. Ignoring the hunter, she focused on Walcott instead.

"Can you help us, or not?"

"Of course," he reassured instantly. "Tensions are high between the Council and the Court right now. The last thing we want to do is refuse aid to your people. What more can you tell me about your missing delegation?"

"More?" Lizzy asked wearily.

"How many fey are missing? Where did they arrive? Who were they meeting and for what reason? Who knew they were coming, and which portal were they scheduled to return through? For starters."

The questions being flung at her hurt more than the previous disbelief over her origins. The innocent enquiries made it painfully clear to Lizzy how out of their depth she and Booker really were.

Each question was a stab of pain in her chest, and her breath caught in her throat. She couldn't answer any of his questions, because Lizzy simply didn't know the answers.

"I—"

"We can't tell you any of it. It's classified," Booker answered instead.

His voice was cold and detached. Exactly like a court fey should sound. Lizzy had heard Booker use it before, but it was rare that he chose to don that particular facade, and she couldn't stop herself from glancing up at him in surprise.

"You're certain you can't tell me anything of use?" Headmaster Walcott pressed. "They must have been important for the fey to send anyone after them. Isn't it still court policy that you take your lives in your hands if you choose to travel through a portal?"

"They were important. Which is why it's classified. As Lizzy mentioned, we didn't intend to come here. Master Roche was rather insistent, however."

"I understand," Walcott offered gently, "then perhaps our best course of action should be to contact your ambassador at the European Vampire Council. They would be sure to know—"

"No," Booker said sharply, but Lizzy could feel him fumble for an excuse.

She turned back to Walcott and pressed her lips together when she spotted the vampire's eyes narrow. It didn't matter what excuse Booker came up with. Their flimsy cover of being on official business had already melted away and she sighed, patting Booker's hand where it still rested against her shoulder.

"Sit down, Booker," Lizzy muttered when he glanced at her, and as Booker did as she said, the headmaster turned his attention back on her.

"Neither of you are supposed to be here at all, are you?" he asked, and Lizzy hesitated, debating how to answer him.

Considering she'd flung his possessions around the room, and both she and Booker had outright lied to him, Walcott waited with remarkable patience.

"It's like you said," she admitted eventually, "fey who go missing... It's a risk we take. The Court isn't investigating the disappearance. They won't send anyone to find them. It's just us, taking the same risks the portal-party did."

"I don't think so," Walcott prodded gently, "if this was simply you two risking your lives, you'd not have needed such elaborate lies..." He glanced at Booker for a moment before continuing. "You don't want me contacting the Court because you're under eighteen. Am I right?"

"Half right," Booker offered. "I'm eighteen, which puts Lizzy under my guardianship. No one's going to be coming for her, or demanding her return."

His words startled her, and she pressed their mental bond with a light touch, showing her curiosity. Wondering if he'd planned that ever since insisting on coming along.

Booker ignored her silent questions, and the headmaster's voice drew her attention back to the conversation outside her mind.

"But?"

"But... we didn't exactly apply for a licence to activate and use a fairy circle," Lizzy said with a sigh, grimacing at the admission.

A soft laugh came from where Andric stood, but Lizzy refused to look at the vampire, still annoyed at the situation he'd dragged them into. Instead, she watched the headmaster lean back in his chair, shaking his head in disbelief as a small, impressed smile lifted his lips.

"Why are you two looking into this?" he asked, and Lizzy's heart rose to sit in her throat.

After the emotional ups and downs of the night, she didn't want to tell Roche or Walcott it was her mum who was missing.

That her whole world had walked through a portal a month ago and not come back, but she had no other answer.

The sudden flood of emotion made Booker's mind flinch back from hers before coming to her rescue.

"One of the fey in the delegation is very important to me. To us," he corrected quickly. "She's... Maddy might as well be family."

"Speaking of families, won't yours be worried about you?" Andric asked, and despite Lizzy continuing to ignore him, she could hear the curiosity in his voice. She watched as Booker hesitated, unsure how to answer, and forced herself to speak.

"No," Lizzy said, still refusing to look at the vampire. "Booker's eighteen and... and my mum won't be looking for me."

"What about your father?" Headmaster Walcott prompted, but Lizzy shrugged.

"I wouldn't know. I've no idea who he is."

The headmaster hummed in response before steepling his fingers and pressing them lightly to the underside of his chin.

"Well, all your good intentions aside, I hope you both realise this situation leaves us in quite a quandary," he finally announced, and while Lizzy desperately wanted to be offended, the only thing she had the energy for was a weak, mirthless laugh.

"I may have a solution for you both," Walcott continued, "if you'd be willing to hear me out?"

Although their minds were still connected, Lizzy glanced at Booker for his reaction, only to find her friend already watching her.

"*Hear him out?*" Booker suggested. "*He could have called the Court already...*"

"*At this point... Well, it can't do any more harm. Just to listen,*" Lizzy agreed. "*What a mess. I'm sorry I dragged you into this—*"

"*Don't,*" Booker growled. Lizzy forced her mind into silence and pushed back the urge to apologise.

"We're listening," she said instead, surprised when the headmaster tilted his head in a small sign of thanks.

"I can make some enquiries with the Vampire Council about the comings and goings of recent delegations. If they never made it to the Council, it's highly likely a fey delegation going missing will have raised some eyebrows," he explained.

"If they made it to the Council, then their presence will have been noted, and the portal they were scheduled to return to Arbaon through will be somewhere on record.

"I'm confident I can use whatever I find to determine some logical next steps, and we can figure out how you may proceed in your search from there."

"Alright," Lizzy said slowly, eyes narrowing in open suspicion, "but I can sense a 'but' in there."

"You're a clever young woman, Miss Hail," the headmaster agreed, smiling, "the 'but' is that, in return for my help, you two will need to do something for me."

"Like what?" Booker asked, suspicion colouring his voice and his mind's tone, feeding back into Lizzy's caution.

Despite that, Walcott's smile widened and he opened his hands in a placating gesture that did nothing to reassure Lizzy before he answered them.

"Stay at Speculo School."

"That's..." Lizzy spluttered and shook her head as though the words could make more sense after rattling around her mind for a moment. "Why?"

"Firstly, because while you say no one's looking for you, and I believe you, the tensions between our realms are high right now. The last thing we need is for one of you to end up hurt, or worse, and for the Court to believe we did nothing to prevent it. To allow the Court to use such an event as an excuse to break off negotiations, is not an eventuality I can risk."

Booker groaned loudly and slumped back into the chair. "And they would, " he muttered, even as Lizzy wrinkled her nose.

"And the other reason?"

"You're under eighteen, and should finish your education."

"You want us to enrol here? Actually attend classes?" Lizzy spluttered in surprise.

"I'm over eighteen," Booker repeated quickly, and Lizzy could practically taste his aversion to sitting in a classroom when he'd so recently escaped it, but Walcott shot him a look full of undisguised amusement.

"Barely."

"But the classes are going to be completely different," Lizzy argued, drawing the headmaster's attention away from Booker's sudden scowl, and he nodded.

"Yes. Which should make them an interesting challenge for you both. Something to keep the pair of you out of trouble, while I make some initial enquiries."

"How long will this take?" she asked, bringing Booker's incredulous laughter to a sudden stop.

"Lila! The only two fey in a school of vampires? We'll be outsiders. Anomalous. The odd ones out—"

"Well we're used to that, aren't we?" she shot back, and Booker quickly fell silent.

"...could be a few weeks. Maybe a month or two," the headmaster was saying when Lizzy pulled back from Booker's mental voice and returned her attention to the room.

"A compromise then," Lizzy offered. "We'll stay for three months. After that, you let us leave with any information you manage to dig up so we can try other ways of finding the delegation."

The headmaster hesitated, lips pursed in consideration. "I'm hesitant to allow the pair of you to wander the mortal realm alone," he admitted. "What do you intend to do if faced with another kavian?"

"I'm sure we can spend the time here, stuck inside a school, learning something about how to evade them," Booker scoffed.

"Evade, or fight," Lizzy agreed, nodding at Booker, but the headmaster's eyebrows rose in surprise at her words.

"Fey are notoriously peaceful," he said, his unspoken question about their willingness to fight hovering in the air, and Lizzy swore silently.

"Fey have no reason to fight in Arbaon," she replied, "that clearly doesn't seem to be the case here."

The headmaster considered her in silence for several long seconds. The longer he stared, the more Lizzy could feel her heart beating harder against her chest. Eventually, the headmaster hummed before he seemed to accept her explanation.

"In that case, I have a counteroffer for you both. You may leave in three months, on the condition that during your stay here you both attend an additional class."

"What class?"

"All vampires are taught to fight, and to defend themselves against kavians, from the first day they set foot inside a vampire academy. For obvious reasons, neither of you are capable of joining the classes full of your peers. Those vampires who have been training to do battle since they were eleven years old.

"However, since you have both implied a willingness to resist your natural disinclination towards fighting, then I suggest your extra class be with Hunter Roche. He will teach you both the best way to survive or escape a kavian attack."

"Headmaster—" the vampire in question began, but a single glance from Walcott silenced him.

"You aren't even supposed to be on Speculo grounds for another week, Andric," the headmaster warned. "It's this, or you can continue your assigned period of official leave."

Lizzy heard nothing more from Roche, but the headmaster turned back to her so she assumed he'd agreed to their private lessons. A quick glance at Booker told her that the decision was hers, and she considered Walcott's deal carefully.

"You know, it's oddly satisfying. Not one of us likes this deal, but we're all considering it," Booker announced, buying her a few moments to think. He was lounging back in the chair, and Lizzy cracked a grin for the first time in what felt like days.

"He's right," she said simply, "and... we don't really have a choice. While I'm loath to admit it... Master Roche might have been right in claiming you're our best chance at finding out what happened to the delegation."

At the very least, there were currently no better options, Lizzy admitted to herself. A quiet sense of amusement, and a subtle glance from Booker, told her he'd sensed at least part of the stray thought.

She found herself caught in his calm, mint-green gaze, wondering if what they were about to do was the best course of action, or if she was missing something obvious, but a moment later, Booker gave her a nod. Just one, not bothering to resort to telepathy.

With their minds linked, Lizzy could sense he wanted the two vampires to see his agreement before Lizzy confirmed their decision. A united front. She let the sensation of a grateful smile shimmer across her thoughts before she turned back to Headmaster Walcott.

"Okay, Headmaster," she said, "we agree."

At Lizzy's announcement, the old vampire offered them a wide, pleased grin.

"Excellent," he said before he turned his attention to Andric once more. "Hunter Roche, I trust you can ensure our two new transfer students are given accommodation and can find their way to their rooms?"

The slight shuffle of movement made Lizzy wrinkle her nose. She couldn't deny he'd been indirectly helpful, and he had saved their lives. But the kavian hunter's attitude irritated Lizzy an unreasonable amount, and now she and Booker were stuck taking lessons from him.

"Of course," Andric confirmed, and the headmaster nodded.

"Speak to Miss Harris outside," he instructed, then turned back to Lizzy and Booker. "I'll do my best to get you both some answers, or at least some leads you can follow on your own," he promised. "In the meantime, learn what you can from my staff. You are not the first fey I have met, and almost all of your people have a severe lack of knowledge about the mortal realm upon their arrival here."

Lizzy winced at the reminder.

"Speaking of a lack of knowledge, I brought some gemstones

for trade—" she began, but Walcott's soft laugh cut her off, and her expression sank into an open grimace. "Exactly. Booker mentioned something about selling them. Would you know how I could go about doing that?"

"Leave them with me, Miss Hail, I'll ensure both of you are set up with bank accounts and funds," Walcott promised, eyes sparkling with what Lizzy suspected was politely suppressed mirth.

"*Not all of them,*" Booker warned as she stood up and placed her bag on the chair so she could dig through it. "*They seem helpful, but let's leave ourselves a backup plan.*"

She gave the mental equivalent of a nod and handed the headmaster one of the two small cloth pouches she'd packed before lifting her bag back onto her shoulder.

Booker rose to his feet to join her, his bag held at his side, and when they turned, they found Andric Roche already standing by the door waiting for them. She'd not noticed him move, and that fact brought a scowl back to her features.

Halfway across the office, the headmaster called out to them, pulling them both to a stop.

"One last thing," he said, and Lizzy forced herself not to tip back her head in open frustration and let loose a groan. She could feel Booker smothering complaints too, and it gave her the strength to hold Headmaster Walcott's piercing gaze without wavering.

"Only a handful of my students will have ever encountered a fey before, and while you may not know it, the scent of fey blood is particularly potent to our kind so, on occasion, they may forget their manners."

"What?" Booker spluttered, and Lizzy could feel her mouth fall open in shock.

"I'm not telling you this to scare you," the headmaster continued, lifting his hands in a way Lizzy assumed he intended to be reassuring. "We don't lose control like the kavians do.

Neither of you are in any danger staying here, but you may draw more attention than usual. Particularly if either of you become injured in any way."

"What kind of attention?" Lizzy snapped.

"You may find yourself stared at. Held under intense scrutiny, for example. Or, to give you a worst case scenario, a student may ask if you're willing to share your blood. That's all."

"What makes you think either of us would give our blood to anyone?" Booker snapped, and Lizzy could feel his outrage thrumming through her head, mixing with her shock and making her dizzy. "The only way that would happen is if one of you attacked us!"

"You would never be attacked by a vampire, from the scent of your blood alone," Andric said from behind them.

Despite his words, the image in her mind's eye of him lunging for her in the alley still made Lizzy flinch, and she stepped closer to Booker.

"I've only brought it up, because drinking from a live subject is highly restricted. And on school grounds, forbidden entirely," the headmaster continued, voice softening. "I'm telling you only so that you can be aware. No matter which friends you may make, or what a student might ask of you, neither of you should agree to share your blood with a vampire within these walls."

"And you couldn't mention any of this before we agreed to stay here?" Lizzy growled, but the headmaster offered her an unapologetic smile.

"Would you have agreed to stay if I had?"

She pressed her lips together, biting back sharp words as anger fought to spark through her again, but Lizzy was too tired to fight another battle. Especially one she'd already lost.

"A minor amendment to our arrangement, then. We are allowed to leave the instant a vampire attacks either of us... In a situation that's not part of Master Roche's lessons, of course,"

Booker said.

"That will not happen," Walcott repeated, but Booker tensed beside her.

"If you're so sure, then you've got no reason not to agree," he snapped. Lizzy sent a pulse of gratefulness across their linked minds, and Booker let his hand rest on the small of her back, the familiar touch grounding her.

Walcott hesitated, and Lizzy wished she could hear the thoughts going through the old vampire's mind, but it was Andric who broke the silence.

"Headmaster," the hunter called softly, and Walcott's gaze drifted past Lizzy and Booker to settle on the figure behind them. "Trust goes both ways, and you're asking them to put a lot of faith in us. We should trust they won't use this as an opportunity to leave Speculo grounds ahead of the agreed upon terms."

Lizzy glanced back at the vampire in surprise, but his attention was fixed over her head, holding the headmaster's gaze.

That's what had been concerning the headmaster?

She was careful to keep the thought away from her connection to Booker, but the irritation at being doubted for the third time in the same night was something she couldn't bury.

"Lizzy's never made a promise in her life that she's not kept," Booker snapped, her irritation fuelling his anger, and Lizzy pulled her attention away from Hunter Roche to elbow her best friend, but he didn't so much as flinch.

"And what about yourself?" the headmaster asked.

"I'm not the one you're making a deal with," Booker sidestepped the question carefully before lifting his hand away from her back, only to sling his arm around her shoulders with practised casualness, "but I go where Lizzy does."

At that, the headmaster's gaze shifted back to her, and she swallowed down her embarrassment at Booker's indirect praise and open loyalty. It always left a warmth sitting in her chest that she never quite knew how to handle.

"If I was going to try and wiggle my way out of our arrangement, I wouldn't have agreed to it in the first place," she added, and the headmaster's features turned contemplative, a small frown settling between his brows.

"My apologies," he offered after another beat of silence, "neither of you have done anything yet to earn my distrust. If you are attacked by anyone at Speculo School, our arrangement for you to remain here will, of course, be negated."

She wasn't feeling particularly grateful, considering the situation he'd manipulated them into, but the headmaster also held their best hope of finding out what had happened to her mum, so Lizzy bit back her more sarcastic retorts. It wasn't worth getting on the old vampire's bad side just to make a point, so she settled on a simple "Thank you."

The headmaster inclined his head slightly in response, and Lizzy heard Master Roche move behind her.

"Follow me, Miss Hail, Mister Reed," he instructed, and when Lizzy turned away from the headmaster, she found the kavian hunter already holding open the office door for them both to step through. "We can talk to Miss Harris about where you can stay during your time with us."

As Lizzy moved past the vampire, Booker at her side with one arm still protectively slung over her shoulders, they heard the headmaster's voice reach them one more time.

"Once you have our guests settled, come and find me, Hunter Roche," the headmaster added. "I'd like to know why you were in Hockley tonight."

She glanced at the kavian hunter, but couldn't read his features. He simply nodded once and followed them both out of the office into the reception area, the door clicking closed behind him with a finality that made Lizzy's stomach lurch.

10

As the office door clicked closed with a deceptive softness, Andric couldn't help but release a soft huff of frustration.

He'd thought, for a moment, he'd gotten away with being in Hockley without drawing Walcott's attention. That the arrival of two fey would be enough to distract the headmaster.

He was already going to get badgered half to death by Nameer the moment his friend caught up with him, but it had obviously been too much to hope that he wouldn't also have to explain his presence in the nearby town to his employer.

Andric was painfully aware he should have known better than to try and slide anything past the wily old vampire.

Still, it could have gone worse, he admitted. Walcott keeping him at the school to train the fey was better than having to return to his family home.

He knew, without a shadow of a doubt, that if Walcott had ordered him home, he wouldn't have been able to endure his mother's grief without going insane.

Mentally shaking himself out of the downward spiral his mood had begun to take, Andric glanced around the reception area.

Taking stock of the lay of the room, the way his training had taught him, Andric automatically noted the distinct lack of exits.

The door at his back led to Walcott's office. A sealed room that probably held a hidden escape passage, but if so, then only the headmaster was privy to that knowledge. The reception area was just as well fortified, no windows and only one door out.

The lack of escape routes made his skin itch but as a fortified location to make a last stand, it had been well designed and served its purpose.

Mia Harris stood from her desk, a smile spreading across her face, and Andric suppressed the wince he could feel wanting to escape him. Especially when he noticed the fey watching him too.

He'd known they'd been lying about something, but illegal entry into the mortal realm hadn't even been on the list of possibilities. Let alone that the pair were barely old enough to be called adults.

That's not fair, he corrected himself silently. They were young, but at twenty-two, he wasn't much older than them.

Which was probably why Miss Harris believed she could get away with her constant, and insistent, flirting.

Clearing his throat, he stepped towards the woman's desk and gave a small nod in greeting, moving his hands to clasp against the small of his back, and out of Mia Harris's reach.

"How did it go?" she asked lightly.

Andric bit back his initial response that the meeting had been private and nothing to concern herself with. But taking a sharp tone with Mia Harris would only be asking for trouble.

Instead, he reminded himself he only had to endure her persistent presence for a short while longer, just until she finished her last year at Speculo, and he forced himself to answer.

"It went as expected. Miss Hail and Mister Reed will be joining Speculo School as transfer students, starting immediately. Headmaster Walcott would like you to arrange housing for them, and a class schedule."

"Transfer students?" Miss Harris repeated, hazel eyes widening in open surprise, and he watched her carefully as she turned her attention to the two fey.

She'd dismissed them as troublemakers the first time they'd

passed through her office, and he'd not made any move to correct her assumptions. With the additional information, he could almost hear her mind reevaluating them, and he smothered another sigh.

"Housing, and a class schedule please, Miss Harris," he prompted, ignoring the flush of embarrassment colouring her cheeks at his gentle reprimand.

"Oh, of course, I'm sorry. One moment," she murmured, turning to the computer and bending over to use the keyboard, ignoring the perfectly good chair right beside her.

"You're very lucky, you know," Miss Harris called over her shoulder, glancing back at the two fey. "Speculo School's one of the best in Europe. To be transferring here at all is an honour, but especially halfway through the year."

"Yeah. Lucky us," Miss Hail drawled, not making any attempt at covering her sarcasm, and Andric forced himself to swallow down a laugh.

Her irreverence was refreshing. It wasn't the first time that night he'd had to bite back a grin in response to something the woman had spat out in anger, or frustration.

Miss Harris, on the other hand, didn't appear to find Miss Hail amusing in the slightest. A scowl flashed across her features, squashing Andric's amusement, and a moment later, she began peppering the two fey with questions, her voice sharp and probing.

"Names?"

"Lizzy Hail, and Booker Reed."

"Ages?"

"Seventeen and Eighteen."

"Birthdays?"

"Umm..."

"Skip it," Andric instructed, but Miss Harris straightened up from the computer, her lips pressed together in irritation.

"I need to know what year to place them in, Andric," she explained, her voice slow as though he didn't understand how schools worked.

Forcing himself to reign in a sudden flash of temper, Andric made a concerted effort to keep an even tone as he responded.

"Place them in the final year. Skip the birthdays."

Mia took a slow, deep breath, but she didn't argue again. Turning back to the computer, her fingers tapped away at the keyboard a fraction harder than necessary as she muttered to herself.

"This is most irregular," she breathed before raising her voice and directing her next question back towards the fey. "Which school are you transferring from? I can have them send your records over in the next few days."

"Arbaon Academy," Miss Hail answered, and Andric bit back a curse. He'd hoped to keep their origins a secret for a little longer, but the moment Mia froze at the name, it was clear she'd figured it out.

"Arbaon?" she repeated, straightening up from the keyboard again and turning to face the two fey this time. "The fey realm, Arbaon?"

"Is there another Arbaon we don't know about?" Mister Reed quipped wearily, and Mia's mouth snapped shut as she considered the pair in silence.

"I don't know what you or the headmaster expect me to do," she said finally, crossing her arms and turning back to Andric. "I cannot request records from the fey realm, and I doubt they have half the same classes, even if I could."

"Then it will have to be a customised schedule," Andric said. "In addition to the standard subjects, get them into beginner finance. First year history should cover some of the basics of the mortal realm."

He paused, running through the classes the school offered, and trying to figure out what might help the two fey adjust, before adding, "Home economics too, to give them a solid basis for figuring everything else out... and they might find fey-vampire relations interesting.

"Also, schedule them in for fight training once a day, excluding Sundays, and change the location to the back field. They'll be training with me."

By the time he'd finished, Miss Harris was staring at him with her lips pressed tight, and he could all but feel the eyes of the fey on him too.

Regardless of how unnerving their combined focus was, Andric didn't let himself shift under the scrutiny, only raising his eyebrows after a moment of silence.

"Headmaster Walcott's expecting me back once I have them settled, Miss Harris, so the faster you can set up their schedules and lodging, the better."

"They're training with you?" she asked, her voice low and edging into an angry growl that had Andric biting back another groan.

He could ignore the inconvenient flirting, but the young vampire's badly concealed jealousy often left him praying for her graduation sooner rather than later.

Nameer, on the other hand, found it to be an endless source of amusement.

It wouldn't be the first time Mia Harris had gone out of her way to make her classmates' lives difficult over some perceived favouritism on his part, but her mother held a seat on the European Vampire Council. It made rebuffing her advances difficult and disciplining her nigh on impossible.

The last thing he wanted was to paint a target on the fey's backs, however, so he forced his features into a calm mask and nodded.

"Yes. As per the headmaster's instructions."

Her anger melted away at his words, replaced with a look of sympathy that was simultaneously annoying and easy to disregard.

"Oh, yes. I see. It must be so frustrating for someone as skilled as you to be reduced to teaching fey."

"What in the realm is that supposed to mean?" Miss Hail growled, and Andric sent up a prayer for strength to any deity that might deign to listen.

"Well, your kind aren't known for your proclivity towards violence—" Miss Harris cooed, her voice turning syrupy with condescension, and Andric interrupted with a sharp cough.

"The schedules, please, Miss Harris," he cut in, praying it would be enough to interrupt the animosity he could already sense building between Mia and Speculo School's two newest students.

"Of course," she said, turning back to the computer and leaning over the keyboard again. "How about I put down a training session three times a week instead?" she offered. "Give you a break from teaching children the basics?"

"Miss Harris, my arrangement with the headmaster requires that I teach our guests how to defend themselves, or I can return to my official leave. Please, enter the training as requested."

Miss Harris didn't answer or turn back to him, but even from where he stood, Andric could see the pout that had painted itself across her face, and he smothered another tired sigh. With luck, blaming the headmaster for the training would keep the two fey safe from Mia's jealousy, and he glanced at the two teens as Miss Harris continued entering the information into the computer.

It might keep them out of the young vampire's line of fire, but the excuse didn't look like it was going to keep him safe from the pair's wrath. Both of them were glaring at him with various levels of irritation, but Miss Hail looked ready to fling another stack of books at him and he shifted his weight, half-prepared to dodge another telekinetic attack.

"Done," Miss Harris said, and the printer at the back of the room burst into life. She straightened and blurred across the room, using her enhanced speed to collect the timetables and room assignments and bring them back to Andric a second later, startling a gasp from one of the fey at his side.

He didn't like the almost predatory smirk the vampire shot at the pair as she handed over the documents, but he bit back the sharp reprimand on the tip of his tongue as he accepted the paperwork.

"Thank you, Mia," he offered, the use of her first name drawing her attention away from the fey instantly. Her attention snapped back to him, and a bright smile softened her features as she flicked her long hair over one shoulder.

"My pleasure, Andric," she replied, and he stepped back from the desk with a polite nod.

He was careful not to look at the two fey. Heading towards the exit without a word, he listened carefully to make sure the pair were following, and only turned around when he stopped to hold the door open.

Miss Hail appeared to have given up on her glares having any effect on him.

Or maybe she's simply too damn tired, he thought to himself.

As she stalked past, she kept her gaze focused forward, but Mister Reed continued to study Andric with narrowed green eyes.

Andric didn't risk glancing back at Miss Harris, not willing to encourage the young woman any further. He'd already pushed his professional boundaries further than he was comfortable with. He stepped into the hall behind the two fey, firmly tugging the door to the office closed behind them.

Wordlessly, he beckoned Miss Hail and Mister Reed to follow him down the hall, moving at a more sedate pace than he'd taken the first time.

Rushing them through the halls of the castle had been a weak ploy to keep the pair off balance. The best he could manage on short notice, but he hadn't expected Miss Hail to keep up as well as she had.

Once again, she'd surprised him.

"Where are we going?" Mister Reed asked, pulling Andric from his musings, and when he turned to study the pair, he found the young man already watching him, his arm still slung around Miss Hail's shoulders like it lived there.

His pale green stare was disconcerting. It was like the young man could see beneath Andric's skin, and he found himself glancing away at the thought. The memory of the fey slipping into his mind and forcing a buzzing pressure against the inside of his skull, had bile burning at the back of his throat.

"All the students live and study within Speculo," he explained as they moved back down the first of three stone staircases that would return them to the ground floor of the school. "You've been assigned rooms for your stay here. The classes I signed you both up for should give you some basic understanding of the mortal realm, but there's a substantial library here too if you'd like to do your own research."

"This place is huge," Miss Hail muttered, "it'll take us three months just to find our way around."

"I'm sure once you've had a day or two to settle in, and make friends, one of your classmates will help you find anything you need," Andric reassured.

He didn't notice the pair's reactions, distracted by the number of vampires still milling around in the hallways as they stepped back into the student areas of the school.

Classes had ended for the night while they'd been meeting with the headmaster, and while many of the students had already found the library for the morning or had returned to their dorms ready to sleep the better part of the daylight hours away, there were still many curious eyes settling on the pair of fey as Andric led them through the school.

"Andric Roche, the last person I expected to see break the rules. What are you doing back on school grounds?"

The cheerful voice pulled him to a stop, and he turned to greet the familiar face of the school's deputy with a genuine smile of his own.

The woman only came up to his shoulder and still stood almost a head taller than Lizzy Hail. Despite her size, Andric knew better than to underestimate Hilda Gladstone. Before becoming Walcott's right-hand woman, she'd had a long and illustrious career as a kavian hunter. Despite the light, kindly smile aimed at him, she was one vampire Andric didn't want to anger or disappoint.

"Thomas knows I'm here," he reassured, and Hilda gave a soft hum in response.

Turning her gaze on the two fey, she lifted a hand to casually rub at the back of her neck, fingers trailing down the long, thin braid of rich chestnut hair that hung over her shoulder as she studied them.

"Aren't you going to introduce me?" she asked, and Andric offered a small grimace of apology before turning to the tired-looking teens.

"Booker Reed, and Lizzy Hail," he said, remembering the girls preferred name this time, "this is Miss Gladstone, the deputy headmistress of Speculo School."

She smiled at the two teens, despite the cool mask one of them had thrown up and the suspicious glare from the other.

"Fey in Speculo, Andric? Can you elaborate, or should I speak to Thomas?" she asked, eyes as rich brown as her hair sparkling as she shifted her attention back to him.

"Should probably speak to the headmaster," he admitted, "I'm not entirely sure what he plans to share," Andric warned, receiving a simple nod of acceptance in return.

"I'll do that right away then," she added, rubbing her hands together lightly as she turned back to the teens, moistening her lips a little before she continued, "and if either of you need anything during your stay here, don't hesitate to come and find me. Any of the students will be able to direct you to my office," she told them, her lips curving into a warm smile, open and welcoming.

In the face of her easy kindness, Andric watched the two fey soften and their wariness fade a little. They both nodded, mumbling promises to seek her out if they needed to, and Andric smothered a sigh of relief.

As the deputy moved past them, Miss Hail twisted under Mister Reed's arm to watch Hilda head up the same staircase they had come down. This time there was no narrowing of her electric-blue eyes, and no scowl marring her features, so he let the hope catch in his chest.

Neither of them had seemed particularly comfortable around him, or the headmaster, and it was a relief to think the fey might have found an ally in Hilda. Someone they might be able to lean on and trust as they adjusted to the mortal realm.

Andric waited patiently until he had their full attention once more, then nodded down the hall that would lead towards the final-year dorms.

"Come on, let's get moving before you draw a crowd of curious vampires," he teased softly, turning to guide them the rest of the way across the school grounds.

Lizzy paid more attention to their surroundings as they passed through the school this time. The task was made that much easier by the fact that Roche wasn't rushing them through the hallways at breakneck speed.

Solid stone stairs and thick rugs transitioned into polished wooden floors as they moved down into the lower levels of the school.

The hallways were wide enough for three or four people to walk side by side without a struggle, and the ceilings were so high, Lizzy began to wonder if they'd originally been designed by fey from before the separation.

It wasn't hard to imagine them flying through the castle. Streams of fey weaving their way above the heads of the vampires, and that of their wingless male counterparts, long before the creation of Arbaon.

Before the fey had left to reside in isolation.

Every level they went down, the larger the windows grew, letting in more and more light as pinks and peaches of a sunrise painted the horizon. Lizzy watched the sky change colour through the clear glass panes of each arched window they passed.

The building felt too large, too imposing, and Lizzy struggled to find anything homely or comforting about the place, even with paintings scattered along the walls, and side rooms filled with soft chairs and warm carpets. She didn't know if it worked for the vampires, but it didn't help Lizzy.

Wordlessly, Booker's mind pressed against her own, and she took comfort in the familiarity of his presence.

Even the weight of his arm around her shoulders spelt safety to Lizzy, and it was a comforting warmth against the early morning chill. By the time Andric finished leading them across a grassy square in the middle of the castle, Lizzy found herself struggling to stay on her weary feet and eventually had to step away from Booker to prevent the extra weight of his arm from sending her stumbling.

Their encounter with the deputy head of the school, Mistress Gladstone, had been the last thing Lizzy could bring herself to handle. Since she and Booker had snuck out of Arbaon, she had encountered more new people in one night than she ever had before, and Lizzy found herself drained and running on the last dregs of energy.

"*Think of it like the first day of school, all over again*," Booker tried reassuring her across their bond. His mind brushed light and gentle against her own, as though he could sense how fragile she felt.

He probably can, Lizzy mused. Her head was a mess of emotions and she had no idea which of them Booker might be responding to, or if he was responding to all of them, and she pushed back as much gratitude as she could muster before responding.

"No. *We've got that delight to look forward to tomorrow.*"

His mind grimaced, and Lizzy glanced up to study his wrinkled nose. His expression brought a weak smile to her face, which prompted him to roll his eyes dramatically.

The pair of them were so distracted by their loop of reassurance, that they almost walked into Andric's back when he stopped outside another door. It was plain wood this time, Lizzy noted as Andric knocked sharply, marked by nothing more than an intricately carved number: 1952.

Before Lizzy could ask him where they were, the door opened to reveal another young woman, one hand holding her door wide, with the other braced against the doorframe.

She looked about their age, and Lizzy lifted her chin, prepared for the vampire to study and then summarily dismiss them, as Mia had done. Instead, her mead-coloured gaze flicked across each of them in turn, as confusion worked its way onto her soft features.

As she moved, a thick braid fell over her shoulder. The style wasn't unlike Mistress Gladstone's but the young woman's braid of honey-brown hair was thick and chunky. Lizzy suspected when worn loose, her hair would be a veritable cloud around her.

"Uh... hello?" the vampire said, eyebrows lifting as she finally focused her attention on Andric.

"I'm Hunter Roche," he introduced himself. "Are you Cara Evelyn?"

The woman's features fell into a concerned frown. "I am. Is there a problem?"

She let go of her door and crossed her arms tight over a plain black shirt. The style was unfamiliar to Lizzy and seemed to stay up with only thin straps of fabric over the vampire's shoulders. Her wide-legged trousers in a soft, smoky-grey fabric were at least recognisable and relief at the familiarity pushed aside some of Lizzy's anxiety.

"Not at all, Miss Evelyn," Andric continued. "I'm here to inform you that you've had a new classmate assigned to your room."

"This late in the year?" she asked, her crossed arms dropping to her sides, and Lizzy finally found herself meeting the other woman's gaze.

"Your new roommate, Lizzy Hail," Andric introduced her. "She and Mister Reed will be transferring here for the remainder of the school year."

"Hang on, we're not staying together?" Lizzy asked, and the hunter who had been causing her nothing but problems since the moment they met sighed as though she were the annoying one.

In an instant, the sound brought a fresh scowl to Lizzy's face and she grit her teeth, struggling to bite back a sharp comment in response.

"The school doesn't let us share rooms with guys," Cara explained, a smile curling up the corners of her mouth. Her rounded jaw and button nose gave the vampire a soft look that matched the gentleness of her voice, and Lizzy's temper sputtered and went out beneath her words.

"You know," Cara continued, shrugging, "just in case we're irresponsible enough to sleep with one another—"

"Don't put that thought in my head!"

"She's like my sister!"

The telepathic connection with Booker's mind snapped as they both recoiled from each other in horror at the vampire's implication. Lizzy winced and shook her head, glancing at Booker, only to find him reacting similarly, but the moment their eyes met, they both broke into soft laughter.

"It's just... too weird to even think about," Lizzy reiterated, not bothering to mask a shudder.

"Regardless, you're to room with Miss Evelyn and Mister Reed has a room in the opposite wing of the school."

Lizzy focused on Andric, sobering at the vampire's statement, despite the small grin he seemed to be sporting in response to their reactions.

"You're really splitting us up?" she demanded, and his smile vanished.

He hesitated at her question. For a moment she thought she spotted regret flicker across his features, but before he could say anything, Lizzy's new roomate answered instead.

"It'll be fine!" she promised, stepping out of her room and

linking her arm with Lizzy's. "I'll bet if you're transferring together, you'll have similar classes. So you can meet up at breakfast tomorrow."

"I guess we don't have a choice," Lizzy muttered, letting Cara tug her one step towards the room before she paused, and turned back to Booker.

One familiar, telling lip-twitch, and a moment later, Booker was back in her mind and Lizzy's shoulders lost a little of the tension that had gathered there.

"*I can't keep this up indefinitely*," Booker reminded her.

"*I know, but just... as long as you can?*" Lizzy pleaded, and a soft wave of reassurance washed across from Booker.

She'd lost nearly everything when her mum had left. Her family, her home, her sense of self and belonging. Booker was her last constant. Her last anchor in the storm her life had become, and their imminent separation left a cold dread sitting in the pit of her stomach.

"Your schedule for classes," Andric said when Lizzy dragged her eyes away from Booker's, holding out a sheet of paper for her to take.

"Breakfast tomorrow," Booker reassured her out loud, and Lizzy nodded, fingers tight around her schedule. She couldn't make herself step into the room, and Booker cleared his throat before turning to Andric.

"Lead on," he said, and Lizzy forced herself to watch the two walk away and disappear through a door at the end of the hall, only Booker's connection to her mind reassuring her that he was still nearby.

"Hey, are you sure there's nothing going on between you two?" Cara asked beside her, and Lizzy snapped her head around from staring down the empty hall to glare at the woman.

"No! Booker's like family," she snapped, and the vampire released Lizzy's arm to raise her hands in surrender.

"I was just checking," she said, "you seem pretty close."

"You're not close with your family?" Lizzy shot back, but Cara simply shrugged and beckoned her into the room.

"Not really."

Lizzy followed the other woman inside and slowly closed the door behind her. Her fingers stayed curled tight around the handle. It was a reassurance. A reminder that she could still leave, if she wanted to, but the rest of her was busy absorbing her new surroundings.

The room was large and designed for comfort, but simple. There were two single beds on opposite walls, a couple of desks, and a single large wardrobe with double doors and a couple of draws in the base.

The floor was dark wood, like the hallways, but a large rug had been spread across the floor between the two beds. It softened the otherwise harsh feel of the room. Thick, heavy-looking curtains hung on either side of a large window, currently letting the morning light trickle in.

A jacket hung from the footboard of one bed, and Cara's desk was all but invisible beneath piles of books and paper. While it was clear Cara had been rooming alone for a while, her belongings hadn't spread across the invisible divide down the centre of the room.

"Shared bathroom through that door there," Cara explained, pointing out another door that had been left ajar as she moved across the room to sit at her paper-filled desk. "I usually shower before bed. If you want to use it in the evenings when we get up, we won't get in each other's way. Where did you two transfer from?"

"Uh, Arbaon Academy," Lizzy answered. Releasing her death grip on the door handle, she stepped towards the neatly made bed, placed her bag at the foot, and ran her now-free hand over the soft mink-coloured covers.

"Arbaon?" Cara repeated. "The fey realm? You're both fey?"

"That seems to be a common reaction, but we've been re-establishing contact here for decades now. What's so surprising about us being fey?" Lizzy grumbled as she moved on from the bed to inspect the matching wooden desk on her side of the room. The only difference to Cara's was that this one was empty, and when Lizzy opened the single drawer, it only contained an old pencil, its tip worn down to the wood.

"Sure, your Court has been negotiating with the Council," Cara agreed, leaning against her desk and folding her arms, "but most vampires have still never actually met a fey."

The quiet note of curiosity in her voice made Lizzy's shoulders tense, and she closed the desk drawer as her mind reached out for Booker's, seeking reassurance that returned to her quickly across their connection.

"So, how long are you here for?"

"At least a couple of months," Lizzy said, dropping her class schedule on top of the desk and turning to face Cara, mimicking the vampire's pose by leaning back against the desk and crossing her arms. "Why?"

"Oh, uh... I suppose that makes sense. You're probably staying until the end of the year, right? But, if we're rooming together, we should probably get to know each other better..."

Lizzy narrowed her eyes as Cara stumbled over her explanation. The woman could be trying to be genuinely friendly, but Lizzy admitted to herself, she didn't have enough experience to be able to tell for sure.

She tried to remind herself she wasn't there to make friends. She wanted to find out what happened to her mum, that was it, but as Cara met her sharp gaze with what Lizzy would almost call a hopeful expression, she couldn't find it in herself to push the woman away.

It would have been easy to do with any of the court fey who

tried to worm their way into her life. The manipulations of the Court were never obvious but always going on underneath the surface, and Lizzy wouldn't trust any of them as far as she could throw them, but the way Cara was staring at her, tentatively hopeful and a little nervous, she found her resolve to keep the woman at arm's length crumbling.

"Sure, I guess," she said slowly, still wary about any concealed motivations the vampire might have, but the bright smile spreading across Cara's face at her acceptance surprised her.

"What about your friend?" she asked, gesturing to the door, and Lizzy smothered a groan as the pieces began to fall into place.

"Booker?" she asked, watching Cara's grin widen slightly.

"Yeah, is he going to be here until the end of the year too?"

"That's the plan."

"I hope I can get to know you both while you're here," the woman pressed, and Lizzy almost laughed. As far as motivations went, the woman's interest in Booker was as benign as it could get.

"Sure, I'll introduce you at breakfast," Lizzy promised, trying not to roll her eyes when a soft blush crept over Cara's cheeks. "Look, I'm not trying to be rude, but it's been a long day—"

"Oh! You're probably exhausted," Cara cut her off, standing up straight from against the desk and gesturing towards Lizzy's bed. "I'll go and take my shower, get out of your way so you can get changed. The sheets are clean, the school staff change them every few days..." She paused, gaze darting around the room like she was trying to remember something before Cara simply shook her head.

"I can't think of anything else you might need to know, but breakfast opens around six in the evening, and classes start at eight. My alarm might wake you if you're a light sleeper, but if not I'll get you up in time. Promise."

Before Lizzy could say anything in response to the rapid

flood of information Cara had handed her about the school, the vampire darted around the room in a burst of speed, and vanished into the bathroom faster than Lizzy could track.

The rapid movements startled her, and as the bathroom door snapped shut, she slammed a hand to her chest, her heart racing and her stomach churning as memories of the kavian's taunts echoed through her head, and Andric's snarls as he lunged for her flickered through her mind.

"Rot and termites! I wish they'd stop doing that," she swore softly, her breath coming in short, sharp pants. Booker's soft concern echoed across her mind until she sent back a wave of reassurance.

It wasn't possible to send words across the distance that now separated them, but it was impressive Booker could maintain the link at all. She knew if it had been down to her, the connection would have failed already but Booker's telepathy had always been strong.

Strong or not, it had been a long day for both of them, and maintaining the link would be draining. Lizzy summoned every shred of weariness she currently felt before projecting it towards Booker, and a moment later, she felt their connection dissipate.

A soft smile crept up on her at the care he took when disconnecting their minds, but she wiped it away when she heard the water begin running in the washroom Cara had vanished into.

Moving her bag from the bed onto the desk, she began working to unpack the belongings she'd only put together several hours earlier.

So much had happened since she'd tied the bag closed in her room that Lizzy paused with her fingers resting on the drawstrings. Had it really only been a few hours?

A wave of genuine exhaustion hit her when she realised that, yes, it had been.

She'd broken out of Arbaon, illegally activated a portal-tree, been chased by a monster, rescued by a vampire, and negotiated help from the headmaster of a vampire school to find her mum, all in one night.

Despite all that, she didn't feel any closer to success, and Lizzy swallowed back tears. She knew why, and it was because she was stuck, again. Confined to one place, with no way to get answers, waiting on others to find her mum for her, and she hated it.

But she'd agreed to stay still and wait for news, because as much as she wanted to walk out the front doors of the school and scour the mortal realm for her mum, she didn't know where to start looking, and if Thomas Walcott could give her a direction, a hint, or some clue, she would take it.

Shaking her spiralling thoughts and building tears away, Lizzy sucked in a deep, bracing breath and tugged open the drawstrings on her bag. She began pulling her belongings out, movements fast and sharp. Desperate for a distraction before she broke down in tears, Lizzy focused on finding a place for her meagre collection.

The blanket she'd shoved in at the last minute got spread across the foot of the bed, her clothes were placed in the empty side of the wardrobe, as it was divided in two much like the rest of the room, and her spare shoes were placed in the empty bottom drawer of the wardrobe.

The pouches of nuts and dried fruit went into the desk drawer alongside the stray pencil, and she tucked the second bag of loose gemstones between the mattress and the wall, secure and hidden from sight long before Cara turned off the water in the next room.

In minutes, Lizzy had undone the work of the previous week. It had taken her time to gather everything she thought she'd need without Booker noticing, and now all her work at packing and preparing to flee Arbaon had been practically cast aside.

As she changed out of her clothes into her sleepwear, a light shirt and pants loosely laced closed, and slipped into the surprisingly soft bed, Lizzy dared to hope her bargain with Walcott would be worth it.

It was only that tiny spark of hope that helped her avoid crying herself to sleep.

Andric knocked on the door to the headmaster's outer office for the second time that morning. He stepped inside, resisting the growing urge to blur across the grounds and out the front gates to avoid the imminent discussion with Walcott entirely.

Truth be told though, it wasn't Walcott he wanted to avoid. Andric braced himself and let his gaze sweep the office, but there was no sign of Mia Harris, and Andric blew out a soft breath of relief, closing the door behind him as he moved further into the room.

It had taken less time to get Mister Reed settled into his room than it had to convince Miss Hail to accept their separation, but getting the pair of them set up for the night and making arrangements for the following evening, including directions to the breakfast hall for Mister Reed, seemed to have been enough time to avoid a second encounter with Miss Harris.

Unless she's speaking with the headmaster...

The thought drifted through his mind unbidden, and Andric grit his teeth, not letting himself hesitate. It was only a few months until the young woman graduated and she already had a job lined up at the European Vampire Council.

After that, he wouldn't have to deal with her or her never-ending flirting ever again, Andric reminded himself firmly, before stalking across the reception area and knocking on the door to the headmaster's office.

"Come in," Thomas called.

Andric opened the door and stepped through, bracing himself for Miss Harris but finding the welcoming smile of Hilda Gladstone instead.

He almost wilted in relief. Andric thought he'd masked his reaction, but there was a slight widening of Hilda's smile that said he'd not been as successful as he'd hoped.

"Ah, Andric, thank you for being prompt," Thomas greeted. "Come in, take a seat."

"I thought being prompt would be better than avoiding you," Andric offered with a grin, only half joking as he moved across the office, but the wry smile he got in return eased the worst of his nerves.

"I hope you don't mind that I stayed," Hilda said, her hands resting in her lap, fingers lightly twisting together. "I was curious to know what brought you back so soon."

"I don't mind," Andric said with a shake of his head before sinking into the chair that, less than an hour ago, had held an irate fey woman flinging books at his head.

"It's nothing... elaborate," he began, aware he owed the two older vampires some sort of explanation. "I just... I couldn't stand being in that house."

"I can't imagine how difficult—"

"No," Andric agreed, cutting Hilda off, his voice quiet, "you can't. Dad's near catatonic with grief, and when he's not he's destroying the house, or picking physical fights with anyone who can punch back harder than him. Mum's splitting her time between crying, and blaming me for—"

"Your brother's situation is not your fault, Andric," Thomas growled. The sound was primal, predatory, and it reminded Andric how much older Walcott was than the average vampire. Slowly, the breath that had caught in his throat released into a sigh and he shrugged.

"I know that... even if I don't believe it all the time," he admitted. "I wasn't even with him... but it doesn't stop Mum thinking I should have been able to help him, or at least find him now he's a kavian." His voice caught slightly, and Andric had to swallow hard before he was able to continue, softly but with a hint of bitterness. "Family duty to put him out of his misery, and all that."

Andric shook his head and leant back in the chair, letting the tension leach away from his shoulders for the first time in weeks. "I wasn't breaking the terms of my employment, I'm not that stupid," he promised, "but I couldn't be in the house any longer. I've been staying at a hotel in Hockley for a week now... patrolling the surrounding areas at night.

"It was pure chance I stumbled over the fey. I could have let them wander off on their own if I'd been trying to hide that I was nearby. But I wasn't hiding. I wasn't working for Speculo, and I wasn't on school grounds... I just wasn't in the family home either. But there's no law against that," Andric added before his lips twitched into a faint smile. "I know because I checked."

Thomas snorted a soft laugh at his words. His amusement turned Andric's nerves into relief. Combined with the realisation that he'd managed to avoid an official reprimand, the last of Andric's tension left him.

"Sometimes, you're almost too smart for your own good, Andric Roche," Hilda offered, grinning. "One day that's going to bite you in the arse."

"One day, but I don't think today is that day... Am I right, Thomas?" Andric asked, glancing between the two heads of the school, and after a moment, Thomas sighed and shook his head.

"I should find something to pull you up on, just on principle, after this stunt... but I do understand," he said. "The problem is you're still on bereavement leave, and I can't have you working here until it's run its course."

"I understand," Andric muttered. "I still have my room in Hockley—"

"Oh, really, Andric," Hilda scoffed. "When have you ever known Thomas to play by council rules? Be realistic," she scolded, rubbing her hands together and grinning. "You do have a plan, I'm assuming, you old fox?"

"I had an idea in mind," Thomas agreed, "if you're willing to play bodyguard, Andric?"

"What are you thinking?"

"I, and through me, Speculo, cannot employ you as a guard for the school because you are on bereavement leave, but there is nothing to say you cannot accept a private contract of employment during your time away from the school. Such as acting as guard and guide to two visiting fey. You have already agreed to private tuition, this would simply formalise that arrangement, and allow you to remain on Speculo grounds as a private contractor."

"Seems too good to be true, what's the catch?" Andric asked, and Walcott's grin widened.

"Well the pay isn't fantastic, and there's no pension plan to speak of."

"Hang on," Hilda cut in as Andric laughed softly. "A private contract's all well and good, but it needs to be a paid contract if you want to circumvent the council's laws. How are two teen fey going to come up with those kinds of funds?"

"Ah, that actually brings me to the second order of business," Walcott said, shifting forward in his seat. "Whether you agree to the contract or not, Andric, I'll need you to take Miss Hail's gemstones to one of our contacts. Have them appraised and sold, and then arrange for a broker to set up accounts and the appropriate identity documents for her and Mister Reed.

"This will need to be done tonight. I don't want the young lady's valuables lying around a school unsecured. Like most fey new to the mortal realm, I suspect Miss Hail has no idea how valuable her Arbaon-sourced gemstones truly are."

"What makes you think that?" Hilda asked, stealing the words from the tip of Andric's tongue, but both of them fell silent when Thomas picked up the small pouch, untied the strings, and carefully poured the contents out onto his desk.

A small shower of gemstones spilt out across the wooden surface, a kaleidoscope of colours glinting and glimmering.

"Sweet mercy," Hilda swore, and Andric's jaw dropped open in surprise.

"Miss Hail has brought with her a veritable fortune," Thomas said, "so I don't think paying you for your services will be beyond her means."

It took Andric a moment to find his words again, still staring at the gemstones scattered across the desk. Sapphires, emeralds, rubies, and what looked like diamonds were all sparkling in the artificial warmth of the electric lights. All Arbaon-sourced, making them not only rare but of pristine quality too.

"If... if you can, uh, convince Miss Hail to hire me, then I'll take the position," Andric said, stumbling over his words as he tried not to calculate an estimated value for the gemstones that the young woman had been carting around, protected by nothing more than a piece of fabric.

"I'll have the paperwork drawn up," Thomas said, carefully collecting the gemstones and returning them to the drawstring pouch.

"Once the gems have been appraised, sold, and a bank account opened for the two of them, perhaps you can get them some basic supplies too? Bags, school supplies, a few changes of clothes, and the like."

"Sure."

"You've been awake all night, Andric," Hilda interjected, frowning and fidgeting in her seat, "drive carefully. You might survive a car crash, but—"

"I was thinking I'd blur," he reassured her with a smile, "it'll be faster. I can cut through the forest, and I'd have to leave the car outside of Hawkwell anyway, the roads are too narrow to get that monster of a vehicle through without drawing unnecessary attention."

"If you're going to blur the distance, keep an eye on the time," Walcott added. "We don't want to incite more of Miss Hail's wrath by sending her to her first lessons without workbooks and pens."

Andric laughed and nodded, but Hilda frowned at the headmaster.

"Why do I feel like there's a story there?"

"I'll let Thomas tell you," Andric said with a grin still curling his lips, and it felt like weeks since he'd smiled as much as he had that night. "I should get going if I want to make it to Hawkwell and back before the fey get to their first lessons."

"I'll get the contract written up, and you can collect it off my desk when you return," Walcott instructed as Andric pushed against the arms of the chair and rose back to his feet, smothering down a weary sigh and nodding.

"Travel safe," Hilda warned again, and Andric offered her another soft smile before he turned to leave the office.

By the time he stepped into the reception area and closed Walcott's office door, the old vampire was already telling Hilda about Miss Hail's attack-by-books.

"Andric!"

For a split second, the high-pitched voice calling his name made his heart still in horror. The thought that he'd walked, unprepared, straight into another encounter with Mia Harris made his stomach drop, but then the voice fully registered.

The false pitch, the awkward vocal tics as the speaker tried to make themself sound feminine and failing miserably, had Andric growling at the beaming face of his best friend.

"Don't do that!" he snarled.

"Oh, my friend. I'd say I'm sorry for startling you, but the look on your face just now was entirely worth any retribution you bring down upon me at a later date," Nameer said laughing, leaning against the door that led back to the rest of the school with his ankles and arms casually crossed.

He was still dressed in the uniform of a kavian hunter, so Andric assumed he'd come straight from his post at the front gates.

The black T-shirt with short sleeves looked simple enough, but reinforced with tiny strands of woven plastic it doubled as armour and was highly resistant to the scrabbling claws of a rabid kavian. The trousers were thick leather, strengthened in key spots, with built-in sheaths for the daggers that hunters always carried.

Nameer preferred his gun, Andric knew, but nothing took a kavian down faster than a severed carotid, and no hunter would refuse to carry a blade on principle alone.

"What are you even doing here?" Andric demanded. "Shouldn't you be sleeping, or preparing the next round of torture for your students?"

"And let you skitter off into the unknown without an explanation?" his oldest friend asked. A black eyebrow arched over warm brown eyes that were still glimmering with open amusement, and his dark clothes and umber skin almost let him disappear into the shadows of the windowless office. Then his lips parted into a familiar, cheeky smile, flashing sharp, white teeth at Andric playfully. "Not bloody likely."

Andric stared at Nameer for a long moment, holding the other man's gaze, before he let a wide grin spread across his features. It was mirrored by Nameer, the other vampire's smile widening as Andric paced across the room. The two came together with the casual ease of familiarity, hands clasping around each other's forearms, while they tugged each other into a hug, laughing.

"Ah, I have missed you," Andric sighed when they stepped back, and Nameer's mirth quietened in response. He studied Andric's features with careful intensity and Andric let him until the other man released a soft hum.

"It's rough, back home?" he asked, voice quiet, and Andric nodded.

"Of course it is," Andric scoffed. "Mum blames me—"

"She shouldn't," Nameer muttered, frowning and ruffling his loose curls with one hand in open agitation. "Isaak was her apprentice. It was her training that failed him."

"Harsh," Andric muttered, pressing his lips together at Nameer's glare and finally releasing the other man's forearm. "But... you're not wrong. Still, in her eyes, it was me who talked her into letting him become a kavian hunter. Ergo..."

"I don't think she's blaming you, Andric. I think she blames herself, and you happen to be an easier target right now."

"Maybe," Andric allowed, with a small shrug.

"So that's why you're back?" Nameer asked.

"Sort of... I had a room in Hockley. Was hunting for kavians in the local area to keep myself busy, waiting until my mandatory leave had run its course," Andric said, "and then I stumbled over a couple of fey and now everything's a mess."

"That'll teach you to skirt the rules—"

"Like you've never pushed the line!"

"Ah! But I have never been caught, my friend," Nameer teased, and Andric groaned under his breath.

"So, tell me about these fey?" Nameer said, changing the topic smoothly, but Andric was used to the man's whirlwind conversations. "There are already rumours they will be staying at Speculo. Truth?"

"Oh yeah," Andric sighed, "It's been a bloody long night." He nodded towards the door, before adding, "Come on, I've got to get to Hawkwell and back before the first lessons start tonight. We can talk while we walk, and I'll tell you all about how two fey can turn your entire life upside down," Andric groaned.

Reaching for the door handle as Nameer chuckled, Andric braced himself for the teasing his friend was sure to dish out when he explained how he'd come to the rescue of his two new protégés.

Cara woke her the following evening as promised, and Lizzy struggled to stumble through the motions of a shower and crawling into a fresh set of clothes while still half-asleep.

A mug of coffee settled in front of her, and Lizzy blinked at it slowly. The rich scent drifted up on thin streams of steam and she drew in a slow, deep breath.

It was only as Booker claimed the empty spot on the bench seat to her left and slung an arm around her shoulders, that Lizzy started to come around properly. Glancing around, she assumed that she must have followed her new roommate, half-asleep, into what appeared to be a large dining hall.

"Drink," Booker insisted from beside her, and the amusement in his voice had her jabbing at his ribs with her elbow instinctively, even as her hands curled around the mug, sliding it across the surface of the long wooden table in front of her to gulp down the warm drink in half a dozen mouthfuls.

"If you're planning on dragging her to breakfast without giving her at least an hour to wake up, you're going to need to provide coffee," she could hear Booker saying. "Milk, with two teaspoons of honey... or whatever you use for sweetener here in the mortal realm."

"Why are you such an insufferable morning person?" Lizzy grumbled, prompting Booker to snicker at her misfortune.

"It's not morning, Lizzy, it's late afternoon, at best."

"We just woke up. That makes it morning."

"Why does the school run at night?" he asked.

She glanced up at him in confusion, trying to figure out why Booker thought she'd know the answer. It was only when she saw his attention focused across the table, it dawned on Lizzy that the question hadn't been meant for her.

Cara was sitting opposite them, watching them both with wide eyes, a blush on her cheeks and an expression of surprise on her soft features.

"Cara," she blurted out, "I'm Cara."

"Booker."

Lizzy watched her friend introduce himself, his features curling into a slow smile, and she smothered a sigh. His next trick would be to hold out his hand, and when the poor unsuspecting victim of his flirting accepted, he'd plant a delicate kiss on it.

Before he could make good on the well-practised move, Lizzy kicked his ankle beneath the table.

"Is there any more coffee?" she interrupted, and he smoothly redirected his raised hand to push over a second mug from its previous place in front of him.

"So, why?" he asked again, and Cara shook her head.

"Oh! Right... Uh, I'm sorry," she spluttered, "we're rather light sensitive. It doesn't hurt us, or anything, but too much sunlight can bring on headaches. It makes it harder to concentrate, so the Council decreed that to enhance our learning environments, vampire schools should function on a night class schedule."

"More importantly," Lizzy interrupted as soon as Cara paused to take a breath, "are we in the same classes?" She waited until Booker turned back to her before adding, "We didn't check the schedules last night."

"I brought yours. It was on top of your desk," Cara said, holding out the sheet of paper Andric had given Lizzy the night before, and she reluctantly took it from the vampire, cradling her second coffee in one hand and sipping on it as Booker shifted and pulled his timetable out of a trouser pocket.

"What's your first class?" Cara asked while Booker compared the papers.

"It looks like English, followed by com-put-ing?"

"Computing," Cara corrected, flushing again when both of the fey turned to stare at her, and Lizzy raised an eyebrow, waiting for an explanation. Neither of the classes were ones Roche had named the previous day, and she wondered if they were part of the standard subjects he'd mentioned.

"I'm sure Mister Root will explain it to you in class," she said. "What's after the evening break?"

"Home ec, then lunch, vampire-fey relations, and another break, followed by fight training and showers—you have scheduled shower time?" Booker asked, and Cara nodded while she crunched through a slice of toast.

"Oh sure," she said once she'd swallowed, "the training can be intense. Really get you working up a sweat. Especially if you have Hunter Khatri."

"Sounds... delightful," Booker muttered, and when Lizzy shot him a grin, he was openly wrinkling his nose in disgust.

"Roche might go easy on us," she tried to reassure him. "He knows fey aren't fighters—"

"Hunter Roche? Go easy on someone?" came a new voice, and Lizzy stiffened as she turned to face the stranger who was already dropping into the seat beside Cara.

He had the darkest skin she'd ever seen and a smirk on his thin lips that Lizzy took an immediate dislike to.

"Not a chance," the newcomer snorted, crossing his arms against the table and leaning his lanky frame across the top. He almost knocked over a stand of cold toast before Cara was able to grasp the back of his shirt and tug him back into his seat. "The only hunter who's more of a hard-arse than Roche is Khatri—"

"Don't be rude, Blake!" Cara growled when she finally got him to settle back on the bench, but he rolled his eyes before turning sharply towards her.

"Oh, lighten up, Cara," he grumbled before returning his attention to Lizzy and Booker.

"Mia mentioned there were a couple of fey transferring to the school. You two are all anyone wants to talk about this morning, so I thought I'd come on over, introduce myself—"

"Then how about you do that, instead of waffling?" Cara interrupted.

"Blake Allbrook," he continued, ignoring Cara as though she hadn't spoken and stretching his hand out across the table towards Lizzy.

She stared at it for a moment, but she could remember the dozens of times Booker had made the same move. The same too-casual offer of a hand she'd only recently stopped him using on Cara. She flicked her eyes back up to Blake's smiling face, offering him nothing more than a tight smile in exchange.

"Lizzy," Booker introduced her, scooping up the offered hand in his, "and I'm Booker."

"Uh... right..." Blake spluttered, pulling his hand free from Booker's grasp quickly and glancing between them, lips pressing together.

"Was there something else you wanted to say?" Lizzy asked while turning her attention to the long table they were sitting at, finally awake enough to take in more of her surroundings.

Glancing over the various serving plates, racks of toast and jugs of milk, she was looking for something that was both appealing and recognizable as food. Finally settling on an apple, she leant forward, snatching one out of a nearby bowl of fruit while waiting for Blake to answer.

"You're rooming with Cara, right?"

"Why?" Lizzy shot back, casually tossing the apple from one

hand to the other, settling back into her seat, and leaning her shoulder against Booker's side, his familiar presence giving her the confidence to meet the stranger's stare.

"Ah, well, you must have done something to annoy Mia for her to shove you in there. But I can get her to assign you a different room. Don't worry."

As much as Lizzy didn't want to share her room with a strange vampire, her gut was telling her that she shouldn't accept Blake's offer. Apart from the sudden tension radiating from Booker, Cara had gone silent too. Her mead-brown eyes, fixed and unmoving, stared at an empty patch of table before her.

Instinct told Lizzy whatever Blake was willing to help her with would come at a steep price. And with far too many strings attached.

"Why?" Lizzy repeated, her voice harder this time.

"Why... what?" Blake spluttered.

"Why would I want you to get me a different room?"

"Oh. Well. It's just... No one wants to room with Cara."

It was on the tip of her tongue to repeat her question, to ask him why, but another glance at Cara, and the embarrassment painted across her cheeks in a bright red flush, changed Lizzy's mind.

It was too familiar. Too similar to when children of the Fey Court would try and tempt Booker away from her side with promises of friendship and positions of power. Lizzy could feel her anger bubbling up, but she pushed it down and forced herself to shake her head.

"I'm fine, thanks," she said with feigned lightness to her voice before turning her anger onto the apple and biting into it with a satisfyingly sharp crunch that almost drowned out the dual squawks from the vampires.

"What?"

"What?"

"She said, she's fine where she is," Booker answered for her as she chewed on her apple.

Both Cara and Blake were staring at her with expressions of surprise and confusion, but Lizzy ignored them, turning to Booker and nudging his arm with her elbow.

"What's that first class again?"

"English."

"We should probably find the classroom now," she grumbled, swinging her legs over the bench and rising to her feet before taking another bite of the apple as Booker followed her lead.

"Maybe social cues are different in Arbaon," Blake growled, his voice changing from its previous overly friendly tones to a low warning that made the hair on the back of Lizzy's neck stand on end. "This was an olive branch. An offer of friendship. You should accept it."

Lizzy paused and turned back to Blake slowly. His hands had curled into fists and were resting against the tabletop. Although he hadn't stood up he was leaning forward again, and there was a sharpness to his narrowed eyes. It gave Lizzy the uncomfortable impression of being studied.

"An olive branch implies I'm in some sort of fight with someone."

"I told you, you pissed off Mia," Blake repeated, finally standing from the table. "It doesn't matter what you did, not really, but trust me you don't want to make it worse. Sit with us in English. I'll help you get on her good side."

"What's in it for you?" Booker snapped, and Blake's features lit up with a disarmingly soft smile.

"Can't I simply want to be friendly? If Mia marks you as trouble, you're going to have a very lonely time at Speculo." He paused before glancing down at Cara's still bowed head. "Just ask Miss Evelyn here."

Lizzy slid her gaze over to Booker, confirming the anger she felt was being reflected back at her, before she shook her head.

"I think we'll manage just fine without Mia's endorsement."

In the time it took Lizzy to blink, Blake's encouraging smile had vanished. It was swiftly replaced with a sneer, and his previously welcoming attitude had shuttered and turned cold.

It left behind a chilling essence hovering between them and Lizzy shivered at the sensation, like wet mud stuck to her skin, leaving behind a trail of cold slime.

"That would be a mistake," he muttered. "I hope you change your mind," he added before turning and walking away as though the entire conversation hadn't happened.

Lizzy watched him move across the large dining room and settle at another table full of smiling faces that, as she watched, began shifting into surprise, and anger.

With the sounds of breakfast echoing off the stone walls and the acoustics from the high vaulted ceiling, Lizzy couldn't hear what was being said over the buzz of voices in the room.

Based on the reactions around the table, however, Lizzy suspected Blake had passed along their refusal to socialise with Speculo's more influential students.

As she glanced across the collection of vampires, Lizzy found Mia staring back. Her features had already hardened into a glare, and Lizzy quickly turned away.

"Let's go," she insisted, and Booker slung his usual arm around her shoulders, leading her towards a large set of double doors that Lizzy assumed Cara had guided her through on their way to breakfast while still mostly asleep.

It wasn't until they were outside the dining room and standing halfway along the cool stone hallway, well away from any prying eyes still eating their breakfasts, that Lizzy let out a breath of relief and allowed herself to lean into Booker's side.

"Didn't think we'd run into that kind of elitism outside of the Court," Booker grumbled under his breath, and Lizzy nodded.

"Should we have—?"

"No," he cut her off. "It's not like we need their help. Walcott's helping us, Master Roche is teaching us how to defend against kavians. We don't need to ingratiate ourselves with anyone else here."

"Hey!"

The shout made Lizzy pull back from Booker, and they both turned to find Cara approaching them at a jog.

"Everything alright?" Booker asked and Cara nodded, flicking her braid over her shoulder and lacing her fingers together around the strap of her bag slung over one shoulder.

"Oh, yeah... only..." She paused, her gaze still fixed on Booker before shaking her head and glancing back down the hall towards the dining room, "the English classrooms are that way."

"Ah, thank you."

Lizzy watched the same slow smile from breakfast curl around Booker's features and rolled her eyes. "Come on, Booker, let's go," she prompted, and he turned to her instantly, smile widening into a grin.

"Cara, care to show us the way?" he asked.

"Oh," the vampire said, startled. Delighted surprise splashed briefly across her features before it vanished behind hesitation, and she glanced between Booker and Lizzy, her fingers twisting around the bag strap. "I mean—I could, but..."

"But?" Booker prompted.

"What you said... at breakfast. What Blake said... I mean. Thank you, but..." She paused, not quite smothering a wince, before she shook her head and continued, "But you'd be better off staying on their good side," Cara murmured, and it was clear to Lizzy how much that admission cost her.

"I didn't say it for you," Lizzy said, her voice sharper than she'd intended, and Cara's gaze snapped up from where it had dropped to the floor, making Lizzy swallow hard and try to soften her tone.

"I don't know anything about you, and I don't know what their problem with you is, but I also don't care. I don't plan to spend time with people who only want to get to know me because of where I come from. People who are only interested because of some perceived advantage they might gain. It's not like I'm here to make friends."

"Then... why are you here?" Cara asked, head tilting slightly in curiosity, and Lizzy's breath caught in her throat as she realised her mistake.

She didn't know how to answer the woman. Why were they at Speculo School?

Because some kavian hunter had dragged them there. Because Walcott was the only person who'd been willing to try and look for her mum. Because Lizzy didn't have any other good options.

"To attend classes, of course."

Booker's voice snapped Lizzy out of her stunned silence, and she cleared her throat, nodding sharply.

"Right. Where did you say English was?" she asked Cara quickly.

Cara stared at them both in silence. For a heartstopping moment, Lizzy didn't think she would let the matter drop, but when neither Lizzy nor Booker elaborated, the vampire sighed.

"This way," she offered, turning to lead them back down the hallway and past the dining room. None of them glanced into the hall as they passed, and Lizzy found herself hoping her principles wouldn't come back to bite them.

Literally.

14

Almost ten minutes later, Lizzy was certain students only reached their lessons on time thanks to flagrant use of vampiric speed. She and Booker only barely managed to settle into their seats before a loud bell rang out across the school grounds, and Cara claimed a chair beside them.

Vampires quickly began to fill the room, and Lizzy's skin began to crawl at the numerous eyes passing over them. Booker, on the other hand, seemed to be basking in the attention, shooting his most charming smile at any vampire bold enough to meet his stare, and Lizzy sighed under her breath.

"Can you stop flirting for twenty-four hours? At least until we know what we've gotten ourselves into?" she muttered, but his grin just widened.

"There's no harm in flirting, Lizzy."

"That you know of," she grumbled.

A student stopped beside their desk, arms crossed over her chest, her presence silencing their quiet argument. She hovered there for a moment until Lizzy turned to face her.

Dark streaks, the same colour as her coppery skin, ran through her short, straight hair, and she wore a red dress that ended in a flared skirt above her knees.

"I hear Blake invited you to sit with us," she said, raising a sharply arched eyebrow. The motion almost made it disappear into her golden-brown fringe, cut into an artfully jagged edge, and Lizzy blinked at her in surprise.

"I don't know. Who are you?" she asked, her tone pointed, but the girl just clenched her jaw.

"We're sitting at the front," she continued, as though Lizzy hadn't spoken.

"We're sitting here," Booker shot back before Lizzy could answer, his voice playful and his grin widening into something less light and more taunting. "Why don't you join us?" he offered, his voice low and purposefully tempting, and Lizzy heard Cara splutter from her nearby seat.

The young woman he'd focused his attention on, however, merely scoffed and stalked to the front of the class without another word, and Booker sat back in his chair with a sigh and a shrug.

"Well, that didn't go down well."

"You're going to get us into trouble," Lizzy scolded, but his green eyes were glittering with laughter and she couldn't make herself sound genuinely irritated with him, turning to Cara instead and ignoring the other girl's blush.

"Who was that?"

"Um... Kelsey. Kelsey Garrick. She's Mia Harris's best friend. Between them and Blake, the three of them pretty much run the school's more influential circles. Mia's work in the headmaster's office gives her power over assigning teachers and rooms, and Kelsey and Blake make sure no one gets to Mia without going through them first... and everyone wants to get on Mia's good side."

"See?" Lizzy shot back over her shoulder at Booker. "You're making enemies already."

"I could be making influential connections," he retorted, "but so far no one's taking the bait."

Lizzy gave a quiet groan, but before she could remind him he wasn't bait, or scold him further, she was interrupted again.

"Miss Hail, Mister Reed," came a voice from behind them, and when Lizzy turned in her seat, she found a tired-looking Andric Roche standing with his hands held behind him, studying them both. "I see you found your first class without any trouble."

"Cara gave us a helping hand," Booker said, and Andric offered him a small nod in response.

"I was hoping to catch you both at breakfast, but I was a little delayed. Headmaster Walcott arranged for some supplies for you both," he explained before holding out a bag for each of them, one in each hand.

Lizzy's brow furrowed, even as she reached out to accept the bag he was offering her, Booker moving to do the same at her side. She fumbled with the fastening, taking a moment to figure out how to open it, and eventually tugged on a small piece of metal that parted the fabric as it slid past.

"The documents for your... finances, are in your bag, Miss Hail, I would recommend reviewing all the paperwork when you have a moment in private," Andric explained. "Beyond that, both of you have some basic supplies. Pens, pencils, some empty workbooks for your classes, some books I thought might help you both acclimate to the mortal realm, that sort of thing."

Lizzy nodded, shifting through the contents. She fingered one of the empty workbooks and eyed a small transparent pouch. It contained pencils and what she assumed passed for pens in the mortal realm. It was only when Booker nudged her arm that she pulled her attention back to the waiting vampire.

"Oh, um... thank you," she added, lifting her head from the bag to offer a polite smile, only for it to freeze into place on her face when she caught sight of Mia stepping up beside Andric.

"What's this?" she purred, "Does the headmaster have you running errands now, Andric?"

Her hand settled on Andric's arm, but he stepped back and folded his arms behind him once more, hands clasping together in the small of his back as he offered her a polite nod in greeting.

"Miss Harris."

"It's Mimi right?" Booker asked, turning around fully in his seat, and Lizzy felt her heart raise to settle in her throat anxiously.

She recognised his tone. The one that said he was irritated, but was refusing to show it. The overly friendly voice Booker liked to use when he wanted someone to let their guard down long enough for him to get revenge.

"Booker..." she warned quietly, but he ignored her.

"It's Mia."

"Ah, of course. My apologies. That privilege was only bestowed on Hunter Roche. I remember now."

"Booker," Lizzy hissed, trying to split her attention between Andric, who was shifting uncomfortably, and Mia, whose eyes were flashing with anger and her lips pressing tight, but Booker still didn't stop.

"So far this morning, Blake Allbrook and Kelsey Garrick have both approached us about sitting with you. May I suggest if you are that desperate for more friends, that you be a little more approachable?" he taunted. "Perhaps be a touch more open to people using your adorable little nickname?"

Lizzy didn't wait for Booker to finish provoking the vampire. Shoving the new bag Andric had handed her onto the desk, she stood up quickly, stepping between Booker and Mia as the woman advanced forward a step. Mia's fury was almost palpable, her cheeks flushed dark and her focus fixed on Booker as her hands curled into fists at her sides.

"How dare you—"

"Back away—" Lizzy snapped, blocking Mia's path and lifting her chin to meet the taller woman's gaze.

"That's enough," Andric growled, interrupting their sudden standoff and placing a firm hand on both their shoulders. "Miss Harris, Miss Hail, both of you take your seats. Mister Reed, please refrain from insulting your fellow classmates."

Despite the firm note to his voice, Lizzy didn't move, and neither did Mia. Mia's lips were still pressed together in barely restrained anger, and the muscle in her jaw twitched as she clenched her teeth. The part that concerned Lizzy the most, and the reason she refused to back down first, was that Mia still had her entire attention fixed over Lizzy's shoulder, glaring at Booker.

Lizzy didn't need to look at her best friend to know he'd be sitting calmly, leaning back in his chair. Maybe with one leg crossed over the other and with the smallest hint of a light, mocking smile on his lips.

He trusted her to handle any fallout from his taunting, but where the children of the Fey Court would back down when Lizzy challenged them, more comfortable with words than the threat of a fight, here in the mortal realm, surrounded by vampires, Lizzy no longer had the advantage.

If anything, she was at a distinct disadvantage, and she could almost feel the hush that had fallen over the classroom as more and more students noticed the confrontation, and Lizzy's shoulders tensed.

There was no way Mia could let her challenge slide. Not without damaging her position in the school.

Lizzy's fingers curled into her palms as she prepared to push the woman back with telekinesis, wondering if she would be fast enough to combat Mia's speed, or if she would be outmatched, as she had been when trying to fling books at Hunter Roche.

"Mia... That's enough."

Andric's voice was quiet this time, but the soft use of her name seemed to draw Mia's attention back to where she was standing and the audience their spat had garnered. Her frame gave a small shudder, and her lips twisted up into a tense smile, but she slowly stepped back from Lizzy.

"Of course," she purred, but Lizzy didn't let herself relax.

She could still see the fury simmering behind the woman's diamond-hard gaze, and she swallowed nervously.

"I wouldn't make an embarrassment of myself by sparring with ignorant children," Mia spat before tossing her long, copper-red curls over her shoulder and turning away to stalk towards the front of the class, head held high.

As Mia passed each row of seats, Lizzy watched the other students break out into whispers, and finally relaxed enough to shoot a glare at Booker. His smug smile vanished, replaced with a sheepish grin she was sure he intended to double as an apology.

"You two have caused nothing but trouble since I found you," Andric muttered under his breath, and Lizzy spun back to him, letting her irritation with Mia and Booker rise to the surface to find a target in Andric Roche.

"Oh, I'm sorry, did we ask to come here?" she snapped, turning to grab the new bag from her desk, before thrusting it back out towards the hunter. "Thank you for the supplies, but I doubt we'll need them. I agreed to attend classes; I never agreed to complete the work."

Andric's lips parted, but he paused. Lizzy watched him glance around the room, as though suddenly remembering they were surrounded by dozens of students, eagerly listening for gossip. A moment later, his mouth snapped closed and he swallowed hard. His hands returned to clasp together at the small of his back once more and he straightened his posture.

"Keep it," he muttered, and when he glanced back down at her, he'd pulled on the cold mask that Lizzy had been faced with several times the previous evening, but his grey eyes were still brimming with irritation. "I'll relay your message to the headmaster."

Lizzy frowned, unable to tell if the words had been a threat or not.

Before she could decide how to respond, or whether to throw

the new bag in his face, Andric had turned and walked away. His long strides propelled him out of the classroom so fast that he only narrowly avoided colliding with the English teacher as he finally arrived, a folder full of loose notes tucked under one arm.

Indecision held Lizzy in place. The urge to go after Andric, to challenge his last statement and demand he explain whatever he'd been implying, was strong. But she also didn't want him to know how desperate she was for the headmaster's help.

She stood, frozen in place, even as the teacher moved to the front of the classroom and began calling for quiet and for everyone to take their seats.

It wasn't until Booker hooked a hand around her elbow and gave it a light tug that Lizzy shook her head and sank back into her chair, the bag of supplies still grasped in her hand, her fingers clenched hard enough into the fabric that they were beginning to ache.

"Lizzy?" Booker whispered. The questions hovering behind her name were unspoken, but still clear enough for her to understand.

Was she alright? Could he help? Did she want him in her mind?

Lizzy forced a brief, tight smile onto her lips, but didn't let her eyes wander to meet Booker's. She tangled her fingers in the pearl pendant strung around her neck, lifting it to run soothingly across her bottom lip and tried to focus on the teacher at the front of the classroom, muttering a soft, "I'll be fine."

She quietly hoped that she wasn't lying.

15

Andric stalked out of the English classroom as fast as he could without resorting to blurring.

His temper was pushing against his control, barely being held in check, but he kept walking. The last thing Andric wanted to do was get into an argument with an insolent teenage fey in the middle of a classroom full of students.

Since the night he'd killed the kavian attacking the two fey, they'd proven themselves to be stubborn, headstrong, argumentative troublemakers.

They'd broken laws of their own realm and put themselves in danger. Had lied about their motives and negotiated to get the assistance they wanted, with little to no sacrifice on their part.

And now she had tried to twist the terms of their arrangement.

It was infuriating... and, Andric reluctantly admitted to himself, impressive.

Stubborn and headstrong. But also clever, resourceful, and brave.

When he finally slowed his pace and glanced around, Andric found himself on the opposite side of the school to Walcott's office and grimaced.

I'll relay your message to the headmaster.

He wished he could take back the parting words he'd shot at the fiery fey. They'd been born from frustration, and Andric admitted that they'd been a low blow on his part.

Something about the young woman's abrasiveness sparked his temper. Like a match igniting from friction, Lizzy Hail frayed at his control.

He backed up until he could lean against the stone wall of the hallway. With a sigh Andric ran both hands through his hair, clasping them together at the base of his skull, before he tilted his head back, and sucked in several deep breaths.

As he calmed, his eyes slid shut and he let the scenario from the classroom replay in his mind, then winced when he realised it had been almost entirely his fault.

His irritation at having to use Miss Harris's affection to convince her to back down from the confrontation had made him careless, and his muttered complaint about the two fey had been bitterly unfair.

Miss Hail had been well within her rights to call him on it.

"Damn it," he muttered, suddenly remembering the contract for his employment sitting in the depths of her new bag. It had already been a coin toss whether the woman would sign it. After their argument, Andric suspected he might have to get on his knees and beg.

"Now that is a position I have not seen you take for many years," came the familiar voice of his best friend, and Andric cracked a single eye open to stare at Nameer balefully.

"What do you want? Isn't there a class full of wannabe hunters you can torment, instead of me?"

"Not at all, Andric. I'm entirely at your disposal."

"Lucky me," he muttered dryly, catching sight of Nameer's growing grin before he closed his eye again.

"Seriously, Andric, the last time you were so worked up you had to ground yourself like this, we were still one of those wannabe hunters getting tormented. What happened?"

Andric pressed his lips together, considering if he really wanted to open himself up to the good-natured teasing he was certain to get about Miss Harris's behaviour, but the opportunity for some unbiased advice was too good to pass up, and he heaved another weary sigh, bracing himself.

"I may have, possibly... fucked up," he admitted. Silence was his answer. Andric had no trouble imagining shock and surprise flickering across Nameer's face. Probably followed by a look of calculation as his friend judged how many jokes Andric was willing to take.

He and Nameer had been inseparable friends since they were eleven. There was little they didn't know about each other. It wouldn't take Nameer long to figure out that Andric had very little patience left, and almost as soon as he thought it, Andric heard Nameer settle against the wall beside him.

"Alright," he said quietly, and when Andric cracked a hesitant eye open again to check on his friend, Nameer was staring straight ahead, gaze fixed out the window on the opposite side of the hall, watching the empty gardens with his hands shoved into his pockets, a picture of patience. "Tell me everything."

The details fell from his tongue, almost without Andric's conscious permission.

It was a relief he'd almost forgotten, being able to confide in a friend, without reservation, and the longer Andric spoke, the more he thought he might be able to understand the connection between Miss Hail and Mister Reed.

Also, the longer he spoke, the clearer his choices became.

He had underestimated Mia Harris's possessive streak, and when he admitted as much to Nameer, his friend finally reacted, grimacing and giving a full body shudder.

"For all that I tease you, the faster that one graduates the better," Nameer muttered, and Andric huffed a small laugh.

"She'll never sign the contract now," Andric muttered. He'd long ago dropped his hands from the back of his neck, but now he found his arms crossing defensively.

"The fey girl?"

"Lizzy Hail, yes."

"I'm sure you could find a way to convince her—"

"You've not met this fey, Nameer," Andric cut him off, shaking his head. "She's the most stubborn, bullheaded, determined person I've ever—"

"Oh, do you mean to tell me you've finally met your match?" Nameer teased, and Andric gave a quiet groan.

"There's only one thing to do," Andric said, ignoring his friend's taunting. "I just won't mention to Walcott that it's not been signed. If he doesn't know, he can't remove me from Speculo, and he won't be liable for my presence here."

Nameer sobered and turned to stare at him properly. He shifted until his shoulder pressed against the stone wall, and lifted his arms to cross over his chest, mirroring Andric, but it was the frown furrowing his face that held Andric's attention.

"That is singularly the most stupid idea you've had since our graduation celebration."

"What else am I supposed to do?" he asked, exasperated.

"Bribe her. Forge her signature, for all I care. But lying to Walcott isn't an option."

Andric groaned and let his head fall back against the wall, fixing his stare on the ceiling. Even knowing Nameer was right, it didn't help give him any viable options.

"I can offer her nothing," he admitted. "I'm going to have to stay as far away from the pair of them as possible. They're already in Mia's crosshairs. The last thing they need is an even bigger target on their backs."

"Andric," Nameer sighed, pushing off the wall and taking a moment to stretch, arms above his head and back curving like a cat, before he turned back to his friend. "I love you like a brother, but sometimes you overthink things."

"What do you mean?" Andric asked, and Nameer shook his

head, a small smile lighting his face as he laughed.

"Why don't you start by offering her a bloody apology, and see where it goes from there?" he suggested before turning and walking down the hall. "Now stop moping," he called over his shoulder, "class is about to let out. And I believe you have a grovelling apology to practise in a mirror, somewhere that's not here."

"So much for moral support," Andric muttered as Nameer disappeared around the corner at the end of the hall. A quick glance at his watch told him that his friend was right, however, and he pushed off the wall, making a beeline for the safety, and relative privacy, of his rooms.

The last thing he needed was for the student population to witness him loitering in the hallways. Especially after the rather public argument in Miss Hail's English class.

To keep an eye on the pair, without drawing down more of Mia's wrath, Andric had taken to lingering outside their classrooms, listening for trouble through the door. Sometimes, he would claim a chair at the back of the room, but as he watched over them, their behaviour remained the same.

If Andric had thought, for a single moment, Lizzy's threat to do nothing more than attend her assigned classes had been a bluff, the young fey had rapidly managed to disabuse him of that notion.

The two fey spent more time talking to each other, than listening.

Occasionally they attempted to draw Miss Evelyn into their discussions, but more often than not she scowled at them until they fell into reluctant silence.

Andric had high hopes the computing course at least might capture their interest. The entirety of the internet's knowledge at their fingertips, the answer to any question they might have about the mortal realm only a few keystrokes away, but once they had discovered the course was supposed to help teach vampires how to integrate into human society, or find jobs, the two fey discounted the lessons and didn't even feign paying attention.

By the end of their second week, their teachers had either given up trying to keep them engaged, or were busy lodging complaints with the headmaster.

The only thing that stopped Andric from giving up hope completely was their continued association with Cara Evelyn. While the vampire was Miss Hail's assigned roommate, he noticed that the fey always found themselves seats near her. Even in the classrooms where they had other options.

He rarely saw the three apart. When Cara and Lizzy arrived for breakfast, Booker joined them, and the trio only separated again at the end of the day when the fey split from Cara to head out to the field for their training sessions with Andric.

The training sessions were also the only time Lizzy and Booker's united front against taking part in classes appeared to fracture.

Booker seemed to delight in complaining. Insisting he wasn't built for the kind of physical activity Andric pushed for. That running laps around the field was demeaning, and how working hard enough to build up a sweat made him feel physically ill.

Miss Hail, on the other hand, sank into the additional exercise like a comfortable, familiar, old chair.

Beyond basic warm ups and stretches at the end of their sessions, Andric had only asked the pair to run laps around the field. He intended for them to build up their general health and stamina before he moved on to other things, but, while Booker slowed to a walk after fifteen minutes and sank to the ground in protest after half an hour, Lizzy just ran. Without comment or complaint.

Not particularly fast, but a consistent sustained jog, for two hours, during which time she seemed to lose herself in her thoughts.

It was something Andric had noticed the first night he'd brought them through the school. When he'd been rushing them through the halls, Lizzy had kept pace, even when he'd been forced to stop and wait for Booker.

It made him curious about what she could be capable of if she applied herself. He could see potential in the young woman and itched to push her to her limits, but until Andric could figure out a way to get them both invested, he didn't dare risk it.

Didn't dare risk another argument.

Not when, as far as he knew, the contract that allowed his continued presence at Speculo School remained unsigned.

Miss Hail hadn't approached him about it, and Andric had yet to find the courage to ask her. Nameer's suggestion of a basic apology taunted him, but every time Andric tried, something else jumped to the tip of his tongue. Like, "Run ten laps around the field, and I don't want to hear a complaint out of you until the second circuit at least, Mister Reed."

So he let Booker complain. He let Lizzy take a lazy jog around the field for two hours a day without challenging either of them, and he let it continue until the day neither of them showed up on the field.

Their last class was the only time, outside of their rooms, where Andric didn't shadow the pair. He was always careful to leave early so that he could be waiting on the field for the fey, prepared for their arrival, but when they didn't show up, his concern began to grow.

He paced impatiently, wondering if the teacher had held them back or if Miss Harris had decided to exact her revenge. The revenge he was sure was building in response to being shown up by Booker on the fey's first day.

His unease and irritation grew in equal measure the longer they remained absent, but eventually, his concern for the missing fey drove him back inside the school.

There were too many students at Speculo to be able to track the fey by their blood. No matter how distinctive it was, the scent was simply drowned out by the sheer number of vampires in the school. After eliminating the obvious locations, including their history classroom and the dining hall, Andric finally found the pair in the library.

He stood in the doorway for a few minutes, relief hitting him harder than he'd expected it to and sending his heart pounding.

They were both fine. Neither in trouble with a teacher nor in danger from a classmate's retaliation. They were sitting around a study table and throwing screwed-up balls of paper at one another. Occasionally, one of the makeshift projectiles was knocked out of the air or redirected with, what Andric could only assume was, telekinesis from one of the two fey.

Alone, and without witnesses, they were laughing together and smiling freely.

It was a relief to discover the pair could behave like normal, happy teenagers. Much of the time they were wearing stoic masks or stony expressions of bored disinterest, but as swiftly as the smile spread across his face at their lighthearted banter and as fast as the relief had flooded him, irritation with the pair hit too, replacing the more positive emotions in an instant.

Before Andric could rethink his decision, he entered the library and blurred across the room to stand beside the table, snatching the most recently tossed ball of paper out of the air.

Both Lizzy and Booker jumped in their seats, Miss Hail jerking back from him as soon as she registered his presence, and their laughter died. Guilt fought to replace his irritation, but he pushed it down and focused on how much of his time they had wasted and how concerned he'd been, letting it fuel the glare he locked onto the pair.

"What do you think you're doing in here?" he demanded, and Booker swore under his breath.

Lizzy did what he expected her to do. Recovering from her shock, she lifted her chin to challenge the anger in his tone, narrowing her electric-blue eyes.

"Well, we were having fun, but you've ruined that."

It was a well-placed blow, and Andric ground his teeth together to stop himself from flinching at the accusation.

"You should have been on the field nearly an hour ago."

"Why? So you can have us run a path into it? No thanks."

"If you have a problem with what I'm teaching you—"

"Well that's the problem, isn't it? You're not actually teaching us anything. We already know how to run."

"Based on Mister Reed's performance these last couple of weeks, I'd beg to differ," Andric shot back at her, and Lizzy's hands instantly curled into fists, her anger spiking in her friend's defence, and Andric silently cursed his miscalculation.

Nothing got the woman angrier, faster, than someone aiming a verbal blow towards Booker. He'd seen the same behaviour mirrored in Mister Reed, and Andric understood. Some of the worst fights he'd ever been involved in had been helping Nameer out of a situation he'd gotten himself into, and vice versa.

They protected each other, and with his thoughtless comment, he'd given Miss Hail something to rail against.

"You want me to show you something more substantial than running, is that the problem?" he continued, interrupting whatever tirade Miss Hail had been about to spit out, and the pair of them froze.

"Alright, fine. We start tomorrow," he growled, forcing himself to still sound annoyed, even as amusement bubbled at the panic-filled glance they had exchanged at his declaration.

"You two had better be on the field by 4am tomorrow, and ready to learn how to fight. Without complaining about working up a sweat, Mister Reed, or you'll need to come up with a better reason for breaking your word when I drag the pair of you in to explain to Walcott."

Their other teachers only knew them as the troublesome transfer students, but Andric knew their real reason for being at Speculo. He knew their real motivation for agreeing to the classes, and he knew his threats carried more weight than their other teachers.

Based on the look the two fey shared, they knew it too, but Miss Hail surprised him when she turned back to him and threw down a challenge instead of conceding.

"Are you sure you can afford to?" she asked, arching an eyebrow. "After all, you're not supposed to be here at Speculo at all, right?"

And there it is, Andric thought to himself, careful not to flinch in the face of her pointed accusation, even as his breath caught in his throat.

She'd found the contract in her bag. Had understood enough of it to know he was supposed to be working for her, and based on her pointed questions, it seemed as though she'd figured out he would be in a precarious position until she signed it.

Andric took a moment to study her and weigh his options.

He could admit he needed her help and lose all leverage over the pair. He could try to lie, but her voice held a thread of cold steel that told him she'd call him on a bluff. And the arch of her eyebrows confirmed his own suspicions. If he lost her trust, he risked losing everything.

Or, Andric could be honest with them.

Why don't you start by offering her a bloody apology, he remembered Nameer insisting and blew out a harsh breath through his nose.

"You're right, I'm not supposed to be here unless you sign the contract stating I'm working for you as your teacher, guard and guide," he admitted, watching her harsh mask fall and her lips part in surprise, and Andric smiled. "But don't think that'll stop me taking you both into Walcott anyway... You both gave him your word that you'd attend the classes. You might have found a loophole with the rest of them but our agreement hinged on me teaching you how to escape a kavian alive. You need to be on the field for me to do that."

He hesitated before quickly adding, "And... I apologise for my comment on your first day. I was... frustrated. But not with either of you, and my words were uncalled for."

The pair glanced at each other again. It was brief, but he'd been watching the two fey for weeks now and knew how much information the pair seemed to be able to convey to one another with little more than a shrug, a nod, or a wrinkled nose.

It only took a split second for Booker to nod and Lizzy to grimace in response, followed by a heavy sigh.

"Fine," she muttered, reluctance written all over her face. "You're right, and... we're sorry."

Andric didn't move and waited until Lizzy met his eyes again. It took her a moment, but when she did, the reluctance melted away into guilt, and her delicate features settled into something that felt a little more genuine.

"We'll be there," she responded, her voice softer and Andric finally found he believed her, nodding his head just once in acceptance before shifting his attention to Booker. He found the other fey leaning back in his chair, a wide grin on his face that vanished quickly under Andric's scrutiny, morphing into a light smile before he added his agreement in the form of a nod.

"And, hey," Lizzy said, lips pressed together for a moment when Andric turned back to her. "I was bluffing. I signed it."

The contract, he realised, and relief hit him like a physical blow. For a moment he thought the fey had struck him with telekinesis as he struggled to suck in a breath, but then the weight that had been sitting on his chest since their argument in the young woman's English class lifted and Andric could breathe.

"Thank you," he offered, not knowing how else to put his relief and gratitude into words. Lizzy nodded before glancing away, and Andric sighed as he collected his scattered thoughts.

"Okay then. Tomorrow we start your training properly, 4am. Don't be late," he finished, a growl of warning to his voice.

He tossed the ball of paper he'd snatched up upon his arrival into the air, and blurred away from their table, not giving either of them a chance to respond.

He stopped inside the library doors and briefly glanced back. One of them had telekinetically caught the ball in midair, letting the crumpled paper levitate as it spun from its halted momentum, and as he finally forced himself to leave the library, a light spring to his step, Andric found himself grinning.

Sixteen days, and who even knew how many wasted hours, spent sitting in classrooms while teachers talked nonsense.

Lizzy sighed and leant back in her chair, tapping against the open notebook on the desk with the pen sitting between her fingers as she tuned out the vampire-fey relations teacher, Master Heyward.

Her eyes stayed fixed on the clock on the wall as her mind drifted.

Despite having attended the Arbaon Academy classes about the mortal realm, Lizzy had found her knowledge to be consistently outdated.

But she'd told herself it didn't matter. That she had no intention of staying in the mortal realm long enough for any of it to matter.

The classes were designed for vampires who wanted to live and blend in amongst the humans who dominated the mortal realm, but Lizzy had no such intentions.

Struggling to understand lessons not meant for her, and letting herself look like a fool in the process, wasn't on her agenda.

And after the argument with Roche on their first day, Lizzy hadn't been even remotely inclined to try.

As far as Lizzy was concerned, Cara had been the only bright spot in their welcome to Speculo School. She'd gone above and beyond to help them both acclimatise, and while Lizzy suspected a large part of her motivation was her interest in Booker, Lizzy couldn't fault the woman for that.

She'd offered her aid from day one. When Lizzy had returned to their room at the end of the first night to find piles of strange clothes on her bed and shoes she had no idea how to fasten, it had been Cara who'd offered her help.

Cara had taught both of them more about how to navigate the realm they now found themselves in than any of their teachers or any of the classes they were being forced to attend.

Nothing matched up to what Lizzy had learnt in her mortal realm lessons, and even Booker's knowledge from his father's journals had only taken them so far. When it became obvious to the fey that Cara had no real friends to speak of and only a handful of friendly acquaintances in the school, a brief discussion between Lizzy and Booker's linked mind was all it took for them to agree; her assistance had earned her their loyalty.

But even Cara's encouragement, and her offers to help them both study, couldn't convince Lizzy to waste her time on the Speculo classes she had no hope of grasping in three months.

Sitting at a computer, learning how to turn it on and navigate the internet while her mother was still missing, made her sick to her stomach. Learning the currency of the mortal realm, while she still had no answers about how or why her mum hadn't come home, made her heart ache. Studying mortal sciences, and hearing nothing from Walcott, filled her with frustrated rage.

And while Lizzy had spent the last sixteen days complaining with Booker about the training sessions with Andric, the daily laps around the field had been the only thing keeping her from going mad.

Every time Lizzy found Mia and her friends' snide little comments pressing hard on her last nerve, and she was ready to walk her way off Speculo grounds, it was time for training with Andric.

Every time she thought she couldn't take anymore and was

ready to scream at the sky, 4am rolled around and she could fall into the familiar rhythmic beating of her feet against the earth.

Every time it hit her anew that her mum was still gone, she could run. Away from everything at the school, away from the swirling in her mind and the constant anger bubbling beneath the surface, leaving it all behind her.

By the time the two hours passed, her frustrations would be settled, and her fury calmed, at least temporarily.

But the longer it went on, the less effective it had become. No matter how soothing she found it, she could run anywhere. Unlike Booker, running had always been something she enjoyed.

The longer Andric had them running, showing them nothing else, and standing in the middle of the field for two hours, watching them with his arms crossed and a frown on his face, the more her irritation with the kavian hunter continued to grow.

The new supplies and clothes he'd delivered on their first day, and the kind intentions behind them, had made Lizzy sign Roche's contract for work that she'd discovered in her bag, in spite of the argument they'd had. But the same argument, and her persistent, growing irritation with the vampire, was also the reason she refused to approach him directly.

As far as Lizzy could tell, every class at Speculo was useless to her, except Roche's. Learning how to fight and defend against a kavian might very well save their lives if only Andric had been willing to actually teach them something useful!

It had taken sixteen days before Lizzy finally gave in to Booker's complaints. He'd spent the previous two weeks doing little else. Splitting his time between flirting with anyone who wasn't part of Mia's crowd of tagalongs and whining to her or Cara about Speculo and how he'd already graduated from Arbaon Academy.

When he'd spent an entire history class connected to her mind, begging and pleading to skip Andric's repetitive lesson on running in circles in favour of doing something else, anything else, Lizzy had finally agreed, slipping off to the library when Cara left them to head to her advanced kavian hunter class.

What Lizzy hadn't anticipated was Andric's response.

Unlike every other teacher in the school that had reacted somewhere between gentle cajoling and badly hidden exasperation at their lack of engagement, Andric hadn't even tried to hide his annoyance.

Instead of working around them or pandering to their whims and desires, the vampire had insisted on their presence. Even when Lizzy had tried bluffing her way out, he'd merely called her on it.

It was irritatingly effective, but he had agreed to teach them something more useful than running laps around a field, and Lizzy couldn't help but find that opportunity a tiny bit intriguing.

She found herself watching the seconds tick by at a glacial pace. The hands of the clock slid closer to 4am, and her pen continued to tap an impatient rhythm against the desk.

"Are you actually that eager?" Booker's voice thrummed through her mind, and her tapping stilled.

"Not eager," she defended quickly, *"just... curious."*

"Whatever he shows us is going to be painful, physical, and exhausting. You realise that, right?"

"But useful. Which is more than I can say for Master Heyward's long-winded speech about... What is he talking about right now?"

"The re-establishment of contact between the mortal realm and Arbaon."

"Still?"

"He's very passionate about it," Booker drawled, and Lizzy had to smother a grin, but her gaze never strayed from the clock.

"Why are we still sitting here?" She didn't realise she'd broadcast the frustrated thought until Booker's curiosity pressed against her mind, and he shifted in his seat until he could stare at her.

"What do you mean?"

Lizzy kept her thoughts carefully still for a moment as she considered whether she wanted to explain before giving into Booker's patient presence in her mind.

"This is useless. Why does it matter who contacted who first, and how? We could be learning to defend against a kavian. Which is something we might actually need to know, if the headmaster can't come up with answers."

"What do you want to do? Get up and walk out? We agreed to attend the classes—"

"And we have. Now it's time for our next class. We can't blur like the vampires, so is leaving ten minutes early to get to our next lesson really a problem?" she shot back innocently.

Booker's emotions and thoughts were moving so fast she couldn't pin down his reaction, so Lizzy finally tore her gaze away from the clock, turning her head just enough to catch Booker's sharp green eyes and study his expression.

He was considering her words, thinking about the school, the classes, their options. It was a near whirlwind of information, and she shook her head slightly before disconnecting their minds.

"Sorry," Booker muttered. His voice was low, but they'd quickly learnt that no matter how quietly they spoke, the vampires would hear them. They'd kept their minds connected more since arriving at Speculo than they had since they were children.

"Well?" she whispered. Lizzy glanced at Master Heyward, still pacing and lecturing at the front of the class, before she let her attention slide back to the clock. Quarter to four.

There was another beat of silence from Booker before his familiar sigh of surrender brought a grin to her face, prompting Lizzy to snap her notebook shut and shove it into her bag, lifting it onto her shoulder as she stood up from the desk.

"Excuse me, Miss Hail, is there a problem?" Master Heyward called, not making any effort to mask the exasperation in his voice, and Lizzy gave the teacher a carefully crafted expression of innocence that had Booker snorting a soft laugh at her side.

"Oh, no. No problem. Please, continue," she responded, stepping away from her desk as Booker stood to follow her, his bag hanging loosely from his hand.

"Where do you think you're both going? There's still fifteen minutes of my class left!"

"Well, don't let us stop you," she said cheerfully as she began backing out of the room, peering around Booker's larger frame to offer the now-spluttering teacher a grin. "We've got another class to get to. On the other side of the school. And Hunter Roche did specifically tell us not to be late, so. You know how it is. Gotta get ahead of the crowds!"

They made it to the door of the classroom just as Master Heyward found his words, but by the time he'd snarled their names, Booker and Lizzy had slipped into the hall.

"Miss Hail! Mister Reed! Return to your seats!"

His voice faded as the door snapped shut behind them, and Lizzy blew out a breath of relief as Booker grabbed up her hand and they began moving together through the empty halls, as far away from the vampire-fey relations classroom as quickly as possible.

"So why are you so interested in this... fight training?" Booker asked once they were several hallways away, and Master Heyward hadn't blurred after them.

"I told you," Lizzy muttered, "it's because it might be useful."

"Any of these classes might be useful," Booker scoffed, "why this one, specifically?"

"Oh, you think we're going to find Mum with a history lesson, do you?" Lizzy muttered, and Booker released her hand to sling his arm around her shoulders and tug her into his side.

"Are you sure that your interest isn't in the teacher?" he teased, his arm keeping her upright as she stumbled at his question.

"What? What are you talking about?"

"I just mean that you and Master Roche do an awful lot of arguing—"

"That's because he's annoying. At best!" Lizzy hissed, but her frustration did nothing more than add fuel to Booker's already widening grin.

"You both bicker very passionately—"

"Oh don't be ridiculous," Lizzy growled, shoving Booker but he refused to release her, still laughing at her reaction.

"You're blushing, Lizzy."

"And you're squirrel shit!"

The insult washed right over Booker, and he tightened his arm enough that his grip turned into a hug and Lizzy settled against him with only minimal muttering.

"If you want to start something with Cara, you don't have to try and pair me up with someone first," she grumbled, and Booker finally let go of her, stopping dead in the middle of the hall.

Lizzy kept moving a few steps until she realised he wasn't following and turned back to find him frowning at her, his hands shoved into the pockets of the trousers Cara had called jeans, and his shoulders hunched slightly.

"What makes you think I'm interested in Cara?" he asked, and Lizzy huffed an exasperated sigh.

"Are you serious? You're rarely not flirting with her."

"I flirt with everyone."

"Yes," Lizzy agreed, forcing her words out slowly and pointedly, "you do flirt with everyone. Right up until the moment Cara sits with us and then you stop flirting with anyone but her."

Booker winced and sighed, glancing away from Lizzy as his shoulders lifted a little more and he cursed under his breath, "Rot, was I that obvious?"

"Probably only to me," Lizzy reassured, voice softening at her friend's admission. Booker recovered from his embarrassment faster than Lizzy had, and his shoulders relaxed as he turned back to her, a sharp, almost calculating expression drifting across his features.

He paced forward to stand in front of her, hands still tucked into his pockets as he studied her for a moment, carefully choosing his words, and Lizzy found herself feeling a little nervous about whatever he was about to say.

"That wasn't why I was asking about Roche though, Lizzy," he said after a moment, "there's some definite sparks there."

Despite her best efforts, she flinched, her attention flicking away to settle on anything that wasn't his suddenly serious green eyes.

"Sparks of irritation, maybe," she conceded. "I'm here to find out what happened to Mum. That's all. And, look, just because you're interested in someone, don't cast the same shadow over my interactions."

Silence was her answer, but Lizzy refused to glance up at Booker and after a moment, he sighed, the sound full of reluctant resignation.

"Alright, fine. Perhaps I misread it," he offered, voice light.

"How very generous of you—"

"But if it turns out I didn't, and you end up fucking the vampire, you owe me a favor."

"What? Why? I didn't agree to bet on this!" Lizzy spluttered, wide eyes snapping back to Booker's grinning face, features alight with open amusement.

"No, but I like being right too much to let it go entirely."

"Urgh," Lizzy groaned and spun on her heel, continuing to march through the halls towards the field at the back of the school, and a moment later, Booker caught up with her, hands no longer shoved into his jeans, and wound one arm around her now-tense shoulders once more.

"Oh, and Lizzy?" he prompted.

The laughing in his voice told her she was going to regret responding, but she hummed a questioning sound anyway, only to elbow the fey at her side when he answered with a delighted, "You're blushing again."

17

As usual, Andric was already waiting for them when they arrived at the field he'd laid claim to for their classes.

As they approached, he turned to face them, stepping away from two large oblong sacks. Each sack was hanging from a frame that left them freestanding in the middle of the field, and Lizzy eyed them with a healthy dose of suspicion.

"You're early?" he asked, the surprise in his voice ringing clear, and Lizzy grit her teeth, tearing her gaze away from the bags.

"You said not to be late," she snapped as they came to a stop in front of him.

"So we bailed on vampire and fey relations fifteen minutes early," Booker announced. Lizzy sighed as Andric's surprise got replaced with a frown, bracing herself for the reprimand she was sure he was about to fling at them.

"Ah," he sighed, "you're probably going to regret that."

It wasn't the reaction she'd expected. She'd braced herself for annoyance, frustration, or disappointment, but instead Lizzy found actual concern in his voice.

"What?"

"Heyward's not known for being particularly forgiving... and we've got to wait for Miss Evelyn, so you've likely got on his bad side for no reason."

"Cara's joining us?" Booker interrupted, and Andric nodded.

"I'll need a second pair of hands, you'll both need a sparring partner to practise with. She's got the best grades in her own training, so isn't likely to fall behind, and more importantly, the pair of you seem to trust her."

"Is trust important?" Lizzy asked when Booker fell silent and turned his attention to the school, already watching for Cara.

"It'll stop you flinching when one of us tries to attack you."

"What if we don't trust you?"

Andric hadn't exactly been pacing, but he froze at her question, going unnaturally still for a split second before his eyes met hers. "Then this is going to be exponentially more difficult for you."

Andric's features lunging at her from a dark alley flashed across her mind again before she swallowed and turned away.

"While we wait, tell me about your telekinetic abilities. How do they work? Can you both use it?"

"We can, but Lizzy's better at it," Booker answered when Lizzy stayed silent. He turned away from watching the school and paced back to her side, his arm falling around her shoulders as a familiar, comforting weight.

"Better in what way?"

"Stronger. And she can use it consistently for longer." Booker shrugged. "Whereas I can maintain a telepathic connection for longer than Lizzy."

"What do you mean by stronger?" Andric pressed, frowning as he clasped his hands in the small of his back, "You mentioned it was like a muscle. Could you simply practise it, and exceed Miss Hail's abilities?" he asked and Lizzy sighed, relenting to his questions.

"Fey have a natural affinity for one or two specific uses of our magic. Booker excels at telepathy, I'm skilled in telekinesis. Some fey can create wards, invisible protections. Some have a connection and affinity with plants. Some are empathic. I could practise telepathy every day for the rest of my life, and I still wouldn't be able to do some of the things Booker can already accomplish, but the reverse is also true. That's what he means by *stronger*"

"Andric had been nodding slowly as she spoke. "So, what can you do?"

"I'm sorry?" Lizzy said, eyebrows raising, but the vampire just smiled.

"What can you both do?" he repeated. "The reason I ask is I'm trying to figure out if your abilities can be used to defend yourselves. You mentioned you held back the kavian that attacked you?"

"Not... not easily," Lizzy muttered, frowning.

"And I certainly couldn't have done it," Booker added. "I've never seen Lizzy get that dizzy from using telekinesis, and my telepathy had no effect on the kavian whatsoever."

"You can lift and move objects though, yes?"

"Inanimate objects are easier," Lizzy agreed. "They have no force or movement of their own, they're not actively fighting against my hold like the kavian was, so the only real limitation is the size and weight of the object."

"Of which Lizzy has a greater upper limit than myself," Booker added.

"Okay," Andric said as he seemed to consider their words, "so what about your range?"

"My... what?"

"How far away from yourself can you reach with your abilities?"

"Most of the time, telepathy requires eye contact," Booker said, shrugging again.

That wasn't a lie but it wasn't the whole truth either Lizzy noticed, and she flicked her gaze up to Booker, catching the tension in his shoulders. For most fey, eye contact was a requirement, but Booker could push his way into a mind without it.

Lizzy knew he hated that it was possible for him, however, so she didn't call him on the omission but it made her hesitate.

Booker had seen into Andric's mind the first time they'd met, and whatever he'd seen had made him willing to trust the vampire. But not enough to share everything about his abilities. It made her reconsider how much to tell Andric about her own powers.

"Standard telekinesis requires line of sight," she said slowly, still watching Booker for a moment before she turned back to Andric. "With size and weight of the object still being the greatest determining factors."

Not a lie, but not the whole truth.

"Alright, it's not important for today, but I'll try and come up with some ways we can incorporate your abilities into your training," Andric said, nodding.

"There's no point letting your skills go to waste," he added before he seemed to focus past her and Booker, prompting Lizzy to narrow her gaze into the beginnings of a glare as a small smile curled up the corners of his mouth.

"Morning, Miss Evelyn," he called, "did Hunter Khatri explain everything?"

"He just said you needed to see me?"

Lizzy glanced back to find Cara approaching them, and Booker let go of her shoulder to run his hand through his hair.

"I'd like to ask you for a favour, actually," Hunter Roche said as Cara stepped up beside Booker, and dropped her bag onto the grass. She'd changed clothes since they'd last seen her in vampire and fey relations, and was now wearing some loose black trousers and a tight shirt in a dark, stretchy-looking material.

"Okay?"

"How would you feel about helping me teach Miss Hail and Mister Reed how to survive a kavian attack?"

"What?" Cara spluttered, her eyes widening as they danced between Hunter Roche, Lizzy and Booker. "But... I'm still learning myself—"

"You have the highest grades in your class," Roche interrupted her, lifting one hand to halt her refusal. "I'm confident you won't fall behind and Namee—Hunter Khatri, recommended you as someone he would trust to teach others. Despite this, please understand, you are free to refuse," he reassured.

Cara bit her lip and stared between the three of them again, only this time she had a small frown on her face as she considered the offer. It made Lizzy nervous. It was too much like being back at Arbaon academy. It was not being good enough, not being worth the effort, all over again, and Lizzy fixed her gaze on the spot where the sky met the treetops surrounding Speculo.

"I'll agree, on one condition," Cara said, and Lizzy's breath caught. Her shoulders tensed as her skin began to crawl, even as Booker wordlessly slipped his hand into hers.

"What's that?" Hunter Roche asked.

"That we can use each other's first names."

Lizzy could see Andric cross his arms from the corner of her eye but didn't let her gaze waiver.

"Why?" he asked, and Cara blew out a long breath that was almost a sigh. Lizzy was sure she could hear frustration and impatience in the sound, and she hoped Cara was scowling at the hunter.

"Well, fey have different honorifics, right?" she said. "I really don't want my friends calling me 'Mistress Evelyn'."

"I second that request!" Booker blurted out, and Lizzy finally shifted her attention from the horizon, nodding her agreement when Andric's grey eyes fixed on her.

"I third it."

Andric stared at each of them in turn, unmasked surprise on his face before he huffed a single, short laugh of surrender.

"Sure," he agreed wearily, "but using my name is limited to out here on the field. If kavians attack the school, the students need to react to my orders as a hunter, not see me as a friend or equal. The title helps us keep a professional distance, okay?"

Lizzy opened her mouth to ask why Mia got away with it so frequently, but Cara's agreement cut her off before she could.

"Deal! When do we start?"

"Right now," Andric answered, a grin creeping across his face. It held an edge of impish amusement that made Lizzy shift her weight nervously.

"What are we showing them?" Cara asked, and Andric quickly turned serious.

"Fey aren't natural fighters, which is why I've been having you two doing so much running," he explained, nodding at Lizzy and Booker. "Given a choice, you don't want to find yourself facing off against a kavian. They have strength and speed on their side, giving them a hefty advantage."

"Stop telling us why it's a bad idea. We already know that part," Lizzy growled, kicking at the grass in frustration.

The next second, Andric had vanished, and she felt a pressure against her back, his arms wrapping around her and pinning her arms to her sides as she gasped in surprise. His grasp wasn't painful but it was firm, and Andric's voice vibrated through her back where he'd pulled her tight against him.

"If a kavian gets to here, you're already dead," Andric said, his voice soft and close to her ear. Lizzy shivered as she realised his lips were inches from her neck, but a moment later he released her.

Stepping back Andric returned to his previous spot, at a normal speed, and nodded at Cara. "So, the first thing we show them is how to get out of a hold. To create some distance between them and a kavian."

"What are the punching bags for?" Cara asked, indicating the hanging sacks, and Andric grinned again as Lizzy tried to slow her breathing.

"Those are for the last half hour, strength training."

Lizzy watched Cara's features contort into a grimace and her heart sank when the vampire shook her head. "You really know how to make friends."

"I'm not here to make friends, I'm here to keep these two alive," Andric shot back before moving on. "Miss—Cara, if you can work with Mister Reed—Booker, I'll work with... Lizzy."

He stumbled over their names but quickly recovered, and Cara nodded, suddenly seeming all business as she beckoned Booker to follow her across the field.

Lizzy shared one last commiserating look with her best friend before he turned to follow Cara, and Lizzy let herself concentrate on the kavian hunter now watching her, standing with his arms crossed in the middle of the field.

"Does the new training meet your approval?" he taunted quietly, and Lizzy shot him a sharp look and had to clench her teeth together before she could force herself to answer without snarling at him.

"I wouldn't know, we don't seem to have started yet."

For a moment, she was sure he was about to laugh, but he turned away instead, heading for the opposite side of the field from Booker and Cara.

"There's only one rule when fighting a kavian," he offered over his shoulder, "and it's that there are no rules."

Lizzy fell into a light jog to catch up, only slowing when she was walking by his side.

"What do you mean?"

"You strike out with everything you have. Anything you have. And you do as much damage as you possibly can to give yourself whatever slim chance there might be at escaping alive.

"You can kick, or use fists, or claw with your nails. Strike out with weapons, or use a stick picked up off the ground. Anything at all," Andric continued. "They're insane, and there's nothing left in their minds except the desire to consume blood. They can't be talked down, or reasoned with. It's kill or be killed."

"Then why teach us to escape? We can't run from a kavian, they're too fast," Lizzy muttered.

Taking hold of her wrist, Andric pulled her to a stop, his grip gentle, and Lizzy glanced up at him in surprise.

"I'm not teaching you to escape, I'm teaching you to avoid being torn apart long enough for help to arrive." His voice was quiet, and Lizzy wanted to be angry with him. He was supposed to be showing them how to fight and win so that if they had to leave Speculo without answers from Walcott, they could survive the mortal realm, but she couldn't summon the fire of her anger.

There was a soft concern in the hunter's grey eyes that silenced her and held her in place at the same time. She could see the genuine worry in his face, and Lizzy swallowed hard, pressing her lips together and silencing her complaints.

Andric dropped his hand from her arm with a sigh. "I don't know how you survived as long as you did against the kavian—"

"I formed a wall," Lizzy said, interrupting him with her quiet admission. She stared out across the field as she hesitated, considering whether she wanted to explain further or not. After a moment, she continued, voice soft.

"It's... instead of grasping at a specific object, at her, I created a broad barrier with my telekinesis. An invisible wall to hold her back. It took less effort than trying to hold her directly... and she did push against it. Fought me. Would have won, eventually, but..." She paused, turning back to Andric and considering him carefully as she finally began to see his point, and sighed, "but... help arrived."

He was watching her in silence, and she couldn't read anything on his features, so she swallowed hard and shook her head, lowering her gaze. "I don't want you to be right about this," she admitted.

"Why?"

"Because it means I got everything wrong. Again. I miscalculated. Again," Lizzy snapped, but she still couldn't summon the heat of her anger; bitter disappointment was the only thing staining her voice. "Coming here, looking for... for the delegation. It was always a gamble, but kavians? Putting Booker at risk? None of this was supposed to happen. I can't even break the law right."

"I think you'll find that part of your plan was perfectly executed," Andric offered, and she could hear the amusement in his voice. She shot him a glare and he instantly sobered, offering her a small smile of apology.

"I'm sorry," he added, "but you're not giving yourself enough credit, Miss—Lizzy"

Why? was on the tip of her tongue but she didn't ask, holding his gaze until his smile widened and he continued.

"Just think about it," Andric prompted, like he was linked to her mind with telepathy as Booker so often was. "You successfully organised a breakout from a magically protected realm. That's no small feat. You prepared a survival pack, including what you believed to be items of trade value—"

"But they weren't—"

"Not in the way you thought, certainly, but that doesn't matter," Andric cut her off, "to your knowledge they were. That kind of preparation wouldn't even occur to most people. And then," he continued, not letting her object further, "you managed to hold back one of the most dangerous creatures in the mortal realm long enough for help to arrive—"

"But I didn't even know anyone would be coming!" Lizzy burst out, flinging her hands into the air, but his next words had her stilling in surprise.

"We never do," Andric said softly, and Lizzy blinked at him, startled. "We never know if help's coming, or if it's going to come in time. You've just got to hope it is, and do the best you can to survive until then."

He took a slow, deep breath, and his curls of reddish-brown hair brushed against his shoulders as he shook his head. "Survival is always about chance, Lizzy. Everything in the world wants to kill us. Even time."

Lizzy didn't know what to say or how to address the vampire's statements, but as he fell silent, she realised he was waiting for an answer. She shook her head, ponytail flicking against the back of her neck as "Fey don't die from old age" escaped her.

She winced at how petty the comment sounded aloud, but Andric laughed, shoulders shaking as he chuckled. The corners of his eyes crinkled with open amusement, and Lizzy felt her cheeks heat from embarrassment.

"Well then, you're already surviving better than we are," he told her, still grinning, and Lizzy relaxed slowly, a smile lifting her features without her permission, and she smothered a soft laugh behind her hand.

"So you can smile," Andric teased, and she lifted an eyebrow, but couldn't quite push the grin off her face.

"Sometimes," she admitted reluctantly, but the vampire didn't push and glanced across the field to watch Cara and Booker instead.

"There's a couple of ways kavians like to pin their targets for feeding. We'll start with a frontal attack, and I'll show you how to get out of each type of grip," he said, moving smoothly from quiet reassurance into teaching her how to survive. Lizzy forced herself to focus, finally willing to listen to the vampire for the first time since bumping into him in a dark alley.

"Alright," she agreed, letting her determination rise to the surface, "let's get started."

18

Since Andric had received his assignment to work at Speculo school, he'd lost count of how many times he'd silently thanked Walcott for separating out the hunters' dining area from the students'.

The series of smaller tables at one end of the dining room were reserved for staff only, and it meant he could angle his seat away from Mia Harris and avoid catching her attention.

He was certain that, if given even the smallest opportunity, Miss Harris would have claimed the seat beside him and made a pest of herself. As it was, he could eat his meals in peace, and keep a careful watch over the two fey he was being employed to protect from the corner of his eye.

They only had six lessons worth of training under their belts, but the pair had already realised their escape from their first kavian had been nothing short of miraculous.

"Andric."

The greeting was quiet, but he immediately recognised the light cadence of his oldest friend and turned in his seat to offer Nameer an easy smile.

"Morning," Andric said as the other vampire slid into the seat beside him, but he spotted the tension in Nameer's shoulders and his smile faded.

"Thanks for lending me Miss Evelyn," he continued slowly, and Nameer gave an almost imperceptible nod, while his dark eyes swept around the room.

It was late enough in the lunch period that most of the students had eaten and left, and the majority of teachers were in their classrooms, preparing for the morning lessons.

There were still a few pockets of students scattered around the room, Lizzy, Booker and Cara amongst them, and the staff tables held a few kavian hunters but none within casual hearing distance, as long as they kept their voices down.

He could tell when Nameer came to the same conclusion. Andric watched him pick up his fork and begin moving his food around his plate, feigning eating as he spoke in a near-inaudible mutter.

"That private contract you've been employed on," Nameer said carefully, and Andric was instantly alert, his attention immediately focussing on his friend as he hummed a soft sound of acknowledgement.

"I don't know what your terms are, or what it covers, but you might want to sit in on Heyward," Nameer warned, and Andric forced himself not to react.

He picked up his mug of blood-dosed water, and used it to mask his response, as he mimed taking a drink.

"Why?" he asked, and Nameer shrugged one shoulder.

"Rumour is, he's on the warpath. Does it matter why?" he asked, sighing before uncapping their prescribed daily dose of animal blood and stirring it into his mashed potatoes, giving Andric the perfect excuse to grimace in disgust.

"We all know he's a prideful little shit," Nameer continued. "Just figured you might want to be on hand, in case someone needs to have their back."

"Yeah, thanks," Andric murmured, glancing away from the ruined mash and blood and letting his eyes skip across the hall to settle on the two fey. "Any idea what—"

"I've got nothing, I'm sorry. It could be anything, but I'd lay bets on embarrassment," he answered, still keeping his words vague, and Andric nodded before tearing his gaze away from the two fey to offer Nameer a grateful smile.

He'd warned the pair of them to expect Heyward's wrath after they'd left the man's class early, but he hadn't expected the teacher to draw the attention of the hunters with his open irritation.

"I recognise that look," Nameer said, voice low with an unspoken warning, "you're getting protective."

"That is part of the terms of my employment," Andric muttered, averting his gaze, but he could still feel Nameer's focused attention and swallowed nervously.

"I think it might be more than that. I know that you're still reeling from Isaak, but it's no reason to get reckless."

The sudden tightness in his chest at the unexpected mention of his brother made Andric's breath catch, but he nodded regardless. If anyone else had tried to wield his brother against him like that, Andric wasn't entirely sure he'd have been able to maintain his composure, but Nameer was... Nameer.

He was family, so Andric took the concern in the spirit it had been intended.

"I'm pretty sure that's why Walcott suggested this course of action," Andric tried to reassure him, "so I'm too busy to run off and do something reckless."

Nameer chuckled and shook his head, returning to his meal without comment. There was a small smile tugging at the corners of Andric's mouth, but he resisted the urge to let it take hold.

"Miss Harris left the dining hall several minutes ago," Nameer commented casually. "You can smile without fear of her simpering," he added, and Andric gave a soft groan, letting his shoulders slump.

"Honestly, the sooner she takes that job at the Council—"

"Do not say that," Nameer teased. "It's only the propriety of her status as a student holding the poor young woman back!"

"What propriety?" Andric grumbled, shooting his friend a sharp glare, but it only prompted Nameer to laugh harder.

Lizzy and Booker rising to their feet, quickly followed by Cara, caught Andric's attention, and he downed the last of his drink, rising to his feet to follow the teens.

"Good luck," Nameer offered, glancing between Andric and his charges. "Let me know if I can help," he added, and Andric grunted a quiet thanks, his hand resting briefly on Nameer's shoulder before he stepped away from the table.

He waited until the three teens disappeared into the hall before he followed after them, not wasting the energy needed to blur. He kept his hands clasped against the small of his back as he moved through the halls, letting his mind drift to Daniel Heyward.

He was a strict teacher, and not one for letting slights against him slide, but Andric had expected the man to go to Walcott or Gladstone. Not resort to petty revenge in the classroom, where his students were at a disadvantage. The knowledge that he was willing to strike such a low blow sat uneasily in Andric's chest.

Absorbed in his thoughts, Andric didn't see who grasped at his arm but their grip was sharp and tight, and his instincts kicked in.

His assailant pushed against him. Forcing Andric into an unwilling blur, and moving them into one of the students' communal lounges. The sensation of nails pressing against his arm drew a snarl from his throat, and he twisted, snapping around and breaking their hold. He shoved hard, forcing his attacker against the nearest flat surface, pinning them in place with a bruising grip.

The fastest way to kill a kavian was to bleed them out before they had a chance to feed and recover. Andric's blade was drawn, aiming for the throat, before their scent told him this was no kavian.

Fear closed his throat, and Andric scarcely managed to redirect his strike in time, the dagger sinking deep into the bookshelf beside her head. As Andric's heart thrummed in barely suppressed panic over almost killing a student, Mia Harris smirked up at him.

Like it had all been part of some master plan she'd had entirely under control.

"You know, if you wanted to pin me to a wall—"

"Damn it, I could have killed you!" he shouted at her, baring fangs at the young woman before pushing away from her. He ran both hands through his hair as he tried to calm his breathing and force his predator instincts back down under his control.

"You wouldn't—" she started to scoff, and any progress he'd made at control vanished.

Andric was back in front of her in an instant, a genuine snarl curling his lips and bringing his fangs close to her face once more.

For the first time, a flicker of fear lit up her face as her back straightened and she pressed herself against the bookshelf.

"It was only your scent that saved you! I almost couldn't stop in time!" he growled at her, but it was only when her expression softened that he realised his mistake.

"You... recognize my scent?" she pressed, fear vanishing and a slow smile replacing it.

How can I not when you keep throwing yourself at me? he wanted to snarl, but there was no way Miss Harris wouldn't consider that a positive outcome. Andric bit back the words and took several steps away from her when she began to lift a hand towards his face.

"What possessed you to do something as stupid as ambush a trained hunter?" he demanded instead, and Mia pushed off the bookshelf, advancing on him with a pleased smile still dancing around her face.

"I wanted to warn you, but I thought a little time alone wouldn't do any harm either."

"Warn me?"

"I saw you and Hunter Khatri talking at lunch," she said, her smile widening. "He couldn't seem to take his eyes off me; care to tell me what the two of you might have been discussing?" she teased, leaning towards him as her grin widened further, and Andric scowled.

"Not you," he growled, and he felt his fangs finally retract as his pounding heart slowed. Mia didn't seem put off by his dismissal, however, and shrugged one shoulder as she began to circle him. As he watched her, Andric got the uncomfortable sensation that, despite his training, he wasn't the one in the role of hunter for this discussion.

"I thought it fair payment in exchange for my warning," she wheedled, but Andric just crossed his arms over his chest and waited, frowning at her until she sighed and rolled her eyes.

"Fine, keep your secrets," she muttered, before clasping her hands behind her back in a passable imitation of a hunter at ease. "The Council is sending a representative to the school soon, I thought you might like to make yourself scarce, since you're supposed to be on leave."

It would have been a fair warning, Andric admitted to himself, if he'd been working for Walcott, but there was a sharpness to her words and in the way she held herself. Something calculating in how she was watching him, and he pressed his lips together.

Miss Harris was digging for information, and he took a moment to consider how best to answer her. The problem was, he couldn't tell what she was digging for. Without knowing, there was no way to avoid giving her what she wanted, and he released a soft sigh before tilting his head in reluctant thanks.

"The... warning... is appreciated, even if your method of delivery leaves much to be desired," he muttered, "but I'm not under the employ of Thomas Walcott, so I have nothing to fear from a council officer."

"You're not working for Walcott?" she repeated, her voice turning from sweet to sharp and demanding in a heartbeat, and although Andric hesitated, he nodded a moment later, confirming it.

Mia tilted her head, considering, and Andric could see her turning his response over in her mind as he waited for the realisation to hit. As much as her pursuit annoyed him, and for all the advantages her parents being on the Council gave her, there was no denying Mia Harris was smart.

"The fey," she snapped, leaning away from him slightly with a frown marring her features. "You're working for the fey."

The bell signalling the start of classes rang out across the school, and relief flooded Andric.

"You're late for vampire and fey relations, Miss Harris," he told her, but she didn't flinch. She held his gaze, her hazel eyes flicking over his face. For a moment he thought she wasn't going to let it go. That she would keep pushing and pressing for answers, but then she scoffed and tossed her long hair over her shoulder.

"Master Heyward likes me," she said, making her way past him and towards the door at his back. "I'll be fine."

Andric said nothing in response. He didn't even let himself turn and watch her leave, waiting until the door clicked closed behind her and the cloying bitterness of her favourite perfume dissipated from the room before he let his shoulders slump.

He leant forward and took several deep, gasping breaths, bracing his hands against his legs as the realisation hit.

He'd almost killed a student.

Fear flooded his mind again, and his eyes stayed fixed on the dagger still buried in the wooden bookcase of the communal lounge.

Bile stung the back of Andric's throat as he struggled to calm his breathing. It forced him upright again before his lunch could make an unscheduled reappearance, and he made himself walk back across the room to pull his weapon free.

It slid back into its sheath smoothly, despite his still trembling hands, but anger was beginning to replace the sickening mixture of shock and horror.

Miss Harris wasn't stupid. She knew how deadly kavian hunters could be, and her actions had been nothing short of reckless.

Vampires were natural predators, and before humans had inadvertently made their blood toxic, vampires had been at the top of the food chain. Any vampire caught unawares would react with violence, so he didn't understand what she had hoped to gain by ambushing him.

Unless she had truly believed him incapable of harming her, he realised with growing horror.

That possibility was even worse than the idea she'd merely had a moment of unprecedented stupidity.

It meant her attention was more than a simple teenage crush, and if she believed them to be mates, he might have more trouble shaking the woman after she graduated from Speculo than he'd hoped.

Andric shook his head and pushed the troubling thoughts of Mia Harris aside. She'd pulled him away from the fey, and Nameer wouldn't have warned him about Heyward for no reason.

Whatever rumours Nameer had heard, it was concerning enough for him to mention it to Andric, and he cursed as he remembered Mia's parting shot. Moving into a blur, Andric sped from the lounge and made a beeline for the classroom, hoping he and Nameer were overreacting and he wouldn't be required to intervene.

" ...so who can tell me some unique abilities of the fey?" Daniel Heyward was asking the class as Andric approached the door. Slipping inside the room, careful not to draw attention to his arrival, and quietly settling into the shadows at the back.

"Miss Harris?" Heyward called, and Andric clenched his teeth, arms crossing over his chest as he frowned, watching Heyward and the classroom full of students with sharp eyes.

"Telepathy," Miss Harris offered. "They can strip the mind of higher cognitive functions, leaving the subject braindead."

Booker's flinch was almost imperceptible, Andric admitted, but he'd been watching the two fey as Miss Harris spoke. It was quickly followed by Lizzy's hand settling on her friend's forearm.

Andric couldn't see her face, but the way her head had snapped around to stare at Miss Harris, he suspected the vampire was being subjected to Lizzy's darkest glare.

"Correct," Daniel Heyward said, and Mia preened, tossing her hair over her shoulder as her friends complimented her, but Andric turned his attention back to Heyward. He paced across the front of the room, his attention fixed on the two fey with uncomfortable intensity.

"That is just one type of the fey's power. Along with their ability to create wards, control nature, and, of course, telekinesis, to name a few. And yet they fled the mortal realm, leaving the vampires to face the rabid kavians alone—"

"That's not what happened!" Miss Hail snapped, taking the bait and Andric let his eyes slide closed with a sigh.

"Oh? You were taught differently?" Heyward asked, and when Andric focused on the teacher once more, there was a cold smile on Heyward's lips. "Well, please, if you think you can teach the class better than me, step up and do so."

Lizzy didn't move, and Heyward's smile vanished.

"Oh no, Miss Hail, you do not get to slink back into your seat now. I think the pair of you have been wasting enough of my time in this classroom the last few weeks. If you are not willing to listen and learn, then you will help me educate the rest of my students."

The chilling smile was replaced by an icy glare, and Andric knew, he just knew, Lizzy was offering the man the same expression in return. He'd not seen her back down from anything yet, and something told him Daniel Heyward wasn't going to be the thing that cowed her.

The whole class seemed to be holding their breath, waiting. Then Lizzy sat up straighter, and growled out a quiet but determined, "Fine."

Booker shifted in his seat as she spoke, head turning away from the front of the class, and Andric found himself meeting the young man's gaze. His brow furrowed over green eyes, and there was a tension in his face that Andric hadn't noticed before.

"Well, stand up, Miss Hail. You can hardly help teach my students while slouching in a chair," Heyward insisted, his sharp tone pulling Andric's attention away from Booker and back to Lizzy. Andric didn't think her shoulders could get any more tense, but she pushed back her chair and rose to her feet, despite the clear reluctance in every slow movement.

"Please, Miss Hail, tell us how the fey fled to Arbaon."

Andric could almost feel her weighing her words, and Booker was staring at the side of her face intently, the frown still etched into his features.

"When vampires began attacking fey, no one knew what the cause was. Just that you were all going insane for no reason, and tearing us apart. Fey, humans, fellow vampires," Lizzy began slowly. "We are a peaceful people. Our abilities can be dangerous, which is why we don't use them offensively. So when, what you all now call kavians, began to decimate our numbers, our people asked for your help. It never came."

Andric winced at the coldness in her voice, but she wasn't wrong. Even vampire history books talked of how they hadn't been able to aid the fey.

Too many of the vampires had turned rabid at once. Clan leaders turned on their communities, the various councils were left in shambles and it took months for the vampires who remained in control of themselves to track down the source of the disease; human blood.

They'd barely been able to save themselves, let alone the fey, but Andric could also understand why the fey would still hold the massacre of their people against them.

"We were hunted mercilessly," Lizzy continued, "and when Brigett Elestov used her power to create the realm of Arbaon, there were less than a thousand fey left alive to go with her. She sealed it off from the mortal realm for our protection, and if she hadn't we wouldn't have survived. How long did it take the vampires to bring the kavians under control after we left?" she challenged. "Because according to our records it took them less than two months to reduce our people to near extinction."

Andric glanced at Heyward, but the man no longer wore a smug expression. Instead, he was standing with his arms folded, fixing Lizzy with a narrowed stare.

"And how did a fey manage to create an entire realm?"

"Queen Elestov could travel through portal trees to anywhere in the mortal realm with the same species of tree," Lizzy explained. "It's a rare nature-based ability. She theorised if all fey connected to and bolstered her power, there was no reason she couldn't travel to a location she imagined. The legends say that when the fey arrived in Arbaon it was a land of white mist and grey clouds, and only the memory of the mortal realm contained in Queen Elestov's blood brought life and form to the realm."

Lizzy shrugged one shoulder. "How much of that has been romanticised, I couldn't say."

"So what you're postulating then, Miss Hail, is that the fey could have also provided a safe haven for the vampires, but instead chose to abandon us, as I—"

"No," Lizzy growled, "that's not what I'm saying at all—"

"If they could make one realm, what was to stop them creating a second?" Miss Harris called out, her voice smug, and Lizzy's head whipped around to stare at the other woman. Andric only caught a glimpse of her profile but the outrage on her features was clear.

"We were dying out—"

"That sort of sounds like an excuse, doesn't it?" Miss Harris pressed, and her friends snickered under their breath. Andric glanced at Heyward to see if the man was going to intervene, but he'd simply leant against his desk, watching, the smirk returning to his lips the longer the two women argued.

"An excuse?" Lizzy spat, but Mia just hummed an agreement.

"If fey have all these abilities, I don't see why they couldn't have found another way of handling the situation. Warding safe locations, for example. Some of them shedding the pacifism they're all so proud of. Why, female fey even have wings, don't they?" Miss Harris pressed, leaning forward in her seat a little, and Andric watched Lizzy tense again and Booker's hands clench into fists.

"Why could they simply not fly away?" Miss Harris continued to question. "Create their communities up beyond where the kavians could reach, while still giving aid to our people?"

"Not... not all fey have wings..." Lizzy started, but her voice had lost its fire. Andric wasn't sure why, until Miss Harris pushed her final blade home, and Lizzy visibly flinched.

"Like you?"

Andric straightened from where he'd been leaning against the wall, not quite believing what he'd just heard, wondering if it would help or make things worse if he stepped in. Another glance at Heyward told him the teacher had no intention of doing so, but before Andric could speak, Booker had slid to his feet.

"Fey like me, Mimi," the young man said. His voice was bright and distractingly cheerful, but from his position at the back of the classroom, it was impossible for Andric to miss the way Booker's hand settled against Lizzy's back.

Beyond her initial flinch, Lizzy hadn't reacted to Miss Harris's words, but Booker had risen to her defence regardless, and Andric found himself studying the pair closely.

The small touches. The slight tilt of a head. The way they could come to a decision with nothing more than a glance. All of a sudden, it made a startling amount of sense, and Andric briefly wondered how often the two fey communicated with their telepathy.

"Fey like—"

"Not all fey have wings," Booker repeated, cutting Miss Harris off and arching an eyebrow. "If we'd followed your suggestion half our people would have been left behind. There were so few of us still alive by then, there's no way we could have endured such a huge loss."

Booker's voice had changed from bright and cheerful, to cold and cutting the longer he spoke, and although Miss Harris spluttered a little, he didn't give her an opportunity to cut in, simply speaking over her.

"What a relief you weren't around to make suggestions when the survival of the fey hung in the balance," he sneered, voice smooth. "As for your other, frankly ludicrous, suggestions, let me explain why they would all have been entirely useless..."

As he spoke, Lizzy had backed away from him. She'd paused when she'd spotted Andric, but had turned away before he could catch her eye and made a beeline for the door. Lizzy slipped out without a word, while Booker held the attention of their classmates, and Andric found himself torn.

He could leave Booker without backup, and let him verbally spar with Miss Harris while Andric checked on Lizzy.

Alternatively, Andric could leave her to wander the halls of Speculo alone, and remain in case he needed to reign in Heyward or Miss Harris.

He hesitated, gaze shifting from the closed door of the classroom to Booker, only to find the fey staring at him while Miss Harris fumbled over some kind of argument.

It was a tiny movement of one hand. Nothing more than his fingers flicking towards the door, but Andric took it as the instruction he hoped Booker had intended and immediately turned to follow after Lizzy.

19

Stepping into the corridor, Andric took a deep breath and pushed his frustration aside. Instead, he focused on finding Lizzy amongst the various scents filling the halls of Speculo.

Her trail was fresh and, after his recent training sessions with the fey, also familiar to him. In minutes he was catching up to her, but the closer he got the greater his concern grew. There was more than just her scent in the air. Andric could smell magic and blood. Fey blood.

He could feel his heart thud against his chest, concern rising as he tracked her to an empty classroom. The smear of blood on the handle revealed her hiding place, even if he hadn't been able to find her any other way, but it doubled his worry. A dozen scenarios began flitting around his mind as he stared at the faint smear of shimmery red on the handle.

How had she injured herself? Was it serious? It didn't smell serious, but he couldn't know for sure until he stepped into the room. Had someone attacked her after she left the classroom—

He forced his thoughts to still and, braced for the worst, he cracked open the door. Stepping into the room, Andric found himself slowing to a stop in the doorway as awe replaced concern and his breath caught in his throat

It was like stepping into a maelstrom.

The room was empty of furniture, books, or detritus, but Andric was certain that if anything had been left behind, it would have been flying past his head.

Her power wasn't visible, but the energy surrounding Lizzy was tugging at his clothes, and her hair moved like a storm was blowing through the room.

Andric's awestruck surprise melted back into concern when he took in her small form crouched against the far wall. Her elbows were pressed against her knees, and her arms had curled up and over her head. He traced the scent of blood to her fingernails digging into her palms, her knuckles white with tension where they'd curled into fists.

"Lizzy," he said softly as he closed the door and her head sprang up from its place pressed between her elbows and knees. Her bright blue eyes were rimmed with red, but there was no evidence she'd let a single tear fall, and Andric felt an ache build up in his chest at the sight.

"Leave."

It was the only thing she said, her voice low, quiet, and absolutely vibrating with fury. It didn't take a genius to figure out that a refusal would ignite her temper like a firecracker, and Andric paused as he considered his options.

He could walk away. Turn around, leave the room, and let her calm down alone as she'd all but demanded. His other option was to risk her wrath and stay.

It was the look Booker had given him before Andric had followed after Lizzy that made him determined to stay.

The young man seemed to know Lizzy Hail almost better than she knew herself, so Andric braced himself with a sigh and shook his head. He moved to lean against the wall opposite her, leaving the centre of the room empty, filled only with her buzzing power.

"No, I think the last thing you need right now is to be alone," he said, keeping his voice quiet and soothing. Despite that, the pressure in the room grew heavier and shifted like a living thing, like an extension of the turmoil swirling behind the mask she'd made of her anger.

"What do you know about what I need?" Lizzy hissed from her position on the floor, legs pressed against her chest. "You don't know anything about me! Get out!"

Andric held her gaze unflinchingly. She was defensive and hurt, and he didn't understand her well enough to know the best way of handling the situation. But he wouldn't walk away.

Mia's attack had been, at least in part, his fault, and Andric wanted to apologise. He wanted to find a way to fix it, so he shook his head again.

"Has anyone, other than Booker, ever had your back?" he asked gently. "No matter what?"

She flinched again, looking as stricken as when Mia had asked about her lack of wings, and some of the tiny facets that made up Lizzy Hail began to fall into place.

"Family? Any other friends—"

"Shut up," Lizzy hissed, but Andric approached instead. Stepping away from his position against the wall opposite her, he advanced towards the centre of the room, his steps slow and gradual. He ignored the way her power pulled at him, tugging against his hair, and focused on steadying himself before each step, like walking across the swaying deck of a ship.

"You came running headlong into the mortal world. No one searching for you back in Arbaon. Only Booker at your side. You don't know your father, and your mother—"

It was like shackles holding her back had snapped open. Lizzy sprang to her feet and flew at him. None of their training was brought to bear, no finesse or technique, just pure emotion raging at him as her hands connected with his chest and shoved hard.

"You don't get to say anything about my mum!" she screamed, any shred of restraint or control gone, and Andric stumbled back a step, hands raising but Lizzy kept advancing.

Her hands lifted to shove at him again, but Andric caught them gently, holding her in place, "Okay," he offered, pausing to toss his hair out of the way as the whirlwind of her power blew it across his face, "then tell me why she's not here looking for you?"

"Get out. Let me go!" Lizzy snarled, tugging against his gentle hold around her wrists, but he wouldn't let her retreat. "Go back to your stalker, and leave me alone!"

Her temper sparked his irritation once more, the dig about Miss Harris cutting close to the bone, but he forced it down and studied her instead. "You defend her with the same ferocity you do Booker," he said, "and you only offer your loyalty in return for loyalty. I've seen it with Cara... so why isn't she—"

"Please stop," Lizzy said, and the energy in the air drained away. It was like her outburst of fury had exhausted her of the will to fight, and as she settled, Andric swallowed hard, carefully uncurling his fingers from around her wrists.

She kept her head down, refusing to look at him, but he could smell the saltwater tears in the air and it struck him just how much he wanted to help her.

Her and Booker. Neither of them seemed to have any sort of support network. No friends, or family... and a sickening thought stole his breath.

"Oh," he sighed, eyes closing for a moment as he prayed he was wrong. When he blinked them open again, Lizzy had curled her arms around her waist, her shoulders tensed again and she was still refusing to lift her head, staring determinedly at the floor.

"The delegation?" he asked, but her flinch confirmed it. "Your mum was part of the delegation."

"She'd be looking for me... if she could," Lizzy muttered. Andric was half convinced she had meant the words to be flung at him as a snarl, but when Lizzy finally dragged her electric-blue gaze up from her feet, her fury was gone. Replaced with exhaustion and bitter resignation.

"Are you happy now? You've got all the answers you wanted. Now get out, and leave me alone."

Andric sighed and shook his head once more, watching the motion bring a scowl back to her features. "Lizzy, I wasn't—"

The sound of the door opening halted his words, and Andric snapped around. He placed himself between Lizzy and whoever had walked in, but stopped abruptly when he found Hilda Gladstone standing in the doorway.

The tapered fingers of her hand rubbed over the handle in an anxious motion, and she stared at them both, expression startled.

"Andric?" she asked after a moment.

"Everything's fine," he reassured, shooting a brief glance over his shoulder at Lizzy, only to find she'd turned her back on the deputy headmistress and had shifted so her arms were crossed instead of curled around her waist.

"Did you need the room?" he asked, turning back to the deputy, her restless stroking of the door handle drawing his gaze for a moment.

"Oh, no..." she answered slowly, her worried gaze flicking past him to settle on Lizzy once more. "Only, I... I thought I heard..."

"Miss Hail can be very passionate about certain... topics of discussion," Andric deflected, letting his hands clasp against the small of his back, shifting instinctively into the stance of a hunter at ease and drawing Gladstone's attention back to him.

"I see," she murmured, tongue darting out to moisten her lips while hesitating in the doorway.

Her hesitation stung Andric. That the woman didn't trust him alone with a student hurt, but if she'd overheard Lizzy's shouting, he reasoned, he could understand her caution.

"If there were something wrong, Miss Hail, please remember you can come and find me at any time. For any reason," Hilda Gladstone prompted, glancing past Andric again, and he forced himself not to turn and watch Lizzy's reaction.

There was a heartstopping moment of silence from the young woman before a resigned sigh emerged from behind him.

"I'm fine," she said, her voice low and quiet. "I had a disagreement with Mia Harris. Andric was helping me get control of my temper."

"I see," Hilda repeated, a frown growing on her face. When she glanced at him again with one eyebrow arched, he nodded, backing up Lizzy's half-truth.

"Perhaps," Hilda continued, "someone should remind Miss Harris that her position within the school demands a certain level of responsible behaviour in exchange."

"You might want to remind Mister Heyward of that too," Andric muttered, and Hilda's second eyebrow rose to meet the first before she hummed.

"Very well," she said. "If you have everything... in hand?"

When Andric nodded she only hesitated for another moment, fingers still tracing over the door handle with a nervous kind of energy before she seemed to shake herself and turn to leave, closing the door gently behind her.

He let his arms drop to his sides with a sigh and turned back to Lizzy. She was already staring at him, one arm still held across her body, and the other lifted, her fingers curling around a small pearl pendant that she ran against her bottom lip.

"So where does this leave us?" she asked, voice hard and cold. "Are you going to tell Walcott?"

Andric hesitated, but slowly shook his head. "I don't see that it makes any difference," he offered and was rewarded with open surprise splashing across her face. She seemed to freeze, blinking up at him startled as the pendant dropped from her fingers.

"You... What?"

"It doesn't change anything. Everything you told us was true," he said, shrugging. "So you left out a few details... they weren't important details. Not details Walcott might need to help you find answers, at any rate."

"So... you're just—you're going to do nothing?" Lizzy spluttered, and Andric smiled before letting himself take another, closer, look at her.

She was small, but there was an inner strength to Lizzy. He should have seen it the first night they'd met, when she'd recovered from her fear fast enough to stand her ground and argue with him, but he'd dismissed it. He'd assumed it was due to shock or the woman not being aware of how close to death they'd been.

But even now, even believing she'd revealed a secret he could wield against her, even after breaking apart just a little, she stood with her chin raised.

Lizzy met his gaze and held it. She was terrified, it was hidden there in the darkest depths of her gaze, but she refused to flinch. Andric couldn't help but find that deeply impressive.

"I'm going to guard your vulnerabilities," he said, "as per the terms of my employment contract with you," he added, smile widening teasingly. "And maybe, if I'm very lucky, earn a little of your trust."

"Why?" she asked, and Andric's smile faded as he sighed.

"Because you're clever, funny, and you've got potential... and I don't think I was too far off the mark. Apart from your mum and Booker, do you have anyone back in Arbaon?"

She didn't flinch or order him to be silent this time, but she went very still. Like an animal startled in the wild. Andric waited, not pushing her, and a second later, her mouth tightened and she glanced away, shrugging one shoulder.

"Mia wasn't... wrong. Entirely," Lizzy muttered. "All female fey have wings. Or, we should. The fact that I don't... well. Until Booker, I'd only ever had my mum. And now I only have Booker."

Arbaon was, as far as the stories went, a single realm with a small population. Andric couldn't imagine living his whole life knowing an entire realm believed you to be lesser because of an accident of birth.

That same urge from earlier rose up again. The desire to help, to guard, and to protect.

"Trust me?" he asked, letting a hint of playful challenge enter his voice and hoping it rallied her stubbornness back to the surface.

Instantly, her head whipped around to study him as she openly considered his question. Eventually, Lizzy offered a tiny nod and Andric let his lips curl back into a smile.

"Your hands. At least one of them is bleeding," he said, holding out his own. "I can smell it," he added, watching Lizzy swallow hard before she slowly put her hands back in his.

Andric lifted them, the motion tugging Lizzy a step closer as he inspected her palms, and he hummed.

"It's just the right," he told her, releasing her left hand and cradling her injured one in both of his before bringing his gaze back to hers.

"Vampires have a venom in their teeth that can stop a wound from clotting and closing. It's how we used to feed on humans... but our saliva counteracts it, and encourages injuries to heal over at an advanced rate," he explained, pausing to give her a moment to absorb his words before he grinned again. "Still trust me?"

"Not as much as before you grinned at me like that," Lizzy muttered, scowling at him, and Andric laughed, prompting her to roll her eyes in response. "But... enough," she added, despite the nervous swallow he caught sight of.

He didn't give her a chance to second-guess her decision or worry about what he planned to do. Andric brought the pad of his right thumb to his lips and ran his tongue over it before bringing it down to her hand.

His thumb swept across her palm, pressing featherlight against the crescent-shaped wounds where her nails had sliced into her hand, and Lizzy gasped. He hoped it wasn't caused by fear, but he couldn't bring himself to look at her and check. Instead, he waited until the small cuts closed, leaving only faint red lines in their wake, before he released her.

"There. Good as new."

Her other hand came up, and Andric watched her stroke over the freshly healed marks in silence for a moment before he could bring himself to look at her. He wasn't sure what he would find in her expression. Nerves, shock, or open distrust, but he hadn't expected wide-eyed fascination.

"Lizzy?" he asked, and she snapped her head up, quickly lowering her hands.

"Thank you."

He wanted to know what she'd been thinking. What had been going through her mind behind those entrancingly electric-blue eyes, but Andric didn't know how to ask her, so he just nodded.

"You're welcome. Can't have half the school getting distracted with the scent of fey blood now, can we?" he teased, keeping his voice light before nodding towards the door. "Come on. Knowing you and Booker, I can't see either of you going to the rest of your classes for the night. I'll walk you back to your room. I'm sure he can find you there."

"Yeah," Lizzy agreed, but her tone and energy had dropped again, and Andric frowned.

"What is it?"

"It's nothing... It's just. Well, I'll have to face them sometime," she sighed, shrugging one shoulder. "It's usually easier to get it out of the way sooner rather than later. They don't get any big ideas, like what they've said actually affects me," she admitted, and all over again, Andric's chest tightened.

"I'm going to ask you to trust me one more time tonight," he said, and Lizzy glanced at him and arched an eyebrow high enough to make him grin. "Once more, I promise, but... go back to your room. Wait for Booker and Cara. Call it a night, you look exhausted," he suggested, shooting her a wordless, pleading look and after a moment, she relented.

"Alright, fine," Lizzy muttered, crossing her arms again, but Andric noticed there was no tension in her frame this time.

He had to smother a smile by turning his back on her and heading for the door when he realised he was starting to get a handle on the girl's tells.

"Thank you," he offered instead, holding the door open for her, ignoring the eye roll the action received. Lizzy marched out of the empty classroom with her chin up and shoulders back, like she hadn't just clawed herself back from the edge of a breakdown, and he found himself relieved that she'd relented to his request.

He moved to wipe the remnants of her blood from the handle, faltering for only a moment when he realised it was already gone, a flicker of gratitude for Gladstone's quick thinking thrumming through him.

He could thank her properly later, though. For now, he had a couple of ideas he needed to run past Walcott before he wanted Lizzy or Booker back in any class containing Mia Harris.

20

Lizzy managed to sit at breakfast the following evening with her spine straight and head up. A mug of coffee in hand, as though nothing out of the ordinary had happened the previous day.

As Andric had predicted, Booker found her as soon as he could escape Heyward's class. After one look at her face, he'd settled on her bed, pulling Lizzy down with him until he could hug her, letting her curl against his side and fall into sleep.

But he'd known better than to try accessing her mind.

When Cara's alarm had gone off, Lizzy woke to the sound of her roommate and her best friend talking in whispers, while Booker's fingers stroked soothingly through her hair. An action that had warded off her nightmares for as long as she could remember.

A quick shower later, the three of them headed directly to the dining hall for breakfast, keeping their discussions light. The previous day's events were only conspicuous by their absence in the conversation.

Booker kept himself glued to her side, one arm slung over her shoulders a little more tightly than usual, and Lizzy was grateful. It wasn't only Mia she was dreading bumping into, but Andric too.

She hadn't told Booker that Andric knew about her mum. Hadn't wanted to speak about anything at all when he'd pulled her into a hug, and she hadn't had the chance to mention it since waking up.

She truly didn't know what to make of the hunter's actions the previous day. His determined support, his quiet acceptance, and his request for her trust, but when he broke his self-enforced pattern of watching them from a distance and slid into the seat beside Cara, sitting opposite her and Booker, Lizzy's stomach gave a nervous flutter.

"Evening you three," Andric greeted, voice soft as his eyes flickered over each of them in turn, before meeting her gaze. "I'm glad I caught you all early," he added, and Lizzy forced herself to swallow hard before she could answer.

"We thought it might be best to try and miss the main rush," she admitted, realising a moment later, when Booker's arm tightened enough to become a hug, that it was the longest sentence she'd strung together all evening.

"Smart," Andric agreed, nodding before leaning his arms against the long table and lacing his fingers together. "I spoke with Headmaster Walcott yesterday," he said, "and I have a proposition for you three."

"What sort of proposition?" Booker asked, and Cara hummed in agreement to the question, prompting a tiny upturn at the corners of his mouth that made Lizzy want to grin in response.

"Neither of you have found the classes very... hmm, engaging, let's say. And I know you've recently recommitted to giving them a chance, but I think there are some teachers here at Speculo who might not be willing to give you that second chance," Andric said carefully, and Lizzy found herself quickly scowling.

"You mean like Heyward?" she snarled, and although Andric didn't answer, she spotted his laced fingers flex slightly, like they wanted to curl into fists.

"So, here's the proposition," he continued, as though Lizzy hadn't interrupted, refusing to confirm or deny her accusation. "You keep attending the basic finances, computing and home economics classes. You both seem to be enjoying home ec, you need the finances class, and I think if you give computers a fair chance, you'll love that too.

"As for everything else, we drop the core subjects from three to two lessons a week, remove you from vampire-fey relations and history entirely, and replace them for more time on the field training with me."

Booker groaned at her side. "Still insistent on these rotting lessons then, are we?" he complained. "Surely Mimi's little verbal—"

"What would that make the new schedule look like?" Lizzy asked, cutting Booker off gently, but she still saw him stare at her in surprise out of the corner of her eye.

"It would put the two of you training with me for almost twenty hours a week. With that kind of dedicated training, you could advance very quickly, but neither of you are used to that level of physical activity, so we'll take it slow at first. Build you both up to it... Still, your muscles are going to hate you for a while."

"Lizzy..." Booker muttered softly, and she turned to catch his eye but no tap of telepathy came. He stared at her, eyes flicking over her features and reading her that way instead, then he pressed his lips together and sighed in open surrender.

"I guess we're listening," Booker grumbled, "but how would Cara helping us tie into this new plan of yours?" he asked, and Andric grinned, turning to the vampire at his side.

"Well, Khatri's agreed to graduate you out of hunter training now, if you're interested," he offered, and Cara's eyes widened.

"Wh-what?"

"After looking over your midyear exams, and recent homework grades, Headmaster Walcott has also offered to let you take your choice of exams early. And, of course, I would never, under any circumstances, recommend doing exactly that for vampire-fey relations and history, since neither teacher appeared particularly pleased about the arrangements," Andric added, raising an eyebrow at Cara as the woman stared at him, lips still parted in shock.

Slowly she seemed to recover and shook her head.

"Hunter Khatri... I don't mean to be ungrateful, but he didn't agree just because you asked, did he?" she questioned, frowning at Andric. "Only, I know you're friends, and—"

"No," Andric cut her off, shaking his head, and Lizzy found her attention bouncing back and forth between the two.

"It's just that I want to make sure my scores are high enough to be selected in the first round of apprenticeships—"

"Cara," Andric said simply, laying a gentle hand on her shoulder as her arms began to wave and gesture erratically, and Lizzy hid a grin behind the rim of her coffee. "Nameer's an old friend, yes, and a good one, but there's nothing I could say or do to convince him to let a student graduate early. Not unless he thought they were ready. You're the only name he suggested when I asked for one of his students to help me teach these two."

Cara seemed shocked all over again, but after a beat, gave him a wordless nod.

"Why are you and Walcott suggesting this?" Lizzy asked, as soon as it looked like Cara wasn't going to spiral into another pit of self-doubt and Andric had settled his hands against the table again. Lizzy finally let herself meet Andric's gaze, and almost recoiled at the quiet understanding she could see there.

"I suggested the changes, and Walcott agreed, because you've both been here a few weeks now and you've got a feel for the school, and for the subjects. Settling your timetable into something you can both... if not enjoy, then not actively dislike, seemed like the best way to ensure your time here at Speculo is productive."

There was something careful about Andric's phrasing that made Lizzy frown.

It sounded like he was trying to convince them, and she

narrowed her eyes.

It sounded like something he might have told Walcott, to convince him to agree.

Lizzy shifted in her seat and turned to pull her schedule out of her bag. Skimming over it, she mentally erased the lessons Andric had suggested dropping, and she felt the growing tension leave her as she fought back an amused grin.

"Mia's not going to be in any of our remaining classes, is she?"

Lizzy shifted her attention from her timetable back to Andric, but the vampire never flinched, he just raised an eyebrow and blinked slowly. Too slowly, for Lizzy to believe it.

"Isn't she?"

Lizzy couldn't smother her grin this time and had to turn away, catching Booker's eye and prompting him to burst out into snickers of amusement.

"Alright, fine," he chuckled, shaking his head, "that's how you convinced Walcott, I'll buy it," he said, and Lizzy found herself relieved he'd also caught wind of Andric's evasiveness, "but why are you doing this? This will be time out of your week to help two complete fighting-newbies. I don't see what you get out of this, or why you're willing to help us."

Andric sighed, and Lizzy saw his gaze shift to scan across the dining room behind them. She wondered if he was looking for a particular person, or simply an escape route from their questions, but after a moment he focused on them both again.

"You've both said the fey are peaceful people," he said quietly, "but both of you have potential, and both of you are picking this up faster than I expected. I don't like seeing potential go to waste... and that's exactly what will happen if you... leave Speculo too soon."

Get driven out by Mia Harris, went unspoken but Lizzy heard the implication.

Booker released a heavy sigh, almost a quiet groan, and Lizzy turned back to him, eyeing him carefully. He had his eyes closed and head tilted back, with resignation settling across his face that left her frowning at him in confusion.

"What are you thinking?" she asked, and Booker blinked slowly, meeting her gaze and a second later, their minds connected. His thoughts were hesitant, still wary of overwhelming her, but she sent a wave of reassurance in his direction and the bond settled.

"I'm thinking... Maddy knew more than she let on," he muttered, but the emotions spinning out from his mind made Lizzy swallow hard. Frustration, irritation, betrayal, all tinged with grief, and Lizzy's heart ached.

"Maddy?" Andric asked, and Lizzy shut her eyes for a moment, giving herself time to summon the words.

"*He knows*," Lizzy warned Booker, "*that we're here for Mum.*"

"*Yesterday?*"

"*Yeah. I wasn't... in the best state to be keeping secrets.*"

"*And yet, no one's summoned the sentinels to drag us back to Arbaon, and he's still helping us. Almost like he's invested, wouldn't you say?*" Booker teased, and Lizzy whipped around to shoot a glare at her friend. She could sense the implication he was barely holding back and knew from the glittering amusement in his mind that she was blushing again.

"Maddy. Madeline Hail," Lizzy said aloud, answering Andric's question before the pause in the conversation could grow long enough to draw attention to her and Booker's silent discussion. "My mum, she..."

Lizzy paused and sucked in a deep breath. A sharp pain lanced through her chest, and Booker moved to grasp her shoulder, his fingers pressing hard against her skin in a firm, grounding grip.

"Careful," he warned, and she nodded.

"Are you okay?" Cara asked as Lizzy took another deep breath.

"Maddy's... no longer with us," Booker said, keeping his voice soft. Lizzy could feel hysterical laughter threatening to escape at the strangely appropriate euphemism. She swallowed hard, trapping it at the base of her throat, like a too-large chunk of bread she couldn't choke down as Booker continued.

"And fey... well. Fey can die from a broken heart," he said, voice barely above a whisper, almost inaudible over the bustle of the busy dining hall.

"She would encourage us to run," Lizzy said before Cara could summon a response, and Lizzy let herself concentrate on Andric's sharp grey gaze. He was watching her intently, frowning but focused on listening to her and Booker.

"Neither of us could fly, so she encouraged us to run through the forests of Arbaon. And if we got too angry at one of the visiting court fey..."

"She filled sacks with sand, and taught us how to hit them until we weren't angry any more," Booker finished. His grip on her shoulder eased as the internal pain settled, and he tugged her against his side once more. "I outgrew that, learned to turn their words against them instead."

"I get too angry for that. Words escape me," Lizzy muttered, rolling her eyes at the shimmer of smugness coming across the bond connecting her mind to Booker's.

"So... the pair of you already have a foundation, then?" Andric asked, but Lizzy shook her head.

"I wouldn't call it that. Mum always said it was emotional management," Lizzy explained. "We're a peaceful people, but fey are highly emotional. It's why losing someone we love can... can hurt enough to kill us." She paused, before glancing up at Booker again, "But you think—"

"I don't want to," Booker muttered, "but think about it. No one else we know ever did those things. Other fey weren't encouraged to run through the forest or hit things when they were angry. That's just not how it's done in Arbaon."

"It set us further apart," he added, *"and I know neither of us*

minded that, Lila," he continued swiftly, as her defensiveness rose, "*but it's still true.*"

"And then Maddy just ups and leaves for the mortal realm out of nowhere?" Booker continued aloud. "No indication she'd ever been here before, and no explanation about why she came here now?"

"Mum knew more than she let on," Lizzy whispered in realisation, repeating Booker's words back to him and grimacing.

"That's why you're here?" Cara asked. "You're not transfer students at all?"

"*Rot and termites,*" Booker cursed silently, "*I'm sorry—*"

"*It's fine,*" Lizzy sent back as she sighed and looked over at Cara, letting the girl's hurt expression wash over her and summon up just enough guilt to make the act of admitting the truth to someone else a little bit easier.

"Not in the... traditional sense, no," Lizzy offered, "it's not like the Court would let a couple of vampire students into Arbaon... we agreed to the schooling in exchange for the headmaster's help."

"They're students of Speculo, that much was not a fabrication," Andric chimed in, pulling Cara's intense gaze from Lizzy for a moment.

"Neither is our friendship," Booker added, and Cara's head whipped around to stare at him.

"Okay," she said slowly, and Lizzy felt Booker's frame slump a little in relief. "I understand why Lizzy is here, what about you? Did you just come to help, or is there another reason?"

And just like that, Booker had tensed up again, until Lizzy nudged him and he glanced down at her in surprise.

"*Tell her,*" Lizzy prompted.

"*Lila—*"

"*You like her. And from what I've seen, she likes you. Tell her.*"

Booker swallowed hard, his gaze sliding back to settle on Cara once more, but the almost bruising grip on her shoulder told Lizzy he was still listening.

"If you don't, you know it'll come out later. She's been hurt too often to forgive a lie. You know we wouldn't in her place."

Booker stayed silent. Cara's eyes were growing wide, gaining a hint of hurt, and for a moment, Lizzy thought Booker might not answer. That it might be too painful to share, no matter how much he liked the girl, but then she felt his grip loosen and he took a slow, deep breath, dropping his head to stare at the table.

"My—"

"Not now," Andric interrupted, making all three of them jump, and when Lizzy turned to him, it was to find his attention focused on the dining room behind her, and her stomach dropped.

"I shouldn't linger. Are we in agreement?" Andric asked, still scanning the room, and Lizzy would have bet almost anything Mia Harris had arrived for breakfast. She gave him a quick nod, feeling Booker do the same beside her, and Cara sighed before agreeing too.

"Sure. Can you pass along my request for early exams to the headmaster?" she asked, "I think clearing my schedule of two classes should be enough stress for now," she added, nodding when Andric glanced at her, accepting his recommendations without repeating them.

"Very well," Andric said quickly before rising to his feet, "and to keep you motivated on the work, the headmaster has also agreed to allow all three of you into Hockley for a weekend, with supervision, of course."

"We can get out of the castle?" Booker asked, relief clear in his voice, and Lizzy grinned.

"And we have mortal realm money, so you know what that means?" she teased, transforming his relief into a playful groan.

"Oh fire ants," he swore, "shopping..."

Cara chuckled lightly, and even Andric gave a brief smirk of amusement. "Ten days," he promised, "and I'll help jailbreak you for an afternoon."

He didn't linger, turning and making his way over to one of the staff tables, but Lizzy's good mood vanished as she counted the days in her head.

She knew the exact moment Booker figured out the same thing she had from the way her loss was echoed back at her from his mind.

Ten days was a Saturday. Ten days was exactly nine weeks since they'd last seen Madeline Hail. Ten days was Lizzy's birthday.

The birthday her mother had promised to come back for, and that thought made Lizzy more determined than ever to find out what exactly had happened to stop her mum from fulfilling her promise.

Those ten days passed in a blur for Lizzy.

She didn't need to face Mia in classes any longer, and the red-haired vampire appeared to go out of her way to avoid Lizzy and Booker at mealtimes, both of which took a weight off Lizzy's mind.

The first few days of their adjusted schedule were hectic. Cara was either sleeping, or studying her notes in preparation for her early exams.

Meanwhile, Lizzy and Booker struggled to adjust to the amount of time spent running, hitting punching bags, and learning how to break out of grips and holds.

Andric hadn't been joking when he'd warned them their bodies would ache, and it was rare Booker went more than an hour without complaining.

The pair of them often ended Andric's lessons laid out on their backs on the grass, staring up at the sky, Booker panting in exaggerated protest and Lizzy giggling breathlessly at his dramatic suffering.

More often than not, Andric indulged them.

Lizzy suspected it was because twenty minutes later the bell would ring for the next lesson and, more often than not, that meant Andric got to torture them for another ninety minutes.

Between Cara's exams and Andric's exhaustive training, ten days slipped past Lizzy almost before she noticed, and when she woke up on the Saturday of her eighteenth birthday, it was as shocking as it was painful.

She lay in a strange bed, in a strange realm, and stared at a ceiling made of stone instead of thatch, swallowing hard.

Eighteen for fey meant adulthood. Signalling the transition from a child relying on their parents, to the life of an adult fey, expected to live alone, and survive alone. A fey who could be held accountable for their own actions.

It would have been her mum's responsibility to make sure there was a home, fully stocked and furnished, ready for Lizzy to move into at the end of the day. Her last week would have been filled, much as Cara's had been, with exams at the Arbaon Academy. Those scores would tell her which career paths she could pursue.

But none of it felt real anymore. Arbaon was an entire world away, and the only thing different about today, over yesterday, was the promised escape from Speculo School.

"Lizzy?" Cara said, standing from her bed. Lizzy glanced at her roommate, her friend, and tried to summon a smile. Based on Cara's grimace, she failed.

"You thinking about... your mum?" she asked hesitantly, and Lizzy sighed, shrugging.

"Sort of," she admitted, and a heartbeat later, Cara was sitting on the edge of Lizzy's bed.

"Want to talk about it?" Cara offered, and Lizzy was able to summon a genuine smile for the vampire.

"It's my birthday today," she said simply, "I'm eighteen."

"What? Really? Why didn't you say anything?!" Cara asked, and the excitement in her voice startled Lizzy. She blinked up at Cara and shook her head.

"Uh... because... well, I didn't realise at first. The calendars are all different here. And then, well it's not that important—"

"But this is perfect! We're heading to Hockley, so I can get you a present, and we'll have to find a cake store," Cara babbled, and Lizzy frowned.

"What? Why?"

"What do you mean why? For your... birthday..." Cara trailed off when she finally seemed to notice Lizzy's confusion and returned her frown. "How do fey celebrate birthdays?" she asked, and Lizzy shrugged again.

"We don't really. Verbal congratulations on making it another year older. Eighteen is the... the big one. The important one. We're finally recognised as adults. We move out of our parents' homes and into our own, get jobs, live our lives our way... It just doesn't feel the same, a whole realm away, without..."

"Your mum," Cara finished, and let her hand rest against the back of Lizzy's. The touch was light but genuine, and Lizzy was grateful so she forced a smile onto her lips and nodded.

"But you guys do... cake?" Lizzy asked, trying to bring back the other girl's enthusiasm, and while Cara wasn't quite as excitable as she had been, the grin Lizzy got in return was worth the effort.

"Cake, and presents, and sometimes a party," she said, before moving over to the wardrobe to start rummaging through it.

"Every year?" Lizzy asked, sitting up in bed and watching Cara, bemused, as half her body vanished into Lizzy's side of the wardrobe.

Digging through the half-dozen outfits Walcott had somehow managed to supply the fey with on their first day, Cara's answer became muffled and lost, but a moment later she emerged from the wardrobe, tutting and shaking her head.

"That won't do. You can borrow something of mine."

"What are you talking about?" Lizzy asked, laughing when Cara scowled at her.

"It's your birthday, Lizzy. I can't manage a party, but we're going to get dressed up and go into town. I'm going to show you how to go shopping until you can't carry any more bags. Then we're going to do something fun, like a movie, and after that we'll go out for a meal somewhere."

"I'm not sure Andric planned to give us the whole weekend," Lizzy said in amusement. Cara scoffed lightly and blurred over to her side, tugging Lizzy up and out of bed.

"Come on, go take a shower while I find something of mine that will fit you," she instructed, and Lizzy chuckled as the vampire pushed her into the bathroom.

It wasn't the birthday she was supposed to have, but a new friend was a pretty good substitute, she admitted to herself.

21

Lizzy had almost scowled when Cara handed her a skirt, but the hopeful expression pasted across her friend's face forced her to relent.

Despite her reservations, the blue denim paired with a small pair of black shoes that slipped onto her feet without fastenings, and one of the linen shirts she'd brought from Arbaon, suited her.

It wasn't until they reached the front of the school, where they'd planned to meet Booker and Andric, that Lizzy began to regret her decision.

"Fire ants, what did you threaten Lizzy with to get her into a skirt?" Booker teased, but he scooped her up into a hug before she could do more than glare.

"Put me down!" she growled in his ear, unable to kick at him with the stiff denim restricting her movements, but he followed her demands, snickering.

"Well don't you ladies look lovely," he purred playfully, as his attention shifted from Lizzy to settle on Cara and his grin transformed into a smirk.

Cara had also chosen a skirt for herself in a soft, caramel-brown fabric she'd called suede. It had matching boots and paired with a cotton blouse in the same colour it complimented her skin beautifully

Unfortunately, Booker was ruining the entire effect by making the poor vampire blush to the roots of her hair, so Lizzy promptly jabbed her elbow into his ribs.

"Oof—what?" he grumbled, glaring at her, "It's true!"

"He's not wrong," Andric said, sounding amused, "but the question is, why?"

"It's Lizzy's birthday," Cara said, pretending she wasn't still blushing, and Lizzy rolled her eyes.

Cara slid the straw sunhat she'd been carrying onto her head. The orange band of fabric encircling it was the brightest splash of colour in her outfit, and Cara busied her hands by fussing with the ribbon tails as they trailed off the wide brim, and halfway down her back.

"It's... your birthday?" Andric asked, switching his attention from Cara to Lizzy mid-sentence, and Lizzy shrugged.

"It's not that—"

"It is important," Booker cut her off with a growl. "You're eighteen. This one's important... even without Maddy," he added, voice softening.

"I was thinking, shopping, movie, meal," Cara said quickly, stepping closer to Andric, and Lizzy watched in bemusement as Andric got hit full blast by her roommate's wide-eyed pleading.

He hesitated, and Lizzy half expected him to shut down Cara's extravagant plans, but then she leant forward and added, "Did you know that fey don't do birthday parties?" And Andric caved.

"Sounds like you've got it all planned," he said, holding out an arm towards the front doors of the school. "If we want to fit it all in, then we'd better get started."

"Yes!" Cara celebrated, jumping on the spot and throwing one hand in the air as Lizzy looked on bemused.

"Looks like you're getting a mortal-style birthday," Booker teased as Cara and Andric moved towards the door. "Whether you wanted to, or not!" he chuckled before dragging Lizzy after the vampires with the arm he still had curled around her shoulders.

"Hmm, the weather could have been better," Cara complained as she stepped out of the car. She'd spent most of the journey into Hockley changing the channel on the radio, playing Lizzy and Booker different songs while trying to narrow down their favourites.

Stepping out of the car, and into the bustle of people shopping, was almost a relief from some of the sounds Cara insisted were considered music in the mortal realm.

Distracted from staring at the crowds by Cara's mention of the weather, Lizzy turned to her with a frown. Following her line of sight, she looked up to where Cara was staring and studied the overcast sky. The sun sat hidden behind thick grey clouds, the same colour as Andric's eyes, and the air had a hint of a chill to it.

"It's not forecast for rain," Andric reassured, sliding on a pair of darkened glasses as he and Booker joined them, and Cara hummed.

"Alright, fine. I'll believe you," she muttered, and by the time Lizzy pulled her attention down from the clouds, Cara was already hovering by her side. "Okay, so I'm thinking you two go shopping," Cara said, pointing at Andric and Booker, "and I'll take Lizzy."

"Miss Evelyn—" Andric started, frowning, but Cara scowled at him.

"No. No," she insisted. "It's Cara. Especially now I'm halfway to graduating. And I know what you're going to say, but it's the middle of the day! And there's one of us with each of them! We're as safe as we possibly can be outside of Speculo."

"You've never faced a kavian before," Andric said firmly,

his voice lowering, "and you've still got two years of an apprenticeship to get through. You don't even have any weapons on you..."

Cara stared at Andric, eyebrows raised, and for a long moment, he simply held her gaze. Lizzy glanced at Booker, but he just shrugged, apparently as confused as she was.

There was another moment of silence, before Andric sighed through his nose, his lips pressing together and his jaw clenching. Then he pulled away from the staring contest with Cara, and his gaze flicked over both of the fey.

"For the record, I don't like this," he said, and Lizzy thought it was particularly brave of Cara to grin at Andric in response. "Can you two keep in contact without line of sight?" he asked.

Lizzy startled, a denial halfway to her lips before he caught her eyes and she froze instead, swallowing the lie back down. At some point, he'd figured out how she and Booker were so in tune with one another. He'd known about their use of telepathy, and he'd said nothing.

The bloody vampire was only bringing it up now because he was questioning their range. Lizzy found herself scowling at him, irritated with how observant he was, and even Booker had shoved his hands into his pockets, his shoulders hunched with tension.

"Most people don't notice that," he muttered, prompting Andric to smile slightly.

"It took me a while," the vampire admitted, and Cara shook her head.

"Notice what?"

"Booker and I can, and often do, use telepathy to speak with each other. Particularly when we don't want to be overheard," Lizzy explained.

"And yes," Booker added, leaning against the car, "we can stay connected... but we won't be able to speak across this kind of distance. I'll get vague impressions, or if one of us is experiencing a particularly strong emotion, that can get pushed across too."

"Like fear?" Andric asked.

"Anything strong," he confirmed, and Andric nodded, eyeing Cara's hopeful expression with his arms crossed. Another moment passed in tense silence before he relented with another sigh.

"Fine. If the fey keep in contact, we can split up," he grumbled, and Cara beamed before grabbing hold of Lizzy's hand.

"Woah, hang on," Lizzy yelped, shooting Booker a panicked glance.

Seconds later, his laughter was dancing through her mind, and she spat silent curses at him in response.

"*Have fun, Lizzy*," he drawled. The moment he'd given Cara a nod, Lizzy was being dragged away, devoiding her of the chance to hit her best friend.

Lizzy admitted to Cara an hour into their shopping expedition that she hadn't expected to enjoy herself. She admitted to the vampire she'd been going along with it to make her newest friend happy. She also admitted she'd been wrong.

Cara had been delighted by the admission, and promptly ushered Lizzy into the next shop.

What Lizzy had the most trouble wrapping her mind around was the sheer choice available in the mortal realm. Fabrics, styles, colours. Shoes, boots, slippers. Trousers, shorts, long skirts, short skirts, dresses, and she'd lost count of how many different styles shirts came in.

In between filling her arms with bags of new clothes, Cara took her into two bookstores and a sweet shop, followed by several jewellery stores where they browsed before leaving empty-handed. Eventually, Lizzy had to beg for a chance to stop and catch her breath.

She dragged Cara over to a bench, made of speckled stonework and wooden beams, and collapsed. More shopping bags than she could count slipped down her arms, their handles tangling around her wrists as she slumped back against the seat and laughed, while Cara settled beside her.

"You know, now we've stopped, we'll never get that momentum back again," Cara whined, but she was grinning and laughing along with Lizzy.

"I'm not like you vampires, I can't blur to get my shopping done at breakneck speeds," Lizzy said, and Cara snickered as her gaze flickered around the bustling street, adjusting her straw sunhat.

"It's probably best that you stopped me," Cara admitted. "It's getting a bit late. We should head back to the car and wait for the guys, before deciding where to go next. I was thinking movie then a meal, but a meal first might be better..."

"Thank you," Lizzy said, her voice quiet, but Cara's head whipped around to stare at her like she'd shouted it.

Lizzy kept her gaze on the bustling street. The crowds had begun to thin out as the afternoon wore on, but it was still busy. She'd half hoped it would drown her out, but Cara was watching her, waiting for her to continue.

"This... It could have been a disaster of a day. Nothing but reminders of what should be happening, and wasn't. Of who... who should be here, and isn't. You've turned it into something fun."

Cara hopped up from the bench and grabbed hold of all their bags in one hand, before looping her free arm through Lizzy's and tugging her onto her feet.

"Well, we're not done yet. Let's head back to the car—"

Relieved, Lizzy used their linked arms to tug Cara to a stop, offering her a soft smile of thanks.

"Actually, I can use the link with Booker," she explained, already tugging on the connection in her mind. She pressed a flurry of feelings across the link that implied searching, and it echoed back a moment later. It was stronger than she expected, so he and Andric weren't too far away, and Lizzy turned to face the direction she could sense them, pulling Cara across the wide street and cutting across the flow of other shoppers.

"Booker will head in my direction, we'll head in his, and eventually we'll smack into each other."

"Handy," Cara said, and Lizzy nodded.

"I don't know if it comes from the strength of his telepathy, or just the number of times we've had our minds connected over the years, but we can always find the other if there's a link established. Even across distances where we can't talk." She stopped walking and frowned at the buildings blocking her direct path to Booker.

"This is so much easier when it's only trees in the way," Lizzy muttered, and Cara snorted a soft laugh.

"It's this way?" she asked, and when Lizzy nodded Cara tugged her forward towards a narrow archway between two of the buildings that Lizzy hadn't noticed.

"There's some alleys and quiet backstreets we can weave through," Cara said as she led the way, "they should bring us out the other side. Let's just hope the guys aren't doing the same thing."

The small side street was wide enough for three people to walk abreast. Plenty of room for Lizzy to stay beside Cara once they passed through the arch, but she found her steps faltering as they rounded a corner and stepped into another, painfully familiar, alley. Dropping Cara's arm, she slowed to a stop.

"Lizzy?"

"Nothing. Sorry. It's just—"

Images of a kavian flying at her flashed through her mind.

Teeth bared, clawed fingers grasping, and Lizzy shook her head sharply. It wasn't the same street, she realised, swallowing hard, but it was familiar enough to give her chills.

"Lizzy!" Cara snapped. Her sharp tone drew Lizzy's attention, but she had barely registered the panic on Cara's face when the woman blurred forward, grasped her arm, and dragged Lizzy further into the alley, feet stumbling as she tried to stay upright while being propelled at vampire speed.

Lizzy turned and froze as a man stepped into the alley behind them. He was tall, like Andric, and broad enough that it would be impossible to slip past him while also staying out of reach.

When Cara dropped their shopping bags and fell into a stance Lizzy recognised from their training with Andric, she felt her nausea rise in her throat.

"Peace," the man said simply, raising both hands palms out, and Cara stilled.

"W-what?"

The stranger smiled, but there was no warmth there. Just a flash of sharp teeth paired with an amused grin, and Lizzy shuddered.

He wore a long-sleeved shirt with a single, large pocket in the front. It was a style Cara had called a hoodie only a few hours ago in one of the shops she'd dragged Lizzy into. It fell low on his hips, covering dark jeans, and there were wisps of dark blond hair emerging from under the edge of his hood.

The colour reminded Lizzy of the bottom of a riverbed in summer, but it was the bloodshot eyes staring out at them, and the slight waxiness to his skin, that gave him away as a kavian.

Lizzy hadn't noticed the telltale details during her first encounter, but Andric had been adamant about drilling into her and Booker the features that distinguished a kavian from a vampire.

Waxy skin, sharp nails, bloodshot eyes, and an insatiable desire to rip, tear, kill, and feed.

"I said peace," the creature spoke again, gaze sliding between Lizzy and Cara. "I wish only for a moment or two of your time."

Booker had sensed her panic. Lizzy was getting flashes of concern pushed along their link, but her focus was on the kavian. He'd made no move to approach, and his request for a peaceful exchange seemed to have stunned Cara into silence.

"What do you want?" Lizzy asked, and Cara hissed.

"Lizzy! Don't—"

"I'm looking for my wife, Raine Caldwell," the creature said, and Cara fell silent again. "She was passing through this... quaint little town about a month ago. We were supposed to meet in Hawkwell, but she had a bad habit of getting sidetracked."

"Why... Why are you asking us about this?" Lizzy asked, cautious, as the kavian slowly moved to cross his arms over his chest. "We're not—"

"From around here?" he said, and the words were almost playful. Teasing, if only the amusement registered on the rest of his features. "I know," the kavian purred, his gaze losing focus as it raked down her frame. "I can hear fey blood. It sings..."

"We don't know anything about your wife," Cara snarled, stepping between Lizzy and the kavian, breaking his line of sight, and the creature inhaled, eyes sharpening as they settled on Cara.

"Well, that's not entirely true," he said. "See, I was looking for her. Knew she had to have passed through Hockley, so I tracked her scent and found what little remained of her corpse. It was in an alley, not too far from here, and smothered in the pungent aroma of fey."

Fury flashed across his features, and the brown leached from his gaze, turning to rich red as his attention slid past Cara to settle on Lizzy once more.

"That fey."

Cara backed up a step, her arm outstretched to push against Lizzy, but the kavian didn't advance and despite the thundering terror flooding through her, Lizzy couldn't move.

"I'm not going to kill you—"

"Why not?" Cara spat.

For the first time, hints of his amusement lit up his features, and the red drained from his pupils, leaving them a dark, wood-brown once more. He almost looked normal, only the bloodshot whites of his eyes betraying his true nature.

He appeared no more deformed or monstrous than the vampires Lizzy had been surrounding herself with for weeks.

"Do you really want to complain about that?" he taunted, grin widening to flash sharp teeth at Cara once again. "Do you really want to make me question that decision, baby hunter? Make me think about changing my mind?"

"We have names," Lizzy growled, and his focus flicked back to her in an instant. Like a light bulb going out, his temper and threats evaporated leaving only Cara's ragged breathing behind, and Lizzy's pounding heart.

"And what might they be?"

"I'm not giving you my—"

"Lizzy Hail."

"Lizzy!" Cara hissed, but Lizzy refused to tear her eyes away from the threat at the end of the alley.

His features smoothed out, and there was a beat of tense silence before the kavian bowed his head in acknowledgement.

"Alex Caldwell," he introduced, voice calming and he swallowed visibly. "I think you have answers for me, Lizzy Hail, and I'm fairly certain I can make your cooperation worthwhile."

"What are you—?"

"Ah! Ah! My questions first," the kavian said, a low growl to his voice that snapped Lizzy's jaw shut with a sharp click. "How did you and Raine cross paths?"

Lizzy was silent. Cara's hand was trembling against her arm. From fear or anxiety, Lizzy couldn't tell. The telepathic bond with Booker was growing stronger as he got closer, but it was too slow. The kavian scowled at her hesitation and her gut said she needed to find a way to stall.

To survive until help could arrive. With as frequently as Andric repeated it, the words had branded themselves into her mind. Lizzy moistened her lips before swallowing down her nerves and forcing herself to answer the kavian, while holding his sharp gaze.

"She stalked me through the town, I don't know how I drew her attention—"

"Simply existing draws attention to you," Alex interrupted. He took a step deeper into the alley but paused when Lizzy backed up and Cara snarled.

"Stay right there! Not another step closer, or this discussion is over," the vampire spat. Lizzy glanced at her friend and her breath caught at the sharp teeth Cara had bared, her mead-brown eyes flashing a deep red.

When Lizzy turned back to the kavian, Alex was also studying the irate vampire at her side before he shrugged and pushed his hands into the pocket of his hoodie.

"Have it your way, baby hunter," he said, shrugging before his attention settled back on Lizzy, and her heart thundered in her throat all over again. "Your question, Lizzy Hail."

"You said... You said that you could make my cooperation worthwhile," she said. His lips quirked into a shadow of a smile that continued to leave his eyes icy cold, and Lizzy shivered.

"I did."

"How?" she asked.

"I think I know why you're here in the mortal realm, and yet so very far away from any of the Vampire Council's designated outposts," he said, but there was an edge of taunting to his voice that made Lizzy bristle.

"That doesn't tell me how you can—"

"You are not the first fey named 'Hail' to have crossed my path."

"What?" Lizzy choked out, breath catching in her throat. She stepped forward, only Cara's hold on her arm halting her. "What did you say?"

Panic, hope, fear. Her emotions were a whirlwind and she knew Booker was getting it all. She was too unfocused to even try and block them from reaching him, but Alex simply grinned at her.

"What happened to Raine?" the kavian asked, and Lizzy ground her teeth together.

"Careful, Lizzy," Cara whispered, and Lizzy swallowed hard at the warning, grateful for the reminder. It was possible, probable, the answers she sought weren't good ones, but she had to have enough cards in her hand to keep Alex Caldwell speaking.

"She confronted me in an alley, and... we exchanged a few... words."

"She taunted and then attacked?" Alex asked, sounding weary, but Lizzy didn't answer. She raised an eyebrow, challenging his second question, a little surprised when the kavian grinned at her.

"Fair enough. Your question?"

"The fey called Hail you claim to have crossed paths with," Lizzy said, choosing her words carefully as her heart thundered in her ears, the beat of it throbbed through her throat and made speaking difficult. "What... What happened to them?"

"That's a very broad question," Alex said, his frown returning and Lizzy licked her lips.

"Is... is she...?"

"The last time I saw her, she remained alive," he offered, a sharp smile spreading across his features one more time, and Lizzy's world tilted on its axis.

"*Alive*"

She hadn't meant to project the thought, but it rang through her mind like a bell. Vibrating down to her core and shaking everything she knew to be true to its foundations.

Alive was more than Lizzy had dared hope for.

"How did Raine end up dead?" Alex's voice cut through her spinning thoughts, and Lizzy's eyes snapped open. She didn't remember letting them fall closed.

"What?" she breathed, and the kavian loosed a soft growl, Cara tensing at her side.

"How did Raine end up dead?" he repeated. Her relief and growing hope withered as she considered the answer to his question. If he was asking her another question, it was possible the kavian still had more answers for her.

Where had he last seen her mum? How long ago had that been? Did he know where she was? Could he lead her there?

But asking any of those questions meant giving him his answer. And that meant giving up Andric Roche.

It had been Andric who killed the kavian woman, Raine, saving her and Booker in the process. Andric who'd tried to get them answers. Andric who was teaching them how to survive an encounter with a kavian... and Lizzy hesitated.

"She attacked me," Lizzy said weakly, stalling, "I defended myself—"

"You're lying to me!" Alex snarled, his features twisting and pupils turning red once more. Sharp teeth began to emerge from beneath his parted lips, and Lizzy shuddered, shaking her head as Cara dragged her back. Chillingly, he matched their movements, step for step.

"I could smell you there. Smell the other fey with you, but you know what else I could smell, Lizzy Hail?" Alex growled, and his hands emerged from the pocket of the hoodie, flexing as the nails elongated into vicious claws.

"I smelt vampire. Someone came to your rescue. Not this unblooded youngling. Even if I couldn't scent the difference, she's shaking too hard. She's never killed more than an insect in her life. Someone aided your survival, and I want the name of the vampire who killed Raine, or I swear I'll tear out the throat of your—"

A loud snarl drowned out Alex's threats and pulled a shriek from both Lizzy and Cara, but it was Booker's voice in her head, ordering her to go left, that kept them both on their feet.

Lizzy reacted, her instinctive trust in Booker pushing her into motion. Her hands grasped at Cara, tugging the vampire aside, pressing them both tight against the alley wall as a blur of dark jeans, a blue shirt, and auburn-red hair blurred through the spot they'd been standing in mere moments before.

With a second, furious growl, Andric launched at the kavian. Lashing out with his blades drawn, he was flung into the brickwork of the nearest building with little more than a sharp, twisting motion, leaving Lizzy staring at the failed attack in shock.

But she didn't have time to worry about Andric, as Alex turned to her with a snarl. His hood had fallen back, leaving the dirty blond strands to hang limp around his face. His fingers were twisted into the claws of a predator, and as his bloodshot eyes landed on her, his lips peeled back to reveal bared fangs and a snarl.

22

Lizzy's blood turned to ice and her throat closed up. She couldn't breathe, and she couldn't scream, but Alex only managed to take one step towards her and Cara before Andric was on him again.

A dagger buried itself in the kavian's shoulder before Lizzy had even noticed Andric get back on his feet. Red brick dust coated his shoulders as he leaned heavily against the blade buried in the kavian's back. His second dagger lifted towards the creature's throat almost faster than Lizzy could follow, but not fast enough.

With a grunt of pain, Alex spun. The movement tore the blade from his back, sending blood splattering across the ground. The damage left one arm hanging limp as he thrust out towards Andric with his uninjured hand. The flat of his palm slammed against the centre of the vampire's chest with a sickening crunch and sent Andric staggering back against the side of the building once more.

"*Lila,*"

"Lizzy," Booker's voice in her mind collided with her name spoken aloud, both filled with relief as his hand slid into hers. "Cara, are you both alright?" he whispered, but Lizzy was too transfixed on the fight to answer him.

Beneath the gaping fabric of the kavian's torn hoodie, there was a deep gash running across his back. Lizzy felt her stomach roll when the muscle and skin began to knit itself back together as Alex advanced on his prey.

Andric was still trying to reclaim his footing and catch his breath from the last blow. One dagger was missing, his back was pressed against a literal wall, and Lizzy couldn't tear her eyes away.

Between one heartbeat and the next, the world slowed.

She could see the talons tipping the kavian's fingers. Hear the snarls and the thudding sound of Alex's boots hitting the ground. Strands of dark blond hair hung in a splayed mess around his head, and without his hood, sun-burnished skin shone like candle wax in the weak daylight.

He was heading for Andric. Right hand lifting, fingers extended. Claws readied. Like five razor-sharp blades prepared to tear out Andric's throat, or cut out his heart, and Lizzy felt a stab of pain through her chest.

Alex drew his shoulder back, and she sucked in a breath.

She saw the beginnings of a blur around the kavian's elbow as Andric lifted his head, a furious, silent snarl curling the hunter's lips, and Lizzy reacted.

"No!"

Lizzy flung herself forward, body and mind. Reacting on instinct, as she had when Raine had lunged for Booker. Cara's grip on her arm, and Booker's hand in hers, stopped her physical advance.

But their hold didn't stop her mind. Her power stretched out, reaching for Andric, and placing a barrier between the kavian's claws and their intended target.

The blow landed, and time sped up again as the creature's hand crumpled against the solid force Lizzy had formed.

The strike rang against her mind like the blow had been physical, and Lizzy swayed on her feet. A soft, whimpered cry escaped her, drowned out by the kavian's snarl of agony, but the sound of snapping bone rose above them both.

Through the pain-fuelled tears stinging her eyes, she could see the mangled mess of his hand and bile burned her throat, but it had given Andric time to recover, serving its purpose.

She saw him push off the wall, taking advantage of Alex's pain, and his remaining dagger flashed forward, but Lizzy struggled to focus.

She tore her hands away from Booker and Cara, lifting them to press against the pounding in her skull.

Her eyes fell closed, releasing the stinging tears to slide, unobstructed, down her face. She struggled to draw in enough air through her nose and found herself gasping as she continued to reel from the blow.

Hands pressed against her back and shoulders, but she didn't know if it was Cara or Booker. They were asking her questions, but Lizzy couldn't make out their words past the rushing of blood in her ears.

Forcing herself to stare past the pain, Lizzy tried to follow the fight, but both the kavian and the hunter were making use of their enhanced speed.

They blurred across the narrow alley, too fast for her bruised and aching mind to follow. By the time she dragged in a sharp gasp of shock, the metal dustbin that Alex had thrown at the three of them had already been stopped.

Her wide-eyed gaze locked with Andric's, his usual soothing grey was ringed with red, and she braced herself for the flash of fear. For the memory of him launching towards her to rise up... only it never came, and Lizzy blinked in surprise.

Andric dropped the metal bin to the floor of the alley with a loud crash and spun back to face the kavian, but the alley was empty.

"Fuck!" Andric snarled, pacing forward several steps before halting. Lizzy hadn't seen where his daggers had ended up, but as she watched him, his arms remained tensed at his sides, his fingers curling into tight fists. He stayed alert, readied, and on edge.

"Wh—" Lizzy started but her voice choked slightly, and she had to stop and swallow, shaking hands lowering from her head slowly. "What happened? Where did he go?"

"It fled," Andric snarled, his back still to the three of them, but there were tiny movements of his head that told Lizzy, despite his words, he was still studying every inch of the now-empty alley.

He was leaning forward, weight on the balls of his feet, and for a moment, Lizzy thought Andric was about to give chase. To do as his title implied and hunt down the kavian, but then a single sharp sob pierced the air and the tension snapped.

"Oh God," Cara muttered, one hand fisted in her hair, and the other pressed against her mouth, muffling her words as she fell apart. "Oh shit. Fuck. Oh God. It was... and we were..."

Watching Cara splutter and stumble as she struggled not to break down, Lizzy could feel the torrent of emotions rolling off Booker beside her. At some point, he'd taken hold of her hand again, but his attention remained on Cara as she began to cry, and Lizzy could feel how much Booker wanted to help, he just didn't know how.

"It's alright, Cara," Andric said softly, appearing beside them and looking as though he hadn't escaped death by the skin of his teeth. The only outward evidence of the altercation was a thin layer of brick dust still powdered across his shoulders. "It's gone for now. As long as we head back to Speculo quickly, I can have a unit of hunters out here to take care of the problem, before it kills anyone."

"Take care of the problem?" Lizzy repeated, frowning before realisation broke through her foggy mind and she shook her head. "You can't kill him!"

"That's the only thing we can do with a kavian," Andric growled. "How you've managed to escape in one piece twice, I'll never—"

"You don't understand!" Cara snapped, cutting Andric off sharply. She had lowered her hands but her whole frame was trembling. "It could talk, Andric! It wasn't rabid!"

"That's..." Andric said, trailing off and shaking his head as he blinked at Cara, stunned, "but that's not possible."

"It was alert. It was coherent—"

"You've never encountered one before," Andric interrupted, his voice low and reassuring. "The sounds they make... they can almost sound like words, but there's no intelligence left. They're running on nothing but pure instinct."

His explanation didn't calm Cara's frustration and her shaking hands curled into fists. A ring of red bled into her eyes, filling with fury as her teeth began to elongate.

"Lizzy had a full blown fucking conversation with it!" Cara snarled, and Andric's jaw snapped shut. "They had a game of bloody twenty questions going on! I have no doubt it would have torn us to shreds the moment it got the answers it wanted, but it was coherent, Andric! It wasn't fucking r-rabid!"

Her voice broke on the last word, and Cara dissolved into tears again, her features melting back into the girl they'd been going to classes with, and Lizzy felt Booker waver.

"Go on. Help her," she encouraged, and Booker glanced at her.

"But... are you okay?"

"I'm fine," Lizzy promised, forcing herself not to think about the question and pressed reassurance along their link before she broke it. Still, he hesitated, and she responded with a glare.

"I'm fine, Booker," she muttered, relieved when her voice held steady. It was all the encouragement he needed, and Booker stepped away, releasing her hand to pull Cara's sobbing form into his arms.

Lizzy watched as the vampire collapsed against him, her arms curling around his waist. Clinging on as if her life depended on it, and Lizzy swallowed hard. Cara needed him, but she wasn't used to sharing Booker and it left a strange hollowness in the palm of her hand.

"You're not fine," Andric muttered beside her, and Lizzy's head whipped around to stare at Andric in surprise.

"What?"

"You're bleeding," he said, frowning, keeping his voice quiet. "Your nose."

Carefully Lizzy sniffed and dabbed at her nose with the back of her hand, pulling it away to show shimmery red blood staining her skin and she grimaced. She'd thought her blocked nose had been caused by the tears the pain in her head had brought forth, but apparently, she'd underestimated the kavian's strength.

She dabbed at her nose again, but her hand came away with a new smear even smaller than the first. "I think it's already stopped," she muttered.

"You used telekinesis?" Andric asked, and Lizzy turned to stare at him again. He was standing right beside her, close enough to touch and she swallowed hard. She couldn't quite read the expression on his face, but Lizzy shrugged one shoulder, feeling a little defensive.

"He was about to tear your throat out."

"Did you know what blocking his attack would do?"

His voice was soft, and Lizzy shivered before shaking her head. "I knew it would hurt," she admitted. "I could see he was trying to blur. We've been doing something in science about speed times mass equalling power, and I just... I don't understand it, but... but I knew it wouldn't be good."

She shook her head, swallowing hard. Visions of Andric bloodied and dead flashed across her mind briefly, and she crossed her arms. "I didn't know it would... hurt that much," she admitted, "but I'd do it again."

Andric stared at her, and she scowled, crossing her arms and daring him to chastise her. Silently daring him to tell her she should have done anything else when fighting kavians was exactly what he'd been teaching them to do for weeks, but Andric stayed silent, eyes still locked on hers.

"We should probably get out of here." Booker muttered.

Lizzy jerked back from Andric and turned to find Booker still hugging Cara gently, the vampire's face buried against his shoulder. "We're sitting ducks if he decides to come back."

"And he will," Andric replied, "rabid or not, fey blood draws kavians in like moths to a flame. He won't be able to resist the scent as soon as he picks it up, and I refuse to use either of you as bait."

He paced away from the three of them, moving around the alley and collecting his fallen weapons. His steps were quick and sharp but not a blur, and Lizzy found herself watching him, tracking his movements so the hunter was never entirely out of her line of sight.

"Come on," he said as soon as the blades were sheathed and hidden beneath the leather jacket he'd been sporting all afternoon. "The faster we get back to the school, the faster I can send out a team—"

"Didn't you listen to Cara?" Lizzy cut in, eyes narrowing. "He wasn't rabid. You can't just kill him."

"Lizzy, it would have torn you both apart if I hadn't arrived when I did. If Booker hadn't been able to track you down—"

"He wanted answers! That's all!"

"What kind of answers?"

"He..." Lizzy faltered, and moistened her bottom lip nervously before forcing herself to continue. "He was looking for his wife. It was the kavian who attacked us the night we arrived. He recognised... me. My... my scent," she explained, voice weakening the longer she tried to explain to Andric, and her eyes skittered away from his as the disturbing knowledge the kavian could track her down by smell shook her confidence, and she shivered.

"He just... wanted to find out what happened to her," she said, turning back to the vampire, crossing her arms and lifting her chin.

"And what possessed you to try and talk to a mindless monster?" Andric growled, hands clenched, and Lizzy felt her stomach hollow out when she realised he was furious.

She didn't want to disappoint him, and it shocked her like a bolt of lightning, making her blink rapidly. It stole her words, and for a moment, the two of them stared at each other in silence.

"He claimed to have met another fey named Hail," Cara offered into the silence, and Lizzy heard Booker's soft, choked gasp.

"What?" he whispered, "When? Where? Was... was she...?"

"We can't do this here," Andric interrupted. "I don't understand how a kavian could have been coherent, but sane or not they're still deadly, and your blood will be drawing attention. We go back to the school, and we'll speak to Walcott," Andric said, approaching the three of them once more, and Lizzy noticed he was no longer curling his fingers into white-knuckled fists.

He placed one hand gently against the small of her back, startling her enough that Lizzy unfolded her crossed arms and let him guide her along the alley as he ushered Booker and Cara ahead of them.

"As soon as we're in the car and back on the road, we can talk about it there."

"What about Alex?" Lizzy asked, digging her heels into the pavement. She had expected Andric to drop his hand, but he didn't. Instead, he ground to a halt beside her, frowning, and Lizzy took full advantage of his undivided attention, raising her eyebrows in challenge, "If he's not rabid, then surely he doesn't deserve to be hunted like an animal."

"That kavian tried to kill us. You realise that, yes?" Andric grumbled, but Lizzy didn't back down, holding his gaze until she saw his lips tighten, and then Andric sighed, offering her a single nod of surrender. "Alright, fine," he muttered, "if we leave right now I won't order a team to head into Hockley until after we've discussed the matter with Walcott. Deal?"

"Deal," Lizzy said quickly, turning and avoiding Booker's gaze as she continued down the alley in the direction Andric had been herding them. Trying to ignore the fact that despite no longer needing to be encouraged forward, Andric's hand was still a comforting warmth resting featherlight against her spine.

23

Despite an outwardly calm appearance, Andric made liberal use of his superhuman reactions on the winding forest road and got them all back within the safety of the school's warded walls in record time.

His mind hadn't stopped spinning since Cara's announcement that the kavian hadn't been rabid, and he'd struggled to calm his heart rate since spotting the claws-extended, fangs-bared kavian, with its attention fixed on Lizzy Hail.

Lizzy, who had stood her ground like an idiot.

He thought he'd taught her to run. What had she done instead? Talked to the bloody thing!

Andric spiralled between being furious with her, relieved she'd survived, and terrified that he almost hadn't been fast enough.

Although Lizzy and Cara had relayed the entire event to Booker on the drive back to Speculo, Andric only began to fully absorb their story during the second telling in Walcott's office. When the three students were safely seated opposite the headmaster, and in no danger of another attack.

It was unbelievable. He'd studied kavians as part of his training. Knew their capabilities, and how they functioned. Every part of him that was trained as a hunter scoffed at the story.

There was a voice in his head, sounding suspiciously like his mother, whispering that Cara had never faced a kavian before. Reminding him that while Lizzy had, she had no idea what a kavian truly was.

He'd only had a few weeks to begin teaching the pair of fey what to expect from the mindless monsters. Surely the two terrified girls had been blinded by their fear? Confused, and misinterpreting incoherent sounds from the rabid beast as speech?

But the longer they spoke, and the more they revealed about the kavians questions and the bartering of information Lizzy had engaged in with Alex Caldwell, the more Andric began to believe them.

When Lizzy and Cara finished explaining the events in Hockley to the headmaster, a tense silence fell over the office. Andric stood beside Walcott's desk, leaning against the bookshelves with forced casualness, studying the faces of the room's occupants with concern-sharpened focus.

As soon as they'd arrived, Booker had taken over one chair and immediately pulled a still-shaken Cara into his lap. Despite the blush the move had summoned to her face, the young woman hadn't protested. Although the encounter in town had shaken her, she was recovering.

Not all hunters reacted well to their first face-off with a kavian, but Andric suspected Cara could be one of their best if she continued to bounce back from the afternoon's incident.

Support from her friends would help, Andric knew, and Booker hadn't left her side since she'd burst into tears in the alley. Ever since Lizzy had absolved him of worrying over her, ushering him towards their vampire friend.

It was for exactly that reason Andric couldn't seem to stop himself from worrying about Lizzy.

"This information about kavians who retain enough of themselves to speak. To barter, and restrain themselves from attacking outright, is concerning."

Walcott's careful words broke the quiet that had fallen over the office, and Andric's eyes flicked over to the headmaster as he continued.

"We have survived against them this long because they are wild and uncontrolled. If this is no longer the case... it must be brought to the attention of the Councils."

"Alright, fine," Lizzy said, waving a hand through the air as though brushing aside the headmaster's concerns, "but this kavian, Alex, he claimed to have seen my mum. He said she was alive—"

"Miss Hail," Thomas interrupted her, and Lizzy fell silent. His voice was soft, gentle. From his tone alone, Andric suspected what the headmaster was going to tell her, and braced himself for the argument it would spark.

"Even if you assume the creature wasn't lying about having seen your mother, the chances of a fey surviving an extended period of time around a kavian... well. It's nigh on impossible.

"You had answers the kavian sought... and it told you nothing of worth in exchange. Only what you wanted to hear. The kavian gave you no name or description, not even a location. From what you've said, it didn't even reveal the familial connection to you, only claiming to have met a fey that shared your name. A name you supplied it with. That is an easy lie to tell, Miss Hail, surely you can see that?"

Nothing moved. Lizzy stared at Walcott, Walcott waited, and Andric held his breath for the spark of fire in her that never seemed to go out.

"Lizzy," Booker said, voice barely above a whisper, but in the silence of the office it might as well have been a shout and Lizzy flinched, shaking her head.

"No."

"Miss Hail—"

"No," she repeated. "You don't understand. This feels right. I can't explain it better than that, but it never felt like she'd—" Lizzy cut herself off, a sharp sound of frustration escaping her. "I told myself I was coming here for answers. To find out what happened to her. I couldn't grieve without knowing, not like I was supposed to, but I think I couldn't grieve because she was never really... dead."

She leant forward in her chair, arms bracing on her knees as she stared at Walcott, blue eyes wide and intent on the old vampire's face.

"I need to find Alex," she pleaded, "I have to know what he knows about her. The last place he saw her. What happened when he met her. Anything he knows. Everything he knows. Please, don't send hunters to kill him, we need to talk to him instead."

"Miss Hail," Thomas began again, but the slow way the headmaster said her name told Andric her pleas hadn't moved him. "Let me be blunt. Under normal circumstances, a kavian will mindlessly seek out any source of blood. Human, vampire or fey. They do not care, so long as they can gorge themselves... but given the choice, a kavian will always target a fey.

"Your blood draws them in. They can't resist it. If an entire delegation of fey went missing, it's because they encountered kavians, Miss Hail. And if they encountered kavians, then they're all dead. I'm sorry."

She reeled back from Walcott as though he'd slapped her. Her sharp intake of breath made Andric shift on his feet, letting his focus skim across her form, studying her, but for what, he didn't know.

What did it look like when a fey died from a broken heart?

There was pain in the way her hands had curled into fists, and an ache deep in her eyes, but nothing else gave away what the woman must be feeling.

"Lizzy," Booker said, his voice rough with restrained emotions.

He was staring at Lizzy. His jaw clenched and his expression torn, and for once their shared pain was on open display. Not for the first time, Andric wondered what Booker's connection was to the missing fey.

Lizzy refused to acknowledge her friend, and although his hand twitched towards her, with Cara still on his lap, Booker couldn't physically reach out.

Her eyes fluttered closed for a brief moment as she drew in a slow breath, and the phrase *calm before the storm* flitted across Andric's mind.

"So you won't help," she muttered, and Thomas sighed.

"I am helping you, Miss Hail. You asked me to find out what happened to your mother's missing delegation. That's exactly what I'm working on, but I will not aid you in seeking that which cannot exist, and speeding you towards your own early demise in the process."

"But he wasn't out of control!" Lizzy finally snapped, her temper fraying.

Andric found himself impressed she'd held it together as long as she had, but then she turned to him and a chill raced along his spine. She was looking for someone to concede the point. For anyone to offer her a shred of hope... but Andric couldn't.

He crossed his arms, swallowing back the bitter disappointment that he couldn't give her what she wanted, and offering only a small shake of his head.

"Even if this kavian wasn't mindless and rabid. Even then, he still lacked the level of control he'd need to keep fey blood close at hand, and not give into the temptation it provides," Andric admitted.

His apology was inherent in the softness of his words, but Andric didn't think Lizzy could hear it. Betrayal flashed across her face. Only for a split second, but it hurt more than the blow to his chest from the kavian.

"It's been... weeks, Lizzy. Months," he reminded her, and while he couldn't attest to the creature's ability to speak, he'd seen the fraying control on the kavian as it had advanced on Lizzy and Cara, prepared to lash out and strike.

"You say you spoke to Caldwell," he reminded her. "You tell me. Do you think he had enough restraint to avoid... the worst-case scenario for your mum... for weeks? For months?" Andric continued, pressing gently, and her eyes fell closed again.

She kept them shut, and Andric swallowed back a flinch. The last thing he wanted was to pile more pain on this woman's shoulders.

He glanced at Walcott, and the headmaster gave him a short nod.

It didn't lessen the ache in his chest, but it was enough to reassure Andric they were doing the right thing. They would still help her get the answers she needed, but letting her have false hope that her mum might still be alive, out in the mortal realm somewhere, was a different kind of cruelty.

"Booker?" Lizzy murmured, voice low and trembling.

The young man in question grimaced, glancing between the three vampires before giving a heavy sigh.

"I don't know, Lizzy," he admitted. "You've had doubts since the Court announced her status. But if you're right, then what's stopping her from coming home?" he asked. "Maddy's brilliant, resourceful, and clever. And she loves us. I think..." Booker trailed off with a wince, and Andric's heart ached for Lizzy.

"I think... if she were still alive, two months is more than enough time for her to find her way back to you," Booker admitted, expression pained as he stared at Lizzy's bowed head.

The office filled with silence, and all of them waited for Lizzy to respond. She stayed in her seat for a long moment, perfectly still, and Andric wasn't sure she was even breathing.

Cara shifted in Booker's lap.

The headmaster's hands, resting atop his desk with fingers laced together, brushed against each other. The only sign of his anxiety over Lizzy's reactions.

Booker's fingers clenched tight against the arms of the chair. He looked like he regretted the words that still hung in the air, but he didn't retract them.

Andric watched Lizzy.

She was rigid. Eyes pressed so tightly closed that a frown had formed across her brow. Her frame was frozen, held perfectly still. Even her shoulders lacked the subtle shift of life, and as the seconds ticked by, Andric became certain she was holding her breath. Her hands were still curled into fists and pressed against her thighs, atop the denim skirt Cara had cajoled her into for her birthday.

Happy bloody birthday, Andric grumbled to himself.

There were smaller clues to her building fury too. The straightening of her spine. The way her chin had lifted a fraction, like it did when she was staring him down mid-argument. The press of her lips together. The rapid movement of her eyes, hidden away behind closed lids, as she sought some kind of answer.

Something to say to convince them, or change their minds.

Andric knew right then she wasn't going to drop it, so when the first word out of her mouth was an acceptance, he blinked in open surprise.

"Fine."

Every single one of them flinched at the chill in her tone. The bitterness and barely suppressed fury staining every letter of the single word Lizzy hissed out into the room. It was an acceptance, but not one willingly given.

"Fine," she hissed a second time as her eyes slid open.

They were alight with blazing pain and hurt, spitting electric-blue sparks of emotion, and Andric found he couldn't meet her gaze. For a moment, he dropped his gaze to the floor and forced himself to take a breath before turning his focus onto the other faces in the room.

"If none of you believe me, if none of you are willing to help me, then I'll do it myself."

"Miss Hail, we have an agreement—"

"Oh I've not forgotten our agreement, Walcott," Lizzy spat, and it was the first time since her arrival she'd refused the headmaster his title. "I'll stay for the agreed three months. I'll even keep going to the classes. But don't think for a moment I trust you to find me my answers when you've just admitted you're looking for the wrong thing."

She snorted a harsh laugh, no true amusement in it and more disdain than anything else. "You're not looking for answers. You're looking for bodies."

"What if bodies are all there is to find?" Walcott pressed, and Andric stared at him in surprise. Cara's jaw fell open in shock, and Booker growled a wordless warning. Lizzy was hurting and lashing out, but the headmaster's eyes had narrowed, calculating.

He's assessing the danger, Andric realised in shock, *assessing how much of a risk Lizzy poses to the school.*

Andric swallowed down bile at the cruel prodding of a grieving young woman. His grief for his brother still sat too close to the surface to appreciate the lengths Walcott was willing to go to in the name of protecting the school.

"Then at least I'll have found the bodies by exhausting every last possibility!" Lizzy yelled, shooting to her feet. Andric half expected her to fly at the headmaster but instead, she turned and made for the door.

Her fury-fuelled movements, not quite a run, carried her forward. Then she wrenched open the office door and slammed it closed behind her before Andric could do more than push off the bookshelves and consider blurring after her.

But there were still Booker and Cara to consider, and Lizzy needed a chance to step away, calm down and, hopefully, grieve.

Andric sighed and reluctantly leant back against the shelves once more.

"That was cruel."

It was the first thing Cara had said since stepping into Walcott's office that wasn't directly about the kavian in Hockley.

All eyes in the room settled on Cara, but she didn't flinch. The shaken fear from earlier seemed to have receded, and Andric found himself relieved and a little hopeful for the young vampire.

"I beg your pardon, Miss Evelyn?"

"I said, that was unnecessarily cruel," Cara repeated. "I'm not afraid to say it again. The girl's lost her whole world, and you're telling her you're not even going to try and help her look for answers?!"

"Miss Evelyn, you can't possibly think—"

"Of course kavians killed her mother," Cara snarled, almost baring her teeth at the old vampire, "we all know it. I think even Lizzy knows it, somewhere deep down. But tell me who it would have hurt to let her keep her hope until you found the proof of it?"

She rose to her feet, Booker following her quickly, standing behind the young vampire's shoulders, and staring at her as she glared down at the headmaster.

"It was unnecessarily cruel," Cara said again, "and you should apologise."

Thomas Walcott raised his eyebrows slowly and sat back in his chair. "And how do you recommend I do that, Miss Evelyn?" he asked. "Even if I wished too, Miss Hail has made it clear she won't spea—"

"She won't trust you," Andric cut in, frowning at the headmaster for trying to turn his misstep around on Lizzy. It wasn't about the woman refusing to speak to him, it was that they had shattered the fragile trust she'd placed in them, and Walcott glanced at him in surprise.

"I suggest you instruct the hunters you're sure to send out to attempt a capture instead of an extermination," Cara growled, "at the very least, because you were right about one thing. Its ability to speak is concerning. If they're evolving, we need to know how and in what ways. Capture might be the only way we find that out... and it might be the only way Lizzy gets the answers she needs."

Andric watched as Walcott studied Cara in silence, weighing her words before offering a sigh and a nod.

"You... may have a point, Miss Evelyn," the headmaster conceded.

Booker snorted in response, and Andric bit back a smile when Cara subtly elbowed him, but she didn't tear her eyes away from the headmaster. She waited for him to continue with a level of expectation that forced Andric to lift one hand to his jaw, masking a full grin.

"I'll assign a team of Speculo hunters to scour the local area. With instructions to capture Alex Caldwell, if possible," Thomas said. "But I won't have them risking their lives for this."

Cara was silent until Booker slid his hand into hers, prompting a sigh as she shook her head.

"That is an acceptable middle ground," she said, a faint note of exasperation in her voice, "and it's the offer you should have made Lizzy. We'll be sure to pass it along to her."

It was a dig. Small, and a little petty, but Andric also couldn't find it in himself to begrudge her the comment. She wasn't wrong, after all, and as Cara and Booker turned to leave the office, Andric pushed off the bookcase and followed them.

"Hunter Roche..." the headmaster called, and Andric stiffened.

"I'm afraid I can't stop to chat, Headmaster," he offered over his shoulder, not quite able to bring himself to turn around. "I need to escort Mister Reed and Miss Evelyn back to their rooms, before checking on Miss Hail."

And before Walcott could speak again, he ushered the two teens out of the office and closed the door between them and the headmaster, pointedly ignoring Booker's grin and the smile of approval he received from Cara.

24

Lizzy didn't know where she planned to go after storming out of Walcott's office.

Her chest hurt, her heart ached, and her nails dug into the palms of her hands. Her head was still pounding with a headache from the blow against her telekinesis, and the worst part was... she was trapped.

Trapped by a promise made to a vampire who had no intention of helping her find her mother.

Trapped for another two months inside a school that was teaching her nothing of use.

All while her mum was still alive somewhere. Alone, without help, and probably trapped in some way herself.

And there was nothing Lizzy could do about it.

"Damn it, damn it, DAMN IT!" she shouted, slamming her hand against the nearest wall, hissing at the stinging pain that ricocheted up her arm. It didn't hurt as much as her head, or her heart, but it was a fresh sting that distracted her, for a moment, from the aches winding their way through the rest of her body.

She leant her arms against the wall, and pressed her forehead against the cool stone. Struggling to catch her breath, Lizzy fought back the prickling tears stinging her eyes.

When Andric had seconded the headmaster's opinion, it had hurt. It had been a disappointment. But it hadn't been a surprise.

What had been, was Booker.

She'd thought he believed her. He'd come with her to the mortal realm, after all. To have him also doubt that her mum was alive had almost crushed her and she'd had no choice but to leave the office.

"It would be remiss of me not to point out that if you shout any louder, you are going to garner a larger audience to your display than just myself," came a soft voice, and Lizzy tensed.

She didn't know what to expect but turned slowly towards the voice, one arm still braced against the wall, only to find the small figure of Mistress Gladstone standing in the otherwise empty hallway, watching her intently.

Lizzy didn't know what to say, so she said nothing under the vampire's scrutiny. Gladstone's watery chestnut gaze studied her in silence before her lips pressed tight and her fingers twined together in front of her.

"Come along," she said finally, tilting her head, "my office is this way. We can talk there."

She turned and started walking before she noticed Lizzy wasn't following and stopped again, glancing back over her shoulder, an eyebrow raised in silent question.

"You said I could talk to you about anything," Lizzy said, finally summoning the energy to speak. Mistress Gladstone nodded, but Lizzy couldn't help the sneer curling her lips.

"Are your words as worthless as Walcott's promise to help me find my mum?" she asked, unable to stop the bitterness seeping into her voice.

She half expected a reprimand or for the vampire to leap to Walcott's defence, but Gladstone did neither. For a long moment she didn't even move, but then she stepped towards Lizzy, quickly coming to a stop at her side.

"I am not Thomas Walcott, Miss Hail," Gladstone said, her voice barely above a whisper and her eyes as hard as the stone wall still keeping Lizzy on her feet.

"Now, you can come to my office, so that we can speak in private, or you can go to your room so you don't disturb the rest of the sleeping vampires in this school. The choice is yours, dear," she added, laying a gentle hand on Lizzy's arm before turning and walking away again.

Lizzy struggled to swallow, caution holding her in place, but just as Mistress Gladstone was about to turn a corner, Lizzy was able to push herself into motion once more and ran to catch up.

"Sorry," Lizzy muttered, slowing to walk beside Mistress Gladstone, and the vampire hummed.

"Not to worry, dear. Let's get somewhere a little more private, and you can tell me what the old coot's done now," she reassured, and Lizzy was able to huff out a weak laugh at the woman's words.

It was only a few minutes later when Gladstone ushered Lizzy into an office smaller than the bedroom she shared with Cara.

A desk sat in the middle of the room on a thick rug and a small table was set against the back wall, holding a kettle and full tea service. A thick carpet covered the floor beneath the decorative rug and paintings littered the stone walls of Gladstone's office, rather than the bookshelves Lizzy had half expected.

Once the door closed behind them, Gladstone directed her over to a chair before moving to the back of the room, turning on the kettle, and setting out a couple of cups, casually going about preparing tea like it was a regular ritual.

"Now, while I make us a drink," she said as she added dark brown leaves to the pot, her back still turned to Lizzy, "why don't you start by telling me exactly what happened?"

And Lizzy did.

She hadn't intended to. She'd planned to share the minimum possible before escaping. But, like drawing poison from a wound, Gladstone's sympathetic ear pulled the full story from Lizzy.

She told the woman everything. From how her mum had never come back from the mortal realm, right through to their afternoon in Hockley and Walcott's refusal to help her in getting answers from the sane kavian.

When Lizzy finally got around to explaining how she'd fled Walcott's office, she looked down to find her hands curled around a lukewarm cup of tea and blinked in surprise.

She didn't remember Gladstone handing her the cup, but when she glanced back up she found the vampire sitting behind her desk, sipping at her tea with a small frown.

"Do you feel better?" Gladstone asked, studying Lizzy as her thumb rubbed rhythmically along the rim of her cup.

"No," Lizzy muttered, lowering her gaze to the tea still cradled in her hands so that Gladstone wouldn't see the lie on her face.

She lifted the cup, sipping at the warm drink. Swallowing down the thanks hovering on her tongue, because despite what she'd said, spitting out her fears and ranting about her concerns, had left Lizzy feeling more grounded than she'd expected.

"Walcott's a fool," Gladstone muttered, and Lizzy choked on the mouthful she'd been halfway through swallowing.

"What?" she spluttered, and the vampire across from her smiled lightly in amusement.

"You and Miss Evelyn return to the school with eyewitness testimony of kavians being able to speak, and he doesn't want to investigate the matter?" she asked. "Of course he's a fool. Unfortunately, he's a fool with a great deal of power and influence."

"You... you believe me?" Lizzy asked, blinking in shock.

"You've no reason to lie."

"Well, no. I don't, but... but everyone else... Even with Cara's help, I—"

"I am not in the habit of deluding myself, just because the reality is something I don't wish to contemplate," Gladstone said, lowering her cup to the desk.

"Miss Hail," she continued, sighing, "the way I see it, if this kavian, Alex Caldwell, can speak, then he has regained his intelligence. If a kavian has regained his intelligence, then how can they also be called rabid? All a kavian is, is a rabid vampire. If they're not rabid, then they are not kavians."

"Okay," Lizzy said with a frown, "I can see that... but how do I find Alex before he's killed. Walcott's going to send out hunters, and—"

"Hunters who will believe they are tracking a mindless beast," Gladstone reassured. "A kavian leaves a trail a mile wide, usually of dead bodies. This Caldwell fellow will, presumably, not."

"You think he'll evade the hunters?" Lizzy asked, eyes wide with hope. If he could evade them, and escape them, there was still a small chance she could get her answers.

"He evaded our dear Mister Roche, did he not?" Gladstone said, smiling, and Lizzy shivered at the reminder.

"True. But he wanted to know who killed his wife. That was Andric... and I don't know what he might do with that information."

"One thing at a time. First we have to find him. Or at least make contact. Mister Caldwell cannot be the only sane, coherent kavian around."

"Find...? What?" Lizzy asked, frowning, but she couldn't help the shard of hope piercing her chest like a dagger, stealing her breath all over again. "You—? You're willing to—? You want to—?"

"Contact Mister Caldwell?" Gladstone prompted, her smile gentle before she nodded. "Yes."

"But... why?"

Gladstone's smile faded, and she stared at Lizzy for a long moment in silence, the tips of her fingers tracing seemingly random patterns across the surface of her desk.

Lizzy couldn't quite grasp what Gladstone was offering. Everyone she'd expected to back her had quailed at the chance to contact a kavian who had regained control of themselves. But not Gladstone, and hope had stolen Lizzy's breath as her mind spun.

"Has anyone told you the source of the kavian affliction?" Gladstone asked, and Lizzy shook her head.

"It took us months to trace the source," Gladstone continued. "Our numbers were almost as badly decimated as the fey, by the time we finally stumbled upon the source of the madness: human blood. Our primary source of food.

"Humans have flooded themselves with toxins and chemicals. In hindsight, it was inevitable that their blood would become poisonous. But none of us realised. It never even occurred to us."

Gladstone shook her head, clasping her hands around her empty cup as her fingers stroked over the smooth china while she continued.

"At that time only a few small clans, or rare individuals, had chosen to survive from animal blood alone, but thank goodness they had. As soon as we discovered the source of the madness, consumption of human blood was forbidden. Our numbers recovered over time, but we never found a way to pull a kavian back into its vampiric state.

"Now, we all survive from animals alone. Drinking human blood... it doesn't always turn a vampire into a kavian, but it could. At any time. Without a way to reverse the effects, it's a danger the Councils deemed too great to risk.

"The kavians are not at fault for what they are. It's a sickness. But, if Mister Caldwell has regained his sense of self... I think we vampires owe it to the kavians we've hunted and killed to find out how. To find out if this healing can be replicated."

"You... you want to see if you can help all the kavians? If they can be fixed?" Lizzy asked, and Gladstone offered her a small smile.

"Yes. And, hopefully, get you some answers in the process."

Lizzy glanced down at the teacup in her hand, its contents now cold, and frowned as she turned over the woman's words. It was a kind, altruistic goal.

She wished she could believe it.

"Why does everyone else want to kill them, but you think fixing them is the better choice?" she asked, frowning as she stared at Gladstone, but the vampire just grinned.

"I see there's no fooling you, Miss Hail." She fell silent, but Lizzy didn't speak, and Gladstone sighed, lifting her hands in surrender.

"The blood we consume fuels our abilities. Human blood makes us stronger than animal blood, and the history books say that fey blood made us stronger still. We can survive on the blood of animals, certainly, but fighting against kavians, who consume human blood regularly? We are always at a disadvantage. It's only a matter of time before they overrun us. I'm simply thinking in the long term. A cure for the kavian state of mind would be... nothing short of miraculous."

Lizzy still hesitated. The shattered trust she'd placed in Walcott, and even Andric, still cut deeply at her heart, but she could see no reason for Gladstone to lie.

"Okay," she sighed, nodding a moment later, "fine. But the last time I saw him he was fleeing Andric in Hockley. How are we supposed to find him before the hunters do?"

"Leave that to me—"

"No," Lizzy growled, "I tried that once before with Walcott. I won't do it again."

"If I explain to you what I intend to do, will that suffice?" Gladstone asked, raising an eyebrow as one finger tapped against the desk. "Because truthfully, Lizzy, there is little you can do to help."

Lizzy tried not to flinch at the words, but she suspected she failed when Gladstone added a soft, "for now."

Lizzy knew Gladstone was right but it didn't make it sting

any less, and her fingers tightened around the small teacup. The desire to throw it against the nearest wall in frustration was almost overwhelming, but she pushed the urge aside and slumped back against the chair.

"What are you planning to do?" It was as close to an apology as Lizzy could get, but she needed Gladstone and aggravating the only person willing to help her find Alex Caldwell wasn't an option Lizzy was willing to entertain.

"Before I was a teacher, I was a kavian hunter. And a very good one," Gladstone explained. "What works in our favour is that Mister Caldwell knows you have the answers he seeks. He will not have gone far. In fact, I suspect he will be lingering somewhere in the forests surrounding the school."

"How does that help us? If any of the hunters see him—"

"The hunters at Speculo will stay within Speculo," Gladstone reassured. "Walcott might double the number of hunters on duty, but the teams going out in search of Mister Caldwell will be focussing their attention around Hockley. A mindless kavian wouldn't stray too far from such a readily available source of blood. If he stays in the forest, awaiting the next time you leave the grounds unprotected... well, it's the safest place for him to linger."

"If you think he'll be waiting for me, then—"

"We don't know how in control he is, Miss Hail," Gladstone said, cutting her off sharply. "Please, allow me to approach him first. Explain that you're open to having an exchange of information. Let him know you're willing to work with him, before we put you in imminent danger."

"I... suppose... that makes sense," Lizzy admitted, muttering her concession almost too quietly to hear, but Mistress Gladstone simply smiled at her.

"I understand you want to do more, Lizzy. As soon as I think there's something you can help with, I give you my word I'll come to you for aid."

Lizzy stared at the woman. Her simple clothes, her hair pulled back into a long plait, and watery, chestnut eyes. Lines marred her forehead, and Lizzy got the sudden impression she'd underestimated this vampire.

She pressed her lips together and nodded.

"Give me a week," Gladstone said, climbing to her feet and rubbing her hands together like she was cold as she came around the desk, "two at most," she added, taking the unfinished tea from Lizzy's hands. "I should have some kind of an answer for you by then."

"Thank you," Lizzy said as she rose to her feet, sensing the dismissal and moving towards the office door, Gladstone walking right beside her. "No one else would—and I can't do this on my own, so—"

Gladstone's hand settling against her upper arm silenced her and pulled them both to a stop by the door, but when Lizzy glanced up at her, the vampire was smiling.

"You're not alone, Lizzy," she promised, and Lizzy took a moment to pull in a deep breath. Gradually, the tension eased from her shoulders and she offered Gladstone a small, shadow of a smile.

"Go on, now," the vampire said, opening the office door that led back to the rest of the school. "Back to your rooms. I'll come find you when we have some results," she promised.

Hope sparked through Lizzy for the first time since Alex Caldwell mentioned her mother, and Lizzy quietly followed Gladstone's instructions. Weaving her way through the empty, sunlit halls of Speculo School, Lizzy hesitantly let herself believe that, this time, her trust wasn't misplaced.

When Lizzy returned to her room, she found Cara waiting for her. She could appreciate that Cara had been worried, but the questions about where she'd gone and if she was okay pushed Lizzy to remain silent.

Where had Cara's questions been during the argument with Walcott? Lizzy thought bitterly. Nowhere. She'd kept her silence, and while part of Lizzy understood Cara's input wouldn't have influenced Walcott, Lizzy couldn't quite bring herself to forgive the fact that Cara hadn't even tried.

Not yet, at least.

She wanted to sleep on it. Give her frustration a chance to ease, but her silence upset Cara.

And an upset Cara led to an upset Booker.

She'd never been able to handle Booker's quiet irritation well, so faced with it across the breakfast table the following morning she'd faltered. Instead of apologising, as she'd intended, Lizzy found herself eating in silence and leaving the hall without speaking a word to either of her friends.

She knew it was a bad move, but Booker's wordless reproach and Cara's hurt glances from beneath lowered lids banished the words from her lips every time she tried to speak.

By the time Lizzy had managed to beat her nerves into submission and remind herself that the events in Walcott's office hadn't been Booker or Cara's fault, she'd begun to notice the signs.

The light touches against arms and hands. The way green eyes followed Cara. The fingers tangled together as they walked.

Booker was well on his way to courting the vampire, and Cara all but glowed under his attentions.

Despite the worried looks Lizzy caught Booker sending her way, the last thing Lizzy wanted was to insert herself into the middle of their budding relationship, so she maintained her silence. Ignoring the unspoken apology that hung in the air between them, she focused instead on Andric's lessons.

It was pure avoidance, and Lizzy knew it. Still, she threw herself into the training and pushed herself as hard as she could go.

She ran faster, and for longer. She tried to punch harder, and aim better. She was more vicious and violent when breaking free of Andric's holds.

And while Booker continued to complain about the work and collapse against the grass in protest, Lizzy no longer joined him.

Instead, she insisted on sparring with Andric until the Speculo bell rang to signal the end of the lesson, pointedly ignoring the concern in every frown Andric sent her. Openly scoffing at the silent worry when he knocked her to the ground, and offering nothing but glares when the hunter questioned whether she was sure she wanted to continue pushing.

Lizzy was sure.

If Gladstone managed to make contact with the kavians, Lizzy knew she would need to know how to defend herself. Just in case.

But she wouldn't speak her plan aloud. Couldn't. Not now. Not when all of them had proven they didn't believe in her goal, so instead of answering Andric, Lizzy would press her lips together, climb back to her feet, and throw the next punch.

And in this way, the days began to slip past her.

With Lizzy ignoring Booker's worried looks and silent requests for telepathic connection.

With Cara trying to draw her into conversation, hesitant and prodding, while Lizzy offered nothing but polite, vague responses. Keeping the vampire at arm's length, despite the urge to let her back in.

With the heavy gaze of Andric Roche and his presence shadowing her almost everywhere. His frowning concern near-palpable.

Andric was the one Lizzy went out of her way to avoid. She went to the training. She listened and practised. She threw punches and broke his holds, but she rarely risked speaking to him.

Andric understood her in ways only Booker ever had. He could worm his way under her guard and inside her walls, and see to her core.

He'd proven it when he'd witnessed her crack before. Proven he could find her weaknesses and knew how to press against them, and Lizzy refused to let him wind his way past her barriers a second time.

Not now she knew he wasn't truly on her side.

Stepping out of the computing class almost two weeks later, Lizzy was surprised to spot Gladstone seemingly waiting for her.

A single nod from the deputy and Lizzy felt her heart lift to sit in her throat. One brief glance to ensure Booker and Cara were distracted by each other, and Lizzy had darted across the hall.

Gladstone offered nothing more than a smile before turning and leading the way through the school, and Lizzy followed.

Her fingers nervously twisted around the strap of her bag, and she struggled to swallow down her questions, but they didn't go far before Gladstone pulled her into a quieter hallway, away from the rush of blurring vampires travelling to their next classes.

"I may have had some success," Gladstone said, her voice low and her hands rubbing against each other anxiously.

Suddenly her questions vanished, and it was all Lizzy could do to stare at Gladstone, her mouth open and eyes wide.

"Really?" she asked, voice trembling with terrified hope, and Gladstone smiled.

"I've been leaving... signs. Coded messages, for lack of a better term, that I wish to speak with a kavian. There have also been sightings of the creatures in the woods surrounding the school."

"Isn't that bad news?" Lizzy hissed, keeping her voice low, but Gladstone shrugged.

"Under normal circumstances, I would say yes. But there have been no attacks. Not in Hawkwell, not in Hockley, and none of the patrols scouring the local woodland have encountered anything either. That's unprecedented. Where there are kavians, there are kills. Which implies..." She trailed off, eyebrows lifting, and Lizzy couldn't help the slow smile spreading across her face.

"Just a little more time, Miss Hail," Gladstone murmured, resting a light hand against Lizzy's elbow, "a little more patience..."

Lizzy waited for her to continue, but Gladstone fell silent, her eyes flicking to the end of the hall, staring steadily past Lizzy.

Even before she turned, Lizzy somehow knew it was Andric at her back. She followed Gladstone's gaze and scowled, her smile withering when, as she'd suspected, she found the hunter watching them.

"Go on, dear. Better get to your next class," Gladstone encouraged, patting Lizzy's arm, and she nodded. Trusting Gladstone to continue keeping her secret, Lizzy forced herself to turn and walk away, trying desperately to ignore the weight of Andric's gaze.

As she turned the corner, she could hear Andric asking Gladstone about her. About how she was doing, concern clear in his voice, and a sharp pain made her chest ache.

Pushing it down, she crossed her arms and kept walking, forcing herself to remember the words the hunter had spoken in Walcott's office.

Do you think he had enough restraint to avoid... the worst-case scenario for your mum... for weeks? For months?

Andric had made her hesitate. Made her actually consider her mum being dead, and Lizzy was willing to admit to herself that in the face of his calm logic her certainty had wavered.

And she wasn't quite ready to forgive him for that.

While Lizzy wasn't ready to forgive Andric, she was more than ready to forgive Booker.

She missed him. Wanted his comforting presence back by her side, but the rift that remained between Cara and herself made Booker that much harder to reach.

It complicated things in a way Lizzy didn't know how to untangle, and she'd never been very good at apologies in the first place.

Especially when she still believed she was right.

She desperately wanted to find a way to thaw the ice wall that had sprung up between them, but it was solidifying by the day.

It was only Gladstone's news of the kavians in the surrounding forest that gave Lizzy hope she had something to break through Booker's stubborn silence.

She waited until the two of them were alone. Walking towards the field for one of Andric's lessons without Cara, and cleared her throat softly.

Booker didn't look at her, but his hands curled into fists before he shoved them deep into the pockets of his jeans.

"Can... Can we talk?" she asked.

He stayed silent and kept walking. The only sign he was willing to listen was the way his steps slowed, and Lizzy blew out a relieved breath at the hesitant acceptance.

"I... I've been thinking," she said, turning slightly as she walked beside him so she could watch his face as they drifted towards the practice field. "If the kavians aren't rabid, then they must want something, right?"

At that, Booker stopped, and his features fell into a frown. For a moment, she thought he disapproved, but when he turned to stare at her, she could see confusion instead and rushed to explain.

"Everyone wants something. As mindless creatures, they wanted blood, and to kill, but if they're sane and coherent, then there must be something else they desire, or they'd just keep killing as they were, you see? So if we can try to negotiate—"

"Lizzy," Booker growled, his dark tone shocking her into silence. "This is what you want to talk about?"

Lizzy blinked. "What—?"

"Of course it's what you want to talk about," Booker muttered, turning away from her and Lizzy's temper sparked.

Had he thought she would abandon her mum just because no one believed her?

"They must want something," she snapped, and finally Booker lost his temper. She knew she'd pushed too far when his hands came out of his pockets and his voice dropped low, turning as cold as mid-winter.

"You're absolutely right," he hissed, eyes snapping back to hers, "everyone wants something. You want to find Madeline. The kavians want blood. What are you going to offer when they demand your throat in payment?"

"That's—"

"What if it's just fey blood they need? I'm here, after all. We can offer them my blood in exchange for your information."

Lizzy reeled back a step, a wave of sickness washing over her as she shook her head. "No! Booker—"

"Don't you understand yet, Lizzy!" he spat, words still dangerously quiet. "There is no point finding Maddy if we lose ourselves in the process! The kavians aren't the answer you seem to think they are!"

"So I'm supposed to give up?!"

"That's not what I said!"

"But this is the best lead we've had!"

"Do you think I don't know how much you miss her?!" Booker finally yelled. "Me?"

One hand moved to grasp her elbow, but despite his temper and the pain flickering across his face, Booker's grip was still gentle, and a wave of guilt washed away Lizzy's fury. It welled up, replacing her bitter disappointment and leaving her feeling wrung out and hollow.

"Booker..." she breathed softly.

He released her in an instant, stepping back and running both hands through his hair, sucking in a deep breath before releasing it in a heavy sigh.

"I can't do this today, Lizzy," he muttered, turning sharply and stalking away from the field where Andric was waiting for them.

She watched him retreat. His shoulders slumped, head down, and his hands shoved back into his pockets as guilt gnawed at her stomach.

"Rot and termites," Lizzy hissed, turning to head back into the school. There was no way she was facing Andric's questions about where Booker was when she'd messed up so spectacularly.

And how did I mess it up, exactly? Lizzy thought to herself as she stormed back towards the school, a scowl on her face and a sick feeling in the pit of her stomach.

She could count on one hand the number of times Booker had lost his temper with her, but Lizzy couldn't understand what had set him off this time. She hadn't meant to imply he didn't understand. And she'd never meant for him to believe she would trade his life for her mum's. That was no choice at all.

There were some lines she wouldn't even consider crossing. At least, she hoped so.

But he'd been mercurial, and reactive, and the last time Lizzy had seen him that volatile was...

Do you think I don't know how much you miss her? Me?

Oh.

Oh, squirrel shit.

Lizzy ground to a stop, eyes sliding shut with a groan, cursing herself silently, and repeatedly, all while desperately hoping she was wrong.

Quickly she counted the days that had passed since her birthday and swore again, immediately turning on her heel and chasing after Booker.

This time she really did owe him an apology, and she hoped he wasn't too furious with her to accept it.

26

It was easier to track her best friend down than Lizzy expected.

After heading back to the spot where they'd parted, Lizzy made her way to the nearest castle courtyard.

With the students in their classes, any of the courtyards were a safe bet. Stone benches Booker could settle on, surrounded by beds full of flowers and shrubs. Still, she paused in surprise when she stepped through the archway to the first courtyard and found Booker sitting with his back to her, facing the small fountain in the centre of the decorative space.

Lizzy thanked her lucky stars that, despite the rift growing between them, Booker remained as predictable as ever.

She'd braced herself, preparing to walk right up to him and kneel at his feet. To beg for his forgiveness. It was only Andric's distinctive form sitting beside Booker in silence that stilled her movements and kept her hovering in the shadowed arch.

It didn't look like he'd been there long, still shifting slightly as he settled. Russet curls brushed across his broad shoulders when he turned to stare at Booker, and his fingers curled around the edge of the stone bench.

Lizzy bit her lip as she watched them. Hesitating. Unsure if she should leave or approach, or stay where she was. Hidden, observing, and—*what was the vampire doing there anyway?*

Almost like their minds were still linked, Booker sighed heavily and asked the question still sitting on the tip of her tongue.

"What are you doing here, Andric?"

"I can't just be keeping you company?"

"You could," Booker conceded, shrugging one shoulder, "but you're not."

Lizzy stepped to the side, her shoulder braced against the stone pillar of the arch as she listened. Waiting, half-hidden in the shadows, and wishing Andric wasn't there so she could make her apologies to Booker.

"I might have overheard the tail end of a certain argument and thought you might want someone to talk to."

"Rotting vampire hearing, of course you did," Booker complained, and Lizzy had to press a hand to her lips to smother a smile.

Silence fell again, and neither Andric nor Booker spoke for several long, tense minutes.

Before arriving at Speculo, Lizzy would have believed Booker could outwait anyone, but she'd been on the receiving end of Andric's quiet patience. The longer the pair sat, the more tension gathered in Booker's shoulders, and eventually, he huffed another loud sigh.

"Lizzy and I have barely spoken since Walcott decided to be an arse," Booker muttered, and Lizzy winced.

"I'd noticed."

"I'm not surprised. Everyone's noticed. But it's fine," Booker brushed off, one hand waving through the air. "We argue. We don't talk for a while. We always drift back together."

Isn't that the truth, Lizzy thought, leaning her head against the cool stone. It was her and Booker against the rest of the realm, and she missed him. But she'd been so wrapped up in finding her mum, she'd forgotten the date.

And that might be unforgivable.

"So what's the problem?" Andric asked gently, and Booker leant forward, bracing his arms on his knees and shaking his head.

Lizzy couldn't see his face, but she knew him well enough to imagine it. Green eyes closed, with stoic features that could be carved from stone, while he considered how much to say and how much to reveal.

Booker hated speaking about this. Usually, it was Lizzy who told the story, if it was necessary, but now—

"Have you wondered why I'm here with Lizzy?" Booker muttered, startling her from her thoughts. His voice was low, and it took everything in her not to step closer in support or move to his side and wrap him in a hug.

"She's your best friend," Andric said simply.

Booker was silent for so long, Lizzy's heart settled in her throat before he finally nodded, and the rush of relief almost left her sobbing.

"Yeah, she is... but that's not why I'm here. Or, at least, not the only reason. I wasn't lying that first night in Walcott's office, Andric. Maddy's important to me too."

"Maddy?"

"Madeline Hail. Lizzy's mum... she's... she's special."

"In what way?"

"Maddy's unlike any other fey I've ever met," Booker said. The affection in his voice warmed Lizzy, even as it brought a stabbing pain of loss to her chest, but she forced it all down and kept listening.

"She's smart, and brave. Clever, and kind. She's so rotting kind. When I was eight Maddy came and found me. When I was lost and adrift in an endless sky of grief, she lit a light that helped me find my way back to my sanity. She helped me find my way again, and then Lizzy became my anchor."

"What happened?" Andric asked.

"My parents were murdered."

"What?"

"The court sentinels never found out who. But they were all I had in the realm. No brothers or sisters. No extended family. And after I found them—"

"You found them?" Andric choked out, and Booker shrugged.

"—the grief was killing me, until Maddy came for me," he said. His voice was deceptively calm, but Lizzy knew him better than that and her hands itched to pull him into a hug, even as his next words froze her in place.

"Dying from a broken heart doesn't hurt, Andric," Booker continued. "The grief hurts, but the dying part... It's calm. It's peaceful. A relief. That's what makes it so deadly, you see? You don't have to face the agony of loss waiting for you back in your body, you can just... drift away. It's why I don't care that Lizzy keeps fighting to find Maddy. It's giving her something real, something solid to cling onto. She needs that."

"Then what made you so angry today?" Andric asked, and Lizzy turned away from them, pressing her back against the far side of the arch, concealed from view and hiding from Booker's answer.

She knew what was coming if Booker continued being honest with the vampire. And after everything else he'd revealed, she saw no reason why he would keep this final betrayal of hers a secret.

"It was a misunderstanding," Booker muttered. "She wanted to talk about Maddy. I thought... I thought she'd remembered the date."

"The date?"

"It was today. Eleven days after Lizzy's birthday is the anniversary of their deaths. I guess I thought... But it doesn't matter what I thought."

"Of course it matters, Booker," Andric corrected, and Lizzy found herself agreeing.

She slid to the floor, her knees pulled tight to her chest as guilt overwhelmed her, and her fingers curled around her pearl necklace as hot tears spilled silently down her cheeks.

"No, it doesn't," Booker growled. "I'm fine. It's been ten years since they were taken from me. Today is hard, tomorrow will be better, but Lizzy—"

He cut himself off sharply, and Lizzy tried not to cry harder at the loyalty she was certain she didn't deserve.

"I get it," Andric said, "I understand. I have a best friend like that. Just as close, just as... frustrating..."

"But you wouldn't change a thing about them?"

"Exactly," Andric said, huffing a soft laugh. "Nameer Khatri, he's called. He works here at Speculo—"

"Hunter Khatri?" Booker asked. "Cara speaks highly of him."

"He's one of the best. He's not here right now. He's leading the hunting party Walcott sent to Hockley for the kavian, and I'm just..."

"Adrift. That's why I couldn't let her come here alone," Booker muttered, "I'd have gone mad worrying. Is that why there's more hunters on guard duty than normal too?"

"Noticed that, did you?"

"It'd be hard not to. Half the school's whispering about it. About the reasons why."

"It's just a precaution. For the moment."

"A necessary one?"

Booker's answer was silence, and Lizzy's nerves returned as she remembered Gladstone telling her about kavian sightings in the forest.

"I know you two are arguing right now, but try not to worry too much. I'll keep an eye on her," Andric promised, and Booker swore.

"So it is necessary."

"Not yet," Andric sighed, "but... fey blood draws kavians in, and—"

"The nosebleed. From the telekinesis."

"I'd hoped it was small enough, stopped quickly enough, that it hadn't been noticed," Andric admitted, "but... my gut is saying we're not that lucky."

"What can we do?" Booker asked, and Lizzy held her breath.

Nothing, she pleaded silently, brushing her tears away from her face. *Do nothing. Not until Gladstone has a chance to set up a meeting...*

"For now, nothing," Andric said, and Lizzy exhaled slowly in relief. "You're safe inside the walls of the school. With luck, Walcott will find some answers for you both."

"And if he doesn't?" Booker pressed.

"Then... I'm still contracted to act as guide and guard," Andric said. "So wherever the two of you decide to search next—"

"You know Lizzy could release you from the contract, if you asked."

There was another long silence, and Lizzy frowned as she recognised the note of probing curiosity to Booker's voice, but without seeing his face, or connecting to his mind, Lizzy didn't know what he'd been prying for. With no other way to read him, she could make no guesses and clenched her teeth to bite back a groan of frustration.

"But you're not going to ask, are you?"

"Mister Reed—"

"Ah, back to surnames too?"

Andric growled, and Booker laughed.

"Don't worry, I can't say having someone trained to fight kavians with us when we leave is a bad idea. And you'll probably need help convincing Lizzy of that."

"When?"

"Yes. When. Do you really think Walcott's going to turn up any answers after that last meeting?" Booker asked with a sigh. "Even if there was something to find... he's not looking all that hard."

Lizzy carefully pulled herself back to her feet, peering around the archway to stare at their backs as they fell silent again.

Booker looked better now. More relaxed. His hands were pressed against the bench as he leant back slightly, face tilting up towards the sky.

In contrast, Andric's shoulders were hunched, and he sat facing the small fountain, as though trying to avoid Booker's gaze.

"I'm sorry," the vampire offered, softly breaking the silence.

"Whatever for?"

"I believed Walcott to be your best chance at answers, but—"

"Bringing us here kept us alive. We'd not have survived alone with all the gaps in our knowledge, Andric," Booker reassured, "and, look, if you still think there's some kind of apology owing... keep keeping Lizzy safe."

"I'm not sure that's an apology, so much as a full-time job," Andric mused. Booker laughed, and Lizzy rolled her eyes, but she stepped away from the courtyard, careful to keep her movements slow and as silent as she could manage.

She couldn't approach Booker now. Wouldn't interrupt the warm, and surprising, camaraderie that had sprung up between Andric and her best friend.

Instead, she chose to retreat, and wait for Booker outside his rooms. She could apologise to him later. She knew from what he'd told Andric, Booker would forgive her, but the apology still needed to be made, and the comfort of a sister given.

But first, she had to tell Gladstone what she'd overheard. She needed to warn her that the hunters knew about the kavians in the forest.

It was possible, probable, that Gladstone already knew, but Lizzy couldn't risk it. She adjusted her path through the school, heading directly for the deputy headmistress's office and forced herself to push everything else to the back of her mind, ready to deal with later.

27

After warning Gladstone, who had listened intently and thanked her for the information, Lizzy had gone straight to Booker's rooms.

She hadn't had to wait there long, her friend reappearing shortly before the bell that signalled the end of classes rang through the school.

The moment he'd met her eyes, Lizzy had felt her heart crack again and the guilt roar through her, but the apology had gone as she'd expected. Offered and accepted, without dramatics, and the hug he'd allowed her to wrap him in had healed more than just Booker's hurts, it had soothed some of her own too.

But despite the fragile mending of their friendship, Lizzy couldn't forget what he'd said in Walcott's office, and she couldn't forget what she'd overheard as he spoke with Andric. While Booker's desire to protect her warmed her heart, Lizzy couldn't let it get in the way of finding her mum.

Lizzy needed to be ready for whenever Gladstone could arrange a meeting with Alex Caldwell, and she couldn't do that if Booker was hovering over her.

She needed something to hold his attention, so Lizzy carefully went about trying to repair her friendship with Cara.

It took nothing more than a tentative request for help with her science homework, and Cara grasped hold of her olive branch with both hands. The vampire's eagerness to help, and her obvious desire to return to their easy friendship, left Lizzy burning with guilt.

But a happy Cara meant a distracted Booker, so Lizzy pushed the guilt aside, reassuring herself that her quiet manipulations weren't the only reason she'd reached out to Cara again. Merely the most pressing.

That only left Andric Roche to evade.

He'd become her ever-constant shadow. His promise to Booker to keep an eye on her seemed to be one the kavian hunter intended to take literally. The only time she was free from the weight of him watching her was during the brief walk down to the training field, when he blurred ahead to meet them, instead of stalking her footsteps.

It was irritating to be unable to do anything, or go anywhere, unobserved, but she didn't feel smothered. Lizzy had expected to. Had expected to chafe under his watch. To feel trapped, or hunted, but the sensation of Andric's gaze on her was more comforting than she wanted to admit.

His presence was also, unfortunately, not overtly overbearing, so Lizzy couldn't even call the hunter out on his behaviour without drawing his suspicion.

All Lizzy could do was ignore him, and hope Gladstone would be able to find a way to get her alone when the time came.

She concentrated on nudging Cara and Booker together as often as she could, and her attempts at distracting the pair worked better than Lizzy could have anticipated.

It didn't take long for Booker to begin skipping the training sessions Cara couldn't attend, and although Andric frowned whenever she turned up alone, he also didn't track Booker down and drag him onto the field as she'd half-anticipated.

The unexpected result of having Andric's undivided attention was how hard he began to push her. To run faster, to hit harder, to break holds with more force. No holding back and no hesitating.

She left every session exhausted, certain he couldn't possibly expect more, and yet every time he pushed, she pushed back and met the goals he set. Every time she expected to falter and fail, she simply didn't, and Lizzy didn't know how she felt about that.

And when he swapped from teaching her individual moves to sparring with her outright, she didn't know how she felt about that either.

It brought them physically closer than she allowed anyone, except Booker. Arms curled around her, hands grasping her wrists, and she slammed elbows into his ribs and kicked at his legs until the vampire released her.

Only sometimes Lizzy forgot that getting Andric to release her was what she was supposed to be doing, and regularly thanked her lucky stars Booker wasn't connected to her mind to tease her about it.

The worst part was, it was happening with increasing frequency, and it would only be a matter of time before Andric noticed her distraction. Any other time, any other situation, Lizzy would consider whether that was a bad thing or not, but she didn't want him closer. She needed more distance, more space, more room to escape the grasping hold of Speculo and enact her plans with Gladstone. She couldn't let Andric under her skin, no matter—

"Lizzy." His low voice, a little breathless from the fight, brushed her ear and she shivered in his grasp, her back to his chest and his arms locked around her, trapping her arms against her torso. It was the same hold he'd shown her in their first session. The one kavians liked so much because it brought their victim's neck within biting distance, and she realised she'd gotten distracted. Again.

"Lizzy, you can't freeze," Andric growled, and she instantly reacted. Grasping his hands, she held them against her and dropped, lowering her centre of gravity and forcing him to bend.

She used her shoulders to lift his arms and turned sharply, sliding her body and head out of his grip and twisting his arm hard.

A sharp, snapping pop cut through the air, combining with Andric's grunt of pain and shattering her focus, and this time, Lizzy did freeze.

Horror flooded through her system as she jerked her hands back from his body, letting him straighten. His jaw clenched tight and eyes closed.

"Good," he muttered, and Lizzy gaped at him.

"Good? But I heard... What...?"

"You dislocated my shoulder," Andric growled, but there was no anger there, just a tense kind of controlled pain, "and that's good. A kavian can't grab you if they can't use their arm."

"Andric—!" Lizzy spluttered, part shocked, part horrified at what she'd done.

"But you took too long to react," he continued. "You'd already have had your throat torn out. You cannot freeze, Lizzy," Andric scolded, voice still tense, his breathing a little unsteady, and Lizzy's temper flared.

"Will you stop teaching for thirty seconds, and tell me how to help you!" she snarled, and Andric blinked at her before offering a small, tight smile.

"It's already fixing itself," he reassured, breath hitching for a second before he continued. "And that's your other lesson. Vampires, and of course kavians, heal at an accelerated rate. Kavians faster than us, since they're not limited to animal blood. You've incapacitated me, but it won't last."

His eyes slipped closed and the same sickening cracking sound reached her ears, making her flinch back a step even as Andric released a soft, relieved sigh.

Then those blazing grey eyes snapped open again and locked on her.

"What you should have been doing, from the moment you

heard my arm give way, was turn and start running."

Lizzy stared at him, torn between concern and anger that he was still teaching her lessons when she'd... When his arm had...

Shaking herself and licking her lips nervously, Lizzy glanced away for a second before bringing her attention back to Andric, staring at his shoulder instead of meeting his focused gaze.

"Are you alright?"

"It'll bruise, but it's back in place. I'll grab a dose of blood from the medical supplies," he reassured, voice finally softening and stepping closer. "It's okay, Lizzy. That's exactly what you should have done, what you've been training to do for weeks now—"

"That doesn't make it better," she snarled, and Andric fell silent.

Slowly, he lifted his uninjured arm, letting his hand rest against her wrist. It was warm, steady, and the firm touch pressing against her skin made Lizzy painfully aware of her hands trembling. She sucked in a deep breath and lifted her head to meet Andric's stare, but she wasn't faced with the stoic teacher this time, or the perfectly in-control hunter.

The eyes staring back at her were soft and calm. The same soothing gaze that belonged to the vampire who'd let her cry and rage at him after the disastrous vampire-fey relations class, and Lizzy's throat was suddenly very dry.

"Hunter Roche," came a familiar voice, and Lizzy jumped, stepping back from Andric and turning to stare at Hilda Gladstone where she stood on the edge of the marked training field, hands rubbing her upper arms as though warding off the chilly early-morning air.

Andric cleared his throat, shifting until his hands clasped against the small of his back. Lizzy noticed that he'd moved his right arm slower, twisting it behind his back cautiously and guilt flared in her gut once more.

"Deputy Gladstone," Andric greeted, "I'm surprised to see you out here... is there something I can help you with?"

"Just the reverse, dear," Gladstone said, a smile gathering at the corners of her mouth. "I came to let you know Hunter Khatri and his team have returned to the school. I thought you'd like to catch up with your friend. Find out, firsthand, how the hunt went."

Andric's polite smile had vanished, Lizzy noted, replaced by growing concern. The way his back straightened, he looked like he was fighting the urge to stalk off immediately.

"It's quite alright, Andric," Gladstone added before either he or Lizzy could speak. "I'll walk our Miss Hail back up to the school," she reassured, and Lizzy found herself desperately trying to stamp down on the hope sparking through her. Andric could read her far too well for someone who didn't have access to her mind via telepathy, and the last thing she needed was him getting suspicious.

Still, he hesitated, and Lizzy bit back the urge to chime in some encouragement.

"Besides," Mistress Gladstone added, her smile widening, "I believe I heard you mention needing to get some blood from medical. It might as well be now."

Lizzy grimaced, dropping her gaze, and a second later Andric sighed.

"If it's not too much of an imposition—"

"Of course not," Gladstone insisted, and Lizzy almost held her breath waiting for Andric's decision.

"Alright," Andric said, turning to Lizzy, "we'll skip the 4am class, but you're back here, tomorrow, 2am. And try and drag Booker with you this time," he added, and Lizzy struggled not to grin in relief, nodding her agreement.

She thought that not arguing might have been a mistake when Andric paused, a small frown creeping its way onto his face, but Gladstone interrupted, tutting softly and pulling his attention back to her.

"Go and see to that shoulder, Andric," she scolded, and

Lizzy was surprised to watch the kavian hunter grin sheepishly and duck his head before heading towards the school without another word, only taking half a dozen paces before he blurred, disappearing across the school grounds.

"Finally," Lizzy muttered, turning to Gladstone and stepping up to the small vampire's side. "Have you... heard anything?" she asked, and Gladstone smiled, rubbing her palms together before she interlaced her fingers and settled her hands at her waist.

"Walk with me, Lizzy dear," Gladstone said in answer, and Lizzy bit back a sigh of frustration.

Snatching up her bag and slinging it over her shoulder, she jogged to catch up with the vampire, falling into step beside her and adjusting her pace to match.

It was a slow walk back towards the school, and Lizzy had to fight back the urge to snap at Gladstone for answers. She swallowed down her pleas for answers, for even a shred of hope, but she couldn't bring herself to tear her eyes away from Gladstone's face.

They were halfway back to the school before the vampire finally seemed to relent.

"I've been leaving messages, as you know," she began, her voice soft and low. "In code, using an old hunter signalling system. Not one in use any more. Or even taught to the current generation. But I got an answer."

"You... you did?" Lizzy breathed.

"They're willing to talk."

"Who? Caldwell?"

"Yes, Caldwell, and others." Gladstone paused, tilting her head. With a jolt, Lizzy realised she was probably checking for anyone nearby who might overhear. It was only a second or two until Gladstone stopped and turned to Lizzy, fixing her with a sharp expression that pulled Lizzy to a halt beside her and sent a chill racing up her spine.

"It appears Mister Caldwell is not the only kavian to have regained his wits. I was contacted by a kavian called Sethan Blackwood, and while the details that can be shared via the hunters code are sparse, I was able to convey our interest in the fey called Hail that Caldwell referenced. In response, Blackwood would like to meet."

"Meet?" Lizzy breathed, her head spinning. "But... but if he wants to meet, then... If he knew nothing—"

"If he had no answers for you Lizzy, there would be no reason to meet. Exactly."

A strangled sort of sound escaped Lizzy. Half laugh, half relieved sigh, part sob, and her hands lifted to press against her forehead as the world seemed to spin.

Fingers clasped around her arms, and Gladstone's soft voice echoed through her head, reminding her to breathe, and Lizzy sucked in a sharp gasp of air.

"I'm fine," she whispered, lowering her hands and shaking her head. "I'm sorry, I'm fine."

"It's quite alright, dear," Gladstone said gently, her thumbs stroking across Lizzy's upper arms soothingly. "I imagine the relief must be... quite heady."

Lizzy nodded and swallowed hard, trying to push back the tears of relief at the prospect of some answers.

"The meeting is set for four days from now," Gladstone continued, releasing Lizzy's arms, but one hand stayed settled at her elbow, guiding her forward as they continued across the dark grounds.

"Sunday?"

"Yes. In the afternoon, when the rest of the school is asleep. You'll need to sneak out of your room without waking Miss Evelyn. Meet me at my office, and I'll get us off the grounds without being seen... And Lizzy, you cannot tell anyone about this," Gladstone warned. "Not Miss Evelyn, not Mister Reed, and certainly not Andric Roche."

"What? Why?" Lizzy asked, blinking in surprise. "Now we can prove that the kavians—"

"No one," Gladstone repeated, and Lizzy frowned at her until the vampire sighed. "Miss Evelyn will not want us to go without backup from the hunters, she will want to inform Andric Roche, at the very least. Hunter Roche will either forbid you from going, attack the kavians on sight, or report our activities to the headmaster. It's what his training insists upon."

"And what about Booker?" Lizzy grumbled, crossing her arms, and Gladstone hesitated.

"I... suppose... you could tell Mister Reed," she conceded, pulling her hand back from Lizzy, and wrapping her hands around her upper arms again, rubbing lightly. "Only, do you think he could keep it a secret from Miss Evelyn? They seem to be very close these days, and then the issue of her going to Hunter Roche is, once more, a concern."

Or Booker might go to Andric himself, Lizzy admitted to herself. Particularly after the discussion she'd overheard the pair having, and Lizzy grimaced, shaking her head. She hated keeping anything from Booker, especially something this big, but she couldn't trust him not to interfere. Not this time.

"Okay, fine. I won't tell anyone," Lizzy agreed reluctantly, and Gladstone offered her a gentle smile in response before tilting her head towards the school.

"Come along, let's keep walking," Gladstone prompted. "Two figures in the shadows, talking, will raise more eyebrows than the sight of a teacher escorting a student back to the castle."

The pair of them walked in silence as they approached the school.

Its towers loomed high and blocked out some of the stars. Lizzy stared up at them and blew out a heavy sigh. She was drained and tired from the relief flooding through her, but even the smallest chance at getting some answers had lifted such a weight from her shoulders that she was beginning to think she might be able to fly away, even without the wings of a fey.

"So that's it then?" she breathed, still staring at the sky, blinking back tears again at the emotions still rolling through her. "I sneak out past Cara on Sunday, meet you at your office, and we meet with this Sethan Blackwood person and see if they have any answers about my mum?"

Gladstone hummed a soft affirmative, but when Lizzy glanced at her, the woman's shoulders were hunched, and Lizzy frowned.

"What is it?"

"Well... no. Don't worry yourself, dear."

"No, tell me. If there's something else—"

"It's nothing. Nothing the kavians have requested, anyway."

Lizzy frowned and stopped walking. "But?"

"Keep walking, Lizzy dear," Gladstone warned, and Lizzy huffed but lengthened her stride to catch up with the vampire, scowling pointedly at her. Gladstone's lips pressed together, and her fingers tightened on her arms before she seemed to wither with a sigh of surrender.

"I just think... you're asking for information, and offering nothing in exchange. And while they have requested nothing... I think it would be a show of good faith were you to offer them a small vial of fey blood," Gladstone explained, and Lizzy stumbled, startled.

"What?!"

"Shush," Gladstone hissed, glancing around before shaking her head, "I told you, it's not important."

But it was. Lizzy could see on the woman's face that it was and, as much as the idea turned her stomach, Gladstone was right. She was asking to meet with the kavians, asking them for information on her mother, and offering nothing in exchange.

Her skin crawled but a small vial was a small vial. It was nothing. Negligible. A show of good faith, exactly as Gladstone had described, and Lizzy swallowed back her nausea.

"I... I don't know... I'm not sure I'm..."

Gladstone watched her through the shadows but said nothing, and Lizzy took a deep breath, forcing the bitter words past her tongue. Voicing aloud something she often felt but rarely spoke of and trying not to choke on the words.

"I doubt I'm... fey enough... for that kind of offering," she muttered.

"Because of your wings?" Gladstone asked bluntly, and Lizzy flinched.

"Because I don't have any. Yes."

"You're fey enough," the woman muttered. "I can tell."

"You can... what?" Lizzy spluttered, and Gladstone turned her head to stare at her for a long moment, eyes glinting in the shadows and bringing a fresh shiver slithering along Lizzy's spine.

"Fey blood is... distinctive. It's more potent than either human or vampire blood, and its purity strengthens the drinker more substantially than other kinds." Gladstone paused, tongue darting out to moisten her lips before she shook her head. "Your blood is fey, Lizzy. Wings or no."

"I—I don't—can I think about it?" Lizzy whispered weakly, and Gladstone offered her a wide grin in response.

"Of course, dear. Just don't think too long. We've only four days before the meet."

Lizzy nodded, swallowing hard, and followed Gladstone into the school in silence when the deputy held one of the doors open, lost in thought.

Lizzy barely noticed Gladstone leading her back to the room she shared with Cara. She was only half aware of walking in, wishing Gladstone a good morning, and closing the door between her and the deputy headmistress.

Lizzy dropped her bag on the end of her bed in a daze and showered on autopilot, lost in her mind as she considered blood, and vampires, and kavians.

Hours later, Lizzy found herself sitting cross-legged on her bed, still thinking. She'd changed into some loose cotton pyjamas she'd bought on her birthday: a strappy top, and wide trousers in a dark blue fabric scattered with silver stars.

She didn't remember weaving her hair into a plait but could feel the damp hair pressing along her spine when she got startled from her thoughts. The door opened, and Lizzy's head snapped up as Cara stepped inside, dropping out of a blur as she crossed the threshold.

"Squirrel shit, you scared me," Lizzy muttered, huffing out a breath.

Cara paused before laughing. "Sorry! I didn't expect you to be here," she said, grinning as Lizzy shrugged, accepting the apology without comment.

"What are you doing here?" Cara asked, closing the door and moving to unpack her bag on her desk. "You're usually still walking up from the training field at this time."

"Andric's friend's back at Speculo, so we finished the 2am class early, and he cancelled the 4am."

"So, you've been sitting here for... almost three hours?" Cara asked, pausing her movements to stare at Lizzy. "Alone?"

"What time is it?"

"Six am. Dinner's just started."

"I suppose so, then. Yeah. I mean... I had a shower..."

Cara stared at her, frowning, and Lizzy shrugged one shoulder, drawing one leg up until her thigh pressed against her chest. She wrapped her arms around her shin and let her chin rest against her knee.

"What's on your mind, Lizzy?" Cara asked gently, moving to sit on her bed, and Lizzy pressed her lips together as she considered how to answer.

She knew what was bothering her. The suggestion that she hand over a vial of blood to the kavians. A *show of good faith*, Gladstone had said. The problem was, she didn't know how to ask the questions buzzing around her brain without raising Cara's suspicions.

Without raising them any more than they already are, she admitted, lifting her eyes to find Cara staring at her in open concern and resigning herself to saying something, if only to assuage the vampire's worries.

"It's nothing," she began, pausing as Cara's expression twisted from concern into disbelief, and Lizzy couldn't stop the sheepish grin that crept over her face.

"Alright, fine... it's nothing important. It's just something that's been... on my mind. About vampires." She struggled with how to word her questions, not prepared to reveal her reasons to Cara, then Walcott's warnings their first night sprang to mind. "It was something Walcott said," she added, shooting a cautious glance at Cara.

"Okay," Cara prompted, and Lizzy blew out a soft, nervous sigh.

"He said... he said we shouldn't offer our blood to anyone, and... and I was wondering, well... why? Beyond the obvious, of course. It just—it seemed like there was—"

"More to it?" Cara cut in, and Lizzy blinked at her in surprise but nodded. It hadn't been what she was going to say, but letting Cara lead would, she hoped, make the line of discussion a little less suspicious.

"That's 'cause there is," Cara said. "We're predators at heart, so someone voluntarily offering us their blood is... intense. It's a show of trust, sometimes of loyalty. Blood sharing between vampires is sometimes used as a show of intimacy between, uh—" She coughed delicately, cheeks flushing. "—lovers."

Lizzy shook her head but ignored her blushing. "So... if it can mean all those different things, then how do you tell them apart?"

"It depends how the blood's given," Cara explained. "Trust and loyalty tend to be given in containers. A bottle, vial, bag, cup, whatever. But trust will always require a smaller donation than loyalty. As for the, uh... other type of offering... that's... Well, it's intimate. It's... it's taken... directly."

Lizzy's breath caught, and her eye widened as she stared at Cara, but the woman didn't elaborate. Slowly, Lizzy swallowed and forced the words off the tip of her tongue.

"You... you mean, like... a bite?" she asked, and Cara huffed.

"Not 'like' one," she muttered. "The wrist, throat..." She coughed again before continuing, her voice dropping to a mutter. "The thigh. A direct bite is intimate."

Lizzy was so far away from her original reasons for asking about vampires' relationships with blood, she wasn't remotely worried about Cara guessing her reasons for asking. Despite that, she found herself curious, in a way she couldn't explain, over the various ways vampires viewed the sharing of blood.

"So, vampires mix up their sex and their blood. You just go around biting each other—"

"No," Cara spluttered, and Lizzy couldn't smother her grin at her friend's bright red face, not at all mitigated by the glare she was shooting Lizzy. "I don't understand how you and Booker can be so... so... casual about—"

"Sex?" Lizzy teased, and Cara threw her hands up.

"Yes!"

Lizzy chuckled but shrugged as she answered. "It's fun. It's enjoyable, and it doesn't get us killed. Not like falling in love can," she explained, and Cara sobered.

"Then... offering our blood to... to an intimate partner sounds similar to falling in love for fey," she tried explaining again. "We're predators, Lizzy. Letting another predator drink from us is... it's a level of vulnerability, and it's trusting them not to kill us in the process. It's not something done with every partner, and it's never done lightly."

Lizzy nodded, but the way Cara had described the intimate sharing of blood made her pause, a frown creeping over her features as she turned the vampire's words over in her mind.

"You said... Do both vampires not drink at the same time?" she asked, "Wouldn't that... I don't know, trigger your healing? Negate the risk of one of you killing the other?"

Cara was already shaking her head before Lizzy even finished voicing her questions.

"No. I mean—yes, it would. But no, we don't do that. That's... It would create a permanent blood-tie. Only mates complete that type of bonding."

"Mates?"

Cara sighed heavily and wrinkled her nose. "Sure. I mean,

not the legendary-soul-mate kind of mates. We don't have one person we're destined to spend our lives with or anything," she explained, nose wrinkling again. "But sometimes, we'll meet someone and our instincts will just go, 'Yes. That one. They're a good fit.'

"It's just... a gut feeling. It tells us that we're highly compatible with this particular person, but it's not an instant connection or anything. It takes time. Getting to know them. It's a choice we make, but it's also what made fighting the kavians so dangerous when they first emerged."

"What? Why?" Lizzy prompted, and Cara hummed as she appeared to consider how to explain.

"We're... exceptionally responsive to potential mates. It's one of the early signs, and it grows if we choose to pursue the relationship. Their scent can pull us from a blood frenzy. Their voice can calm us when we're in a temper. We'd have to force ourselves to fight or harm them. Their presence soothes the predator in us, so when mates were forced to battle their kavian-turned partners..." Cara swallowed and shook her head. "I can't even imagine. It was a terrible time. Especially for those who'd completed a blood-tie. That... that's something else."

"I don't understand," Lizzy said, frowning and shaking her head. "How? What makes a blood-tie so different?"

"It's..." Cara sighed and rubbed a hand over the back of her neck. "I don't know how to explain it, Lizzy. I've never done it, so I only know what we're taught but... It's supposed to tell you everything you need to know about each other, and it's permanent. I always imagined it was like telepathy, showing each other the deepest parts of yourself, connecting you together with an unbreakable bond..."

Lizzy shivered at the thought of being known on such a level but shook her head.

"That would take a deep dive," she explained, continuing when

Cara frowned. "Telepathy is only a light connection, just brushing the surface. Communicating thoughts and ideas active in your head in that moment. To know the inner parts of someone, we would have to do what's called a deep dive. It looks at memories, emotions, the core of what drives and motivates a person. If you stay too long in a deep dive it can form a permanent connection, but a telepathy master can unravel the bond. Deep dives are how the Court questions criminals."

And it might be what she and Booker would face on their return to Arbaon, Lizzy didn't add aloud. But she'd decided months ago that enduring a deep dive would be worth it if she could find answers about her mum.

"Lizzy... I—I know it's none of my business," Cara said, and Lizzy blinked, snapping out of her thoughts and glancing back at her friend. The vampire was still sitting on her bed, but her hands were twisting together nervously, and Lizzy frowned.

"What?"

"I don't know what prompted you to ask," Cara began, and Lizzy held her breath, "but you should know, he'd—Andric would never ask you for—"

"Andric?!" Lizzy gasped, spluttering as her eyes widened, and Cara stilled.

"If... if not Andric, then... who did you want to give blood—?"

"I didn't!" Lizzy exclaimed, panic fluttering through her stomach. "I was just curious—Andric?!" she repeated, but Cara's concern was being replaced with a slow-growing grin.

"Well, yes. Who else?" she asked, voice too innocent to be believed. "You spend hours on that training field. In close proximity. Arms wrapped around—"

"Cara," Lizzy growled, "you've been spending far too much time with Booker," she snarled, and Cara snickered.

"You say that, but all he did was point it out," she defended. "I started watching myself, and you're both awfully focused when you're around each other."

Lizzy pressed her lips together to bite back her response, but she couldn't deny it as fervently as she wanted to. Not as violently as she'd been able to the first time Booker had pointed it out.

"Even if Booker had a point," Lizzy forced out after a long pause, after she was certain she wouldn't give away more than she wanted to, "which he doesn't, I'm only here to find my mum," she said. "Then we'll be going back to Arbaon. So there's no point starting anything, with anyone..."

At Cara's stricken expression, Lizzy's voice trailed off. As she realised what she'd said, Lizzy bit back a curse, watching Cara duck her head and stare at her hands.

"It's not... I didn't mean..."

"No, it's fine," Cara said softly, and Lizzy shook her head.

"It's not. And I'm only speaking for me, here. I don't know what Booker wants, or plans—"

"But the fey don't commit, do you?" Cara said, shrugging one shoulder. "Love can kill you, so you just—"

"No," Lizzy cut in sharply. "Not love. It's a broken heart that can kill us. Most of us don't think it's worth the risk. And Booker... Booker's already experienced that loss once," she confided. "It'll take a lot to make him risk it again, but that doesn't mean he never will. Just—" She cut herself off.

Cara was watching her now, and the vampire shook her head. "What?"

Lizzy hesitated. Despite using their budding relationship to her advantage, she was unsure if she should encourage Cara any further. And she wasn't certain of how far to push Booker.

But it was so clear to her how well the two fit together. More importantly, she'd felt how much lighter Booker's mind had grown since meeting Cara, and she sighed.

"Just... be absolutely sure Booker is what you want. Who you want. If you change your mind, and he's already in too deep, you and I are going to have problems," she warned, and Cara sobered. Lizzy held her gaze and waited, but it only took a moment for Cara to offer her a nod, accepting Lizzy's quiet threat.

"We should go to dinner," Cara said, and Lizzy smiled at the peace offering, accepting it for what it was. "But you'll need to get dressed," Cara added, "unless you want to give Mia more fuel for the school's rumour mill."

In an instant, Lizzy's smile had vanished, and she rolled her eyes as she slid off her bed and stomped across the room to the wardrobe. "Well we can't give her even more gossip. She's overworking herself as it is," Lizzy muttered, digging through her clothes for something comfortable she could throw on for dinner, letting her lips curve into a small smile as Cara laughed behind her.

When it came time to return to Arbaon, Lizzy already knew she was going to miss Cara enough to hurt, and she felt a sharp pang of sorrow for the loss Booker would endure.

But, for now, they could enjoy each other's presence, and Lizzy couldn't convince herself it was a bad thing.

29

It was too quiet, Nameer had told Andric the night before, standing in the hunters' equipment room and peeling off weapons and armour so they could be serviced.

The forest. The animals. The hunters had seen signs of kavians but not encountered a single one.

Andric had been able to see the anxious tension on his friend's face but hadn't been able to offer the man any reassurances.

And now? Now Nameer's instincts had been proven correct. Too quiet. The calm before the storm.

Andric found himself striding through the halls of Speculo, trying not to fall into an urgent blur, and keeping a half-asleep Booker at his side as they headed towards Lizzy and Cara's room.

"Try and keep up," he forced out, voice rougher than he'd intended, but Booker didn't seem to take offence. The running Andric had spent the last two months putting the young man through was paying off now, and they moved through the halls and down a flight of stairs quickly.

He could see the questions on Booker's face as they passed groups of hunters, all of them armoured, all of them carrying weapons, but Andric couldn't explain. Not before they'd reached Lizzy, and not where someone could overhear.

He'd been foolish. Lax. He couldn't believe he hadn't noticed the signs—

He interrupted himself by knocking on the door to Lizzy's

room, hard and fast. He could see Booker lean against the opposite wall, yawning and folding his arms across his chest, as Andric shifted his weight impatiently.

"Come on, come on," Andric muttered, knocking again, louder; the firm thumps against the wood bordered on thunderous and, finally, he could hear scrambling movement on the other side.

It was Cara who answered, with sleep-mussed hair and confusion growing as she stared at them, but Andric's gaze immediately went over her head to lock on Lizzy, the fear curling around his heart eased a little at the sight of her.

She was only half-awake. Her blue eyes still glazed and the blankets pooled around her waist as she sat up, her legs sliding off the bed to rest against the floor.

"What's going on?" Cara hissed, clutching a dressing gown around her form, and Andric sucked in a sharp, bracing breath, before clenching his teeth.

"I can't say."

"I can hear boots... Are the hunters—?"

"I can't say," Andric ground out again, meeting Cara's eyes and watching the girl's concern grow as she snapped her jaw shut.

Even without the order from Walcott not to reveal the events of the night before the two fey had reached the headmaster's office, the last thing Andric wanted was to start a panic. While he was confident Cara could keep her head, he didn't know how many other ears might be listening, awakened by the heavy boots of the kavian hunters patrolling the halls.

"Miss Hail, the headmaster has requested you and Mister Reed in his office," Andric said. He glanced back at her and watched as she reacted with a slow blink, still sleep dazed.

"Right. Let me... let me get dressed," she called wearily, but Andric shook his head.

"No time. Throw on an overcoat and some shoes. But make it fast," he added, and Lizzy startled at the command, lifting her head and frowning, but before she could summon a response, Cara had nodded and shut the door.

The second she was out of Andric's sight, the fear began clawing at his mind again and he began pacing, the rhythmic fall of his feet against the carpet-covered stone helping him to stay focused, but he could feel Booker's sharp green gaze watching his movements.

If he listened, he could hear the two women moving around in the next room. He let the sounds reassure him and his movements smoothed out, becoming a soothing, regular beat.

"What does Walcott want in the middle of the afternoon, that couldn't wait until we woke up?" Booker muttered, leaning his head back against the wall, and Andric shot him a sharp look. It drew a scoff from the young man and he shoved his hands into the front pocket of the hoodie he'd thrown on after Andric had hammered on his bedroom door.

"Right. Yes. You can't say," the fey complained, and Andric's hands flexed in silent frustration where he had them clasped at the small of his back.

It was only a minute or two before Lizzy re-emerged from her room, but Andric still had to bite back an impatient "Finally" when she stepped into the hall.

She tugged the door to the room closed behind her, and he noticed she'd done as he instructed, only adding a light jacket and a pair of leather ankle boots to her pyjamas.

"Alright," she sighed, rubbing a hand over her face before dragging it through her mussed hair, "I'm here. What's going on?"

"Not here," Andric said, ignoring Booker's shrug in answer to Lizzy's question. "Walcott's office. I'll explain everything there. Now, stay close to me," he warned, turning to lead the way down the hall, "and keep up—"

"Andric!" Lizzy snapped, and he ground to a reluctant halt.

Glancing back at the pair, he watched Booker push off the

wall and sling a casual arm around Lizzy's shoulders. The motion didn't divert the young woman's attention, but it gave them a distinct impression of presenting a united front. Lizzy crossed her arms, glaring at him, her eyes spitting blue fire despite still being half-asleep, and Andric bit back a sigh.

Stubborn.

"Tell us what's going on," she demanded.

"I—"

"And if you say you can't, I swear..." Her voice trailed off, and she left her threat unfinished, but it still made guilt bubble up in his throat.

"The sooner you come with me, the sooner you can get your answers," he growled, but Booker's quietly drawled voice silenced him.

"You do remember you don't work for Walcott anymore, right?" Booker asked. The playful smile dancing around his lips replaced Andric's guilt with annoyance.

"What is your point?" he asked, frustration making his words short.

"My point is every single time we've set foot in his office, something's gone disastrously wrong. And from the look on your face, the third time isn't going to be the charm," Booker said. "You don't take orders from the headmaster, and while I can't speak for Lizzy, I'm not inclined to go running off to his office, with no reason or explanation, just because he demands it."

Andric blinked at Booker, before glancing down at Lizzy. She was watching Booker, frowning, arms still crossed, and Andric hoped her sleep-smothered mind, in desperate need of coffee, would simply encourage Booker to follow him to the headmaster without a fight.

But he knew her better than that by now and grimaced when her jaw clenched, and she leant into Booker's side more firmly.

"Booker's right," she said, and Andric loosed a quiet growl of frustration, but Lizzy wasn't done.

"Nothing good's come of us listening to the headmaster so far," she snapped. "Tell us what this is about, right now, or I'm going back to bed."

"Bloody hell," Andric groaned, fingers lacing against the back of his head as he turned away from them, glancing down the hall, considering his options. He could probably force one of them to Walcott's office, but not both. And he couldn't leave either of them undefended. Not now.

His mind raced ahead, mapping the familiar paths through the school. Considering weak points and defendable positions, before he scowled and turned back to the two fey.

"Compromise," he growled, lowering his hands from the back of his neck. "No Walcott, but we can't talk here either. We'll commandeer a student lounge. Now follow me. Quickly."

The orders were short and sharp, but to his relief the pair didn't argue, stepping forward in silent agreement with his swiftly negotiated middle ground. Andric led them through several corridors before he ushered the pair into one of the smaller rooms set aside for students to relax in.

There was a soft leather sofa before an empty fireplace and two matching, deep-seated armchairs at either end, with another two scattered around the room. The walls were solid, no windows for a surprise attack, and lined with books. Andric did a quick blur around the edges of the room. His boots made little to no sound against the thick rugs laid across the hardwood floors, and he checked the second door on the far side of the room, making sure it was locked before returning to Lizzy and Booker.

"Take a seat," he prompted, but while Booker let himself collapse into one of the deep leather armchairs, sprawling over it with one leg tossed over the arm, Lizzy refused. Crossing her arms, a frown of irritation marring her features, she stood beside the chair and glared up at Andric.

"Tell us what's going on!" she snarled, and Andric sighed, following it up with a deep, bracing breath before he spoke.

"A short while ago, a kavian was discovered on Speculo grounds—"

"What?"

"How?"

"Please," Andric said, holding his hands up and halting their questions, "let me finish. Standard protocols are in place for a kavian breaching the outer defences, but... but we weren't prepared for someone within Speculo to be a threat." He paused and shook his head. "Although, in hindsight, we should have been."

"Why does Walcott want to see us about this?" Booker asked, frowning up at Andric from where he was lounging across the armchair, one arm flung across his stomach and the other stretched languidly over the edge of the seat.

"Walcott's office is the most easily defendable room in the castle," Andric explained. "Having you two sequestered there is only logical with a kavian on the grounds."

"Fey blood calls to them, right?" Lizzy muttered, and Andric nodded.

"Exactly. But, also... I think he was planning to apologise."

"Apologise?" Lizzy repeated, openly startled, and he watched her share a confused glance with Booker.

"For putting you both in danger," Andric explained, his voice catching, and he had to swallow hard before he was able to force himself to continue. "For... for none of us noticing the signs, for not seeing the threat she was—"

"The threat who was?" Booker asked, his eyes narrowed, and Andric shook his head again.

"The vampire that turned kavian tonight was Hilda Gladstone."

30

The vampire that turned kavian tonight was Hilda Gladstone.

Shock flittered over Booker's face, and he sat up straight in the chair he'd sprawled over, but it was Lizzy's reaction to the news that concerned Andric. She went completely still, and he was fairly sure she'd stopped breathing.

"Some hunters on patrol heard growls emanating from her office," Andric explained, keeping his attention fixed on Lizzy as she stood staring straight ahead, her eyes unfocused. "But when they checked on her, they weren't expecting to encounter a kavian. It lunged for them, and they narrowly escaped serious injury. Especially in such close quarters."

Still nothing, although she did suck in a small, shuddering breath. Andric wished he could find it reassuring.

"She fled from her office, into the school. We're locking down dorms and guarding them. A majority of the hunters are sweeping the school room by room, but it's possible, probable, she scaled the outer walls and fled into the forest."

"Scaled the walls?" Booker repeated, voice strangled. "I thought you said the school was safe from kavians!"

"It is, from external attacks," Andric explained, "but we never anticipated one of our own... Not any more. Not now we know the cause. It's only the hunters that protect us inside the grounds."

"But why would Mistress Gladstone—?"

"She... she didn't—" Lizzy interrupted Booker, her voice hollow before she cut herself off. Her left hand lifted until her trembling fingers could curl around the pearl pendant. Her words lacked the usual thread of steel running through them, and the shakiness hovering there instead made Andric wince.

"She can't be—" Lizzy tried to deny it again, shaking her head as though the motion would help her make sense of what Andric had told them.

The urge to pull the woman into a hug made his hands itch until he clasped them together at the small of his back.

"I'm sorry, Lizzy," he said softly, but she flinched like he'd shouted, and Andric could feel himself crumble slightly at the reaction. "The hunters she attacked got a good look at her. Up close. Closer than they wanted to be. It was definitely Hilda."

Lizzy shook her head again. She released her hold on her necklace, dropping her hands to her sides as they curled into tight fists, and Andric braced himself... but the indignant fury never lit.

"She wouldn't have—" Lizzy's voice died again, but this time her eyes flicked up to meet his and Andric could read the myriad of swirling emotions in their blue depths.

Confusion. Anger. Hurt. Despair. The one that broke his heart was pleading hope. She wanted him to tell her the events of the night weren't real, and Andric couldn't do it.

"She wouldn't..."

"We'll never know the why," Andric said, keeping his tone gentle, "but she must have felt it was worth the risk. Consuming human blood doesn't infect us instantly, Lizzy. For some, it will only take one feeding, but some vampires can drink human blood for weeks, or months... only then, between one meal and the next, our minds snap beneath the pressure."

"But... but we were..." Her voice trailed off, and Andric sighed.

"I know you two were getting along well. You were close. It's why, I think, Walcott wants to apologise. Putting two fey into the path of a kavian... You're both lucky she didn't turn on you without warning."

They were all lucky she hadn't. In hindsight, Andric didn't know how a building full to the brim with hunters had missed all the signs. The constant rubbing or itching at her skin. The way she'd been drawn inexorably towards the fey. The greyness to her skin that, to Andric at least, had been put down to her age.

The guilt wouldn't stop plaguing him.

He'd missed the signs in his brother and he'd made exactly the same mistake with Hilda Gladstone. It had only been little more than a day since he'd allowed her to escort Lizzy back to the school alone. If her control had shattered only hours earlier... without warning... without Lizzy having any defence besides what little he'd managed to teach her... Andric shuddered at the thought and pushed the guilt away to deal with later.

"No. Wait," Lizzy breathed, pulling his attention back to her and Booker, "the kavians aren't rabid. We've encountered two now that haven't been. Raine and Alex. So it's possible Gladstone—"

"No. It's not."

Lizzy had looked so relieved at her potential solution, but the moment Andric had realised where her train of thought had led, regret took hold around his heart, knowing he would have to shatter those fragile hopes.

"What?" Lizzy asked, voice trembling, and Andric swallowed hard.

"It's not possible," he said, "even if we assume the two kavians you've encountered weren't flukes, Gladstone was a quintessentially rabid kavian. She had no restraint. No control—"

"She fled the school instead of killing those hunters!" Lizzy snapped.

"That's survival instinct. Nothing more. She was outnumbered. Even rabids have basic instincts for survival. Especially ones recently turned, they retain... shadows of their memory, and

Gladstone would have known that, being in the centre of Speculo, her best chance at survival was to run."

"So you're just going to give up on her?" Lizzy snarled, and Andric flinched. Gladstone had been one of his teachers, one of his mentors, for years, and her loss hurt, but he pressed his eyes closed and swallowed it down.

"I'm simply being realistic, Lizzy," he began, but the young woman scoffed and tossed her hair.

"Being realistic," Lizzy muttered. "You don't believe there're kavians out there who've retained their minds. You've made that perfectly clear!" she snapped.

"It doesn't matter if I believe it or not," Andric growled, struggling to keep control of his temper, "because it doesn't make them any less dangerous. In fact, it probably makes them more so!"

He paused, taking advantage of Lizzy's stunned silence to draw in a single, deep breath, hoping his next words would sound like a request instead of the order they were.

"Now, since neither of you seem willing to go and see Walcott, I need you to go back to your rooms while—Yes, Booker, you can join Lizzy and Cara," Andric said as the young man opened his mouth to speak, and Booker settled again, a grin dancing around the corners of his mouth. "The hunters will continue their sweep of the school building and grounds, but until then I want both of you shut up somewhere safe. Just in case."

"Gladstone wouldn't—"

"You're right," Andric growled, and he clenched his teeth as his fangs began to elongate in response to the worry and irritation rushing through him. He glared at Lizzy, frowning at her, silently pleading for her to understand the seriousness of the situation. "Hilda Gladstone wouldn't have hurt a hair on your head. The kavian that might be hiding somewhere in the school, on the other hand, would wrench back your head, tear out your throat, and drown themselves in your blood! Go back to your room, Lizzy, and stay there until the school's been cleared!"

Even as the words spilt over his tongue and across his lips, Andric knew his tone was too hard, too harsh, and her shell-shocked expression only reinforced that.

Booker was glaring at him, and Andric sighed, "Lizzy—"

"Don't," she hissed. "I don't want to hear it."

She spun on her heel and stalked over to the door, yanking it open and disappearing into the hall before Andric was able to shake himself out of his shock.

Her voice had been cold, her eyes like shards of ice. He was used to her temper being white-hot and burning out fast, but he'd never encountered the quiet rage she'd just displayed.

"Well, you made a complete compost heap out of that," Booker sighed, rising smoothly to his feet, and Andric shook himself out of his shock. Snapping his gaze around from the still-open door to settle on Booker, the fey let his hand settle on Andric's shoulder, and the look of sympathy on his face made Andric flush.

"I don't know what you're implying, Mister Reed, but—"

"Lizzy doesn't take orders, Andric," Booker said simply, cutting him off. "Not from anyone. She'll consider advice, suggestions, instruction, she'll even contemplate requests, but never an order."

"Damn it," Andric cursed, tilting his head back with a heavy sigh, and he could feel Booker's hand pat against his shoulder.

"How risky is it for her to wander the school right now?" Booker asked.

"Probably not as dangerous as I fear," Andric admitted after a momentary pause. "Gladstone could have tried to hide within the school. It's daylight, and kavians shy away from the light, but it's just as likely, if not more so, that her instincts told her to get as far from the building full of hunters as she could."

"And Speculo is crawling with hunters right now?" Booker

asked, prompting a nod from Andric. "So a cry for help...?"

"Would have aid to her side in moments," Andric finished, the tension finally falling away from his shoulders. He lowered his head to glance at Booker, and the young fey offered him a lopsided grin.

"I'd highly recommend apologising when you see her next," Booker added before turning to head out of the room, his hands slipping back into the pocket on the front of his hoodie. Andric matched his stride, turning Booker's words over in his mind.

"Why is she so against orders?" Andric asked. "I understand not every situation calls for them, but..."

"She's been told too often, by too many people, what she can and cannot do, Andric," Booker explained, shrugging one shoulder. "Lizzy's stubborn. To a fault."

They paused in the doorway to the student lounge, and Booker sighed, turning to gaze down the hall that would lead him back to Cara's rooms, but Andric kept his attention on Booker. He didn't sound like he'd finished, and after a moment, the fey grimaced.

"Neither you or I are going to be able to convince her to change her mind about something she believes to be true," Booker said calmly, "not without proof she can see with her own eyes. That's just who she is."

Booker smiled softly, "I can't speak about Caldwell, but the kavian the first night? The one you saved us from?" Booker turned to him and lifted an eyebrow. He paused, waiting until Andric nodded before adding, "She spoke, Andric. It was twisted. Most of it was nonsensical taunting... but it was clear, understandable speech.

"You might not be wrong about kavians... but neither is Lizzy," Booker added simply before heading off down the hall, not bothering to wait for Andric to recover from the shock of his words.

Booker had a point, Andric realised reluctantly as dread began uncoiling in the pit of his stomach.

He'd been so focused on being right. So sure he and the hunters knew everything there was to know about kavians, it hadn't occurred to him that Lizzy's experiences could be something new. He'd needed them to be false or flawed, or else everything he knew was a lie... but Booker had found the middle ground.

What if they were both right?

With a groan, Andric pressed his hands against his face as he considered Booker's words. He scrubbed his palms across his cheeks and let his fingers scratch through the scruff of a half-formed beard in desperate need of a trim as he turned the situation over in his mind.

But it didn't change anything. It would still be world-shattering to the hunters if kavians were beginning to evolve and regain some semblance of sanity, and on the flip side, it made the rabids no less dangerous.

Somehow, Andric had to get Lizzy to understand that. But first, he had an apology to make.

As he lowered his hands, with a final heavy sigh escaping him, he caught sight of a flash of red hair turning a corner at the end of the hall and frowned.

It had looked like Mia Harris, and he hesitated. The last thing he needed was the vampire spreading rumours and gossip across Speculo, but Andric decided she couldn't have overheard anything of importance and turned on his heel, letting her make her escape.

Enough hunters were patrolling the halls to escort her back to her room. Andric had more important things on his mind. Like explaining to Walcott why the two resident fey wouldn't be making an appearance in the headmaster's office.

31

Lizzy spent the afternoon walking the grounds.

She lost count of how many groups of hunters she passed. How many times they paused in their tracks, suspicion in their gaze, before they relaxed and moved on.

Lizzy didn't care. She was furious and keeping moving was the only thing stopping her telepathy from escaping her control.

There was a scream of pure frustration threatening to gather in the back of her throat, and she didn't know how to soothe it.

Gladstone had been her best hope of finding information about her mum. She'd been Lizzy's only hope of contacting the kavians.

And it was gone. All gone in the space of one afternoon, just because Andric wouldn't listen. Wouldn't help her track down Gladstone and see, just see, if the woman could be reasoned with.

But it wasn't Andric's fault. Not really. No matter how incensed she was at him for issuing orders like they were out on the training field.

It was Gladstone she was angry with. The woman had known Lizzy was relying on her. She didn't understand how the kindly old vampire could have risked their plans, risked everything, by consuming human blood. Not when she knew it was tainted, not knowing how it could affect her, even after only one dose.

And how many times had the woman consumed it? Was that afternoon the first, or had Gladstone been drinking it for some time?

The betrayal stung, but... but if Lizzy was being brutally honest with herself, she couldn't blame Gladstone either.

Replaying their conversations in her mind, Lizzy reached the gradual conclusion that Gladstone had to have been drinking human blood in an attempt to help.

It was the only thing that made sense.

They were supposed to meet the kavians in less than twenty-four hours, and for Gladstone's corruption, Lizzy blamed herself.

Hadn't it been Gladstone who asked her for a donation of fey blood?

Fey blood that was stronger and more potent than human blood?

Fey blood that wouldn't taint or corrupt, but fuel and power a vampire about to walk into a meeting with kavians?

She must have wanted it for herself and maybe if Lizzy hadn't hesitated, everything wouldn't have

As her mind continued to spin in circles, Lizzy found herself on the training field where Andric taught them to fight. She'd spent so many hours there over the last few weeks, she knew almost every dip in the dirt and every tuft of grass by heart, taking comfort in the familiarity.

Stepping up to one of the punching bags still hanging from a freestanding hook, Lizzy began to hit it. Moving through each of the blows Andric had taught them, losing herself in the motions that were, gradually, becoming second nature.

If only she hadn't hesitated.

Punch to the nose.

If only she'd believed Gladstone, that her blood was fey enough. magical enough.

Elbow to the jaw.

If only she hadn't taken so long to think it over. If only she'd gone and found the vampire sooner, and let Gladstone know what she'd decided.

Knee to the groin.

If only she hadn't planned to leave her decision to the last possible moment. If only she hadn't chosen to wait and tell Gladstone in her office before they left. If only she'd let the deputy headmistress take her blood in advance.

Foot to an imaginary shin.

If only. If only. If only. It ran around her head so many times it made her dizzy, and yet it changed absolutely nothing.

One more blow against the bag and Lizzy stumbled forward in surprise. The material gave way beneath her fist, splitting apart, and it took her a moment to notice the fine grains of sand spilling out over her arm, gathering in a heap beneath the bag.

Slowly, she pulled her hand back. Breathless, tired, muscles aching. With her body covered in sweat and her hair clinging to her face, Lizzy tried to brush the sand off her hand and arm, but it only spread further and clung more tightly to her skin.

It was all her fault.

She knew it without a shadow of a doubt, and now she had no way of making the meeting with Sethan Blackwood.

"Rot and termites," Lizzy hissed quietly into the evening light, the sun beginning to dip behind the treetops.

She pressed her eyes closed and forced down the sob building in her chest. It took half a dozen slow, deep breaths before she turned and made her way towards the student shower block to avoid running into Cara.

To wash away the sand, the sweat, and to give herself time alone to hide the tears against her cheeks that she refused to acknowledge.

When Lizzy slunk back to her room, in desperate need of clothes more substantial than her pyjamas, Lizzy half expected to be faced with at least Cara, and possibly Booker as well.

She was, admittedly, relieved to discover she was wrong.

Instead, she found a scrap of paper on her pillow—a note in Booker's familiar looping script—telling her they'd meet her at breakfast.

Her heart warmed, then went cold again and Lizzy shivered, biting her lip. She couldn't even tell Booker why she was so upset.

He'd been furious with her for even considering seeking out the kavians, and Lizzy knew her plans with Gladstone were a secret she'd never be able to tell him. It hurt almost more than the lost opportunity for finding her mum.

Putting the note back on her pillow, she turned away and moved around the space she shared with Cara, trying not to think about having a secret from Booker.

She'd never kept a secret from him, not for long, and the thought that this might forever be between them was enough to bring fresh tears to her eyes.

In her rush to distance herself from the emotions shooting shards of pain through her chest, Lizzy threw on some loose cotton trousers over the ankle boots she'd slung on that afternoon, and a long-sleeved shirt got tugged over her head as quickly as she could manage.

Lizzy fled the room in minutes, the light denim jacket hanging around her shoulders, and her hands roughly dragging her hair, still damp from her shower, into a high tail as the door clicked shut behind her.

She wouldn't let herself think about it, she decided firmly, pushing all thoughts of secrets and kavians from her head and heading towards the dining hall.

There's no reason to mention it, she reasoned as she moved through the quiet halls.

Most of the students hadn't woken yet, or staggered from their rooms for food or to prepare for classes, and Lizzy let the rare, peaceful atmosphere soothe her as she considered her new options.

Without Gladstone, there was no meeting with the kavians. Without the meeting, there was no reason to ever mention to Booker what her plans had been.

Instead, she would have to rely on whatever Walcott could dig up, and Lizzy pressed her lips together as her last remaining shred of hope sputtered and died.

"Well, well, well, don't you look a state," came Mia's sharp voice, and Lizzy sucked in a breath as her feet ground to a halt, almost against her will.

Ignore her. Ignore her. Ignore her, she chanted to herself, but Mia made it impossible, standing in the middle of the hall and blocking Lizzy's path.

As she watched, Kelsey and Blake took up positions on either side of Mia, a little behind her, both of them were sporting amused grins.

There was an air of excitement around them as they glanced between Lizzy and their illustrious leader that made Lizzy cautious, and she considered the trio carefully.

They outnumbered her, and despite Andric's lessons, she stood no chance against vampires with years of training.

She could try walking around them or back down from Mia's challenge, but as she considered her options, the most unnerving part about their blockade was that they did nothing. Mia seemed content to give her time to think, and Lizzy moistened her lips, growing nervous at the self-satisfied smirk on the vampire's lips.

Dismissing Kelsey and Blake as nothing more than Mia's backup, she let herself meet the other woman's hazel eyes and lifted her chin.

"I'd like to get to the dining hall in time to actually eat something, Mia. What do you want?" she said, trying for a growl but the events of the day were still wearing on her, and Lizzy's words escaped her as little more than a harsh mutter.

"Temper, temper," Mia scoffed, "I simply wanted to check on you. I couldn't help but notice you running off this afternoon—"

"Stalking, Mia?" Lizzy asked, crossing her arms, her suspicions about the encounter growing as Mia's smile widened and grew sharper.

"You seemed so very distressed," she all but purred, and Lizzy shifted her weight as Kelsey and Blake snickered. "Running from Hunter Roche like that. I assume he gave you the news about our dear deputy?"

"Ah and here it comes. Your obsession with—"

"We're not talking about me," Mia cut her off, the saccharine quality to her voice finally draining away sharply.

Lizzy grit her teeth, eyeing Kelsey and Blake again before continuing. "What, exactly, are we talking about?" she ground out. Mia's lips twitched up into a smirk, but there was nothing warm about it, and Lizzy could almost feel the biting cold radiate out like a physical thing.

"Why, Deputy Gladstone, of course," Mia said simply. "After all, you must have cultivated a... close relationship over the last few weeks."

"What makes you say that?" Lizzy asked, her hands curling into fists, the motion hidden from view beneath her still-folded arms.

"Why else was Hunter Roche informing you of her new status as a kavian in the middle of the afternoon, while the rest of the school was left to sleep?" she asked, the sharp smile returning to her lips, and Lizzy found herself swallowing hard at the predatory glint to the woman's gaze.

"Hilda Gladstone was ninety-three, you know. A hunter herself in her youth, before she became a teacher. I wonder. What new upheaval in her life could possibly have tempted her to consume human blood, after so many years of ironclad control?" Mia purred, and Lizzy froze.

A brief glance at Mia's friends, laughing to themselves, told Lizzy neither of them had picked up on their leader's implications, but it didn't stop Mia's unspoken accusation slicing through her.

My fault. My fault. My fault—

"I thought if anyone was gonna turn in this school, it'd be bloody Evelyn," Blake drawled out.

"What?" Lizzy breathed out, blinking out of her thoughts and trying to focus past the guilt roiling in her stomach. She couldn't trust any of the vampires before her. She needed to be on her guard, but she couldn't make herself focus.

"You didn't take my advice then?" Blake sneered, "Didn't ask her why she's got no friends here at Speculo?"

"It—"

"Who'd wanna be friends with the kavian spawn," Kelsey spat, cutting off Lizzy's defence of Cara and leaving her even more confused.

"What?" she repeated, frowning and glancing between Blake and Kelsey for an explanation, while Mia continued to stare at her, like a cat about to pounce on a mouse.

"Her parents turned kavian," Blake tossed out, shrugging one shoulder. "Both of them. At the same time. That kind of weakness? Could run in the blood. No one should want to be around that," he said, eyes trailing over Lizzy from head to toe. He shot her a grin, lips curling into a smirk, then added, "Especially not a fey."

"Maybe Cara will be next," Mia mused, taking a single step closer to Lizzy. "After all, lots of things seem to be going disastrously wrong around you, don't they?"

"You—you don't know what you're talking about..." Lizzy said, but there was no strength to her voice.

Her mum. Ending up at Speculo. No one believing her about the kavians, and now this... Gladstone's new condition ensuring Lizzy couldn't make the meeting with Blackwood.

Mia was right. Lizzy hated it, but she also had no defence, and her eyes dropped to the floor.

Like a wolf scenting fresh blood, Mia moved closer still, her voice dropping to a dangerous hiss.

"Do you know how a hunter kills a kavian? They have to bleed them out. Drain the human blood from their system so they can't heal. It's a rather gorey affair. And now the hunters will have to track down Gladstone, and tear her apart, or slice up her throat, until she's nothing but froth and bile upon the forest floor."

Mia's words summoned Lizzy's memory of Raine Caldwell, the kavian Andric had saved her and Booker from on their first night in the mortal realm, and she shuddered before something in Mia's words caught her attention, and her head snapped up.

"Track her down?" she asked, "They didn't find her in the school?"

"No," Kelsey chimed in, "she must have braved the sun. Escaped the grounds, and taken shelter in the forest. How she got past the hunters on the walls as a mindless beast, I'll never—"

"So she's still alive," Lizzy breathed, hope sparking through her as Mia scowled.

"Not for long," she snapped, "her demise is now inevitable, so why don't you crawl back into whatever hollowed out tree you escaped from and—"

"How did she get past the hunters on guard duty?" Lizzy asked, cutting Mia off, but she ignored the growing fury on the redhead's face and focused on Kelsey instead.

"Why?" Blake asked, voice suspicious, but Kelsey didn't appear to have the same reservations and snorted inelegantly at Lizzy's question.

"Sheer luck, most likely. The majority of the hunters scouring the school, means there were less manning the perimeter. That's my guess. Now, of course, most of them are out in the woods looking for her."

"Which means the walls are still only being patrolled by a skeleton team," Lizzy muttered, breath caught in her throat as she fought not to let hope take hold. If Gladstone had escaped, and she was still alive, Lizzy still had a chance—a small chance—of making her meeting with Sethan Blackwood.

"And I thought you couldn't possibly get any more stupid," Mia sneered, and Lizzy snapped out of her thoughts, shooting the vampire a scowl. "That's a kavian out there," Mia continued, crossing her arms, "she'd tear you to pieces as soon as look at you. And even if that wasn't the case, you'd need wings to scale those walls, and we both know that's something you're sorely lacking.

"The only way out of the school for the likes of you is through the front gate, so do me a favour. Go and tell Walcott you want to go home, and stop leaving a trail of trouble in your wake!" Mia spat before turning on her heel and stalking off down the hall, only waiting until Kelsey and Blake were following before she blurred away, her two friends copying her motions a moment later.

Despite Mia's words, Lizzy wasn't stupid. But she was desperate.

She considered going to Booker, or Andric. Even Cara. But as she stood in the quiet hall, frozen and alone, she imagined their reactions. She imagined telling them how she wanted to go after Gladstone to find out if she'd kept hold of her mind. To find out how the woman had scaled the walls without being caught if she was truly insane.

Booker would be angry with her. He wouldn't want her to take the risk.

Andric would forbid it. Probably suggest speaking to the other hunters, or he might go straight to Walcott.

And Cara... Cara might be willing to listen, but she wouldn't keep it from Andric, and she definitely wouldn't keep it from Booker.

If this was Lizzy's only chance, she couldn't risk any of them stopping her.

Seconds later, she turned and began making her way towards the front gates.

Lizzy reasoned she had until the end of breakfast to find a way out of the school before Booker began to worry, and she was determined to make the most of every last second.

Lizzy hadn't exactly run to the front doors of Speculo, but she had allowed herself to move at something close to a jog.

The grounds were dark, the moon had not yet risen above the tree line, but there were lamps powered by the strange electric energy common in the mortal realm, and Lizzy used their intermittent pools of light to guide her.

She didn't head for the front gates but aimed instead for the thick stone battlements encircling the outer edges of the castle grounds.

The wall had been a looming shadow over her time at Speculo, always hovering in her peripheral. It kept the vampires safe from the threats outside, but to Lizzy, it was a reminder she'd agreed to stay put for three months.

To stagnate and let whatever little remained of her mum's trail go cold.

The further she got from the castle, the fewer lamps there were to light the way and the darker the night became.

It turned the almost sixty-foot-high outer wall into a formless shadow as it rose before her, with an ominous aura she struggled to ignore. It separated her from her goals, and from an escape, but she continued to move closer until her hands pressed against the icy stone.

Ancient, weathered, and yet still rough against her palms, Lizzy stared up at the last barrier between her and the forest surrounding the school in surprise.

It hummed with fey magic. The ward was old. Worn, and weak, but still there beneath her hands, and she suddenly realised why Andric was so certain the kavians couldn't gain entrance to the school.

And why the hunters had risked vacating their posts on the wall.

She'd seen the guard towers scattered along its length when Andric had first driven them up to the school, but if Kelsey's mindless babble could be believed, they were practically abandoned right now.

The hunters were trusting in the magic still running through the stones, while they moved through the forest, trying to follow Gladstone's trail.

If she wanted to do the same, or contact Blackwood, fleeing Speculo now was her best chance.

She turned, and with one hand trailing along the cold, dew-dampened wall, Lizzy began to follow the line of stone around the school. She stuck to the deep shadow it cast across the ground and watched as best she could for any flaws or weaknesses she could make use of.

It was only as the barrier began to curve, leading her back towards the front of the school, that her fragile hopes crumbled.

As much as she hated to admit it, Mia had been right. To scale the walls of Speculo, Lizzy would have needed the wings of the fey.

She stilled as the stone beneath her palm changed from smooth to something ragged, then turned her head, her eyes wide.

Or be a kavian, powered up on human blood, she thought as she stared at the deep gouges torn deep into the rock.

There was a guard post almost directly above her. The dim glow from the outpost's electric lanterns barely gave her enough light to make out the chunks of stone scattered across the grass at her feet, but Lizzy could also feel the hum of the wards as they gave a dangerous quiver.

She found herself swallowing nervously. The sheer strength Gladstone would have needed to exert to sink clawed fingers into the stonework and scramble sixty feet straight up, moving fast enough so the hunters didn't catch her, made Lizzy's head spin.

Stepping closer, she ran both hands down the wall, her fingers dipping into the deep grooves with a mixture of fascination and horror.

She half expected a shout to echo down from the top of the wall at any moment. A hunter warning her away, but nothing cut through the evening air.

Even with the school on high alert, Lizzy hadn't seen a single kavian hunter on patrol, and she had to shove aside a flash of bitter disappointment that she couldn't flutter a set of wings and drift over the wall to freedom.

Resigning herself to the fact that scaling the walls was outside her abilities, Lizzy turned sharply. She shivered as the ends of her damp ponytail brushed against the base of her neck, chilled from the night air, but ignored the discomfort as she began tromping across the grass towards the front gates.

She didn't want to run and draw attention to herself, but Lizzy was also hyper-aware that when she didn't show up for breakfast, Booker would likely begin searching for her.

And she'd wasted too much time already investigating the walls.

She was preoccupied, trying to come up with a believable excuse for her absence, when a hunter blurred into her path. Lizzy came to a startled stop, sucking in a sharp breath as her feet ground to a halt.

"You shouldn't be out on the grounds," he said simply. Her surprise had eased the frown from his face, and his tone was light, but the implications set her temper flaring.

"Oh?" she growled, "And where should I be?"

The young hunter didn't look any older than herself and seemed surprised by the question, blinking at her in stunned silence.

"Uh, at... breakfast?" he half asked as a second hunter blurred into existence behind him.

"No one should be wandering the grounds right now," the second hunter said with a scowl, her hands moving to hover over the daggers hanging from her hips.

"I'm not a prisoner," Lizzy snarled, crossing her arms as her heart began to pound. She'd spent so many hours with Andric, she'd almost forgotten the hunters of Speculo could also pose a threat.

"Evans! Fernsby! Stand down!" called a new voice, and Lizzy watched as the two hunters that had blocked her path immediately relaxed. Their hands fell from their weapons to clasp against the small of their back as a third hunter approached, jogging towards them all at a normal, human-like speed.

He wasn't quite as tall as Andric, but he still stood a full head above her, with a mop of loose curls that fell into his eyes, and Lizzy's anger was smothered by confusion when she got the distinct impression she recognised him from somewhere.

It wasn't until he shot her a bright, lopsided grin she was able to place him as the hunter who had been guarding the front gates when Andric had first driven them into Speculo.

"I apologise for these two," he offered, pointing with his thumb and slowing to a walk as he drew level with the other hunters. "They're a little... overeager, shall we say."

"Hunter Khatri—" the woman began, and Lizzy startled at the name.

She recognised it as belonging to Andric's friend, but as she turned her attention back to him, he cut off the other hunter and his lighthearted grin melted away.

"The young lady is correct, Hunter Evans," he scolded, "no one within the walls of Speculo is a prisoner. They should not be treated as such."

"But it's safer—"

"The kavian is not on the grounds," Khatri interrupted her again, his warm mahogany-brown eyes narrowed, and Lizzy watched the woman's frame wither in response before Khatri continued, his voice growing softer.

"The kavian is not on the grounds," he repeated, "and so it is no safer within the heart of the castle, than it is right here by the front gates."

There was a beat of silence, where Khatri raised an eyebrow and the woman, Evans, pressed her lips together tightly. Lizzy almost held her breath, but then Evans backed down, her shoulders slumping further as she dropped her gaze.

"Yes, sir."

"Hmm," he hummed, jerking his chin up and towards the school. "Go on ahead," he instructed, "the next watch should be along shortly, and I can catch up with you when they arrive."

"But-but, sir. Shouldn't we...? I mean—" the young hunter spluttered, stumbling over his words, and Lizzy tensed as Khatri approached her, placing one warm hand against her shoulder as his bright grin returned.

"Hunter Fernsby, this young lady is a fey," he explained calmly, and Lizzy blinked up at him in surprise as the young hunter glanced between them both, looking anxious. "The next shift for gate duty shouldn't be too long now, and in the meantime I do not think one fey is cause for concern."

Lizzy's curiosity about the man vanished. She grit her teeth, shooting Khatri a sharp glare, but he surprised her with a grin and a wink in response, throwing her instantly off balance. Unsure what to expect from the strangely cheerful hunter.

Hunter Evans pulled her hands out from their position at the small of her back and cuffed her younger partner around the back of the head. It was a light tap, but Fernsby flinched anyway, although Lizzy suspected it was more from surprise than anything else.

"Don't argue with your superiors, Hunter Fernsby," she scolded, flushing bright red as Khatri snickered beside Lizzy, his hand still resting against her shoulder.

"Yes, ma'am," Fernsby said, ducking his head, and Evans rolled her eyes.

"With me, Hunter Fernsby," she ordered before blurring away without waiting for him to respond. Seconds later, he'd followed her order, and Lizzy found herself standing within reach of the school gates.

And only one vampire between her and her escape.

"Nameer Khatri," the hunter said, finally dropping his hand from her shoulder and holding it out for her to shake instead.

Lizzy stared at it before lifting her gaze to glare at the vampire.

"Are you sure you'd like to shake my hand?" she growled. "After all, I'm only fey. I might shatter."

Lizzy didn't know what she'd expected but it wasn't for Khatri to break into delighted laughter, his head tipped back and curls shaking.

"Oh, you are an absolute joy!" he announced, and Lizzy was surprised she couldn't hear a hint of sarcasm in his words. "But you are also correct. I owe you an apology. I'm very well aware that Andric has been teaching you and your friend how to fight."

His grin was open, his expression full of harmless mischief, and Lizzy found herself utterly disarmed. Her irritation dissipated as he continued, despite her best efforts to cling onto it.

"I've been waiting weeks to introduce myself to you, Lizzy Hail, and I didn't want Evans and Fernsby loitering around. The best way to ensure they moved along was to make you appear harmless."

"Fey aren't exactly... known for their ability to fight," she conceded, taking hold of the hand still outstretched towards her. "I'm Lizzy."

"Oh, I know," Nameer said with a grin. "It's wonderful to finally be able to recognise a person behind all the stories Andric's been telling," he said, bringing up his other hand to wrap around the back of hers. Not shaking her hand, so much as grasping it warmly between both of his, and Lizzy blinked, surprised by him once again.

"Stories?" she asked before shaking her head and frowning. "And, I'm sorry, but did you say you've been... waiting to meet me?" she continued. "Why?"

"Ah, well, that would be our dear Andric's doing," the hunter said, finally releasing her and sliding his hands into the back pockets of his leather trousers. It left his elbows bent and shoulders hunched, but somehow the vampire still looked relaxed as he grinned at her.

"He's been determined to keep me out of your path. Yours and Mister Reeds, but mostly yours."

"Why?" Lizzy asked again, suspicions rising as her mind supplied any number of reasons Andric wouldn't want her to meet this specific vampire. If Khatri noticed her wariness, he paid it no mind and broke out into soft snickers instead.

"Because I've been friends with the man forever, and he knows I delight in embarrassing him," Khatri said, and Lizzy couldn't smother a soft huff of amusement.

"I didn't think he was capable of being embarrassed," she muttered, tone sharper than she'd intended and she fell silent as Khatri sobered, shooting her a look of sharp consideration.

"Andric keeps his emotions close to his chest," he confided after a brief, tense silence. "You will rarely catch him flushing or stuttering, or clenching his fists in anger. Those kinds of reactions, he considers them mistakes that reveal far too much. You must read his words instead."

Lizzy frowned and found herself tilting her head as she considered what Khatri had revealed.

"Like, when he'll suddenly revert to calling me Miss Hail?" she asked, and Khatri's broad grin reappeared.

"Exactly like that."

"I hadn't noticed him being all that reserved, actually," Lizzy muttered as she remembered the way he'd snapped at her, ordering her back to her room.

At her words, Khatri sighed, and his features softened into something sad.

"He is not incapable of strong emotions, Lizzy," he explained, voice quiet, as though confiding a secret. "And when you see them, those are moments of overpowering emotion slipping through his ironclad control."

There was a weight to his words she didn't know what to make of, and Lizzy crossed her arms when he paused, studying her with an intensity that made her nervous.

"And that is why I wished to speak with you," Nameer continued. "I have never known him so consistently rattled by a person, before he met you."

"W-what?"

The single-word question slipped out of her mouth without permission from her stunned mind, and Lizzy felt her frame freeze as emotions exploded through her.

Surprise over Nameer's evaluation. Horror that she'd prompted him to continue with her question. Something light and fluttering in her stomach she refused to name. Irritation, when the vampire's face remained alight with unmasked amusement at her reaction.

"As his friend, aren't you supposed to keep his confidence," Lizzy snapped, "not spill his secrets to the first person who wanders past?"

"If I thought the idiot might actually do something about it, certainly," Nameer said with a shrug, appearing unbothered by her outburst. "Or if I believed that he would let slip enough for you to figure it out, I may have held my silence. But I'm a romantic at heart, so I'm not about to let him sabotage the possibility of something between the two of you, simply because he's stubborn."

Nameer skimmed his gaze over her briefly, his grin turning mischievous again in a second. "From what I hear of Andric's moaning, you're rather stubborn yourself," he teased, and Lizzy found herself flushing.

Turning away from him sharply, her mind awhirl, Lizzy found her attention settling on the gates of the school once more as she struggled to find her footing amongst the strange turns the conversation with Khatri had taken.

It was like a blast of icy air to the face, reminding her of what she'd come out onto the grounds for in the first place, and Lizzy had to swallow hard around the sudden lump in her throat.

"I'm here to find my mum," she whispered, "nothing more."

She repeated the same excuse to Nameer that she'd given to Cara, only the more times Lizzy was forced to repeat it, the more hollow it sounded.

"Ah," Nameer sighed, but Lizzy didn't let herself turn back to him, keeping her gaze fixed on the gates. "So that is why you're here."

That drew her attention, and as her head snapped around, she could feel her ponytail swing, brushing against her neck.

"You didn't know?" she asked, unable to stop the surprise colouring her voice, and Nameer shook his head, lips quirked up into a half smile.

"I... I guess I'd assumed Andric would have mentioned it," Lizzy said, frowning.

"Andric said nothing. He is under contract with you," Nameer said, shrugging, "and he takes his commitments seriously. Professional, or personal."

"Look," Lizzy sighed, "I don't know what you're trying to—"

"I'm not trying to do anything," he reassured gently, but his gaze was sharp as he continued to watch her. "If you have no interest in my friend, then you do not. It is that simple."

Nameer paused before he grinned at her again, the smile just as bright as the first time. "But having said that, you made no attempt at denying an interest," he teased. "In fact, your only reaction was to mention your other plans. I cannot say this doesn't give me hope."

Lizzy stared at him in silence. Her eyes widened, her lips parted on words his observations had silenced, and her heart was hammering in her chest hard enough to be almost painful.

"I-I don't—"

She tore her gaze away from Nameer and let it skitter across the ground. Releasing a shaky breath, she lifted her pearl pendant to brush across her bottom lip.

Booker had let the matter drop. Even Cara had backed down. But this hunter, who she'd never spoken to before, had cut her excuses off at the knees, and she didn't know what to say.

Her eyes settled on the gate again. She didn't know how long they'd been speaking but Nameer had mentioned another patrol was coming, and Lizzy shook her head sharply, brushing aside the whirling thoughts of Andric Roche.

"I don't have time for this," she breathed, bracing herself and turning back to the hunter.

He was frowning in response to her words, disappointed even as his expression began to shift into something almost apologetic, but Lizzy didn't wait for him to respond.

"I'm really sorry," she muttered, dropping her pendant and grimacing as she brought her telekinesis to bear.

She wrapped her power around Nameer as fast as she dared. Curling around him from jaw to shoulders. Guilt bubbled up her throat as shock flickered across his features, and he pulled his hands free from his pockets.

He was fast, but not fast enough. She held him firm.

The worst part was he seemed nice. Genuinely kind. But this was her only chance, and Lizzy wasn't going to waste it.

"I just need time," she breathed. "I'm... I don't have another choice. I'm sorry."

"Lizzy—"

With a violent twist of her mind, she spun her power in opposite directions. It twisted his head one way, and his body in the other, snapping the vampire's neck with a sickening crack.

She released her power, letting it dissipate, and Nameer's body dropped to the grass like a bird with broken wings. Lizzy's hands slammed up against her mouth as she staggered back from him.

Bile rose in her throat, and she gagged at what she'd just done, but there was no reversing it. She couldn't take back the action and refused to let herself waste the opportunity it presented.

He'll be fine, she reassured herself. He wasn't bleeding. He would heal. Andric had explained vampire healing capabilities only a few days ago.

The reassurance did nothing to lessen the roiling of her stomach, but Lizzy forced herself to turn her back on Nameer's body and head directly for the gates, without looking back.

The longer she was missing from the school, the more likely someone was already searching for her. Lizzy knew leaving the grounds was dangerous, but if she had any hope of finding Gladstone, or meeting with Sethan Blackwood, this was an opportunity she had to take.

Stepping through the tall, unlocked gates of the school, Lizzy found herself on the road leading down to Hockley and hesitated. The first place they would look would be the road, and a car would be able to overtake her easily.

She glanced left and right instead. Tall, thick trees surrounded the school, and the road that led to it, on all sides. Lizzy studied the deep shadows coating the forest floor, and considered her options.

It was riskier...

More dangerous...

But the forest was also her best chance, and with a single bracing breath, Lizzy began to run.

33

Andric leaned against the wall outside of Lizzy and Booker's finance classroom and rolled his neck. The muscles ached down into his shoulders, stiff with tension, and he groaned under his breath.

It was almost enough to make him wish he'd reconsidered informing Walcott about the fey's refusal to follow him to the headmaster's office. A moment later, he grimaced and pushed the budding regret from his mind.

No. Making the council official come looking for me would have been worse, he decided silently.

Still, walking into Walcott's office and being immediately questioned about the legality of his presence on Speculo grounds hadn't been how Andric had wanted to spend his evening.

With a kavian emerging within the school, the involvement of the Council was unavoidable, but he hadn't expected a representative to arrive within the day. It hadn't been until the weaselly little man was halfway through a highly personal interrogation that Andric remembered Mia's warning.

Officer Wilson had already been on his way to Speculo.

It was just their terrible luck he'd arrived in the middle of a school-wide sweep for a rabid. Andric walking into Walcott's office, when he should have been on official leave from the school, had sapped the officer's already precarious patience.

Andric's interrogation had taken hours, and he'd missed

breakfast, but while Officer Wilson had, reluctantly, cleared Andric of any wrongdoing, the bureaucratic idiot had announced his intention to stick around and investigate how a budding kavian had escaped the notice of an entire battalion of hunters.

Andric sighed and shifted his weight.

Not being within the school in an official capacity, he was escaping that particular council probe by the skin of his teeth. Still, the accusations the smarmy little pencil pusher was sure to fling around made Andric's skin crawl.

When he'd arrived, with only twenty minutes remaining of the class, Andric decided to settle against the wall outside and wait for the fey to emerge. But as the minutes ticked by, and he became more aware of the tension in his neck and shoulders from his encounter with the council officer, the more he wished he'd slipped into the back of the class and commandeered a seat.

His gut told him it was going to be a particularly long night. Especially after the way he'd snapped at Lizzy that afternoon—

Before Andric could get too lost in his thoughts, the bell rang across the school, signalling the end of the lesson, and he straightened up, tucking his hands against the small of his back and focussing his attention on the door, waiting for the now-familiar features of either Lizzy or Booker.

He spotted Cara first, Booker right at her side, his hand clasped in hers. Cara leant up, whispering something he couldn't make out over the crowd of vampires filling the hall, and Booker's eyes snapped over to Andric's.

An instant later, he was pushing against the flow of students and heading for Andric.

That was Andric's first clue something was wrong.

While his relationship with the two fey had drastically improved over the last two months, neither Booker or Lizzy paid his shadowing of them much attention. Certainly, neither of them had ever gone out of their way to approach him between classes, and Andric frowned.

"What is it?" he asked, stepping closer to Booker as the fey and Cara broke free of the flood of students.

"Have you seen Lizzy?" Booker asked, and instantly, Andric began scanning the crowded hall again for her familiar form and electric-blue eyes.

"No," he said slowly, and he heard Booker huff out a frustrated sigh.

"She never showed up for breakfast. I wasn't worried at the time, but then she missed maths class. I couldn't find you anywhere, but I was hoping she'd be here in finance."

"Nothing?" Andric asked, concern beginning to settle into his mind as Booker and Cara both shook their heads.

"I've not seen her since you woke us up this afternoon," Cara said softly, and Booker's arm found its way around her shoulders.

"Same," Booker agreed. "No sign of her since you two argued," he added, nodding at Andric.

"And you can't sense her?"

"No. We haven't... she's been keeping me out since Walcott's office," Booker admitted, grimacing. "I've no idea where she is, but no one's seen her for nearly eight hours now. I'm worried."

So was Andric, but he didn't let it show on his face. He saw no need to concern Booker even further.

A soft, familiar scoff came from behind him, drawing his attention, and Andric found himself smothering a growl as he turned on Mia Harris.

"Miss Harris, if you have something to add, please speak up. Otherwise, it might be prudent for you not to eavesdrop on private conversations," he said sharply, barely controlling the growl in his voice.

He expected a sharp comment to be flung back at him. Or maybe an overly sickly flirt, but instead, Mia hesitated, her eyes flicking over Booker and Cara, and Andric was instantly suspicious.

"What do you know?" he demanded, and Mia blinked, pulling her focus back to him as her lips pressed together.

"Nothing of importance," she said finally. "I encountered Miss Hail at breakfast—"

"She didn't come to breakfast," Booker growled, and Mia's lip curled slightly.

"Fine. Outside the breakfast hall, if you want me to be specific."

"I'd like you to be very specific, Miss Harris," Andric said slowly, and the woman's features fell. She glanced away, forcing a soft sigh through her nose before returning her attention to Andric, but he noticed her fingers were stroking anxiously over the strap of her bag.

"It was near the beginning of the breakfast shift, about two corridors over from the dining hall. The last time I saw the girl, she was still facing in the correct direction to be heading there," Mia said, voice short and sharp, but Andric growled.

"Facing in the direction of. So she was stopped?"

"We had words," Mia admitted reluctantly, "but it was nothing—"

"About what?"

"Andric," Mia growled, "I don't appreciate being interrogated—"

"Miss Harris. What did you and Lizzy discuss?" Andric demanded. He knew this would cause trouble. If Lizzy was merely hiding out in a classroom somewhere, Mia would make the girl's life a living hell for the interrogation he was putting her through, but if she wasn't... If Lizzy was actually missing...

Mia Harris holding a grudge was a price he would pay.

"Fine," Mia hissed, fingers clenching around her bag, her teeth grinding together. "She was asking about how a kavian might escape the school. Kelsey pointed out it must have been lucky, to avoid the hunter patrols. Even with as sparse as they've been."

"She was asking how to get out of the school?" Booker

breathed, and Andric's heart sank to settle somewhere in the pit of his stomach.

"Not that it matters," Mia snapped, rolling her eyes. "As I told her, she'd need wings to get over the walls, and it's not like the girl's a proper fey. The only way out is through the front gate—"

"You told her how to get out..." Booker repeated weakly. There was laughter in his voice, but it was bordering on hysterical, and Andric could sympathise.

"No—it's not like—it doesn't matter!" Mia spluttered. "She can't fly over the walls, and the front gates are guarded! It's not like I helped her sneak through a gap in the defences or anything!"

Booker's light laughter was still a touch too close to hysterical, and Andric was struggling not to panic.

"You're right," he said slowly, not sure he could trust his voice not to waver. "There's no telling where Miss Hail is right now, and at least we know she was seen four and a half hours ago, instead of the previously suspected eight. That almost halves the potential time she's been missing for. Thank you," he forced out, and Mia settled in response, sighing as she shook her head.

"That girl is more trouble than she's worth," Mia muttered before turning to Booker. "Perhaps it's beyond time the pair of you return to Arbaon?" she suggested, but before Andric's growl of irritation could escape, or Booker had a chance to respond, they were interrupted.

"Andric!"

Nameer's voice had him reacting instantly, tearing his attention away from Mia as he spun on his friend with a frown.

"Nameer?" he asked, scanning over the other man's face for answers. There was worry there, and a splash of fear. More than enough to make Andric break out into a cold sweat.

"Tell me," he demanded. His voice was sharp, and although Nameer huffed a soft laugh, it lacked his usual levity.

"You're teaching these fey too well, my friend," he said, and

Andric felt his fingers begin curling into fists, shifting his hands to the small of his back to hide the motion.

"Tell me," he repeated himself, almost pleading as his voice softened, and Nameer's hand fell to his shoulder.

"It was my error," he said. "I was speaking to your Miss Hail at the front gate. Sent my team on ahead so that I could talk with her privately. I underestimated her."

"Nameer, please," Andric begged, wincing. He didn't want the man to say what Andric suspected was about to pass his lips, but Nameer grimaced and his heart sank.

"She's left the school. Snapped my neck. Smart girl, that one," Nameer complimented, and Andric's stomach churned. He didn't wait for more information, moving to step past Nameer, but his friend hooked a hand around his arm, tugging him to a stop.

"Andric, you will have to blur. She has too much time on you—"

"So let's not allow her to get any further ahead," Andric growled, and Nameer only paused for a second.

"Very well. I will inform Headmaster Walc—"

"No," Andric cut in, shaking his head, "you can't."

"We cannot keep this a secret—"

"Not from Walcott, no," Andric agreed, grimacing, "but he's not alone. There's a council officer at the school investigating Gladstone's turning."

"Shit," Nameer muttered, but it was Mia who caught Andric's attention once more, resignation settling across her features.

"I can distract the official," she offered, and Andric saw Nameer's eyebrows raise in surprise.

"Why would you help us?" Booker snapped, and Cara placed a hand against his arm.

"Well none of you can do it," Mia sneered, "and as much as I dislike the irritating little upstart, I don't want to see her dead either," she added before turning to Andric.

"With my parents' connections within the Council, any

low-level bureaucratic pencil pusher will be fawning all over me for my good opinion. I can keep him busy long enough for Hunter Khatri to speak with the headmaster," she promised.

Every instinct in him was urging Andric to accept and leave. The sun had set hours ago, and there were kavians in the forest. It would only take one brush against a thorny bush and Lizzy would be tracked and torn apart before he could reach her, and the fear was making his heart slam against his chest.

But he couldn't allow Mia to proceed with the kind of deception she was offering, without clearing up the young woman's expectations.

"Miss Harris," he started, hesitating for a moment before he shook his head. "I'm afraid you've been functioning under some misapprehensions—"

"Oh, please," Mia scoffed, tossing her long, red hair in a manner that told Andric she was more upset than she had any intention of showing. "You are wasting valuable time, Hunter Roche," she said, voice sharp. "I suggest you move quickly."

Despite the sharp edge to her words, Andric caught the tremble around her lips and the hard swallow she gave, and offered the young woman a smile and a nod of thanks.

He turned to Nameer, already finding his friend holding out a spare set of blades that Andric took without question.

"Look after them?" Andric requested, nodding at Booker and Cara.

Nameer grinned, nodding. "Of course. As if they were my own wards."

A final nod was all the time Andric spared the group, turning and immediately stepping into a blur.

The hallways turned to grass, and the grass to the walls of the school, and beyond the walls a road and a forest.

He stepped out onto the tarmac and paused.

Four hours lead time, and Andric could feel his insides shake with fear.

She might already be dead.

Andric shut that thought down quickly. He wouldn't let himself even contemplate the loss before he had empirical proof before him, and taking a deep breath, he considered his options. Left, right, or straight ahead.

He had no idea what Lizzy was looking for, except possibly Hilda Gladstone, but that didn't help him choose a direction.

The road was unlikely, but that only narrowed his search area down to the rest of the bloody forest, so he forced himself to focus. He stopped and closed his eyes. Let his hands hang loosely at his sides and bowed his head.

His heart was hammering in his ears. Panic coated his throat and fear was a bitter tang against his tongue, but Andric concentrated on taking deep breaths. He calmed far slower than he would like, but there was no rushing the process of sinking into his senses.

Like flipping a light switch, everything sharpened.

The ruffle of feathers from some kind of nocturnal bird. The light breeze rustling through bendy, spring-fresh branches in the trees above his head. The soft snuffling of small animals in the underbrush to his right. Andric tilted his head, concentrating his attention away from the abundance of nature.

The crispness of rain was sharp in his nose, but the ground was dry and Andric frowned, taking a slow step to his left and breathing deeply. There would be no trace of her scent after four hours, but instinct made him move towards the edge of the road, stepping into the fringes of the forest as he carefully let his eyes slide open.

The forest was alight with colour. Every curl of a tree root, or tangled knot of climbing ivy, stood out in sharp relief despite the night's shadows, and it took Andric mere moments to track the source of the moisture in the air.

His vision, sharpened by the blood in his system, honed in on the crushed moss, watching the trembling droplets of water that had been squeezed out of its sponge-like structure for a second before he looked further. One pace further on from the crushed moss, breath caught in his throat, and—

Yes!

Another footprint.

The moisture clinging to her shoe had left tiny impressions against the forest floor. They were so small, and without the acuity of his blood-powered vampiric senses, Andric was certain he'd never have found her tracks.

It was a tiny trace, but it was enough, and he moved forward as fast as he dared, unwilling to risk losing her trail.

As he advanced deeper into the forest, Andric kept a constant eye out for kavians, straining his ears for any sign of a rabid.

And with every blurred step through the underbrush, he pleaded with any higher power willing to listen that he wasn't already too late.

She was being tracked.

Lizzy didn't know how she knew, but she was sure.

It could have been just in her head. She'd been walking for hours and the chances of Booker not having alerted someone to her disappearance by now were close to zero. But it didn't feel like it.

It didn't feel like the distant knowledge that someone *should* be looking for her. It felt like someone was shadowing her footsteps, breathing down the back of her neck, and Lizzy found her pace subconsciously quickening.

The part of Lizzy that had set out on the hunt for kavians hoped it was Caldwell on her trail. Or better yet, the mysterious Sethan Blackwood, but after stumbling around in the dark for several hours and not encountering a single kavian, of any kind, she was willing to admit it was more likely to be Andric.

The itching awareness on the back of her neck didn't dissuade her in the slightest, however, and Lizzy continued moving forward through the forest.

It had been slow going until the moon had climbed high enough for the light to filter down through the canopy. The pale glow gave the forest a feeling of movement, as shadows seemed to shimmer around her, mimicking life and doing its best to trick the mind, but Lizzy had grown up playing in the forest of Arbaon.

While this forest lacked the quiet whisper of semi-sentient

trees and the pale blue nightlights of glowshrooms, there was nothing about the tall trunks and thick underbrush that scared her.

She felt the whoosh of his blur before she saw him, and by the time she could focus, Andric had moved ahead of her. He stood in her path framed by two of the larger trees she'd passed in the last few hours, and Lizzy found her feet grinding to a reluctant stop as she met his scowl with one of her own.

"You're still alive, then," Andric growled, and Lizzy swallowed hard.

"Go back to Speculo, Andric," Lizzy said simply, forcing her feet to keep moving and her eyes to stay fixed on a point past the hunter, studying the shadows coating the next stretch of forest.

"And leave you out here alone? Not a chance," Andric spat out the refusal, and Lizzy found her attention snapping back to the vampire almost against her better judgement.

"Why not?" she demanded, snapping at him as a glare worked its way onto her face.

"Why not?" Andric repeated, voice still low, and his expression flickering between shock and frustration.

"That's what I asked," Lizzy said. "You're not going to help me, Andric, so just leave."

"I'm not leaving you out here to be torn apart by—"

"But why?" Lizzy forced out, and despite her best efforts, Nameer's words were swimming around her mind as she watched Andric grit his teeth at her question. "I'm not your responsibility, I'm not—"

"You are," Andric growled, and Lizzy fell silent, eyes narrowing until he continued. "I signed a contract to guard and guide you while you were here. You are entirely my responsibility," Andric said, but Lizzy scoffed, crossing her arms and glancing away as she tried to ignore the throb of hurt cutting through her at his words.

"Then I release you from your contract," she spat, spinning around to march through the woods again.

"I'm not going to let you go and get yourself killed!" Andric growled.

"It's my risk to take," Lizzy threw over her shoulder, "not yours—"

She heard him move, the blur displacing the air around her, and Lizzy reacted. She turned and struck out, her forearm hitting Andric's and redirecting the grab he'd made for her arm.

He tried again, and she redirected his arm the same way. When Andric tried to grasp hold of her for the third time, Lizzy stepped under his guard and shoved hard. His back connected with one of the trees, and her arm pressed against his shoulder, her other hand around his wrist.

He could break her hold. It wouldn't be the first time in their training he'd shown her how to pin him in place before effortlessly sliding out of her grasp, but he surprised her by stilling, and Lizzy found herself copying him.

Their breaths were coming fast from the frenzy of the short altercation, and Lizzy found her eyes flickering over his face, searching for something she couldn't name.

"What are you going to do now, Lizzy?" Andric asked, voice soft for the first time since he'd found her. "I can't risk fighting you. Can't risk you bleeding. Every kavian in the forest would be on us, in a blood frenzy, before I could get you back to Speculo, and you... you can't let me out of this hold and expect me to let you walk away. Not unless you're willing to do what you did to Nameer, and snap my neck."

She should have expected him to throw that in her face, but she hadn't and Lizzy flinched, releasing him and stepping back.

The sound of the hunter's neck breaking still echoed in her ears and made her feel sick, bile burning the back of her throat as she struggled to swallow.

It made her hands shake, her breath catch, and her eyes burn as she tore them away from Andric's.

She turned and ran. Lizzy only noticed what she'd done when she heard Andric swear behind her and give chase.

It was a stupid decision, she realised a moment later.

He was a vampire. He could blur. He would catch up in seconds... but it wasn't Andric that brought her to a halt, it was the dizzying way the forest and trees spun around her.

She couldn't focus and her feet tangled in the underbrush, sending her stumbling forward with a sharp gasp.

Andric's familiar arms curling around her waist were the only things preventing her from crashing facedown against the forest floor. He tugged her backwards, her back pressed to his chest, while his grip kept her on her feet. Lizzy's fingers grasped at his forearms, nails biting against his skin as she swayed, torn between panic over her near fall and fear of his condemnation for hurting his friend.

"It's alright," he breathed in her ear instead. "It's okay. I've got you."

Just like that, her fear melted away and Lizzy drew in a ragged breath. She let herself slump back against his chest, her breath coming in short, sharp pants as she shook her head. The world was no longer spinning, but she half expected it to start up again at any moment.

"Bloody hell, Lizzy," Andric muttered, "I've been trying to get you to do that for weeks, and you decide now is a good time to figure it out?"

"What happened?" she asked, carefully finding her footing, and after a moment, Andric's grip on her waist loosened enough for her to turn around. She was still scared to meet his eyes, but she could see his lips pressed together tightly, hesitating.

"You blurred."

"What?!" Lizzy's head snapped up in shock, only to get hit

by the overwhelming concern on Andric's face. With brows furrowed and eyes hooded by the night's shadows, his expression trapped her in place more firmly than the loose grip he still had on her waist.

"It's... a theory I've had for a while," Andric admitted, voice soft and quiet, but when she continued to stare at him, heart pounding and her silence demanding an explanation, he sighed and continued. "I think you're half-fey... and half-vampire."

"I—I don't—"

"Your colouring. Your lack of wings. Your endurance has always been drastically better than Booker's... and I've not been pushing you these last few weeks for fun. Pressing you to run faster, to hit harder—"

"You were testing me?"

"Training," Andric corrected, lips pressing together for a moment. "We aren't born knowing how to blur, it's a skill we learn and practice."

"But you didn't say anything!" Lizzy snapped, stepping back from him and shaking her head.

"If I was wrong... then nothing would have come from it. You'd have just learnt your limits... but if I was right... Lizzy, you've already said you know nothing about your father. I didn't want to... I don't know. Give you unfounded hope, if I was wrong."

The forest was spinning again, but this time Lizzy knew it was in her head. Her whole reality was shifting, and she clung to the last shreds of what she trusted to be true with stubbornness she could already tell wasn't going to be enough.

"It can't... It's not possible—Mum would have told me. She'd have said something..." she spluttered, shaking her head.

"Can we please discuss this back at Speculo?" the vampire pleaded, but whatever he saw when she met his gaze had his shoulders slumping and a sigh escaping his lips. "Alright," Andric conceded quietly, "what, exactly, did your mum tell you about him?" he pressed, and Lizzy felt her throat close up.

There were no words because she'd never been told anything. She'd learnt very young not to ask. The flash of pain streaking across her mum's face every time she brought it up silenced her efficiently, once she was old enough to understand the heartbreak there.

Beyond the pearl pendant currently hanging from her throat, Lizzy knew nothing about the other half of her parentage.

She let her fingers tangle in the necklace, lifting it to rest soothingly against her bottom lip as her mind spun.

Lizzy would be lying if she said she hadn't imagined what he might be like. If she hadn't considered he might be human. If being half-human might account for her lack of wings, and her distaste of telepathy... but a vampire had never crossed her mind.

"It can't be," she breathed, "it would have been illegal. She'd have been banished from Arbaon, at best," Lizzy explained, but her voice was weak and when she pulled herself from her thoughts, she found Andric watching her, looking about as convinced by her words as she felt.

She couldn't even blame him. She'd blurred, without even knowing she could. It was pretty damning evidence.

But it changed nothing. Lizzy pulled in a deep breath and let her hands curl into fists before she turned and began walking again, trying desperately not to think about anything other than finding Sethan Blackwood.

"Where are you going?" Andric hissed and his fingers gently brushed her elbow before she tugged her arm out of his grip.

"This doesn't change anything, Andric. I still need to find my mum—"

"All you're going to do out here is get yourself killed!"

"By the kavians?" Lizzy challenged, turning back to him, her chin raising defiantly, causing Andric to fling up his hands in unmasked exasperation.

"Yes!"

"You don't understand. They have answers for me. I know it."

"How?" Andric growled, and Lizzy paused, frowning. He wasn't going to leave; she could see it in his face, her own stubborn determination mirrored back at her. There was nothing else she could do.

"They..." she started before pausing and her arms came up to wrap around her waist as she glanced away from Andric. "It's... It's my fault Gladstone changed," she admitted, avoiding Andric's eyes as she breathed the answer into the night. "She was in contact with the kavians in the forest. She arranged a meeting with them. We were... we were going to speak to Sethan Blackwood today, while the rest of Speculo was asleep."

She glanced back at Andric, but the frown on his face sent her anger sparking again.

"See? You don't even believe me when I say—"

"How does that make her changing your fault?" he cut her off sharply, hand raised to silence her words, and Lizzy stared at him.

"She must have been drinking human blood in preparation."

"And how did you arrive at this theory?" he pressed, and Lizzy huffed an irritated sigh.

"She asked me for a vial of blood," Lizzy snapped, falling silent at the growing look of genuine anger building in Andric's face.

"Did you give it to her?"

"No," Lizzy whispered, surprised when Andric's eyes slipped closed, and he sighed softly. "But... if I had, maybe she wouldn't have needed to—"

"Stop it," Andric breathed, stepping closer, and Lizzy's breath caught in her throat when his eyes flicked open and locked on hers. "Drinking human blood was Hilda's choice. No vampire would ever ask a fey for their blood, Lizzy. The desire for it, the craving, it would have come from the first cracks in her control. The first poisonings of her mind weakened by the human blood.

She was already drinking it when she asked you."

"How can you possibly know that?" Lizzy muttered. "She seemed perfectly fine. And you don't even believe me about sane kavians anyway—"

"Sane, or rabid, they will still crave your blood. They're drawn to it. It's why I cannot let you risk staying out here—"

"But it's my risk to take," Lizzy snapped, and the softness that had been creeping over Andric's features was washed away by a wave of frustration.

He groaned, hands lifting to clasp together around the back of his neck, head tipping back to stare at the tree canopy above their heads. "Why are you so hellbent on getting yourself killed!" he groaned at the sky.

"I'm not—"

"You're risking your life every second you're out here!"

"I have to find out what happened to her!"

"Answers aren't worth your life!"

The words were so similar to what Booker had told her, Lizzy almost flinched. Instead, her response came roaring up from the darkest parts of her mind, the fragments of doubt she'd never burden Booker with, and she scowled at Andric as she spat out her answer furiously, and without thought.

"Without my mum, I have no life!"

Her words sank in between them like rocks tossed into a lake, the ripples cascading outwards, changing everything.

Lizzy sucked in a sharp breath, as though she could draw the words back past her lips, but the shock she could read in every line of Andric's tense frame told her it was too late.

Slowly, Lizzy staggered back from him, pressed her spine against the nearest tree, and sighed, dropping her gaze to the ground as her stomach churned.

"Lizzy..." His voice was soft, quiet, pained, and she flinched. Andric instantly fell silent, and Lizzy found herself swallowing hard against bitter tears. Once, twice. After the third time, she managed to moisten her lips and summon forth more words in an attempt to explain to the vampire a feeling she barely recognised herself.

"Don't you understand?" she breathed, "It doesn't matter if I'm half-vampire, half-human, or just deformed. I'm wrong, Andric. I don't fit, I don't belong. The only person I've ever belonged with is Mum, and now she's gone. Gone, missing, d-dead. I don't know! I don't know what happened to her, and it's killing me."

"Booker—"

"Yes, Booker," Lizzy muttered, crossing her arms as her heart ached at the thought of her best friend. "Without his friendship with me, he'd be making headway in the Court already," she said, kicking a foot against the forest floor. "He graduated Arbaon

Academy with top scores. His telepathy is incredibly strong... but he'll never be accepted because of me... and I'm not strong enough to let him go," she added.

"Wh—"

"Alright," Lizzy hissed, hiding her clenched fists. She half turned, shifting to stare out into the forest, keeping track of Andric's position from the corner of her eye, "let's play the 'what if' game. What if you're right, and I am half-vampire. How in the realm does that help? It just makes me wrong in two realms.

"Not fey enough for the Court, not vampire enough for the mortal realm. It's only a matter of time before Cara figures that out too."

"And what about me?" Andric whispered, and Lizzy's breath caught again, but she couldn't stop her eyes from sliding back to the vampire.

"What about you?" she asked. She'd intended it to be angry, a growl, but the words escaped her on a quiet sigh and Andric slid a cautious step closer.

"What's your excuse to avoid getting close to me?"

"I-I don't— They're not excus—"

"Lizzy," Andric breathed, a hint of scolding in the quiet call of her name, silencing her spluttered denials and forcing her to drop her gaze again.

"You don't have to be a perfect specimen of fey or vampire to be valued. For your life to have meaning. For people to care about you.

"Do you think Booker would trade your friendship for a career? That Cara would criticise you because... what? You're not as fast as her?"

He stepped closer again. Close enough to reach out and touch, and Lizzy shivered.

"Do you think I'd have spent weeks helping you train, if I didn't see someone worth investing my time in?"

"You needed—"

"I wanted to remain at Speculo, but I could just as easily have gone back to a hotel room in Hockley," Andric corrected. "You're not wrong, Lizzy. You're strong, and smart, and loyal."

His words were sparking hope in her chest, and she didn't know whether to fall into it or snuff it out. Didn't know if it was safe to believe him, or if it was going to tear her to pieces later. Lizzy closed her eyes, jaw tensing as she shook her head.

"Lizzy Hail," Andric murmured, "the five-foot-three bundle of stubbornness and determination. The young woman who won't back down from anything. Not even a rabid kavian. Not even when I've spent weeks teaching her how to run from one. Whose telekinesis was strong enough to protect herself and her friend."

Cautiously, Lizzy opened her eyes and turned to look at Andric. He'd moved even closer and was now leaning one shoulder against the tree she stood pressed against, staring down at her with an infinitely gentle expression that made her heart slam against her chest.

"What are you doing?" she asked softly, and the corners of his mouth twitched up into a familiar flash of a smile.

"I'm being honest with you," he answered. "There is nothing wrong with who you are, Lizzy. Nothing about you that you should be ashamed of. I don't care what kind of priority Arbaon's fancy Court puts on their wings, or telepathy, or how they look down on physical strength or telekinesis. They're wrong. Strength comes in all forms, and you're one of the strongest people I've ever met. You're... you're incredible."

The realisation crept over Lizzy like storm clouds gathering on the horizon and, with a crack of thunder, everything fell into place. Booker's teasing, Cara's curious questions, the way she struggled to focus during their sparring sessions, and Nameer's sharp gaze and shrewd comments.

And as she watched him study her reaction to his words,

Lizzy wondered when, exactly, she'd begun to fall. Between the bickering and the fights, Andric had demanded respect, and given it in turn. Somehow, that had morphed into something else. Something more.

Staring up at his sharp jaw, his lips curled into a small smile, she'd never wished for a pair of wings to help combat their height difference more. Lizzy shifted until she stood mirroring Andric, leaning one shoulder against the tree.

"Nameer said something before... Well, before..." she murmured and Andric hummed, prompting her to continue. "He said I rattle you," she recalled, watching in fascination as Andric's cheeks flushed, the effect mostly hidden beneath the scruff of a beard that shadowed his cheeks.

"Nameer should learn to keep his mouth shut," Andric mumbled, glancing away.

"Is it true?"

He stilled, eyes snapping back to dance across her face again before he slumped further against the tree. "Lizzy, you terrify me," he admitted, and her breath caught in her throat.

He stared at her easily, and it was all Lizzy could do to stare back, heart thrumming in her throat. When Andric shifted, drawing in a breath to speak again, Lizzy was able to snap out of her shock and move.

Her hands lifted to push into his long hair, fingers tangling at the back of his head and tugging him forward gently. Andric was far too tall for her to reach without his consent, but the vampire bowed beneath her touch and seconds later, their lips connected.

Lizzy could feel the arm he wasn't leaning against lift and curl around her waist. Long fingers settled against her back, chasing the shivers dancing along her spine, and the forest fell silent. It was like every living creature was holding its breath.

If the realisation she'd begun to fall for Andric had been thunder, the kiss was the lightning strike. Illuminating, electrifying, and buzzing with undeniable energy.

If she'd surprised him, Andric didn't show it, leaning into the kiss and angling his head to capture her lips more fully, dragging a surprised inhale from Lizzy that escaped her a moment later as a sigh.

The hand that wasn't still tangled in the silky auburn-red strands at the back of his neck lifted to settle against his shoulder, her fingers curling into the stretchy fabric of his shirt. Clinging tightly and tugging Andric closer, he came without complaint, leaning away from the tree and bringing his fingertips up to brush along her jaw.

It was nothing like she'd expected, but everything she'd hoped. It was quiet, and slow, and warm, and Lizzy could feel her cheeks heating, flushing as her mind began to race forward towards the repercussions of her decision.

She began to consider what this might mean, moving forward—

But then Andric pulled back with a soft groan that sent a fresh shiver along her spine and she didn't care about the consequences. They would be worth it.

Despite being the one to pull back, Andric pressed another brief kiss to her lips, and a final one to the corner of her mouth, as though making some kind of apology, before he let his forehead rest against hers.

His features were relaxed, eyelashes resting against his cheekbones, and she took the opportunity to study his features, mere inches from her own.

Breathing through parted lips, the soft rush of air danced lightly across her flushed face. It was as unsteady as her own, and Lizzy was tempted to tilt forward once more, to find out if the second kiss would be as overwhelming as the first, but she resisted.

Instead, she began to untangle her fingers from his hair,

stroking through the strands until the loose curls released their hold on her, and Andric sighed.

Very slowly, Andric's eyes opened and Lizzy felt her breath catch at the tenderness there, radiating out, but she could see him biting back words. Lips pressing together, muscle in his jaw jumping, and she let her gaze skitter over it all, taking it all in.

"What?" she whispered. Nerves began to flutter in her stomach, but Andric soothed them with a tender swipe of his thumb along her jaw.

"I'm just wondering how furious you're going to be when I tell you we can't stay here," he mused, and Lizzy blinked up at him in surprise, but before her irritation could flicker to life, Andric's attention moved away from her, glancing off to the side. "The forest has gone silent."

His words made her pause, and she frowned. "You mean... that's not in my head?"

She hadn't meant to ask that aloud and when he returned his gaze to hers, with a slow grin creeping over his lips, Lizzy blushed. It was her turn to tear her eyes away, and she ducked her head, pressing her face against his shirt with a groan as Andric chuckled. The kiss he pressed against her hair almost made up for her embarrassment.

"I'm flattered," he said, "but no. It's a bad sign.... it means there's a kavian nearby."

In six words the little bubble they'd formed burst, and Lizzy jerked back from him. The fingertips resting lightly against her neck were torn away at the sharp movement, and the warm hand that had found its place settled against her spine dropped, releasing her. She stared at him in silence, and Andric winced.

"Lizzy, please," he begged, not moving towards her this time, his hands hanging loose at his side. "You have my word, I will do everything I possibly can to help you find out what happened to your mum. I swear it. But not now, and not here. Not without a plan, and weapons, and an escape route.

"We can go back to Speculo, you can tell me everything Gladstone had planned, and we'll recreate the meeting she arranged, but... Lizzy, please, this is too dangerous."

Andric wasn't just begging with his words. Lizzy could see it in his stormcloud eyes, his bowed shoulders and his slumped frame. She was half convinced he'd have dropped to his knees, if only it wouldn't put him at a disadvantage should a kavian attack be imminent. Still, she hesitated.

She turned away, glancing around what little she could see of the forest in the dark, and considered her options. It wasn't that she didn't want to return. Now she wasn't wrapped up in... well, in Andric, the sudden silence of the forest was unnerving, but making the meeting Gladstone had set up might be her only chance.

"It's not that I don't believe you," Andric promised, and her attention snapped back to him in an instant, surprised by the agony flickering across his face. "About sane kavians. It's not that I don't believe you. I'm scared to."

"Why?"

He hesitated before shaking his head. "My brother. He turned. A little over two months ago. It's why I was on leave from the school. It's why I was in Hockley."

"You were hunting him?"

"I was hunting kavians," Andric admitted, "any kavians I could find."

"But wouldn't that make the possibility, the chance he still has his mind, a good thing?" Lizzy asked, confused, and Andric sighed.

"It would give me hope," he admitted, "but that's not necessarily a good thing."

Lizzy stared at him in silence. Finally, Andric moved, taking a single step closer before holding out his hand. Waiting, offering.

"I believe you, Lizzy," he promised, "and I will help you, but please, trust me. This isn't the way to find your answers. It's a surefire way of getting yourself killed."

It crossed Lizzy's mind, just for a moment, that Andric could be telling her exactly what she needed to hear. Anything to get her to listen, and to agree, but as she stared at him, she remembered the rough pain simmering beneath his words as he spoke about his brother.

He'd said little, revealed even less, but the grief was unmistakable, and she swallowed hard, shivering as the forest seemed to grow even more impossibly silent, prompting her to step closer to the vampire again and slide her hand into his grip.

"Alright," she agreed, trying not to think of her decision as a surrender. "Take me back to Speculo."

36

The relief when Lizzy had finally given in, sliding her hand into his and agreeing to return to the school, had almost knocked Andric to his knees.

Instead, he'd given himself a moment to smile before getting them both moving.

The deathly quiet that had overcome the forest was making him nervous, and after warning Lizzy to stay as quiet as possible, he began heading towards a soft snuffling sound in the distance. It wasn't close, but a fox or badger hunting for its dinner was safer than heading towards the deeper silence in the opposite direction.

Safer than encountering a kavian in the dark.

It only took a few minutes of walking in tense silence before Lizzy had suggested blurring. A quick shake of his head, and a sharp look of wide-eyed warning, and Lizzy had fallen silent at his side once more.

Even if he wanted to risk it, risk the rapid movements triggering the kavians that had to be drifting through the forest nearby, Andric knew he couldn't. It would be impossible to both blur and track the tiny, distant sounds of wildlife leading them safely away from the rabids.

But the longer they walked, the more distant the sounds of life grew, and the more anxious Andric became.

He glanced to his right and watched Lizzy as she walked beside him, wordlessly staring out into the forest. The hand not clasped within his own had tangled in her necklace, lifting her pendant to gently rub what looked like pearls against her bottom lip.

In a flash, he remembered the soft press of her mouth against his, and the firm pressure of her fingers in his hair, before the frown of anxiety marring Lizzy's face snapped him back to the present.

He'd known since her birthday he felt more for Lizzy than a guard should about the person they were protecting. The fear when he'd realised he might not reach her fast enough had left him with nightmares, but he'd not allowed himself to consider it. Consider them. He'd forced himself to ignore how he was drawn to her and fought to remain professional. For both their sakes.

But the moment she'd snarled that her life had no meaning, his walls shattered. His heart ached for her, and he'd known in an instant he couldn't let her continue through life doubting her worth.

She was worth... everything.

He kept them moving forward, pace smooth and steady. Nothing to trigger any kavians potentially lingering nearby, but he couldn't resist watching her from the corner of his eye.

She'd been frowning since he shot down her suggestion to blur. Her ponytail brushed the back of her neck as she walked, head bowed, watching where her feet fell against the forest floor.

Cautiously, Andric let the pad of his thumb give a gentle brush across her knuckles. It was brief and soft, but her head snapped up to stare at him as they walked.

He waited for her to say something or for her hand to pull back from his, but she did neither. Instead, Lizzy drifted closer to his side, maintaining the silence, but the frown had fallen from her features.

Andric hoped his sigh of relief wasn't loud enough for her to hear.

It became a habit disturbingly quickly. Every time he noticed her frown returning in the pinch of her lips, or the tightness of her fingers, Andric soothed it away with a gentle brush. Every time he had to tug her around a fallen tree, or across a particularly muddy stretch of ground, he stroked an apology across her knuckles.

As the concerning silence spread around them in all directions, it became an action that soothed his growing concerns and reassured Andric she was still beside him.

It was the growing silence that made him grind to a halt, Lizzy almost stumbling into him at his abrupt stillness. He could feel the weight of her gaze on his face and swiped his thumb across her hand again, but he couldn't spare her any additional reassurance, tilting his head to listen to the forest.

His brow furrowed, as he strained his hearing to its limits, but there was nothing.

Not a bird ruffling its feathers, not a mosquito whining in the distance. Perfect stillness, and Andric felt nausea gathering in the pit of his stomach.

Their route back to the school was cut off, but worse, he had no way to tell which direction was safest. Without a clue from the wildlife of the forest, there could be a kavian around the next tree and he wouldn't know until it lunged for Lizzy's throat.

"Shit," he hissed, snapping his eyes open, considering their options.

"What?"

Andric grimaced at the quiet question. He didn't want to tell her, but he couldn't keep it from her either. Not any longer, and not when her life might rely on her knowing exactly how much danger they were in. Not when, less than an hour ago, she'd had every intention of going out and meeting the kavians on her terms, but Andric forcefully set his questions about that aside for later.

"There's a bloody nest," he muttered, distracted as he continued trying to trace any sound of wildlife to guide them to safety. He couldn't hear any stumbling footsteps, or feral growls but it was possible they hadn't tracked Lizzy's scent yet. He saw her shake her head, confused, and Andric bit back another curse.

"A group of them," he explained, keeping his voice to a low murmur. "More than two. I don't think they've noticed us yet," *or we'd already be fighting for our lives*, he added silently. "They've cut off our direct route back to the school."

"Why aren't we running?" Lizzy asked, and Andric glanced around the forest again as he tugged his phone from his pocket. He couldn't see any movement or shadows that looked out of place, so risked glancing down to try and call Nameer, biting back another curse when he found the screen black and the battery dead.

If her plans to meet with sane kavians held any actual merit, and they'd regained the use of logic, it was likely all paths to and from the school were being watched. Instinct screamed at him to head for the road so he shoved his phone back into his pocket and started walking again, gently tugging Lizzy along with him.

"Because," he murmured, answering her question as quietly as possible, "they haven't noticed us yet. Kavians run on instinct. Predator instinct. If we run, and they hear, they'll chase. As long as they ignore us, we keep moving at a steady pace, and we might get lucky."

"But... you taught me to run..." Lizzy breathed, and Andric paused. One glance at her half-accusatory, half-fearful expression, and he turned to face her fully, his free hand lifting to cup her jaw.

"I taught you how to survive an attack," he promised, lowering his head and meeting her eyes, silently begging her to trust him.

"For the moment, they're not attacking. So we keep walking. We keep quiet. No sudden moves. We'll head for the road. If they've cut off the route to the school, we'll head for Hockley instead, alright?"

"And if they attack?" Lizzy asked, barely hesitating, and Andric let his lips twitch up in a relieved smile at her stubborn strength, just for a heartbeat, before he hid it away again.

"Then you do what I taught you. You run."

"What about yo—"

You run, Lizzy," Andric repeated, voice quieter but sharper. Fear lanced through his heart at the possibility of this brave young woman trying to stand and fight.

She would, he realised, if she thought for a second she could help, and he swallowed down his fear so she wouldn't see it.

His insistence only seemed to aggravate her, and he watched with growing horror as her eyes narrowed and shoulders tensed.

"No, no, no," he whispered, dropping his forehead to press against hers, and sighing with relief as her ire began to settle in response. "Now is not the time for your admirable levels of stubbornness," he pleaded. "I have years of training, and multiple weapons. You have two months of running, and hand-to-hand sparring practice. Promise me, if you get the chance, you'll run?"

"...Okay."

There was barely a pause between his question and her answer, and panic filled him again, urgently scanning her face for reassurance.

"Promise me?" he repeated, gaze locked on hers, studying every twitch of her face and every thought spinning behind her vibrant blue eyes.

Despite their rocky start, and the loopholes Lizzy had found in the wording of her arrangement with Walcott, he'd never witnessed the woman go back on her word, and he needed her to keep this promise. He needed to make sure she'd put herself first and stay alive. Needed—

Her fingers tightened around his hand in a gentle squeeze, and

Andric's eyes snapped open. He didn't remember letting them fall closed as he waited for her promise, but when he met her gaze again, there was a soft determination there he recognised.

"I promise," she murmured. Finally, he could breathe again, knowing that her stubbornness was being funnelled in a useful direction, and Andric sighed, relieved.

He pulled back from her, pressing his lips to her temple, muttering, "Good," quietly against her ear before he turned away, focusing on the forest once more.

Despite pulling back the hand that had settled against her neck and jaw so it now hovered over one of his daggers, Andric kept his other hand curled around hers, pressed palm-to-palm as he guided her through the forest, an anchor to his thrumming heart.

"Steady steps, Lizzy," he warned quietly, "and no fast movements."

After getting a silent nod of understanding, they began cautiously working their way towards the road leading to Hockley.

Despite his words to Lizzy, Andric was expecting an attack at any moment.

The forest was perfectly silent in every direction. It was unnerving. It wasn't something he'd ever encountered before, even when hunting nests.

Usually they would group together like pack animals. Their combined heartbeats against the backdrop of silence their presence produced due to fleeing wildlife created just enough of a resonance to track, but Andric had used too much energy catching up with Lizzy.

It left his senses dulled, but even weakened the kind of blanket stillness that had settled over the forest suggested they'd spread out and he could feel his adrenaline-fuelled heart slamming against his chest.

There could be a kavian, or three, around any tree. Hidden in any shadow, stalking them in silence. Powered up on human blood they were faster, stronger, and capable of perfect stillness before their drive for blood sent them spiralling into uncontrolled attacks, and while it wouldn't be his first or even his fiftieth kill, this time he had a fey by his side he desperately didn't want to see hurt, or killed.

It upped the stakes, but he didn't have time to think about it when his instincts had his feet grinding to a halt. Lizzy copied his motions, and although he could read the nervous confusion on her face, he had nothing to reassure her with this time.

He'd thought he'd heard...

He tilted his head, listening, and then snapped his head around to stare to their right.

A soft squeeze against his hand was enough for Andric to draw in a slow breath before nodding in the direction he was looking. "I can hear movement."

"Isn't that a good thing?" she whispered back, and Andric pressed his lips together, debating how much to tell her. One glance at her face, full of genuine curiosity and stubborn determination, with only the smallest dash of fear, made him decide to be brutally honest.

"More accurately, I hear footsteps," he muttered.

"Squirrel shit," Lizzy hissed, and Andric briefly grinned at the distinctly Arbaon curse.

"You remember your promise?" he asked, letting go of her hand to draw his daggers. Lizzy hesitated beside him, maintaining her silence until he shot her a sharp look that finally garnered a nod of assent.

"Wait until we can see them, and I attack," he said quickly

before pointing in the direction they had been walking in. "I'll keep them distracted while you run that way, straight as you can, until you reach the road. When you do, turn left, and keep running until you reach Hockley."

"What happens when I reach Hockley?" she asked, and Andric grimaced.

"I'll catch up with you before then," he promised.

And if he didn't, the kavians would. He didn't say it, but the shiver that shook Lizzy's frame told him she'd heard it anyway.

Keeping half his attention on listening to the approaching footsteps, he ushered Lizzy over to a large tree. He urged her into a position that placed a large tree trunk between her and the direction he could hear the kavians approaching from.

"There's two for sure," he told her. "Wait until they're all attacking me, before you run."

"Two of them?"

"I can handle two," he promised, turning away from her, blades at the ready.

Just.

"Andric," she whispered, and he clenched his jaw. The handles of his borrowed daggers shifted against his palms, but he wouldn't let his attention waver from the shadows.

Tensed, and waiting. He'd have to be fast. Take out one before the other knew what was happening—

"Don't die," Lizzy hissed. The irritation coating her demand had him snapping his head around to stare at her in surprise before offering her a single nod and a brief grin.

It was a shallow reassurance, and his smile retreated as fast as it appeared, replaced with a resigned sigh when he noticed the extra echo.

"Three," he muttered. The third was quieter, their movements almost drowned out by the other two and helped by his own weakened senses, but now he'd noticed it, the echoes were easy to make out. As was the panicked uptick in Lizzy's heart rate.

"It'll be fine."

"Alright," she breathed, but for the first time, it didn't sound like she believed him, and as Andric waited, every muscle tensed in preparation, he couldn't say he entirely blamed her.

Two kavians would have been a struggle. Three... he would need a healthy dose of luck to dispatch three kavians, alone, without suffering injuries that could draw in more.

One of them stumbled. A twig snapped. They were closer now, and he could make out the third set of steps more clearly... and then all three of them stopped.

He could hear his own breathing, Lizzy's heartbeat, and one set of footsteps growing closer.

His fingers clenched around the daggers again as his eyes zeroed in on the approaching sound. Two had stayed back, but he had to draw all three if Lizzy had any chance of reaching the road. The instant he could make out the outline forming from between the trees and bushes of the forest, he launched forward in a blur.

It wasn't as fast as he'd have liked. He'd used too much energy tracking Lizzy, but the figure surprised him.

It didn't redirect his strikes or block his blows. Instead, the figure dodged until they spat out curses that almost made him collapse to the forest floor in relief.

"Put the bloody fangs away, Andric, we've got enough problems without you slicing me up and drawing attention!" Nameer's familiar voice growled, and Andric halted his attack, stumbling as he fell out of the blur, relief hitting him like a physical blow.

"Nameer?" he checked, only half believing his eyes and ears, but his friend's familiar eye roll reassured him, despite the dark scowl on his fellow hunter's features.

"Yes, yes, you're thrilled to see me," Nameer muttered. "Did you find her?"

Andric nodded and glanced back at where he'd left Lizzy, only to see her already approaching. Nameer huffed a sigh from beside him.

"Well that's one piece of good news," he admitted. "Now what the fuck are we going to do about the nest we're surrounded by?"

"Well, who did you bring with you?" Andric asked, turning back to the trees, but his hope of backup withered as Booker and Cara emerged from between the trees.

"Nameer!" Andric growled, but his friend raised his hands.

"Look, I've been hunting the rabids out here for weeks, and not found a sign. How was I supposed to know they'd magically appear the moment you stepped foot in the forest?" he snapped. "Where did they bloody come from anyway?"

Andric shot a glance at Lizzy, but she had her gaze fixed on the forest floor, avoiding looking at anyone, and he grimaced. "It's... a long story. But what possessed you to bring two more students out here?" he demanded, "Not to mention a second fey—"

"It is as I said. You are teaching the fey too well. Mister Reed threatened to repeat your Miss Hail's trick and head out here alone if I refused to assist."

Andric got as far as drawing in a breath, prepared to continue scolding his friend, but Nameer's quiet growl silenced him.

"And besides," he hissed, "it's not like I knew I'd be leading them into a bloody nest." Andric had known him long enough to tell when Nameer's patience was wearing thin, so he relented.

"You're right, I know, I'm sorry," he forced out. His frustration was still simmering, but the source of it wasn't Nameer. As he took a moment to calm himself, he watched Booker and Cara move to stand with Lizzy.

"Are you alright?" Cara asked quietly, and Lizzy nodded, still avoiding Booker's sharp eyes. Andric only hoped they would hold off on the argument brewing between them until they were safely back inside Speculo.

Turning back to Nameer, he shook his head with a grimace. "That still leaves us with three students, two of whom are fey-blooded, and a nest of kavians on all sides. I like our odds better now you're here, but—"

"But it's still not good odds," Nameer agreed. "Not until we know how many kavians there are."

"Can you call the school? Get some more hunters out here?" Andric asked, but Nameer was already shaking his head.

"With the council officer there tying everything up in red tape?" he sneered. "No. They would take too long to mobilise. If Walcott would even authorise it without knowing the size of the threat. The silence is worrying. Have you seen any at all?"

"None," Andric shook his head.

"That is... disturbing and strange."

Andric huffed out a mirthless laugh, glancing back over towards the three gathered friends. As if she could feel his gaze, Lizzy lifted her head, met his eyes, and waited.

He'd told her he believed her, but he hadn't expected to have to prove it quite so soon.

"It's... possible... these kavians have retained, or regained, their minds," Andric said. He turned back to Nameer in time to see him freeze in shock, his features falling into a sharp scowl.

"How?"

"Unclear. Walcott doesn't put any stock in it, but—"

"But we've encountered two Kavians like that," Booker cut in. "Cara met one, too."

Nameer turned to study the three teenagers, still frowning, but Andric could tell he was already considering their words before he turned back to Andric.

"And you?" he asked. "Do you put any stock in it?"

Andric winced at Nameer's directness but carefully considered the question. He'd not seen either kavian speak, but he couldn't entirely dismiss three eyewitness accounts on two separate occasions either. And then there was the nest surrounding them.

He lifted a dagger, twisting it in a circle to indicate the forest. "Have you ever seen a nest act like this one?" he challenged, and a moment later, Nameer shook his head.

"No."

"No, neither have I. The route to the school is cut off... We've seen not a single kavian. No blitz-like, or uncontrolled attacks. They're not grouping together like they should, and if I didn't know better I'd think that they were—"

"Herding you?" came a quiet voice filled with cold amusement.

Andric spun towards the voice. Nameer copied his actions, daggers almost leaping into his hands as he drew them on a blur.

Cara, Booker, and Lizzy spun around too, but slower, and Andric had already paced forward to stand beside them by the time they finished turning.

He found himself meeting the dark, blood-red gaze of a kavian, but it was the bright intelligence there that stilled his hand as shock hit his system.

It was one thing to take Lizzy at her word. It was another to witness the slowly growing smirk on the waxy face, while its words still hung in the night air.

It was the same kavian that had escaped him in Hockley. The one that had almost got the best of him, and Andric found himself shifting his grasp on his daggers nervously.

When Alex Caldwell spoke again, drawling out the final proof that Lizzy, Booker, and Cara's experiences were, in fact, reality, Andric couldn't halt the sickening shudder shooting along the length of his spine.

"Perhaps," Caldwell purred, a dangerous grin dancing around his lips as his bared fangs flashed in the low light from the moon, "it's because herding you through the forest is exactly what we've been doing."

37

Almost as though they'd been waiting for Alex to give some silent signal, four more kavians emerged from the forest behind him, and Lizzy's breath caught in her throat.

They appeared in pairs. Two of them approached in near-silence, alert and watchful like Alex, but it was the second pair that made her shudder. They stumbled forward on unsteady feet and staggered into the moonlight creeping through the breaks in the canopy overhead.

They were skeletal. Skin drawn tight over their bones. Fingers deformed into sharp, claw-like appendages. Their eyes, glazed and spinning in their skulls, like they were searching for something blindly.

Behind her, Andric began cursing under his breath.

To Lizzy, they seemed sick. Half-starved, and all mad. As they were brought forward, they seemed to grow more agitated, and their glazed gazes sharpened as they leaned forward, noses lifting, scenting the air.

They were held back by the two who seemed to retain control of themselves. Each of the kavians stood behind one of the rabids, restraining them with nothing more than their hold on a narrow, metal collar. It was only as Lizzy eyed their tenuous grip, that recognition hit her like a punch to the gut.

It stole her breath, and a pained exclamation escaped her against her will.

"Gladstone?" she gasped, stepping forward before she'd considered the consequences.

Booker's arm shot out, grasping hold of her elbow and stopping Lizzy in her tracks, but their combined movement drew everyone's attention.

The rabids twisted against their collars, clawed fingers stretching out, grasping at the air in front of them, and deep, rumbling growls slithered from their throats, chilling the blood in her veins.

"No sudden movements," Hunter Khatri instructed sharply, and Lizzy shivered as the grin on Alex Caldwell's face widened dangerously before his eyes locked on hers.

"Ah yes, I believe you would be familiar with darling Hilda here, wouldn't you, Miss Hail?"

"What... what happened to her?" she forced out, and although it wasn't as strong as she would have liked, Lizzy was relieved that her voice wasn't quite trembling.

"She drank human blood, and became a kavian," he said simply, like the answer should be obvious, but as Lizzy stared at Gladstone, she found herself shaking her head in mute denial.

She'd only been missing from the school a little less than a day, but Gladstone looked like she'd been starved for weeks. Her body appeared deformed and there was nothing approaching recognition on her face.

"I... I don't understand. Why is she... why is she like that?"

"And not like my companions and me?" Alex asked, and Lizzy snapped back to face him, studying his smile for a moment before nodding.

Alex gave a soft hum before answering. "That would be a question better posed to Sethan," he said, and Lizzy's eyes flared with surprise. "But first, I think introductions are in order."

Alex held out his arm towards the pair of kavians on his left, but didn't spare them so much as a glance, keeping his gaze locked on Lizzy, and she swallowed nervously at his intense focus. "This strapping young man to my left is Logan, and he'll be keeping hold of poor old Patrick tonight."

Alex lowered his left arm and extended his right, but this time his attention slid from Lizzy's to settle on the second pair of kavians and Lizzy followed his gaze. "This other gentleman to my right is Edward, and he'll be keeping a close watch on Hilda here."

The kavian that still retained his mind, Edward, offered Lizzy a nod of greeting. In other circumstances, she would almost call him polite, but considering he was holding back a monster from her nightmares, the stilted manners were bordering on hilarious, and hysterical laughter threatened to bubble up her throat.

"While you and I made our introductions back in Hockley," Alex continued, and Lizzy found she had his full attention once more, "for the sake of your hunters... and your fellow fey, I am Alex Caldwell."

There was a beat of silence as Alex let his gaze skip past Lizzy and settle on the others one at a time. Booker, Cara, Andric, and Nameer. When no one moved, and the silence held, the kavian raised an eyebrow, his smile morphing into a smirk.

"It would be polite to offer your names in turn," he said, prompting a snort from Nameer.

"Polite?" Nameer growled. "I'll politely introduce you to my blades." He stepped forward, daggers drawn, and the kavians all turned on him as one.

The rabids snarled, arms flailing, and although Logan and Edward continued to hold them back, their features had begun to shift too. Eyes bleeding red, fangs bared, and the tension in the air almost crackled, causing the hair on the back of Lizzy's neck to stand on end.

"Ah, ah, ah!" Alex called, and everyone stilled, both Nameer and the kavians although the rabids continued their snarling. "We're not here for you, hunter, but advance another step and we will defend ourselves," Alex warned. He was the only kavian who hadn't let his teeth elongate into fangs, but his eyes narrowed warningly, and Lizzy shivered.

She watched nervously as Hunter Khatri glared at the group, weapons still drawn, but he was clearly hesitating.

"Nameer."

Andric's voice cut through the tense silence. He said nothing more than his friend's name, but Hunter Khatri's head twitched towards him a tiny bit before he took two careful steps back.

Lizzy shivered as Alex's smile slid back into place.

"Why are you here?" Andric asked once his friend had finished retreating, and Lizzy froze when Alex's gaze snapped back to settle on her.

"Miss Hail requested a meeting. Sethan Blackwood agreed. When we observed Miss Hail's liaison fleeing the school, her mind shattered, we knew it would be difficult for Miss Hail to make the meeting. So, when Edward here saw her leave the warded grounds, alone, he brought her presence within the forest to our attention.

"Sethan is still willing to meet with you, Miss Hail, and discuss what he knows of your mother's location."

Her mother's... location. Hope flooded her chest, and Lizzy struggled to push it down before it could overwhelm her, but Booker broke the silence before she managed it.

"She's alive?" he asked, sounding twice as shocked as Lizzy felt and just as hopeful. The grasp on her arm slid down until he took her hand in his, and Lizzy found herself clinging to him, terrified of Caldwell's answer, and yet still desperate to hear it.

The kavian's pause was momentary. Only long enough for his eyes to flicker over Booker, drop to their joined hands, and settle back on her again, but for Lizzy, the wait seemed to last forever. She couldn't breathe, her chest ached with hope she was trying her best to ignore, her thoughts were sluggish with fear...

And then he nodded.

"Yes."

A soft, almost disbelieving laugh escaped her, and Lizzy swayed slightly, staggering right a step into Booker's shoulder.

The relief washed through her like a wave, and the intense urge to turn and pull Booker into a hug followed swiftly, but the soft growling of the rabid kavians at her unprompted movement killed the thought before she acted on it.

"How? Where?" she asked, eyeing the growling kavians, but Alex shrugged and a pit opened up in the bottom of her stomach.

"More things you would be better to ask of Sethan," he said, dismissing her questions easily. A heartbeat later, his features turned sharp and focused once more and a grin lifted his lips. "Will you come with us, Miss Hail? Speak to Sethan, and find out the answers to your questions?"

His words almost felt like a taunt, but even as Lizzy hesitated, the kavian merely raised an eyebrow, waiting patiently for her answer.

"Absolutely not," Andric spat into the silence, her lack of response left hanging in the air, but Alex's friendly camaraderie vanished at the interruption. His grin became a sneer, but his gaze stayed fixed on Lizzy.

"I have warned you once, hunter," Alex growled, "we are not here for you. Do not think that means I won't allow my associates to tear you limb from limb if you continue to interfere with our negotiations."

"Negotiations?" Andric snarled, "This isn't a negotiation, it's a death sentence!"

"Silence!" Alex snarled, finally tearing his eyes away from Lizzy to glare at Andric, and Lizzy pulled in a shuddering breath, finally released from his gaze, and turned to Booker, only to find him frowning.

"Booker?" she asked, and instantly his mind buzzed against

hers, connecting with an ease and familiarity she'd missed.

"*Don't ever try to keep secrets from me again, Lila,*" he growled, but she could feel the terrified affection behind it and her confidence withered in the face of Booker's emotions.

"*I'm sorry,*" she offered weakly, receiving only a quiet sound of acceptance in response.

"*We can argue about that later. Even at the speed of thought, we don't have time right now.*"

"*What do you think? About Alex? About Sethan?*"

"*You're not seriously considering trusting them?*" Booker demanded, and Lizzy couldn't stop the relief at the outrage she could sense.

"*I want to. I really wish I could, but...*"

"*These others,*" he read, pulling the unease from her mind. "*The... rabids?*"

"*That first one, the night we arrived... she was terrifying enough, but these...*"

"*I can see now why Andric calls them creatures,*" Booker agreed.

"*I could have believed Alex. Part of me still wants to believe what he's saying, no matter how unnervingly creepy he is, but...*"

"*But you can't.*"

"*I can't,*" Lizzy agreed. The relief she felt at his silent support, his mind in complete alignment with hers, was almost enough to make her smile. She made no move to disconnect their thoughts when she turned back to Alex only a few seconds later, only to find the kavian and his subordinates all angled towards Andric and Nameer, each of them sporting snarls or glares.

"I believe the offer was made to me," she said, keeping her voice loud enough to cut through the growled threats floating through the air, and her heart thundered in her ears as they all turned to her.

"Lizzy," Andric choked out, and she spared him a small smile of reassurance before turning to Alex. He was already watching her, features narrowed with suspicion, and while she truly had no idea what expression had settled over her face, from the look of Alex's growing frown it wasn't one he was happy with.

"Mister Caldwell," she began, but her voice wavered and she had to pause to clear her throat, Booker's hand squeezing hers reassuringly as she forced herself to continue.

"Please offer my apologies to Mister Blackwood, but..." she couldn't stop her eyes flickering over to Gladstone, or the shudder that shook her shoulders, before she was able to continue, "but I'm afraid I'll have to... decline... his invitation for the foreseeable future."

Alex stared at her for so long Lizzy was beginning to wonder if he'd heard, and she shifted slightly on her feet. She'd just begun to consider whether she could repeat her refusal without her voice failing, when Alex sighed.

It was a deep sigh, long and slow, and she found herself swallowing on a suddenly dry throat.

"That's... unfortunate," the kavian breathed out, and Lizzy saw Andric turn, angling his body in a way she recognised from their sparring.

Readying for an attack.

"Un-unfortunate?" she forced herself to ask, and the kavian gave a soft hum.

"Yes. Unfortunate. You may be willing to back out of this arrangement, Miss Hail, but Sethan would very much like to speak with you."

Lizzy moistened her lips and tried not to stare at the rabids still straining against the collars that Logan and Edward were holding them back by as she struggled to respond.

"Well... uh, maybe in a few days. Once—"

"My instructions were crystal clear, Miss Hail, and I won't be taking no as an answer," Alex interrupted her, and she watched in growing horror as the kavian finally let his fangs appear and his eyes bleed red.

"I'd say I'm sorry about that, but truly, I'm very much not," and with a snarled command, chaos erupted.

38

Andric moved first.

Blurring across the space between Lizzy and Alex, he crashed into the lunging kavian, forcing him backwards, but Lizzy didn't have time to watch the pair fight.

The moment Alex had loosed a feral snarl, Logan and Edward had released their hold on the two chains, and the rabids made a beeline for her and Booker.

She had just enough time to remember that fey blood called to the creatures before Gladstone was right before them.

She flinched away, pressing closer to Booker as Gladstone snarled and lunged forward, claws reaching out—and then she was gone.

Nameer's attack had pushed Gladstone aside, redirecting her strike and flinging her into a nearby tree, with an audible crack.

"Handle the other rabid," he ordered, thrusting a dagger at Cara. She'd barely grasped hold of it before he was gone, blurring after Gladstone.

Cara didn't hesitate. She turned on the second rabid, his form withered and distinctly more sluggish in his movements, and forced him back from Lizzy and Booker with quick jabs of her borrowed blade.

It was chaos. A cacophony of snarls and growls. The snap of bone and the hiss of metal on metal every time Alex's and Andric's blades locked—*where had Alex pulled a weapon from?*

The fight was on all sides, and Lizzy didn't know where to look, or where to turn. She didn't even notice she'd started to shake until Booker wrapped an arm around her and tugged her back against his chest.

"*Lila, focus*," he pleaded, and she found her fingers curling into fists.

"*They're so fast*," she shot back, and even her thoughts were shaking. "*I know Andric warned us but... but they're so fast. I don't know... How can I...?*"

"*Help Cara.*"

It was a legitimate suggestion. The moment Booker's words sank into her mind, she turned to watch their friend, and it was clear why he'd drawn her attention there. The kavian wasn't as fast as the others, but Cara only had one blade and the creature had ten claw-like appendages.

She was beginning to lose ground.

But Lizzy could hear the urgent terror under Booker's request too, and her heart ached as her gaze flicked back to Andric and Alex.

"*Please, Lizzy... I can't...*"

Booker's broken pleading decided her. Alex and Andric were moving too fast for her to intervene, and Lizzy turned back to focus on Cara, Booker's relief slinking through her mind as she brought her telekinesis to bear.

"*I'll watch your back*," he promised, and with a single nod of acknowledgement, Lizzy struck.

Just as she had with Nameer back at Speculo, Lizzy wrapped her power around the kavian's shoulders. The invisible tendrils of her power held him in place from the chest up, crawling around his neck as she prepared for the wrenching twist she needed her mind to mimic to snap his neck, but she paused.

Nameer's shocked face when he'd realised what she'd been planning to do flashed through her mind, and Lizzy flinched, hesitating.

It was only a moment, but it was enough for the trapped kavian to begin flailing against her restraints.

Instinct compelled it to push against the force holding it back from its intended victim, and Lizzy lifted her hands to her temples with a quiet groan. It was taking everything she had not to lose her grip on the power, leaving her entirely unable to complete the neck-snapping motion she'd intended.

Entwined with her mind, Booker sensed her falter, and she felt his panic rising in the back of her throat. She fought to concentrate past his overflowing emotions, gritting her teeth hard enough to hurt and trying to ignore everything but the sensation of her power still coiled around the chest of the rabid like an iron band.

"Now, Cara!" Booker shouted, and Lizzy cracked her eyes open, watering from the strain and blurring her vision. She struggled to blink away the tears, still fighting to keep the kavian from regaining control of its body.

She could see their friend staring at it in shock, her blade raised uncertainly. When Booker's shout registered, Cara's face hardened.

In a blur of motion Lizzy couldn't follow, Cara had stepped closer, dodging the restricted flailing of the creature's clawed fingers, and drove her borrowed dagger up into the kavians chest. Andric's anatomy lessons told Lizzy that Cara had hit the heart, even before the kavian stilled and finally stopped fighting against her mind.

Lizzy released her power and staggered forward with a gasp, pressing the back of her hand to her nose and urgently checking for blood, but this time she'd escaped the use of her powers unscathed.

As the kavian fell from her hold and sank harder against Cara's buried blade, he disintegrated into frothy red, soaking Cara's arm before splashing against the forest floor. Cara stepped back in a rush, a look of disgust rushing up over her features that, under any other circumstances, Lizzy might have found amusing.

A shriek rent the air, ricocheting down Lizzy's spine like ice. Heart hovering in her throat, Lizzy spun around in time to see Hunter Khatri disembowel Gladstone.

A wave of nausea hit and cool sweat broke out across her forehead at the sight of insides falling out of Gladstone's body and dropping to the ground with a sickening splatter.

The newly turned kavian was mindlessly howling her rage and frustration into the night, but Khatri didn't even wait for her to disintegrate before he moved on. Launching himself off Gladstone's collapsing form, he lunged towards Alex and Andric.

Alex turned at the last second, deflecting Nameer's slashing daggers, and Lizzy was finally able to see why Khatri had chosen to target him next.

As Nameer distracted the kavian, Lizzy's eyes settled on Andric. He'd been backed against a tree and slumped against the bark as Nameer pulled Alex's attention away. Lizzy gasped at the blood soaking through his shirt, a gash running across his chest, from shoulder to ribs.

She didn't know what she planned to say, or shout, or cry out to the vampire, but as her lips parted, the last thing she anticipated was the scream of agony that tore from her throat.

A body had slammed against her back and wrapped itself around her, pinning her arms to her sides in a vice-like grip. Agony burnt through her left shoulder and spasmed down her arm like flames as the kavian's fangs ripped deep into her flesh.

"*Lila...!*"

For a moment, Booker's terror-filled cry rang through her mind and muted the bone-deep ache of the bite.

But the kavian flexed—arms tightening, jaw biting—and the pain exploded again, roaring up and shattering the telepathic connection in her mind as she screamed.

"Lizzy!" Andric's shout was almost drowned out by the sob-heavy gasp of air she drew in when her scream ran out. The kavian's hard fingers curled around her throat, twisting her head as he all but gnawed against her skin, fresh agony rippling out from where his mouth connected to her body.

She could feel blood dripping down her arm as it flooded out of the bite, escaping the suckling lips against her skin, and she shuddered, mind reeling.

She recognised the hold, one of the many Andric had shown her how to escape, but she couldn't make her mind focus. Couldn't concentrate past the pain to remember what she should be doing—

"Release her!" Alex snarled, distracting her from thoughts of escape, and Lizzy found herself staring at him in shock as he disentangled himself from Nameer long enough to turn his snarl towards her and the kavian at her back. "Sethan wants her alive—!"

His order was cut off sharply by Nameer, the vampire appearing behind him with blades that he buried in the kavians back. Blood bubbled out of Alex's mouth, and he staggered forward from the blow before dropping to his knees, hands clasping at the dirt as he coughed up more blood.

In a daze, she watched as Nameer's dagger appeared at Alex's throat, a final gash sending his body into a bubbling pile of red liquid at Nameers feet.

A fresh cry tore through the forest, and Lizzy flinched as the sound reverberated against her ears. The kavian at her shoulder was screaming. A sharp, piercing sound of pain, so similar to her own.

She feared the retribution of fresh fangs against her skin for Alex's death, a shudder making its way along her spine, but instead, Lizzy found herself flung forward, pushed away from the kavian as another tormented cry cut through the air.

She staggered forward, then stumbled, falling to her knees and lifting her right hand to press against the still-burning ache in her shoulder. Her fingers were instantly coated in blood, slick and slippery, but she pressed down harder and forced herself to turn around.

The kavian was writhing against the forest floor, still releasing pained shouts, and her eyes widened in horror as his form appeared to contort.

It had been Logan at her throat, she noted distantly, and her mind felt a thousand miles away as he choked, releasing a gurgling sound that might have been another scream.

He began throwing up the shimmering red blood he'd dragged from the bite wound in her shoulder, and Lizzy shuddered as his clawed fingers sank into the dirt, as though grasping for something to hold onto.

"Lizzy."

Lizzy flinched at the soft call of her name breathed against her ear, before recognising Andric's voice. His chest pressed against her uninjured shoulder, one arm slid around her back and settled firmly against her waist, and she collapsed onto one hip, letting her frame sink against his warmth.

"Wh-what's... happening?" she stuttered.

Logan was sobbing now instead of screaming, but even that was slowing into gasps as he panted for breath, tears streaking his face as his arms shuddered.

"I don't know," Andric muttered. "Nameer will handle it."

Her eyes spun to settle on the other hunter, standing by Booker and Cara. He'd placed himself between them and the writhing kavian, with his daggers still drawn. Booker was staring at her, fear painted across every line of his face, but Andric shifting her in his arms pulled her attention away before she could summon the strength to reassure Booker.

Gently, the hand that wasn't helping to hold her upright brushed against the back of her right hand where it pressed against the bite.

"Let me see," Andric instructed, voice shaking, and Lizzy forced herself to pull her blood-slicked fingers away with a hiss, biting back the sharp gasp trying to escape.

He probed the area, but despite his care, Lizzy couldn't smother a whimper, and when Andric put pressure against the bite once more Lizzy's held breath escaped in a hiss. Her fingers grasped hold of the torn edges of his shirt, adding fresh trails of shimmering blood to the already stained fabric.

"It's not a major artery. He bit into the muscle," Andric explained, and despite the agony still flaring from his firm touch, Lizzy could hear the relief there, almost drowned out by the still writhing kavian behind her.

"We have to stop the bleeding, Lizzy. Still trust me?" Andric asked, and she nodded without hesitation. Anything to stop the stinging burn still trailing the length of her arm.

Andric brushed a light kiss to her forehead before curving around her frame and placing his mouth over the open gash Logan had left across her shoulder.

She expected it to hurt, for the tongue Andric laved over the ragged wound to tear at the skin. She whimpered, expecting the burning agony still simmering through her shoulder and arm to light up once more, but instead, a coolness rushed through her, like she'd been pushed into a cool lake during the height of summer.

It was soothing, ice on a burn, and Lizzy found herself pressing closer and dragging in deep, shuddering breaths full of relief. As Andric worked to neutralise the venom of the kavian's bite, Lizzy found her thoughts sharpening, letting her focus on more than the pain.

She noticed Booker watching her, a million questions written all over his face, and Cara leant up, whispering to him. Lizzy hoped the woman was explaining that Andric was helping, not hurting.

She realised she could no longer hear Logan's pain-filled cries and glanced back towards the kavian. He was kneeling, his hands resting against his thighs, while Nameer stood over him, his daggers drawn.

And then reality slammed back into her, and she tensed.

The second she did, Andric pulled back from her shoulder, turning away to spit out the blood that had gathered in his mouth. Lizzy felt her heart thud at the action, but before she could overanalyse the feeling, his grey eyes were back on hers, worried and searching.

"Okay?" Andric asked, and Lizzy shivered but gave a nod.

"What about the other one?" she asked, voice weak with nerves. "Edward?"

"Ran," Andric growled, turning away from her to scan the area, as though trying to seek out the missing kavian, but a second later, his eyes were back on hers, and his features softened. "Think you can stand?" he asked, and after a moment of consideration, she nodded.

Despite her agreement, Andric didn't let her struggle to her feet. He stood with her, keeping his arm curled around her back and guiding her up, careful to keep her steady as Cara appeared at her side.

The vampire wrapped her in a hug, almost knocking Lizzy over again in her blurred rush, but despite that Cara still only barely beat Booker, her best friend not waiting for Cara to release her before wrapping both of them in the same hug, his hands shaking.

Neither spoke, and Lizzy clung to them both, her eyes sliding shut as she soaked in their silent affection, relief making her feel ill, but they snapped back open when Andric stepped away.

"Andric," Nameer called, drawing everyone's attention back to him and the kneeling kavian, and as Andric stepped towards the pair, Nameer sighed and shook his head, adding, "We have another problem."

Leaving Lizzy to the hugging arms of her friends was harder than Andric wanted to admit.

He felt like every nerve ending in his body was alight and trembling, the fear still shimmering through his system like fine threads of fibreglass, but he forced himself to release her and step back.

He didn't think he'd ever shake the image of Lizzy, screaming and bloody, from his mind, but the concern in Nameer's unwavering gaze had him swallowing every roiling emotion back down to the bottom of his gut and approaching the kneeling kavian.

"What problem?" he growled, teeth clenched, and his hands ached to reach for a blade. His chest was tight and itchy where the skin had recently healed over, and burning some frustration by doing away with one more kavian was looking more and more appealing.

"Look at him," Nameer muttered, and Andric blinked hard as he forced himself to do as his friend had asked, to stop and think, and consider the situation objectively.

And when he did, he felt his jaw drop.

The kavian, Logan, was kneeling on the forest floor, his back to Nameer and his shoulders slumped and shaking. He was sucking in deep, unsteady breaths, still recovering from the screaming and vomiting his body had been doing for several minutes. But it was his hands Andric focused on, laying palm up against his thighs.

Loose. Unthreatening. His fingers were normal, and not in the slightest bit claw-like.

His frame had filled out too, in the handful of minutes since he'd attacked Lizzy, and the longer Andric stared, the more changes he saw.

There was no longer a waxy surface to his skin, like leather pulled taut over the spine of a book, and when Logan slowly lifted his bowed head, there was no sign of red in the whites of his eyes. No bloodshot streaks stained his vision, and a shell-shocked look of dazed amazement was taking over his features, telling Andric this was no trick on his part.

If Andric hadn't witnessed the kavian tearing into Lizzy's shoulder not five minutes ago, and if her blood wasn't still staining Logan's chin, Andric wouldn't have known he was a kavian.

"He looks..."

"Exactly," Nameer agreed when Andric's voice died, trailing off into silence. "Entirely vampire. No sign of kavian on him at all," he added, sounding almost intrigued, but Nameer's musings had drawn the attention of the three friends, and Andric could hear the trio approaching, even as he continued to study Logan for any lingering kavian traits.

"What are you talking about?" Lizzy asked, but before Andric could elaborate, Logan's attention shifted and settled on Lizzy, his dazed expression transforming into one of relief and, surprisingly, open adoration.

"You saved me," he whispered, and Andric's eyes shot up to meet Nameer's, his friend's expression filled with the same apprehensive tension Andric could feel bubbling up in his gut.

"What?" Lizzy squeaked, her voice cracking.

"Your blood, it fixed me," Logan choked out, bracing his hands against the earth and leaning forward, only pausing when Andric took a warning step forward.

Logan flinched back at the movement, twisting and turning aside as though expecting a blow, but Andric could still see his eyes. Wide and fearful but painfully focused. Nothing like a rabid, but then he'd not been a true rabid before he bit Lizzy either.

"I can feel it, or I can't," he muttered, "the constant itching, irritation against my skin, the ache in my gums, the craving for human blood, it was relentless, and now it's not. It's gone."

It was impossible, and yet, the evidence was kneeling in front of him, and Andric felt hope slam into him, hard. A cure for kavians.

It might not be permanent. It might have any number of unforeseeable side effects, but Andric couldn't stop the hope rising. Couldn't stop wondering if he might be able to get his brother back.

Moving very slowly, Logan straightened, turning back to stare at Lizzy. "You fixed me," he breathed, shaking his head, and frowning. "What are you—ugh—"

In a move so fast Andric nearly missed it, Nameer had blurred forward and sliced through the vampire's neck. From the rush of blood that erupted forth, Andric knew the man's carotid had been severed. There was no hope of healing him. Not unless Logan could feed, and feed a lot.

He heard the cries and shouts of shock from Lizzy, Booker, and even Cara, but he could do nothing other than stare, lips parted in shock as Logan collapsed, a gurgling sigh escaping his corpse while Andric's hope shrivelled.

"What... What the bloody hell were you thinking?" he snarled, turning on Nameer as the man cleaned his blade, but he paused in the face of Andric's temper, and slowly met his gaze.

"I was thinking that we do not have time for fairy tales," Nameer said simply.

"A cure for a kavian is not—after everything we've seen tonight, you weren't even willing to consider—?"

"It is not about considering, Andric," Nameer said slowly, brow furrowing. "It is about whether the Council would consider."

"We had the evidence right in front of us, and you killed him!" Andric yelled, fury ridding him of reason, and even the gasps behind him weren't enough to calm his temper, but they did draw Nameer's gaze.

The soft, reassuring smile he sent the three witnesses to their argument made Andric's stomach twist in anxiety, and he was suddenly scared to turn and see their reactions.

"Andric," Nameer began, pausing as he turned from their audience to offer a calm stare that Andric found himself flinching back from.

His oldest friend sighed with an understanding that cut Andric to the bone. "I know the desire for a cure. I understand your reasons, but think, my friend," Nameer prompted gently. "Say we brought him in. Say this cure was the permanent kind. The next question the Council asks is how. How was this kavian restored?"

Lizzy.

Andric sucked in a sharp breath as horrified realisation swept through his hope and sent it scattering to the winds.

No. Lizzy's blood.

That was worse. What would the Council do to keep hold of a cure like that? What would they do under the guise of protecting the girl? And how long before they stormed Arbaon, looking for more sources?

Nameer was still watching him, and the soft hum he released told Andric his realisation had been visible on his face.

"Fuck," Andric groaned, rubbing his hands over his face.

"Just so," Nameer said, finally sliding his daggers away. Guilt swirled in Andric's stomach when he realised his friend had kept them drawn because of his reaction, and he swallowed down the bile building in the back of his throat.

"We have enough to explain with kavians regaining their minds. No need to add this to the pile of things they will struggle to believe."

"So... we're not telling anyone about this? About Lizzy?" Cara asked, and Nameer shot her a grin before shaking his head. Andric turned to the three friends, hesitantly finding Lizzy and studying her face.

She looked... tired. But in her defence, she'd had her sleep cut short when he'd come to find her after Gladstone had turned. Since then, she'd been awake almost twelve hours and had spent nearly half of them marching through thick woodland. Not to mention the pain of the kavian bite, and the lingering effects of blood loss.

What he'd feared to see was missing, however. There was no disappointment in the turn of her mouth, and no fear in the line of her jaw, and he sighed in relief.

He'd not entirely fucked up the fragile tendrils of caring that they'd only just acknowledged. He could still see it there in her eyes, forcing him to swallow hard and clasp his hands against the small of his back, lest he step forward and pull her into a hug.

"No," Nameer answered Cara firmly, "let's keep the properties of your friend's blood between us. For the foreseeable future."

"Good," Booker growled, and the hard chips of emerald green his gaze had turned into clearly said that Andric still needed to earn this fey's forgiveness. "Because the last thing we need is your Council turning her into some kind of experiment!"

"Booker," Lizzy groaned, rolling her eyes, and Andric had to fight back the urge to grin, certain Booker wouldn't appreciate the expression at the moment.

"We're not going to let that happen," Cara reassured, turning to Booker and tangling her free hand with his. Andric watched the way the young fey settled beneath her touch, but Booker continued to scowl at Andric regardless.

"No, we're not," Andric confirmed before sighing and turning back to Nameer, "but there is still the last one, Edward," he said, and Nammer grimaced.

"He ran?"

"East," Andric confirmed.

"I should stay out here then, track him down—"

"None of us should stay out here," Lizzy cut in, stepping away from Booker's arm around her shoulders, and glaring between Nameer and Andric. "We don't know if there are more kavians out here. There's probably at least Sethan Blackwood nearby, and besides, it's taken us months to convince you that sane kavians exist. No one's going to listen to Edward if he starts talking about this.

"He ran. At best a talking kavian will be killed on sight, and at worst, others like him will think he's making up an excuse for being a coward. Right?" she prompted, her eyes dancing between him and Nameer, seeking a confirmation.

"Tell me I'm wrong?" she added, and Andric could feel the weight of Nameer's gaze. Andric studied Lizzy's stern features, her arms crossed and legs braced as though expecting a physical fight rather than a verbal argument. When Andric finally flicked his gaze back to Nameer, it was to find his friend grinning in open amusement.

"Stubborn," Nameer complimented, and Andric laughed softly, trying not to notice the scowl settling across Lizzy's features in response.

"Very."

"Just like you," Nameer teased, and Andric sighed.

"She's not wrong though."

"Well, you would say that."

"Nameer—"

"Later, later, I will tease you later," the vampire agreed, lifting his hands into the air in surrender, and Andric sighed again.

Turning back to Lizzy to find her blushing slightly, he didn't bother masking his grin.

"You're right," he repeated, "we'll all head back to Speculo. Cara, keep hold of that dagger," he instructed, moving forward to stand by Lizzy, "and good work with the rabid," he added, watching the young vampire duck her head to hide a small, proud smile.

"I'll bring up the rear," Nameer announced. "We move at a steady pace. No running, try not to stumble in the darkness. Follow Andric, and hope the kavians have vacated the area after losing four of their number in one night."

It was a faint hope, but as Andric tilted his head and listened, he could hear the rustle of birds in the trees far in the distance and blew out a soft breath of relief.

"Alright," he muttered, shedding his leather jacket and sliding it around Lizzy's shoulders to help hide the streaks of blood drying against her chest and arm.

He waited until she'd slid her arms through the sleeves before scooping up her hand and nodding in the direction they needed to head, trying to ignore the sharp looks Booker was still shooting him. "Let's go."

40

As Andric guided them away from the site of their impromptu battle with Alex and his kavians, Lizzy hadn't been able to stop herself looking back.

From a distance, the ground soaked in the red remains of the kavians, wasn't clear. The deep gouges in the dirt from scrambled footwork were masked by leaves, and she felt herself shiver at the thought that the tiny patch of unmarked forest might have been her grave if not for... whatever had happened to Logan.

Movement in the dark space between two large trees caught her eye, and she felt her breath catch in her throat as she saw the kavian that had fled the fight, Edward, hovering in the shadows.

She almost stumbled to a stop, but he moved before she could speak. Blurring forward he scooped up something from the ground before dashing away, vanishing silently into the forest.

"Lizzy?" Booker asked, and she blinked, turning to stare at him as he frowned at her. "Are you alright?"

"Yes, I just..." She glanced back again, watching the forest, but Edward was gone. It was on the tip of her tongue to explain, but the look she'd seen on the kavian's face made her hold her tongue.

"I thought I saw something, but... I think it was just a shadow," she said softly, offering Booker a reassuring smile and turning around, only to find Andric watching her with gentle concern.

Guilt welled in her stomach at another secret, but she still remembered the casual way Hunter Khatri had slit the former kavian's throat and she ducked her head, tugging Andric's jacket around her as they continued forward.

She couldn't tell them what she'd seen without at least one of them dashing off and hunting him down, and she couldn't bring herself to do that to the kavian. Not when the look on his face had slammed into her heart so powerfully. Not when the expression in his eyes, even from a distance, had spoken of desperation and hope.

She doubted she'd ever see him again, and that was the best course for everyone, Lizzy decided, before pushing the guilt and apprehension out of her mind and focussing on putting one weary foot in front of the other.

They made it back to the school in the early hours of the morning, without encountering any more kavians. Nameer ushered them through the front gates, ordering the hunters stationed there to maintain their silence.

It was only with their concerned stares on her back that Lizzy realised she was still covered in her own blood.

While Andric's jacket hid the worst of it, the vampires had to be able to smell it. She shivered, stepping closer to Andric, and he ran his thumb across the back of her hand in response.

The school was quiet, the students still in the final class of the night, and Nameer and Andric wasted no time moving them through the halls and towards Walcott's office.

Lizzy wrinkled her nose when she realised where they were heading, but it was when she spotted Mia pacing the end of the hallway that she found her feet stopping, and the grasp Andric still had on her hand pulled him to a reluctant halt.

"Lizzy—?"

"Stay here," Nameer ordered, cutting across Andric's soft question, and Lizzy watched as Hunter Khatri approached Mia in a blur.

"Ah," Andric breathed out. She only noticed she'd been openly glaring at the other woman when the quiet sound drew her gaze from Mia to Andric and Lizzy struggled to smooth out her features.

"When Miss Harris revealed that she had encountered you at breakfast, we had something of an open discussion about her misdirected affection," Andric admitted.

Booker's snort of amusement pulled her attention from Andric, and she shot her best friend a silent question, eyebrow raised.

"He practically told her she was rotting deluded," Booker announced, smirking.

Lizzy snapped her head back around to stare at Andric, eyes widening as she watched him flush and duck his head a little.

"That's not exactly—"

"Close enough," Booker interrupted, and Andric conceded the point with a sigh and a nod.

"Come on, quickly," Nameer muttered, appearing at their side again. "Mia's agreed to take Officer Wilson on a tour of Speculo to keep him busy."

"That was... helpful of her," Lizzy muttered, and Nameer shot her cheerful grin.

"Apparently we'll owe her a favour," he explained, and Lizzy rolled her eyes.

It only took a couple of minutes before Mia led a tall, spindly-looking vampire past the end of the hall. She was speaking to him animatedly, keeping his attention away from the doorway the group of them were hovering in.

Andric drew Nameer's attention and waved his free hand through the air, but Nameer shook his head, lifting one hand to his ear.

Lizzy watched the hunters continue to communicate with a series of silent gestures, raised eyebrows, and nods, but it meant nothing to her.

Nameer and Andric seemed to have no trouble understanding each other, and after a moment they grew still.

When they made no move to head for Walcott's office, Lizzy turned to ask Andric what they were waiting for, but his thumb brushed a path across her knuckles again and her voice failed.

She glanced up at the vampire, only to find him already watching her. She narrowed her eyes, but it only made him flash her a smile, and before she could summon her irritation, Nameer interrupted.

"Okay, they've cleared this floor," he muttered.

"Cleared the—? You mean your hearing is that sensitive?" Booker choked out.

"Only if we concentrate, and have recently fed," Cara explained.

"Or if we haven't used up all our strength chasing through the forest after a young fey woman," Nameer teased.

Lizzy blushed and ducked her head, but Andric didn't seem to react to his friends teasing at all, moving his hand from hers to settle against the small of her back.

"Let's not waste time," Andric said instead, urging her forward with gentle pressure, and everyone took the silent signal to begin walking again. "We've no idea how long Miss Harris will be able to keep him distracted."

"Long enough," Nameer reassured. "We just need to get in the office, without raising any questions."

"You think the headmaster being in a meeting will stop a council official?" Andric asked, raising an eyebrow, and Nameer shrugged.

"It bloody well should."

The outer office was covered in far less paperwork than Lizzy remembered, but she was too drained to wonder what had prompted Mia's attempt at organising the area.

She was tired, cold, and beginning to stumble every now and then as the ache in her limbs gradually grew and she struggled to keep pressing forward.

And then they were at Walcott's door.

The headmaster took one look at their dishevelled appearances and ushered them into his office without a word.

Lizzy made a beeline for one of the large, plush chairs opposite the headmaster's desk, sinking into it gratefully.

Like their previous visit, Booker claimed the other chair, tugging Cara down to sit with him. She resisted this time and settled on the arm of the chair instead, but Booker just let his arm settle around her hips instead.

Nameer took up Andric's usual position, leaning against the bookshelves, while Andric himself hovered beside her, seeming unwilling to stray too far away from her side. If she thought about it too hard, it made Lizzy's heart flip in her chest.

"Did you lock the door?" Lizzy muttered to Walcott as he passed her on the way back to his chair, and Walcott offered her an amused smile.

"Unfortunately not," he admitted. "If I lock Officer Wilson out, I shall still have to face the young man when I emerge. It's easier to deal with him when he is not in a temper."

Walcott moved around his desk and sat down heavily, sighing as he ran his gaze over each of them in turn.

"Hunter Khatri informed me that Miss Hail had left Speculo grounds, and the means by which she made it past the hunters on guard," he continued after surveying them all in silence, and Lizzy flinched despite the lack of accusation in his voice. "Would anyone care to explain to me, then, why all of you look like you have been marching through the woods for the last four hours?"

"Because we were," Booker said, and Lizzy heard Andric give a quiet groan.

"We should start at the beginning," Nameer said, but Lizzy could hear the smile in his voice. When she glanced over at the hunter, his eyes were on her and his lips curved into a gentle grin.

"Right," Lizzy breathed, sighing and turning to meet Walcott's patient curiosity, "Hockley."

She saw surprise, then the curiosity returned stronger, and Lizzy licked her lips nervously. It wasn't until she felt Andric's hand rest on her shoulder that she was able to suck in a deep breath and summon the strength to begin.

Slowly, Lizzy told them everything she could remember, from the first time Gladstone had approached her. By the time she reached the point where Andric had woken them to tell them about the deputy headmistress becoming a kavian, her throat was sore and she had the dull throb of a headache building in her temples.

She paused in her story long enough to turn to Nameer and attempt an apology for breaking his neck, but before she could manage any more than a soft "I'm sorry," he was waving it away.

"Don't apologise for being ambitious, Miss Hail," Nameer said, eyes sparkling openly. "Andric taught you to fight, that is what you did. You fought for your beliefs. I cannot fault you for that. Besides, look, no harm done," he added, grinning as he held out his arms indicating his healed form, and Lizzy couldn't help but grin at the vampire's lighthearted antics.

"While the lead-up to what sent you wandering into the forest, alone, is... enlightening, I don't quite see how it's relevant," Walcott prompted, and Lizzy sighed.

"That's because you still don't believe me," she growled, frustrated, but too tired to argue. When Andric cleared his throat, she reluctantly settled, pulling her feet onto the chair and curling up, tugging Andric's jacket more firmly around her.

"It's relevant, Thomas, because they were right," Andric said, "all three of them. The kavians are regaining their minds."

Lizzy tried very hard not to feel overwhelmingly smug as the headmaster's face paled and his jaw dropped open.

The others took over the story then. Between the four of them, they regaled the headmaster with the events of the night, and Lizzy let the constant hum of their voices leach the tension from her frame until she was dozing, her head resting against Andric's hip, and his hand resting lightly against her far shoulder.

Lizzy drifted in and out of consciousness. The occasional tendril of the story would draw her attention long enough for her to force her eyes open and focus, but then she'd sink back into the heavy silence of her mind.

Until she heard her name.

"...very glad that Miss Hail is unharmed. All that remains is to decide what to do about the situation moving forward. I am frustrated to admit I have heard nothing back in regards to my enquiries with the Council."

Lizzy blinked hard and pushed herself up from Andric's side, frowning as she shook her head.

"I'm sorry, what was that?" she asked, and Walcott gave her an amused smile.

"I've been making enquiries with the Council, as I promised," he explained, "but I've heard nothing back."

"Did you expect to?" Nameer asked, and Walcott's expression soured.

"Maybe not news," he admitted, "but I expected an acknowledgement of my request at the very least. What I've gotten is complete silence, until Officer Wilson showed up today. And a greater waste of office space, I have never had the misfortune of meeting."

Booker barked out a sharp laugh, and even Cara pressed her hands to her mouth to smother a grin at the headmaster's words.

"I regret, Miss Hail, that I do not think I will have the answers you seek before the end of the school year, as I had hoped."

"I know who has my answers," Lizzy growled. "Sethan Blackwood."

"Yeah," Booker agreed, and when Lizzy glanced over at him he was nodding, but his features were marked with a frown, and his foot tapped against the office floor, "but how do we find Sethan? And even if we can find him, how in the realm do we get him to talk?"

"I've been thinking about that," Andric said, and Lizzy whipped around to stare up at him in surprise.

"You have?"

"I've been considering where we might go for some answers—"

"We?"

Andric paused, shifting as he let his eyes scan around the room. Nameer's grin widened when Andric's gaze settled on him briefly, but then Andric turned back to her and he nodded, clearing his throat.

"Yes. We."

"But... I dissolved our contract," she said slowly, heart pounding in her chest, but the vampire staring down at her just smiled.

"You didn't think you were getting rid of me that easily, did you?" he teased, and Lizzy found she couldn't quite smother the small smile that was fighting its way onto her face.

"Alright, fine," she muttered, ignoring the snickering she could hear from Booker behind her. "So what were you thinking?"

"If we need to track and hunt a kavian that's regained his mind, and therefore his logic, then we're going to need one of the best kavian hunters alive," Andric explained.

"There's not many left who stand out," Nameer warned, and Andric shot him a grin.

"There's Connorbar Moore."

Nameer loosed a scoff that had Lizzy's eyes narrowing, but Andric didn't seem bothered by his friend's dismissive response.

"Moore's a myth," Nameer said, but Andric shook his head.

"He retired. Almost three decades back," Walcott cut in smoothly, and Nameer's laughter died mid-chuckle.

"What?"

"Mum went on a hunt with him once," Andric explained. "That's the only reason I know for sure. He kept trying to get legislation pushed through the Council, and being denied, so he retired from hunting. Hasn't been seen in public since."

"Legislation to speed up the reintegration of fey and vampire societies, yes," Walcott mused. "So he very well might be willing to aid you... if you can find him."

"So no one's seen this vampire in decades, and you want to try tracking him down?" Lizzy asked.

"I—" Andric started but silenced himself, sighing and pressing his lips together. Lizzy held his gaze, and she could almost hear him weighing his words before he nodded, some decision reached behind his eyes.

"We can try going straight for Blackwood, if that's what you want to do," he offered, and Lizzy felt her eyebrows shoot up in surprise even as he continued. "I just feel that... Blackwood's been smart so far. He's kept the emergence of sane kavians quiet. From what Alex let slip it sounds like he may have kept your mum alive. Those are two very specific actions that have very specific purposes."

"Like what?"

"Like he's preparing for something," Walcott said, voice quiet, and Andric nodded.

"Moore will have the skills and experience to not only help us find Blackwood, but to help us rescue your mum safely... and if we're lucky, kill Blackwood and stop his plans, whatever they are, in the process."

"Where would we even start?" Booker asked. "If this guy's been in hibernation..."

"I might... be able to help with that," Cara said hesitantly. "My parents..." She trailed off, and Walcott shifted in his chair.

"Miss Evelyn—"

"No, it's okay," she interrupted, taking a bracing breath. Lizzy watched Booker stroke his fingers soothingly through the ends of Cara's hair, and gradually, the vampire relaxed.

"My parents turned kavian," she explained, glancing between Booker and Lizzy as she spoke, "but before they did they were hunters... They worked for a team on the Council, and answered to Connorbar Moore. And... and I still have their journals."

She raised her hands quickly, "I've never read them. I can't promise there'll be any solid leads in there," she warned.

Despite her hesitance, Lizzy could almost feel that the energy in the room had lifted. Lightening with nothing more than the thin tendril of hope Cara had offered.

"The journals are older even than the last time Moore was seen... but there might be clues in there. Something to give us a starting point, at least."

"Thank you, Cara," Andric said, and the vampire ducked her head.

"I'm just glad they might be useful to someone," she muttered, and Lizzy let out a breath.

"So... are we really going to do this?" Lizzy asked before turning to Walcott, frowning as she added, "Are you going to let us do this?"

The old vampire leant back in his chair, watching her before nodding. "The news of sane kavians is disturbing, and the knowledge that they might be keeping a fey alive is of even greater concern. Hunter Roche isn't employed by Speculo for the time being, so I have no grounds to stop him accompanying you.

Even if I wanted to," Walcott added, offering Lizzy a smile that she tentatively returned.

"I myself need to go to the Council," Walcott continued. "I want to know why my missives are being ignored, and they need to be informed of this new development amongst the kavians—"

"I'll accompany you," Nameer cut in easily, "the Council will want an eyewitness to the changes in the kavians. And if there is political manoeuvring within the Council, you'll need a second pair of eyes to watch your back," he added.

He'd cut off Walcott as though the vampire wasn't employing him, and Lizzy watched in amusement at the brief flash of annoyance Nameer managed to pull from the headmaster before he surrendered with a short nod.

"Very well," Walcott muttered, "Hunter Khatri and I will go to the Council. If we hear anything of use to you while there, I'm certain Hunter Khatri will be able to contact you by phone," he said, turning to Andric as the vampire nodded in agreement.

"In the meantime, Hunter Roche, you plan to accompany Miss Hail, Mister Reed, and—"

"You should stay," Booker muttered, and Lizzy blinked at him for a moment in stunned silence before realising he was talking to Cara.

It seemed to take Cara a moment too, because there was silence until she shot the fey a scowl. "What? Why!"

"Because you have an apprenticeship to qualify for," Booker said simply, and the fury bled from Cara's features.

"This is more important—"

"No, it's not," Booker said with a frown. "Not for you. You worked hard for this. You deserve it. Fight for it."

Lizzy watched them. Watched their eyes meet, and the tiny twitch at the corner of Booker's mouth, told her he'd linked their minds.

The argument passing between them now would be faster,

more direct, more filled with emotions, and Lizzy found herself swallowing hard.

"Alright," Cara relented, voice soft, and her shoulders slumped in defeat.

"I'll write you a letter of recommendation," Andric offered, and Cara's head snapped up in surprise.

"And I'll make sure Hunter Roche receives it," Nameer added.

"You're not going to inflict my mother on the poor girl," Andric groaned, but while Nameer laughed and Cara seemed shocked into silence, Lizzy glanced around the room at them all in turn, hope finally reigniting fully in her heart.

"So... we're really doing this? We're going to find my mum?" she asked, and Andric broke away from his banter with Nameer to offer her a soft smile that made her insides flutter.

Before he could speak, the door to Walcott's office burst open and Lizzy jumped in her seat. Startled, she spun around to stare at the doorway with wide eyes.

It was only Andric's hand on her shoulder that stopped her from leaping to her feet, and she quickly scowled at the spindly vampire she'd spotted Mia leading away earlier.

"Headmaster Walcott, you cannot continue to avoid speaking with me! I insist—"

"Officer Wilson," Walcott cut the vampire off sharply, and Lizzy shivered at the icy tone of the headmaster's voice. "You're right on time, my meeting has just concluded. You needn't concern yourself with writing up a safety report for the Council," Walcott continued. "I've decided to head there myself, and deliver my report to them directly."

"You-you-you what? You can't do that!"

"Why ever not?" Walcott asked, but the council officer simply stood gaping at him, speechless, and the headmaster hummed.

"Thank you, Hunter Khatri, Hunter Roche. That will be all for tonight," he dismissed them, and Lizzy scrambled to her feet as quickly as she could, Booker and Cara following suit.

As Lizzy was edging out of the room past the council official, Officer Wilson sucked in a sharp breath and his head snapped around to stare at her.

At the same moment, Lizzy was acutely reminded of the dried blood caked to her arm and shoulder, hidden beneath Andric's leather coat.

But the leather wasn't enough to mask the scent from a vampire.

"An injured fey? At Speculo?" Wilson snarled. "What is your business with the headmaster?" the man demanded, and Lizzy froze.

"It's fey business," Booker sneered, "and therefore none of yours."

"I work for the European Council of Vampires!" Officer Wilson growled, and Booker took a step forward, placing himself between the irate vampire and Lizzy.

It gave Lizzy a brief respite. Enough for her to escape the tension the vampire's scowl had wrapped her in, and she shivered. Her skin was crawling, and it prompted her to tangle her fingers in the chain of her pendant.

"I am a fey of Arbaon," Booker snarled, "I don't answer to you or your Council."

It had been a long time since Lizzy had heard Booker utilise his court voice, and if the room had been coated in ice it couldn't have felt colder than his hissed words.

Face a mask, Booker looked over at Walcott. "I assume our discussion will remain... confidential, Headmaster?" Booker all but demanded, and Lizzy watched the headmaster raise his eyebrows.

"Of course, Master Reed."

"Good," Booker said simply before turning back around, placing a hand on Lizzy's elbow and marching them both out of the office without another word.

Lizzy stood leaning against the front of Andric's car, blinking sleepily and watching the sun glinting off the treetops.

At the opposite end of the vehicle, the kavian hunter was busy loading their bags into the boot, and she listened to his movements as she struggled to wake up.

Lizzy had showered and packed in record time, but she'd only managed to have a short nap before Andric was knocking on their door as the sun rose.

Not wanting to give Officer Wilson any further opportunities to dig into their presence at the school, Andric had planned for them to leave at first light. Lizzy had agreed to his plan, but although her bags were packed and ready to go, Lizzy herself felt as far from ready as it was possible to be.

And yet, the hope that had ignited within her in Walcott's office was still burning. Still driving her forward. She had a real chance now, not just a faint feeling that could be easily dismissed.

Her mum was alive somewhere. Probably with the kavians, but alive was better than dead in so many ways that relief kept threatening to clog Lizzy's throat with tears.

Even better, they had a plan.

Find Connorbar Moore. Get him to help them track Sethan Blackwood. Rescue her mum.

It sounded simple, and Lizzy was sure it wouldn't be, but it was more than she'd had when she stepped through the arboretum portal from Arbaon to the mortal realm.

It was a lead. A thread they could pull on and see what emerged.

"You okay?" Booker asked, and she blinked the rising sun out of her eyes. She turned to grin at her best friend standing at her elbow, but the smile he offered back was weak, and she sighed.

"Have you said goodbye to Cara?" she asked, and he nodded.

"It won't be for long. We'll find Maddy, and then..."

Booker's voice trailed off and Lizzy looped her arm through his. "And then you'll come back."

"Will I?" Booker mused, sounding half-curious and very tired, and Lizzy shrugged.

"For a while," she said, humming and tilting her head in consideration, "or forever. That's for you two to figure out."

"Oh yeah?" he asked, and she could hear the playful energy she was more familiar with returning to his voice, "and what about you and Hunter Roche?" he teased, and Lizzy instantly flushed.

"We're not talking about that."

"Aren't we?" Booker asked, and Lizzy found herself glancing away, gaze dropping, but she couldn't stop her smile.

"Not yet," she conceded before turning to stare at Andric, only to find the vampire already watching her. "I think... it's still too new for that."

"But it is something?" Booker asked, and Lizzy nodded, watching Andric smile before he ducked back into the boot of the car to rearrange something.

"And are you happy, Lizzy?" Booker asked, and she sighed.

"No. Mum's still missing."

It was a sharp answer, but she knew what he was really asking, and quickly sighed, relenting. "But... I think I could be."

Booker let his arm slide around her shoulders, and Lizzy leaned into his side for a moment before the boot slammed shut and the car jerked.

"Alright, you two, get in," Andric called. "We've got a long way to go, and the sooner we get started, the sooner we'll get there."

Within minutes, they were all settled in their seats, and Lizzy found herself once again staring out of the windows of the car, watching the forest fly by, and wondering where the vampire was leading them.

The only difference this time was that Andric had her hand wrapped in his, and wherever the road to finding Connorbar led, Lizzy knew she could trust him.

Thank You

Thank you so much for reading Changeling!

If you enjoyed this story, please consider taking a few moments to leave a review on your preferred platform. Reviews for indie authors are so important, and I'm very grateful for all your support.

Keep an eye out for book two in the Fey Touched trilogy, Darkling, later this year or you can keep reading to check out a sneak peek of Chapter One!

And if you're looking for more Fey Touched content, want to be the first to hear new updates, or are interested in downloading the prequel short story 'Whatever Happened To Madeline Hail?' for free you can subscribe to my newsletter at;
www.subscribepage.io/changeling

Or by following the QR code below;

About Author

Arista Holmes was raised and resides in the South East of England where she spends her time consuming coffee, cuddling her cat, and crafting her next book. Arista has also written short stories for charity fanzines to raise money for Doctors Without Borders and the IRSSS.

When she's not writing the next adventure she wants to go on, Ari is immersing herself in worlds and adventures created by others.

You can connect with Ari directly via her website;
www.aristaholmes.weebly.com

Sign up for her newsletter to receive a free copy of the Fey Touched prequel, '*Whatever Happened To Madeline Hail?*'

Darkling
Fey Touched Book Two
Chapter One...

After six weeks on the road together, watching Lizzy had become something of a habit for Andric Roche.

He'd been mid-conversation when he spotted her, standing across the road from the hotel he, and the two fey he was travelling with, had spent the night in. He'd been questioning one of the residents of the vampire clan they were currently visiting, but all of that suddenly felt inconsequential.

Andric couldn't decide if he should be irritated or amused at the distraction Lizzy posed.

She'd shoved her way out of the hotel, pushing the door open sharply and stepping out onto the pavement, his attention instantly diverted to her.

The vampire beside him faded, and the story Andric had been listening to about the legendary hunter, Connorbar Moore, became background noise as Andric watched Lizzy's hands sink into her long dark hair and hastily tug it up into a high ponytail.

She didn't turn around. Didn't notice him staring. Just stretched, tilting her face up towards the morning sun. Lizzy was dressed in the loose cotton shirt and trousers she preferred, and she arched her back. His sharp hearing picked up on her soft groan before she turned and began jogging down the street, away from where Andric stood.

He narrowed his eyes as he stared after her. She'd not done her warm-ups, which meant Booker was once again in a miserable mood over not hearing from Cara.

It also meant she'd probably skipped breakfast to get some peace, and Andric sighed in frustration.

The first two weeks, when the flush of a new adventure had been fresh, the two fey had been content to be patient. But as more time passed, and they questioned an increasing number of clans without finding leads on Moore, or answers about Blackwood, the two friends' relationship seemed to be deteriorating exponentially.

The worst part for Andric was he didn't know how to help them, except to keep going. Keep looking, and digging, and asking questions—

"Your mate?"

The question snapped him out of his thoughts, and he turned wide eyes on the vampire grinning at him cheerfully. Andric could feel his cheeks flush at the implication, and shook his head.

"No," he insisted, ignoring the eyebrows that shot up in surprise at his short answer. "Just... someone under my charge."

"Then you better get after her," the man said, elaborating when Andric shot him a questioning frown. "She turned right at the end of the street. She keeps going that way, she'll be outside the clan's influence. I'm sure you know better than me, Hunter, the dangers right on the edges of clan-land."

Andric did, and he felt his stomach grow cold at the stranger's words. Offering a brief nod, and a soft "Thanks," Andric gave a brief check of the street for any lingering human attention before he blurred after Lizzy.

Kavians wouldn't risk attacking a clan. Strength in numbers would make them hesitate, and their survival instincts ran too strong, despite their rabid tendencies.

But that didn't stop them lingering on the outskirts, hoping to catch a stray vampire alone.

Or at least, the rabid ones.

Andric had no idea how the kavians that had somehow regained their mental faculties might function around clan-land, but it made him even more nervous than the risk of a wandering rabid stumbling over Lizzy.

Rounding the corner, Andric saw her turn into some light woodland on the edge of the town and step into a blur of her own, and he cursed.

Lizzy's discovery of her ability to blur, and that it might mean her father had been a vampire and not a human as she'd assumed, had been the source of another argument between her and Booker.

While Andric had made a concerted effort not to listen in on the details of their discussion, the shouted argument from the next room revealed that Booker had already held some suspicions about her father. And Lizzy hadn't been happy about her friend having kept his silence on the matter.

Between their lack of progress in finding a lead to follow, Booker's irritation about missing Cara, and Lizzy's hurt over the secrets surrounding her parentage, Andric was ready to tear his hair out.

He was itching for a good sparring session. Something to work out a little of the tension thrumming beneath the surface, but with the three of them constantly on the move, driving from one vampire clan to the next, there hadn't been the opportunity.

They hadn't even had a chance to test out Lizzy's blurring ability. To test her limits or get her used to the dizzying motions, but after watching her disappear into the woodland, it was clear she'd not been inclined to wait for his help.

He was both impressed and irritated at the risk she'd taken, but the woman stirring up a mixture of emotions was something else he was growing used to.

With a sigh, he followed her. Tracking her scent as he moved, but she knew he was following.

It was obvious when she began zigzagging her trail, and the predator instincts bubbling up through his chest urged him to run faster, to hunt, to catch, to—

He pushed them down and sped up, gaining on her as her scent grew stronger.

She might have taught herself to blur, but it was still a new skill. One most vampires learned when they were children. It would take months, possibly years, for her to teach her body how to reach its full limits, and within seconds, he'd caught up.

He heard her laugh, and then she turned. Changing directions, stepping out of his range, and Andric's control of his instincts slipped. It was enough to send him blurring forward, to grasp hold of her frame before she could flee.

Lizzy didn't hesitate, and her elbow slammed back into his stomach like they were back on the training field at Speculo.

If she were only a little taller, she might have a decent shot at breaking a rib, but Lizzy's small frame always left her at a disadvantage in a physical fight.

Normally, Andric would have given her the win, but he was still fighting back instincts and his arms tightened instead, prompting her to drop in his grip, her frame growing heavy as she slid out from under his arm.

Exactly like he'd shown her.

He found himself reluctantly impressed as she stepped back from him, laughing. She turned and he could see the edges of another blur forming and lunged.

His body collided with hers, arms curling around her frame. One hand settled between her shoulders and he brought the other up to cushion the back of her head as he sent them both crashing to the ground.

Lizzy's laughter stopped with a rough "Oof!"

Andric landed hard on his forearms, his frame caging her in place even as twigs and stones dug into his skin, making him wish for his leather jacket.

The short sleeves of the T-shirt had done nothing to soften his impact, but the sting of the tiny cuts were quickly soothed by the familiar tingling of his body knitting the wounds back together.

Lizzy's hands were curled into fists, grasping hold of his cotton shirt as he hovered above her and the heat of her touch against his ribs through the thin fabric was enough to pull his mind back from the hunt and remind him why he'd been chasing her in the first place.

Right. Kavians...

It was on the tip of his tongue to scold her for going out running without knowing the area. For the risk she'd taken teaching herself to blur without supervision. To ask her what she was thinking running from him... but one look at her face, eyes still closed and lips curved up into a gentle smile that he hadn't seen in weeks as she tried to catch her breath, silenced him.

Slowly, as though she could feel his focus fixed on her, Lizzy let her eyes peel open and her smile widened into a grin.

"Morning," she greeted, and Andric huffed a soft laugh.

"Good morning," he murmured back. "I see you've been practising," he said, his voice teasing and Lizzy's nose wrinkled, telling him she could hear the hint of a reprimand he'd managed to force into his voice.

"Not intentionally," she admitted, and Andric raised his eyebrows until she laughed again. "I promise. I was just... I was running. Trying to clear my head, and it just happened. I figured out how to trigger it so I wouldn't do it accidentally, that's all."

"And today?"

"Well, I knew you were following me," she said, shrugging one shoulder. She shifted beneath him, and Andric suddenly grew intensely aware of how closely they were wrapped around each other.

His heart thumped hard against his chest, and Andric tried to concentrate on keeping his breathing steady.

That was the other thing they hadn't had time for since starting their road trip in search of elusive leads. Them.

ı the forest surrounding Speculo, when
:omfort had been needed, was the only
ɛ what Andric had overheard Lizzy tell
.ey'd left the school behind, neither of
topic or pushed for anything further.

ame caught up in his arms and the almost
es watching him, Andric's control cracked
.d, hesitating at the last second.

er breathing made him pause, and his gaze
: smile to meet her eyes.

just stare at me, or kiss me?" she moaned, and
/ing.

ɲverstepped a line. That he hadn't misread her.
ressing closer until he could slant his mouth
.izzy met his kiss with a soft sigh. Her grasping
against his ribs, sliding around to press against
ıdric's tension fell away...

ıarkling' will be continued 2024!